Bolt's hand moved to the big .44 as two pulsing veins popped out on his forehead. Bodine had finally crossed the threshold and Bolt's warrior spirit was raging to get out.

"You make one move toward that barn and I'll kill all of you."

"Big talk for a man alone," Bodine said. In the twilight, he failed to notice Bolt was armed. The overseer thought he was invincible as he looked back to his men and motioned toward the barn, "Burn it to the ground."

Having despised Bodine for a long time, Bolt never hesitated. The quiet country evening was shattered with a roar and a flash of flame. The demon spirit was unleashed on the world as Bolt's first bullet ripped through the startled overseer's chest, driving him off the back of his horse.

Copyright © 2012 Allen Russell

ISBN: 978-1-62141-806-1

All rights reserved. No part of this publication may be reproduced, stored in a retrieval system, or transmitted in any form or by any means, electronic, mechanical, recording or otherwise, without the prior written permission of the author.

Published by Rough River Press

The characters and events in this book are fictitious. Any similarity to real persons, living or dead, is coincidental and not intended by the author.

Printed in the United States of America on acid-free paper.

Rough River Press
www.RoughRiverPress.com
2012

First Edition

Buffalo Grass Rider

Episode One:

The Lonesome Wind

Allen Russell

Chapter One:
1835, Making of the Man

The relaxed chatter that filled the Walton Inn only a moment before was now replaced with a tense silence. Nearly everyone in the dining room turned to look at the two shabbily dressed backwoodsmen suddenly filling the doorway. One of them was huge with broad shoulders. The other was shorter and lightly built. Both had shaggy black hair, long beards, and an aroma that suggested a complete lack of personal hygiene.

Standing on the threshold, they seemed to be scanning the crowded room, carefully searching for any lurking danger. Finally satisfied all was well, their attention fell on the only table with empty chairs. It was occupied by an older gentleman eating alone near the center of the dining room.

"Oh no, not today," Sarah Ashton whispered, watching the pair in the doorway. An attractive young woman in her late twenties, Sarah was a farmer's wife who worked at the Walton Inn a few days a week to bring in a little extra money for her family.

When the backwoodsmen started toward his table, the older gentleman quickly got to his feet, abandoned his unfinished meal and faded into the shadows. Ignoring the former occupant, the backwoodsmen made themselves comfortable at the table and started looking around for someone to wait on them.

"What do you have to do to get some service in here?" the big one bellowed, slamming an enormous fist down on the table to emphasize his impatience. The smaller one seemed content to pick at the remaining scraps on the plate in front of him.

"I'll be right there," Sarah said from across the room.

It was late October, 1835, in Smith County, Tennessee. The Inn was located near a bustling ferry landing on the Cumberland Turnpike. The turnpike, or Walton's Road, was the main wagon trail connecting Knoxville to Nashville and the Natchez Trace.

The Inn was packed with weary travelers. Tired and nearing the end of a long day, Sarah was still scurrying around, trying to take care of several tables at once. As much as she wanted to, she didn't have the option of avoiding the men at the table. It was her job to wait on them.

When she approached them with a crock of beer and two mugs, the younger man began leering at her and making suggestions that she tried to ignore. When she got around to the big one, he grabbed her at the waist and pulled her down on his lap. Sarah was used to a little teasing now and then from her customers, but she couldn't stand to have this man put his hands on her.

"Let go of me," she demanded as she resisted his primitive advances.

The big man continued holding her down as his companion laughed and clapped at his antics. Sarah turned her head to avoid the odor of old sweat and his horrendous breath.

"Now, Ms. Sarah," the big man said, his tangled black hair covering one eye, "We just want a little company, don't be so uppity." Due to his immense bulk, the big hillbilly was breathing hard from the exertion of holding onto Sarah. His broad grin revealed widely-spaced teeth, stained brown from the ever-present plug of tobacco in his cheek.

"Take your hands off me," she repeated, still struggling to get away from him. There was little Sarah could do alone, and none of the other patrons in the place would even look over at her, much less, try to interfere.

The big man holding Sarah was well-known hell-raiser, Ollie Drinkwater. Ollie had been involved with several brutal beatings and rumored to be responsible for a killing or two in the backwoods. He carried a big bone-handled knife that he wasn't bashful about using. Anyone foolish enough to come to Sarah's rescue would likely get their throat cut for the effort.

Standing more than six feet tall and weighing well over 300 pounds, Ollie was the self-anointed leader of the Drinkwater Clan. The smaller man was Ollie's younger and slightly unstable brother, Saul.

Timber cutters and whiskey makers, the Drinkwater's lived in a ramshackle cabin back in Panther Holler with their widowed mother and half-a-hundred hogs. They were bachelors and likely always would be, as no woman in her right mind would go anywhere near that holler.

The entire population of Panther Holler consisted of Drinkwater's, aunts, uncles, and second and third cousins. That lack of outside bloodlines and the constant ingestion of moonshine whiskey had evidently been a problem for several generations of Drinkwater's. Most of them were severely lacking in the social graces.

Sarah's young son, Bolt, along with her nephew, Sam Boston, was sitting outside with a mule-drawn cart waiting to escort her home. Bolt Ashton was sitting astride the mule in front of Sam. Neither of them wanted to be seen riding in the cart, it was for Sarah.

"Help me down," Bolt said when he heard his mother's excited voice coming from inside.

"We ain't supposed to go in there," Sam said.

Ignoring the warning, Bolt held on to the mule's collar, swung his leg over, and dropped to the ground. Sam climbed off and reluctantly followed the young Ashton toward the Inn. Sam was bigger than Bolt, but he was the quiet one of this pair. Both little country boys were dressed in overalls and barefooted.

When Bolt came through the door he saw his mother struggling to get away from Ollie. The little boy's brow wrinkled up as two bulging veins popped out on his forehead and his face got red.

Like a lot of Tennesseans, Bolt had Cherokee blood running through his veins. The spirit of the blood in Bolt, however, was very different from that of the rest. The savage warrior spirit in him had lain dormant for many generations, patiently waiting for the proper vessel. The ancient curse had been awakened when Bolt was conceived.

Even at his tender age, Bolt had a terrible temper and a mouth that kept him in trouble much of the time. The little Ashton was stubborn and hardheaded. He was only too happy to take on anything or anybody that got in his way. The fiery little warrior knew the Drinkwater's, but he wasn't afraid of them, and he wasn't about to stand by and watch his mother get mistreated by some giant hillbilly and his dim-witted brother.

Ollie wore bulky homemade trousers that his mother sewed for him. Held up by suspenders, those trousers were always gapped open in the back or on the sides.

No one noticed the little boys when they came through the door. The patrons were all watching Ollie. Looking around for a weapon, Bolt motioned to Sam and made his way over to the corner of the room.

There, next to the pot-bellied stove, they found a neatly stacked rick of stove-wood. Leaning against the stove-wood was a broom and a small scoop shovel used to clean out the ashes. Bolt scooped up a shovelful of red hot coals from the open stove while Sam picked up a sturdy hickory stick from the stack.

When the boys got close enough, Bolt emptied the scoop down the back of the big Drinkwater's pants. Everybody in the place jumped when Ollie exploded out of his chair with a shriek. In his haste to get away from whatever had him by the seat of the pants, Ollie leapt to his feet, throwing Sarah to the floor and turned the table over on Saul.

Just as Ollie started doing a jig to shake the coals out of his britches, Sam cracked him on the shin with the stick. When Ollie grabbed for his throbbing shin, the burning coals skittered down his other leg, setting his homemade woolen pants to smoldering and came to rest in his left boot. Ollie was hopping up and down, trying to shake the fire out of his pants, when he realized his foot was burning. Ollie made the mistake of bending over to yank his boot off, and Sam cold-cocked him. The hickory stick smacked Ollie's forehead with a hollow thump, knocking the big man backwards onto his ponderous smoldering backside.

The whole place shook when Ollie went down on his butt. Nearly blinded from the blow to his forehead, Ollie was still on his back holding his throbbing head, and cursing the two little warriors. Saul was no help, he was howling with laughter along with nearly everyone else in the Inn.

"You leave my mother alone, Pig Farmer," Bolt warned, waving the scoop shovel under the big man's nose.

"Your Mother!" Ollie shouted, "Why you little…I'm gonna wring your neck!"

Still in the floor, Ollie went for his knife. The little warriors weren't dumb; they had freed Sarah from the big hillbilly's grasp. When the knife came out, they figured this was about to get serious and it was time to go. Dropping their weapons, Bolt and Sam headed for the door. Ollie struggled to his feet as they disappeared through the open doorway.

"I'm gonna skin both of you little son's o'. . . ."

Sarah tried to grab Ollie's arm, but the raging hillbilly brushed her off like a gnat.

Bolt was running for his life when he crossed the front porch of the Inn. Still looking back over his shoulder, he ran smack into a man that had just ridden up and tied his horse to the rail. Sam was right behind Bolt and crashed into both of them.

"Whoa," the stranger said, catching the boys in his arms, "where you boys going in such an all-fired hurry?"

Before they could answer, Ollie came hobbling out the door, wearing only one boot. His pants were still smoking and a big purple lump was growing on his forehead. Saul was right behind him, anxious to watch Ollie skin the brazen little kids. Bolt and Sam instinctively went around behind the stranger for protection.

The stranger held a Kentucky long-rifle at arm's length, blocking Ollie from the boys. "Whoa…hold on there. You boys kind o' got these youngsters outnumbered."

"This is none…of your…affair," Ollie gasped.

"I think your britches are on fire, friend," the stranger said. He was grinning when he said it, but Ollie wasn't even slightly amused.

"Get out of my way…or you'll taste this blade…before they do."

The stranger's grin began to fade when Sarah got to the porch. She tried to get around Ollie until Saul grabbed her and pushed her back.

The stranger facing Ollie wasn't a big man but he had a commanding presence. He was dressed in buckskins and wore a wide-brimmed hat. In addition to the long-rifle, there was a knife and a steel tomahawk in his belt. The four buckskin-clad men with him were watching from the hitching rail near their horses.

"I'm sorry to hear you say that," the stranger said. Before Ollie could carry through with his threat, the stranger lashed out and stuck him with the butt of the rifle. The stunned hillbilly was trying to keep his feet as blood began pouring from his nose and lip. In anticipation of what he knew was coming, the stranger pulled his tomahawk. Bolt and Sam scattered as Ollie shook his head, wiped his nose on his sleeve, and lunged at the stranger with a roar.

The nimble stranger side-stepped the rumbling hillbilly and struck him in the back of the head with the flat side of the tomahawk. Ollie went off the porch, landed face-first in the dirt and stayed there. He wasn't dead but he would have a skull-busting headache and a few scars to remember the stranger by when he woke up.

After seeing Ollie go down, Saul pulled his knife and began circling, looking for an opportunity to thrust his blade and let some of the wind out of the impudent stranger. When Saul lunged, the stranger hit him across the hand with his tomahawk, cutting off Saul's little finger and knocking the knife from his grasp.

Saul had a confused look on his face as he studied his suddenly-separated appendage lying there on the porch. Before he could figure it all out, the flat side of the tomahawk whacked him just above the left ear, and Saul toppled over to sleep it off next to his brother.

"Colonel," one of the men at the rail said, "danged if we ain't been here less than two minutes and you already started a fight."

"I never started no fight." Using the toe of his boot, he flicked the severed finger off the porch. "It was these two rascals," he said, turning back to Bolt and Sam. The men at the rail were all laughing. "Are you alright, ma'am?" the stranger asked Sarah.

"I'm fine, thank you."

"You boys hungry?" the stranger asked Bolt and Sam.

"Yes sir," they said together.

"Well, you all come on in and join us, but don't pick on anybody else, I'm plumb tuckered out." They were all laughing as they started for the door. Before he went inside, the stranger picked up the knives dropped by the Drinkwater's.

When they were seated, Sarah came back to their table. "I want to thank you, Sir. I was afraid for my son there. No one here wanted to help us."

"This is your boy?" the stranger asked. "Well, he's a ring-tailed wildcat to take on those two."

"The boys were trying to save me from those two hillbillies."

"I'm mighty glad to know you, Son," the stranger said sticking out his hand. "What's your name?"

"Bolt Ashton, this here's my cousin, Sam Boston."

"Well, Bolt, Sam, it's good to meet you both."

"I'm Mrs. Ashton," Sarah said, "Mr. . . . ."

"Crockett, ma'am...David Crockett."

"You're Davy Crockett?" Bolt asked.

"That's right, Son, fresh from the backwoods. I'm half horse, half alligator, with just a touch of snapping turtle thrown in. I got the fastest horse, the prettiest sister, and the ugliest dog in Tennessee. I can wade the Mississippi, leap the Ohio, ride a streak of lighting, and skin down a honey locust with nary a scratch."

The boys were laughing along with everyone in the place at this backwoods legend.

"Do you know Andy Jackson?" Sam asked.

"Know him? I was just with Old Hickory himself up there in Washington City. It hasn't been but a few months ago. Let me tell you about the time me and Andy fought the Creeks. It all started when. . . ."

Bolt and Sam were spellbound for the next two hours listening to Davy carry on with his stories. It was getting close to dark and long past time to go home when Sarah finally called a halt to the storytelling.

"So long, boys," Davy said.

"Will we see you around here again?" Bolt asked.

"Not for a spell. I'm gone to the buffalo grass."

"Where's that?"

"West, Son...Texas. There's land out there for a man to stretch out in. A vast plain, grass as far as you can see, from Texas clear on up to Canada. The Indians call it the buffalo grass and I want to ride across it.

Besides, things are getting a little too crowded and tame around here for me."

"I've been thinking the same thing," Bolt said. "Think I'll go ride that buffalo grass with you."

"Bolt, you're my kind of boy," Davy said with a grin. "We'd be proud to have you. You fight just like me; I always hit the big one first."

"Yes sir," Bolt said, "Me too."

"How old are you?" Davy asked.

"I'm almost eight."

"He's seven," Sam said, "I'm eight."

"In that case," Davy said, "I think you better stay here and watch out for your momma a little longer before you go wandering off to see the west."

"Yes sir, I reckon you're right," Bolt replied, "but I'm gonna ride that buffalo grass myself one of these days." Crockett and the men with him all laughed at the little Tennessee scrapper.

Bolt and Sam were headed to the door when Davy called them back.

"Boys, I want you to have these." He picked up the knife that belonged to Ollie and handed it to Bolt and gave the other one to Sam. "Now if anybody ever asked you boys where you got those knives, you can tell 'em, David Crockett himself gave 'em to you."

"Thank you, Colonel Crockett," Sarah said, "that means so much."

"You're welcome ma'am. They're good boys; I suspect they'll grow up to be something real special."

By the spring of 1846, Bolt Ashton was in his late teens and growing into a fine looking young man. He was well passed the six foot mark, and Cousin Sam was two inches taller. Bolt went to school long enough to learn to read and write. He was a student of American history, reading all he could about the explorers, mountain men, and frontier scouts.

Andrew Jackson died the year before and Davy Crockett died at the Alamo only a few months after meeting Bolt at the Inn. Even though he had been just a kid, Bolt could still remember Crockett's fun-loving ways.

The knife Davy had given him was Bolt's prized possession. He had the local saddle maker create a leather sheath for it. It was inscribed: *A gift from Davy Crockett, October, 1835.*

Bolt was happy working his parent's farm, but he was getting to the age that he wanted to see more of the world. He read about Lewis and Clark and the wonders they found in the west. He remembered Crockett telling him about the buffalo grass.

The young Ashton was thinking seriously about heading out on his own. The one thing holding him back was Ms. Carrie Lynn Morgan. Carrie Lynn was the prettiest thing Bolt ever laid eyes on. He would see her at church on Sunday and occasionally around the small town where he lived.

Her father, Michael Morgan, arrived from Great Britain years before with lots of old family money and made good. In addition to his hired hands, Morgan owned more than twenty slaves that worked his sprawling bottomland farm.

Bolt had spoken to Carrie Lynn at times after church and they gradually became a little more than friends. Morgan, however, wasn't happy about Carrie Lynn getting too friendly with some hillbilly farm boy, having better things in mind for his daughter.

Bolt would ride out to her home on occasion, or Carrie Lynn would meet him in the woods down by the river. They would sit and talk for hours about the things Bolt was going to do.

The young Ashton was a tall handsome young man and Carrie Lynn was completely taken with him. Bolt wanted to go west as soon as he could, but Carrie Lynn was happy right where she was. She was wealthy and stood to inherit a big piece of land. In spite of many a heated debate about the frontier, their romance blossomed.

Lying awake at night, Bolt often wondered if she could be the one thing to keep him in Tennessee for the rest of his life. He wanted to see the frontier, but giving her up would be too high a price to pay for his wanderlust.

On one of his many visits, Bolt met a young black man that was one of Morgan's slaves. His name was Ezekiel. He was roughly Bolt's age and over time they became somewhat friendly. Bolt was the first white person that ever talked with Ezekiel instead of talking down to him. Bolt discovered, the young slave wasn't much different than himself.

Ezekiel couldn't get away from the back-breaking labor of the farm very often, but when he could, he would go fishing down at the river with Bolt. They would talk about many things. Bolt would go on and on about the western frontier and Ezekiel would listen attentively. Freedom to roam, however, was something a slave could only dream about.

One hot evening, Bolt and Ezekiel were walking back through Morgan's fields toward the slave quarters when Morgan's overseer, Dan Bodine, and several men on horseback, rode up and confronted them.

"Where you been, Boy?" Bodine was from Georgia and he wielded a heavy hand over his charges, feeding his self-esteem by beating on the bodies and spirits of the blacks.

"Just down to the river, Sir," Ezekiel answered with his head down, knowing better than to look Bodine in the eye.

"You got no business at that river, Boy. Maybe I better find some more work for you to do."

"No sir, I got plenty of work to do."

"We're looking for some runaway Alabama darkies," Bodine said, "You see anybody like that?"

"No sir, Mister Dan."

"You're lying to me, Boy. You seen 'em, didn't you."

"No sir, Mister Dan. I ain't seen nobody."

"We were just fishing," Bolt said.

"I didn't ask you," Bodine said without looking at Bolt. He picked up the braided leather whip draped over his saddle horn and let it uncoil. "Boy, you better get for home and right now."

"There's no need for that," Bolt said. His wrinkled brow and two bulging veins on his forehead were signs the warrior spirit was stirring in his blood.

Still ignoring Bolt, Bodine lashed the whip across Ezekiel's back. Wincing in pain at the crack of the whip, Ezekiel began to run towards his family's cabin. Bodine turned back to lash out at Bolt, but the hotheaded young Ashton was already moving.

Despite the overseer's suddenly retreating horse, Bolt managed to get hold of Bodine's coat and drag him out of the saddle. As soon as they were both on the ground, Bolt jerked the unhorsed overseer up and hit him with a hard right fist.

Bodine was back on the ground spitting blood from his busted lip when his companions jumped Bolt. There were five of them and they gave Bolt a bad beating. Before they finished, they held Bolt against a white oak, while Bodine gave him several lashes with the whip.

"Don't ever come back here," Bodine warned as he struggled back on his horse, "I'll kill you next time."

Bolt got up from the ground and stumbled away toward home. His shirt was bloody where his back was laid open from the whip. Bolt stopped at a creek to wash it out before going home. He knew his father would kill Bodine if he ever found out about the lashing.

Enraged and humiliated by the whipping, Bolt never told anyone about it, not even Sam. Bolt vowed he would never be beaten like that again by anyone. He would carry the emotional and physical scars of that whipping for the rest of his life. For one awful moment, he experienced the terror the slaves in the south must have dealt with all of their lives.

Bolt heard later that Bodine found the escaped Alabama slaves hiding in the trees along the river. The overseer killed their leader and left him hanging from a limb, but only after shooting him five times. Even though Bolt was still young, his hatred for Morgan, Bodine, and the institution of slavery was growing with each passing day.

The next Sunday morning, Bolt and his parents were at church. Sam was there and the boys sat in the back row. They wanted to be the first one's out the door after services, so they could get to the creek and go swimming.

The Reverend Thomas Gage was delivering the sermon. Mr. and Mrs. Morgan and Carrie Lynn, along with Dan Bodine and his wife, were sitting down front in their own private box. It was a step up from the main floor on the preacher's right.

The Reverend had been preaching there for as long as most of the children could remember. He was a big man with long white hair and a ponderous beard. Despite his years, he possessed a thunderous voice. An imposing figure looking down from his elevated pulpit, the Reverend Gage was much feared by the young people in the congregation.

Preaching from the book of Exodus, Reverend Gage proclaimed the mighty victory Moses brought about in freeing the Israelites from the Egyptians. Bolt was sitting quietly, listening to the sermon. When he finally heard all he could stand he said something to Sam and the Reverend saw him.

When Reverend Gage paused in mid-sentence, an oppressive silence fell over the meeting house. The Reverend thought he'd teach Bolt a lesson by calling him out in front of the whole congregation. Reverend Gage figured he'd embarrass Bolt and the young Ashton would shrink before him. Grasping the lapel on his long black coat, Gage glared down at Bolt.

"If you have something to add, young Mr. Ashton, perhaps you'd like to share it with all of us."

Much to the Reverend's dismay, Bolt started to get to his feet.

"I'll be glad to share it with you, Reverend." With his strong voice filling the room, the entire congregation turned to look his way. Bolt was still swollen and bruised from the beating he had taken from Bodine and his men. "You say Moses was a great man?"

"He was chosen by God to lead the Israelite slaves out of the bondage of Egypt." The Reverend said it in a loud voice, looking around as if to imply everyone over the age of twelve should know that.

"And that was a good thing?"

"Of course, it was God's will they be free."

"Then why haven't you ever said anything about the slaves in bondage right up the road at Morgan's?"

Hearing that, the congregation began to mumble among themselves. Michael Morgan turned bright red, but he didn't say anything. Carrie Lynn had her head down, trying to hide the smile creeping across her lips.

"Well, that's...different," Gage said, his voice lacking the thunder of a moment before. He was struggling, trying to find the right words to explain. Morgan was the church's biggest financial supporter. "The Israelite's were...God's people."

"Didn't you say, just last week, we're all God's children, created in his own image?"

"Well, yes...but...not the darkies."

"Where does it say that in the book?"

"Well, it's not really in the scriptures...not in so many words...but...."

"Then you, Reverend, are a hypocrite and a liar!"

The crowd gasped when Bolt said that. Bodine got to his feet and started down the center aisle with a couple of men. They planned to remove Bolt from the building by force, but stopped short when Sam stood up.

"You best sit back down, Overseer. Or you'll be the one taking this beating."

The Reverend Gage tried to regain control.

"If that's the way you feel, Bolt, maybe you should just leave."

"I am leaving, and I'll never darken the door of this place again."

As Sam followed Bolt out the door, the crowd sat in stunned silence and watched them go. The Reverend was sweating, trying to think of something to say. Bolt's mother was in tears. Many a member of that congregation had thought it, but the hardheaded young Ashton was the first one to ever say it out loud.

Chapter Two:
1861, Civil War

By June of 1861, Bolt was a grown man in his early thirties. He managed to save enough money over the years to buy his own piece of land, near his parent's farm. Sarah Ashton had given birth to another son who turned fourteen that year. Bolt's parents never planned to have another child at their age, but Trace snuck up on them.

Bolt grew into a quiet, easy-going big man with chiseled features and a lean body from constant hard work. He never had much to say to anyone and he preferred his own company most of the time.

A few might take that as a sign of uncertainty or weakness of spirit, but they would be making a serious mistake. Despite his calm demeanor, he was not a man to be trifled with. His parents always knew Bolt was special, but they weren't sure why.

Sam had occasionally seen Bolt's dark side and it frightened him. Bolt remained constantly on guard to subdue the warrior spirit. He knew if ever released, that spirit was certain to bring pain, suffering, and destruction to whomever was foolish enough to call it out.

Bolt was still thinking about the buffalo grass, but it wasn't the obsession it had been in his youth. Now, it was overshadowed by an unshakable feeling of foreboding. South Carolina seceded from the Union late the year before. Many of the other southern states joined them in January and February. By summer, Tennessee had seceded.

Abraham Lincoln was inaugurated as the sixteenth President of the United States that past March. Lincoln was adamant the Union would not be dissolved. Everyone knew civil war was inevitable.

The war actually started in April when the Confederacy fired on the Union Fort in Charleston Harbor. President Lincoln immediately issued a call to arms. Outright open hostility had not yet commenced, but it was coming. Bolt was in a quandary about the war. He was a proud southerner by birth but he despised the institution of slavery and was ready to fight to end it.

Bolt had been living and working on his place alone for several years. His romance with Carrie Lynn was forbidden by her family after that day at church, but they managed to see each other on rare occasions for a while. Despite the years since their last encounter, Bolt's love for her was still strong.

Carrie Lynn's father arranged a marriage for her to a wealthy young man from Ireland. He came to Tennessee and they were married in 1851. Her wedding day was the worst moment of Bolt's life.

Carrie had given birth to a little girl that was now six-years-old. Throughout all those years, she continued to love Bolt. She would never defy her father or express her feelings to Bolt, but the tall Tennessean was in her thoughts every day. When she would catch sight of him in town her heart would ache to hold him again.

After six years of marriage, her husband contracted diphtheria and died. Carrie moved back home to her parent's farm. Being back so close to him, Bolt was always on her mind.

Bolt never married. His love for Carrie Lynn was something he just never got over. If she had simply rejected him and married another, he would have recovered from that, but Bolt always knew she was in love with him. Deep inside, he was still clinging to the hope she would come back to him someday.

Plenty of women would share their charms with Bolt, and he took advantage of them once in a while. He could never get serious about any of them because his lovely Carrie Lynn was never far from his mind and always in his heart.

True to his word, Bolt never set foot in the church again. The Reverend Gage passed away the year before. He wasn't married. Bolt's mother was one of the women taking care of him at the end.

On the day he died, the Reverend was too weak to speak above a whisper. He asked for Bolt to come to him but Bolt refused. He wasn't going to take part in any conscience clearing on the Reverend's part.

Bolt was building a tool shed on his place one morning when he heard someone approaching. When they got close, Bolt could see it was an older black man on a mule.

When the man pulled up to get off, Bolt realized it was Ezekiel. It had been years since Bolt had seen the slave and he couldn't believe he was the same person. Ezekiel looked twenty years older than Bolt, an old man at thirty-two.

"Mister Ashton," the slave said as he got off his mule.

"It's just Bolt. Ezekiel, it's good to see you again."

"It's good to see you too, I didn't know if you'd remember me. I have a letter here from Ms. Carrie."

"A letter?"

"She said to let no one see it, but you."

Bolt took the sealed envelope and opened it. "There's some water in the bucket over there," he said without looking up.

"Thank you kindly."

Most white folks wouldn't dream of drinking from the same dipper as a slave. It never crossed Bolt's mind. Ezekiel got himself a cool drink and sat in the shade while Bolt finished the letter.

Carrie explained she was older and more independent now. Her love for Bolt was stronger than her need to be accepted by her father. She wrote if he still wanted her, she would leave with him and go anywhere he wanted to go, as long as he would accept her daughter as his own.

"Tell Carrie to meet me at our place along the river tonight," Bolt said, "Tell her...just tell her to meet me." In spite of his excitement, Bolt noticed that Ezekiel was nervous and fidgety. "Is something wrong?"

"Things are bad at Morgan's, real bad."

"I wish there was. . . ."

"It's nothing for you to trouble yourself with. I'll tell Ms. Carrie what you said. You take care now."

"You do the same, my friend."

Bolt left his cabin about two hours before sundown. He made the ride to the river and waited for Carrie Lynn in a little grove of trees. She got there a few minutes later. Without a word Carrie fell into his arms.

Finally free to release all those years of forbidden passion, she kissed him hard on the mouth and he kissed her right back. Bolt laid her down in the sweet grass and started to unbutton her dress. He rushed, thinking this would surely end like it always did in his dreams. Carrie was older, but even more beautiful than he remembered her.

Carrie didn't resist, as he held her in his arms. Bolt wanted all of her as he kissed her mouth over and over. He vowed he would never let her go again. They were together there under the trees for over an hour.

When the sun was down, Carrie Lynn finally got up and began to dress.

"It's getting late. I have to get back."

"When can we be together?"

"I'll arrange to leave tomorrow night after everyone's asleep. I'll bring my little girl and come to your place. We can go from there."

"I'll be waiting."

"Where are we going?"

"I don't know…west, I suppose. This has happened so fast, I haven't thought about it. It doesn't matter, as long as you're with me."

Carrie got on her horse and bent down to kiss him one more time, "Goodbye for now, my love."

Bolt stood in the twilight and watched her go until she was out of sight. His heart was full to nearly bursting. This was like one of his dreams only this was actually happening. After all those lonely years he was finally going to have his Carrie Lynn. Bolt mounted his horse and headed home. He had a lot to do before the next night.

When Bolt got home, he went to the corral to put his horse up. When he shut the gate he heard a soft noise, something or someone was in his barn. He carried a sidearm as a matter of habit, a Remington 1858 Army Revolver. He wore it butt forward in a cross-draw holster on his left side. Pulling the big cap-and-ball pistol with his right hand, Bolt entered the dark barn.

"Who's in here?" No one answered, "I know you're here…come on out."

"Don't shoot," a familiar voice said from the dim interior, "It's me, Ezekiel."

Easing the hammer down, Bolt holstered his gun.

"What in the world are you doing here?"

Before the slave could answer, a woman and two young boys came down from the hay loft.

"We got to get away," Ezekiel said. "This is my wife and my boys."

"They'll kill you if they catch you here."

"Better to be dead than go back there."

"What happened?"

"My old daddy was working, chopping wood," Ezekiel explained, "He was too feeble to be doing that. He missed a lick with that axe and cut himself real bad on the leg."

"I don't understand what that has to do. . . ."

"I know I put you in a bad spot by coming here. I'm sorry, but I got no one else to help me. Forgive me for bringing so much trouble to your door."

"Forget about that," Bolt said, "What about your daddy?"

"He was bad off for the last several days," Ezekiel said. "We done the best we could, but his leg got to stinking and hurting real bad. Bodine came down to check on him last night. They took my daddy out into the night, said they was going to doctor him. We heard a shot a little later…we…we ain't seen him since."

"Do you think they just killed him?"

Ezekiel hung his head to hide the tears in his eyes. "I asked Bodine that very question this afternoon. He just laughed, said my daddy belonged to Morgan and it was none of my business. Then he told me to say goodbye to my boys because they was going to send them off to a trader down in Nashville. I didn't know what else to do. I…I can't lose my boys, it just ain't right."

"You won't lose the boys," Bolt said, his face reddening, "What can I do to help?"

"Thank you Jesus," Ezekiel whispered as his faith in Bolt was confirmed. "We got to get up to Kentucky and the Ohio River. There are people there who will help us go north, Pennsylvania they called it. Mr. Lincoln won't have no slaves up there, maybe we can hide out until this war sets us free."

Bolt had three saddle horses in the barn. "Take the two sorrels and go. You'll have to stay in the deep woods and travel only at night."

"Thank you," Ezekiel said, taking Bolt's hand, "I knew I could count on you."

The woman placed her small hand on Bolt's arm. "You're an answered prayer."

"I don't know about that," Bolt replied. "I'm afraid you still have plenty of trouble ahead. I'll gather up all the food I got in the cabin. You all fill that canteen over there, saddle those horses and...."

Bolt was interrupted by the sound of horses approaching. The torch-bearing riders seemed to be coming up the road to Bolt's house. Turning back, Bolt saw the terror reflected in Ezekiel's tear-filled eyes.

"Get back in there and hide," he said. Bolt walked out just as Bodine and three armed men rode up to the barn. "What are you doing on my place?"

"Looking for runaways," Bodine replied, "a friend of yours, have you seen him?"

"Get off my land!"

"We'll go, after we search that barn. By the way, I followed Carrie Lynn this evening, first time I ever saw her naked. Her father knows all about your little plan. She won't be coming here tomorrow night or any other."

Bolt's hand moved to the big .44 as two pulsing veins popped out on his forehead. Bodine had finally crossed the threshold and Bolt's warrior spirit was raging to get out.

"You make one move toward that barn and I'll kill all of you," he warned.

"Big talk for a man alone," In the twilight, Bodine failed to notice Bolt was armed. The overseer thought he was invincible as he looked back to his men and motioned toward the barn, "Burn it to the ground."

Having despised Bodine for a long time, Bolt never hesitated. The quiet country evening was shattered with a roar and a flash of flame. The demon spirit was unleashed on the world as Bolt's first bullet ripped through the startled overseer's chest, driving him off the back of his horse.

Bodine called it forth, now the spirit was focused on the remaining nightriders. Their only choice was to kill Bolt or pay with their lives. The men with Bodine were caught completely off-guard, but it was clear, Bolt intended to kill all of them. It was too late to run and they had precious little time to react. These phony-brave men were used to running down helpless people, not facing an armed and dangerous man.

Another roar split the night as fire and smoke spewed from the muzzle of Bolt's revolver. The nearest man dropped his torch, but he was blown out of the saddle before he could get his pistol out.

Thick white smoke reflected the flickering light from the torches as Bolt cocked the hammer once again. The stench of burning powder was strong amid the chaos of dying men, pistol shots, and stampeding horses.

In a blind panic, one of the remaining men put a ball through his boot trying to yank his pistol out of the holster. The other one got off a hurried shot, but it missed. Before either of them could fire again, Bolt killed both of them.

Even with his companions lying dead all around him, Bodine wasn't done. With his breath coming in wet ragged gasps, he lay on the ground cursing Bolt.

"Damn you…you. . . ." In spite of eminent death, Bodine tried to raise his pistol. Bolt shot him once more, and then again. He continued cocking the hammer and pulling the trigger on empty cylinders until Ezekiel came out of the barn and spoke to him.

"Bolt…Bolt, are you alright?"

Bolt was trembling as he waited for the demon spirit to go away.

"You have to get away from here," he finally said turning to Ezekiel. "When Morgan finds out these men are dead, he'll know you were here."

Bolt returned the empty pistol to its holster as he tried to comprehend the unspeakable violence that had just taken place. It was the first time he ever fired a shot at anyone, now the warrior spirit had brutally slain four men.

The nightrider's horses were gone. Bolt knew it would only be a couple of hours before they would get back to Morgan's and he would come looking for Bodine with more men.

Ezekiel had the horses ready when Bolt came out with the food and an old flint-lock musket. "Take this. It's all I got." He handed the slave a small pouch containing powder and ball.

"Good bye, my friend," Ezekiel said from the saddle. A terrified little boy was clinging to his back. Slinging the pouch over his shoulder, Ezekiel took Bolt's hand. "I know these animals are valuable, but I got no way to pay you."

"Saving these boys is payment enough. Remember, ride straight north, but only at night. Stay in the thickest brush you can find in the daylight. No fires, day or night. Eat everything cold."

"God bless you," the woman said. The other child was up behind her.

"You too ma'am, now get out of here." Bolt released the slave's hand and slapped his horse on the rump. He watched them ride away until they were swallowed up by the night. "Lord," Bolt whispered, "If anybody ever needed your help, it's them."

After they were gone, Bolt gathered whatever gear he thought he would need and saddled his favorite mount, a tall walking horse named General Jackson. The big gelding was jet black, strong and long winded. His endurance was about to be tested on that bloody night. Bolt rode away from his farm and went to find Sam.

Sam had just gone to bed when Bolt rode up to his cabin. Sam and his pregnant wife came out on the porch with a lamp to welcome him.

"It's a little late to be coming around for a visit, Cousin," Sam said with a yawn, "What's wrong?"

"I need some help."

Bolt explained what happened and that he was going to be gone for a while.

"They'll be after you as soon as they find those bodies," Sam said.

"That'll be tomorrow, and I'll be far from here by then."

"Let's go down to Morgan's right now and kill the rest of 'em. We'll throw 'em all in the river and that'll be the end of it."

"There's been enough killing already. You don't need to get mixed up in this. You're gonna have a family to worry about."

"Well, you can't go now," Sam said, "the south will need every fighting man."

"I don't think I can do that."

"What do you mean? We all knew it was coming. We should head down to Nashville and sign up."

"Sign up? You have a baby on the way, this war isn't for you."

"Everybody says the war won't last long, I don't want to miss it. Them Yankee's got no stomach for fighting. We'll probably be back before the baby gets here. Just come with me, they'll forget about Bodine as soon as the fighting starts."

"I'm going to sign up, but not in Nashville."

"Then I'll go with you," Sam said, "where we going?"

"I'm going north; I'll not fight to save slavery."

"You ain't no Damn Yankee!"

"I've been praying for a way to end this for years. Now it seems I've been given a chance."

"You can't do this," Sam pleaded, "Please...think about what you're saying."

"I have thought about it, you can still come with me?"

"I can't do that. Tennessee's part of the south...it's our home. This war ain't just about slavery. The Damn Yankees up in Washington City think they can tell us what to do."

"You're just repeating what you've read in the Nashville papers. The South can't win this war. They're fighting for the wrong cause and God won't stand for it. My mind's made up. I'm going to join Mr. Lincoln's Army."

"What if we meet on the battlefield?"

"Let's pray that never happens. You know I'd never do anything to hurt you."

"I know that, but...Bolt, please...."

"I want you to tell my mother I'm not a murderer, I had no choice. Tell her I love her and get word to Carrie Lynn to wait for me."

"Carrie Lynn, what's she got to do with this?"

"There's no time, good-bye, Cousin."

They both had tears in their eyes as Bolt got on his horse and started to leave. When Bolt was in the saddle, he pulled up, and turned his horse back to Sam.

"There's one more thing. Tell my little brother to stay out of this war. He's too young, mother needs at least one son alive and well, and you watch your butt...you hear me?"

"Damn it, Bolt," the big man said, shaking his head. The tears where running down his cheeks, but he knew there was no use in arguing. "Alright...alright, I'll tell him...and you watch yours."

Sam stood in silence as his oldest and dearest friend thundered away into the night.

It was just after daylight when Michael Morgan and the county sheriff rode up to Bolt's place. The posse was shocked when they found Dan Bodine hanging from a noose in a big white oak next to Bolt's barn. Powder burns on his shirt indicated he had been shot multiple times. Two days later, the whole county was plastered with wanted posters.

WANTED FOR MURDER AND AIDING RUNAWAY SLAVES BOLTON ASHTON $1,000 REWARD OFFERED BY MICHAEL MORGAN DEAD OR ALIVE

The next two years passed quickly as bloody Civil War raged across the land. Sam's prediction of a short conflict never materialized. On the afternoon of July, 2, 1863, Bolt was in a green Pennsylvania hayfield.

"Captain Ashton, are your men ready?" the general officer asked.

"Yes sir, General; just waiting for your orders, Sir." He snapped the general a sharp salute with his drawn saber. Bolt had just received a battlefield promotion in the Union Army's Second Brigade.

"It's essential we take this ground. We can't allow the rebels to occupy the high ground."

"We'll take it, Sir."

"You're from Tennessee aren't you?"

"Yes sir, Smith County."

"That knife, it isn't official issue, is it?"

"No sir, but. . . ."

"Why are you carrying it?"

"This knife was given to me by Colonel Davy Crockett himself."

"You aren't old enough to have known Davy Crockett."

"I was seven-years-old when he put it my hand, Sir. He was on his way to Texas."

"Keep the knife, Captain. I'm proud to have you with me."

"Thank you, Sir, I'm proud to be here."

General Custer returned Bolt's salute, wheeled his horse around, and galloped to the head of the column.

"I didn't think the General even knew my name, much less where I'm from," Bolt said to his big black horse, "I guess us Tennesseans are scarce in this army."

The Second Brigade, Third Cavalry Division was just south of Hanover, Pennsylvania, preparing to engage the army of Northern Virginia. George Armstrong Custer was appointed to the rank of Brevet General just a few days before. He was given command of the Third Cavalry at Gettysburg and was now preparing to ride to glory with his men.

Bolt had great respect for his commanding officer, even though Custer was several years younger. Custer was brash and even arrogant at times, but he never sent his men into battle, he led them. Bolt would do his best and nothing short of death would keep him from following General Custer across that Pennsylvania field to victory.

"Are we ready, Sergeant-Major?" Bolt asked his orderly.

"Yes Sir," the sergeant replied, "We go on your orders, Sir."

Sergeant-Major Benjamin Bailey was the man Bolt depended on most in his command. He had been in the army much longer than Bolt. Ben knew military protocol and he was steady and level headed.

"General Jackson, my friend," Bolt said to his faithful mount. "This may be our last few minutes on this earth or it could be our finest hour." The old horse was battle-hardened from being in the Union Army for two years. He would stand steady at Bolt's side, regardless of how much hell was raging around them.

Bolt's mouth was dry and he was scared, but he would never let that fear be seen by his men or allow it to get in the way of doing his duty. He thought of his mother back in Tennessee, and wondered if he would ever see her again. He whispered a silent prayer that Sam wasn't across that field waiting for him. His thoughts were interrupted when General Custer raised his saber and shouted.

"Follow me you Wolverines, Charge!"

It was an epic scene as the Third U.S. Cavalry launched themselves at the enemy. The bright stars and stripes of the Union battle flag snapping atop the guidons, galloping horses, bugles sounding, and sabers flashing in the hot July sunshine.

The cannon fire was murderous. Swarms of shot and shrapnel were screaming by Bolt's head as he rode directly at the Rebel Army. In spite of the artillery shells exploding all around them, the tall Tennessean was standing in his stirrups, leaning into Jackson's neck, waving his saber, and urging his men on,

The noise was horrendous, smoke from the burning powder was thick and stinging his eyes. Men were falling all around him when a huge explosion erupted in Bolt's face. Searing pain wracked his body, just before everything went black.

General Jackson went down hard and Bolt was thrown onto the bloody ground. When he started to come to, Bolt was lying on his back in the grass, unable to move, and convinced he was dying.

Bolt could hear Ben Bailey urging him to get up, but his body wouldn't respond. There seemed to be a crushing weight on his legs.

His arms and chest felt as if they were on fire. He reached down and felt of his chest, it was hot and sticky. He stared in dazed amazement as he drew back his blood-soaked hand.

Men were running all around him. Even through the fog in his mind, Bolt became aware of a man standing over him with a musket. The man was wearing a faded gray jacket and worn-out butternut homespun trousers. He was shoeless and his feet were covered with blood.

In spite of being aware of every detail of the situation, Bolt was helpless to defend himself. Johnny Reb was screaming at the top of his lungs as he raised the empty musket over his head, preparing to bayonet the helpless Yankee Captain.

Before the Rebel soldier could strike, a .58 caliber mini ball fired in terror by one his own companions, struck him in the temple. The Rebel's head exploded like a crimson melon and he collapsed into a faceless mass of quivering flesh on the ground next to Bolt.

It was late in the day when Bolt began to regain his senses. Through the fog in his brain, he could hear men crying all around him. Occasionally, he would hear some poor soul wailing in pain and anguish. Looking to his right, he saw bits and pieces of shattered humanity discarded in a grotesque pile.

A mangled hand protruding from the mound seemed to beckon to him. Big blue-bottle flies were crawling over its twisted bloody fingers in the hot evening air. The sickly-sweet stench of rotting blood and lingering death was everywhere.

Bolt thought for a moment that he too might be dead and he was in hell. He knew by his faith hell wasn't in his future. He was in so much pain, it certainly wasn't heaven, and he must still be alive. He tried to roll over and get up, but he was too weak. Bolt was suffering from thirst in the stifling heat and needed water.

As his head cleared, Bolt became aware of a man looking down on him. He threw his arms up to defend himself.

"Take it easy, Sir. You're among friends."

"Where…am I?"

"Gettysburg...you just take it easy, Captain. You're going to be...Bolt...Bolt Ashton. Is that you? It can't be, but...sweet Jesus...it sure is you."

"Am I...are we...dead?"

"No, no...you're a hard man to kill, I reckon. You're gonna be fine. You got some shrapnel in your arms and legs, but it ain't that bad. None of it hit anything important. The doctor said you would keep until they finished with the bad hurt men."

"Don't let them cut off my legs," Bolt begged, grabbing the man by the sleeve.

"They ain't gonna do no such a thing," the man assured him, "I told you, you're gonna be fine."

"Where's my horse?" Bolt asked, remembering General Jackson.

"I'm afraid he didn't make it. Your horse took the worst of the blast and probably saved your life. Most of the blood on you is his."

As the fog in Bolt's head cleared, he noticed the man with him was wearing a dark blue woolen jacket with private's stripes. The man held Bolt's head up and offered him a drink of water. As he took a sip from the cup the stranger lifted to his lips, Bolt noticed the pink palm and scared black fingers holding the cup.

Looking up into the stranger's eyes, Bolt realized he had seen them before, but the old fear was gone. Those eyes were clear and bright with the light of freedom.

"Ezekiel, is that you?"

"Yes sir, Private Ezekiel Washington...United States Army. It's me all right...in the flesh."

"Well Private, I guess you made it after all...thank God."

"We made it, thanks to him...and you.

"What about your family?"

"My wife and boys are safe, just a few miles away in Hanover."

"Both of us here," Bolt whispered, "I'll be damned."

"I doubt that," Ezekiel said. Bending down, he rested his rough, labor-scarred hand on Bolt's forehead. "You all take care of this one," he said to the medical team nearby, "he's something real special."

The battle raged for two more days until the Union Army finally emerged victorious. What was left of the shattered Rebel forces limped back across the Potomac to Virginia, away from the bloodiest battle ever fought on American soil. In spite of more than fifty-thousand casualties, the war would rage on for nearly two more years.

Bolt was up and around in just a week or so. His legs were sore, but still there. He was walking by the remount corral one afternoon when he heard another kind of battle being waged.

A big gray outlaw stud was fighting three men who were trying to tie him down and geld him. They had three ropes on him, but it wasn't doing them much good. Squealing, biting, and kicking, the big horse had no intention of being cut on by anyone.

Bolt walked up just as the outlaw hooked one of his attackers with his off-hind foot, sending the man tumbling across the corral. Bruised and muddy, the man got to his feet, went to the gate, and picked up an axe handle.

"Stand down, Sergeant," Bolt ordered, "That'll be about enough of that."

"Yes sir, but this outlaw don't know nothing but fight. I was just gonna show him who's boss."

"I think that's obvious," Bolt said, "You men go take a break."

"Yes sir, but watch him, he's a killer."

When they were gone, Bolt walked into the corral and approached the wild-eyed horse. Bolt figured him to be about four-years-old. The big gray stood sixteen hands and weighed well over half-a-ton.

The big gray outlaw jumped away from Bolt at first, but Bolt kept talking to him in low tones and slowly advancing on him. Bolt never made eye contact or approached him head on. He eased up shoulder-first toward the big horse. After several minutes, Bolt was able to put his hands on the gray and take the ropes from around his neck.

Bolt left orders to leave the horse alone. He would stop by and see him every day for the next week. Bolt would bring him an apple, carrot, or a handful of sugar, whatever he could find.

One hot afternoon, about a week later, Bolt decided he was healed up enough to try and ride the gray. The first five or six times he got in the saddle weren't very pretty. Finally, after nearly an hour, they came to an understanding of sorts.

It was obvious neither of them could be broken, and neither of them would ever quit, but if enough respect was shown, the big gray outlaw would allow the man to stay on his back. A lifelong bond between man and horse was forged there in that corral. Bolt was leading the big horse out of the corral and back to his quarters when the remount sergeant walked up.

"Looks like you got yourself a horse," the sergeant said. "I still think we should geld him."

"He's fine, just like he is," Bolt said. "I like his spirit. What's his name?"

"Sumbitch is all I ever heard him called."

"In that case," Bolt said to the big horse, "I'm gonna call you Rufus."

"Rufus," the sergeant repeated.

"After Rufus T. Russell, back home."

"Funny name for a horse, Sir."

"Maybe, but those crazy Russell boys were mean as they come. They'd fight an alligator and give him the first bite. Rufus T was the worst of 'em and this big outlaw's just like him."

"Whatever you say, Sir, he's your horse."

"Yep," Bolt said, "he sure is."

Early on the morning of April 11, 1865, Bolt and his men were camped on a wooded hillside overlooking Berryville, Virginia, in the northern Shenandoah Valley. Bolt was awakened by the sentry.

"A rider coming hard, Sir."

"Ours or theirs?"

"Looks like one of ours, Sir."

The trooper galloped up to Bolt's tent and bailed off his lathered horse.

"Urgent dispatch for you, Captain!" he said, "It's over, Sir. It's finally over."

Bolt opened the dispatch case and removed the folded paper. It contained news that General Lee had surrendered the Army of Virginia to General Grant at Appomattox Courthouse just two days before. The Civil War was indeed over.

"It's over, men," Bolt told the group gathered around him.

"Who won?" Ben Bailey asked with a grin.

Hosting the paper over his head, Bolt said, "The Union has been preserved." A big cheer went up from the small group of soldiers. The other men in the troop began to get out of their tents as the word spread through the camp. "We've been ordered back to Winchester," Bolt said, "Let's pack up and get out of here, Sergeant-Major."

"Yes sir, with pleasure, Sir."

Their celebration would be short. In just three days, the unshakable force that held the Union together was gone. Abraham Lincoln was dead at the hands of an assassin.

Bolt went home shortly after Lee's surrender. He was allowed to purchase Rufus when he was discharged. Custer asked him to consider staying in the cavalry, but Bolt was tired of regimental life and wanton bloodshed.

He had done what he set out to do. Slavery was now just a shameful page in the history books. Anxious to get away from the army, Bolt pushed Rufus hard to cover the five hundred miles that stood between him and Tennessee.

When Bolt got home, he found the family farm pretty much untouched by the war. His parents, however, had suffered quite a bit at the hands of the roving forage patrols of both armies and the gangs of Partisan Rangers that roamed the countryside.

The Rangers were guerilla fighters organized by the Confederacy. Many of them had no real allegiance to either side and were only in business for themselves.

Much of the Ashton's livestock had been taken from them. The Union Army had taken their horses for remounts. Mules were scarce and expensive if you could even find one for sale. It was difficult to plow and plant without any draft animals and most of the fields were lying fallow.

The elder Ashton had been shot trying to keep the guerillas from the house one dark night in 1863. He recovered, but he wasn't the man Bolt remembered. He was thin and unsteady, using a cane to get around.

It was a great reunion with his mother. She was so happy to learn Bolt survived the war. His brother, Trace, did as Bolt asked and stayed at home.

Bolt unsaddled Rufus and put him out in his dad's pasture.

"I think I'll spend the night and go on home in the morning."

"There are a couple of things you need to know," his dad said.

"What's that?"

"You don't have a home anymore, and you can't stay here."

"Why do you say that?"

"You're still wanted for the murder of those four men. The courts have confiscated your farm. I tried to buy it, but there wasn't enough money. Morgan owns it now and there's a substantial reward out for you."

"Reward," Bolt repeated.

"When they found those dead men at your place and you gone, they assumed you did it. Boy, I tried to warn you about that damn temper of yours. Bodine's body hanging in the tree really got them fired up."

"Yes sir, I suppose it did."

"They all knew you had it in for Bodine, you knew that runaway slave, and after you joined the union army, that's all it took. There was no need for a trial, you were guilty."

"I need to get word to Carrie Lynn that I'm back; then we can get out of here."

His dad looked down at the ground and shook his head.

"I'm afraid, Son, that ain't gonna happen either."

"Not going to happen! She has to be waiting for me."

"Morgan was enraged by the thought of her being with you. He threatened to take her daughter away if she ever tried to contact you."

"I wrote her letters."

"I doubt she ever got them." His dad hesitated for a moment. "I'm sorry, Son, but she's married."

"Married, that can't be. Who did she...."

"Doc Williams."

"Lawrence Williams, he's twenty years her senior."

"That's true, but it doesn't change the fact she's married. They're living down in Nashville now. Doc's running for the legislature."

Devastated, Bolt walked away from his dad to be alone for a while. He spent the last four years fighting a war so he could come home and marry the love of his life. Now that dream was shattered once again.

He asked about Sam, but no one knew where he was or if he was even alive. To make things worse, Sam's wife died in labor along with their baby boy. No one knew if Sam ever received the news or not.

Bolt's whole world had once again been torn completely apart by his stubbornness to always do the right thing. If he had only stayed nearby, he could have stolen Carrie Lynn away and maybe convinced Sam to stay home.

Bolt saddled Rufus that afternoon, kissed his mother, and said goodbye to his dad and little brother. He was heading west, leaving Smith County for good. It was tough leaving his boyhood home behind, knowing he probably would never see it or his parents again.

Bolt had one more thing to do before he left. Michael Morgan had been causing him emotional pain and misery most of his life. Since he was already wanted for murder, one more killing wouldn't make any difference.

Bolt had become a dark and dangerous man during the war. He survived by allowing that demon spirit to live outside of him. The men he killed were innumerable. He was a true paradox, spending time on his knees every night praying to God for strength, and every day ruthlessly slaying his fellow man.

The sun was going down when Bolt neared the Morgan farm. He could almost picture Carrie Lynn sitting on the porch, waiting for him, like she did when they were kids. There was no anger or even revenge in what he was about to do. Bolt was simply going to kill a man he despised. He was quiet and calm as he rode up the lane toward the house.

The slave cabins were empty and silent. The place looked abandoned, overgrown with briars and brush. The horses and cattle were missing and the fields were full of weeds. Bolt was glad to see the farm in such disarray. If anybody deserved poverty, it was Morgan.

Michael Morgan was coming out of the house with a shotgun when Bolt rode up. Morgan was frail and unsteady, much older than the last time Bolt had seen him.

"That's far enough," he warned, "Who's there? What do you want?"

Bolt pulled his pistol and cocked the hammer. "I'm here to kill you,"

"Ashton…you survived."

Instead of raising his shotgun, the old man began to tremble. The shotgun rattled down the steps after he dropped it and sagged to his knees. Morgan knelt there, eyes downcast and head bowed, unable to look Bolt in the eye.

"Then go ahead and do it. It'll be a blessing. My life has gone to hell anyway. There's never been any peace in this house because of you."

Bolt was looking down the barrel of his pistol. "It should have been a lot different. We could have been family."

Tears were streaking the grime on the old man's face as he struggled to speak.

"I know…I know that now," he said, "she would've waited for you, but I lied. I told her you were dead…at Gettysburg."

"Dead…and she. . . ." Bolt was nearly speechless. Once again, the love of his life had been ripped away from him when all either of them ever wanted, was to be together.

"I'm truly sorry," the old man said, "It nearly killed her, but it was too late. I couldn't take it back. I've wished a thousand times. . . ." Unable to finish, Morgan knelt there and waited for Bolt's bullet.

With his heart breaking, Bolt couldn't bear anymore. He forgot the hatred he'd been carrying around for this old man. Morgan was already paying a high price for his actions, killing him would only provide him with an easy way out. Letting the hammer down, Bolt holstered his pistol and turned away.

Bolt had seen a lot of the country during the war. Smith County just held painful memories and faded dreams for him now. The woman he loved wasn't there anymore and he couldn't face the memories of her. Everywhere he looked, he could see her. Sam was missing and probably dead. Bolt's home belonged to a man that he despised more than any other, and he was still had a price on his head. A lot of men would do anything to make a thousand dollars, although, he doubted Morgan could pay it.

Bolt knew he had to go. Maybe this was his chance to finally see the buffalo grass. The country was growing, railroads were pushing westward. There was fortune and adventure on the frontier and Bolt wanted his share of it. He decided to seek his destiny in Texas.

Bolt briefly considered stopping in Nashville to find Carrie Lynn, tell her the truth, and possibly kill Doc Williams to get her back. He decided there was enough blood on his hands already, Doc was innocent in all of this, and seeing Carrie Lynn again would only cause incredible pain and suffering for both of them.

It was best he remain dead to her and get out of Tennessee as quickly and as quietly as possible. Bolt was racked with heartache and doubt as he passed Nashville, but he pushed on, never looking back. He was headed west to outrun his memories and find his destiny, whatever it might turn out to be.

It took him a week to reach the Mississippi River at Memphis. He went down to the riverfront and found a ferry to get across.

"Where you headed, Son?" one of the crew asked him as they secured Rufus on the deck.

"Don't rightly know," Bolt replied. "West...Texas, I reckon."

"You be careful. I hear tales of cut-throat border gangs and renegade Indians in that Texas country."

"I'll keep my eyes open."

Chapter Three:
Journey to the Lonesome Wind

After five weeks, Bolt arrived in San Antonio. He rode passed the battered remains of the Mission San Antonio de Bexar, better known to Texans as The Alamo. The old mission was overgrown with weeds. There were no crosses or monuments to mark the passing of the brave defenders. With their blood soaked into the soil and their ashes mixed with the swirling Texas dust, those men were, and would forever remain, a part of this big country.

Bolt stepped off of Rufus, removed his hat, and stood there in silence. It was his way of showing the respect he had for his fellow Tennessean, and good friend, Davy Crockett, who died there with Travis, Jim Bowie, and a hundred-eighty others, fighting for Texas Independence.

With his hand on his knife, Bolt remembered the day Davy gave it to him. He could still hear Davy giving him the best advice he ever got.

"Son, if you know you're right, then go ahead." Bolt had lived by that code ever since.

The Alamo was a brutal testament that Tennessean's and Texan's were all forged in the same fiery furnace. Hardheaded and independent, neither could be told how to live their lives by anyone. They might grudgingly submit to being governed, but they could never be ruled.

Bolt put his horse up at the livery and got himself a room in the hotel. He figured to sleep in a bed at least one night. He wasn't sure where he was going, and it might be his last chance for a long time.

After a bath and a clean shirt he made his way down the street to a small café. Bolt walked through the door and took a seat at a table in the corner. Surveying his surroundings, he noticed an attractive tanned woman who was standing near the kitchen, watching him. A waiter started to bring him a menu until she grabbed the waiter by the sleeve.

"Evening stranger," she said when she got to Bolt's table, "What brings you in here?" She spoke perfect English but with a sultry Mexican accent.

Bolt pulled off his hat and gave her a smile, "Just need a bite to eat ma'am."

"Well, you've come to the right place. We have the best food in San Antonio."

She was five-feet and a couple inches with long dark hair and brown eyes. Bolt noticed right off she was a well-built woman. She was the first Mexican woman he had ever been around and he was taken by her beauty.

"What's good?" he asked.

"The special tonight is chicken enchiladas."

"That sounds fine. I'll have that."

Bolt had no idea what an enchilada was, but if it was chicken, how bad could it be? He never even glanced at the menu. He was too busy exploring every inch of the voluptuous woman standing in front of him. She was dressed in a long flowing skirt with a low-cut flowery top that clung below her shoulders. Her skin was smooth and tan, she smelled like desert flowers.

"I'll be right back, coffee?" she asked over her shoulder.

"Yes ma'am, thank you kindly."

Bolt watched her walk away with interest. This lady was a lot of woman. She had a way of walking in that swaying skirt that most of the men in the place took notice of.

Returning with Bolt's supper, she sat down with him. He began to eat as she tried to make small talk.

"What's your name, Stranger?"

"Bolt, ma'am…Bolt Ashton."

"Well, Bolt, what brings you to San Antonio?"

"Just passing through."

"Passing through to where?"

"West," he said.

"Where are you from?"

"Tennessee."

This lady was struggling to get a conversation started with the quiet drifter. She was attracted to his rugged looks and she loved his voice. She could have all the attention she wanted from the regular clientele, but it had been a long time since a man like Bolt had come through her door. She was working hard for any attention at all from him.

"Are you married?"

"No ma'am; never found the time, or any woman that would have me."

"I somehow doubt that," she said. With her elbows on the table and her chin in her hands, she stared at the quiet drifter, "You haven't asked my name."

"Sorry," Bolt said, sipping his coffee, "what's your name?"

"I'm Sarah, I own this place."

"Pleased to meet you, Sarah, that's my mother's name. Begging your pardon, ma'am, but that's a strange name for a lady from around here."

"You mean a Mexican?"

"Well, yes ma'am."

"My mother was Mexican. Father was a Baptist preacher from Louisiana."

"Well it's a lovely name for a beautiful lady."

"Thank you for saying so. Let me know if you need anything."

As Sarah got up and walked away, she glanced over her shoulder to see if he was watching. Bolt sat and finished his meal as Sarah took care of her other customers. The food was a little spicier than he was used to, but he liked it. The Tennessean figured he was going to like Texas.

Sarah was closely watching Bolt from across the room. When he was finished she went back to his table.

"Can I do anything else for you?"

"No ma'am, it was a fine meal, thank you very much."

"Anything at all."

Bolt was no stranger to female companionship, and he knew exactly what she was saying. He was tempted but held back. His heart was still heavy from learning the truth about Carrie Lynn. Even though it had been a long time, the thought of being with another woman wasn't really on his mind.

"I'm just fine," he replied, "think I'll turn in."

"Where are you staying?"

"I have a room at the hotel down the street."

Reaching out, Sarah took his hand, "Will you come back tomorrow night?"

"I'm moving on west at first light."

"Well, have a good night."

"Thank you…you too," he said, turning away.

Bolt went back to his hotel and turned in for the night. The cantina next door was still loud and he had trouble getting to sleep. His mind was on the beautiful lady that sat with him in the café.

It was after ten when he finally put her out of his mind and dozed off. Shortly after falling asleep, Bolt was awakened by a soft tapping on his door. He got out of bed, slipped on his pants, pulled his pistol, and walked to the door.

"Who's there?"

"It's me, Sarah."

Bolt opened the door to find his lovely hostess wearing a blue cotton shawl over her head.

"The clerk told me which room was yours," she whispered, her hands on his bare chest, "Are you going to let me in or not?"

"Sorry," Bolt said as he let the hammer down on his pistol and stepped aside, "Please, come in."

As soon as the door was closed behind her, Sarah put her arms around Bolt and kissed him hard on the mouth. There was no need for any further conversation, Bolt knew exactly why she was there and he was happy to supply whatever it was she wanted. Bolt didn't get much sleep that night, but he decided he was really going to like Texas.

Bolt slipped out at daylight the next morning without waking her. He was in a much better mood on that fine Texas morning. The world seemed brighter. Maybe life held some promise after all.

After saddling Rufus, he headed southwest toward the Mexican border. Bolt heard there were cattle ranches there that might be hiring. With his army pay just about gone, he needed a job.

A little reluctant to leave such a sensuous woman behind, Bolt thought for a moment maybe San Antonio might be a good place to settle. That thought evaporated as the memory of Carrie Lynn returned to him. Bolt had never gotten anything but pain from being in love and he vowed to fight against that emotion from then on. If he ever managed to get over Carrie Lynn there would never be another. He intended to take whatever he could from the ladies and move on.

West Texas was a land of cactus, mesquite brush, dust, and drought. Everything growing in that arid country had stickers. Texas longhorn cattle ran wild in the brush. Those bovine will-of-the-wisps were fair game for any man tough enough to catch them. The only problem was they weren't worth anything in Texas. The more Bolt saw of this big country, the more he liked it.

Everett Monday was a genuine, native-bred Texan. Born in Val Verde, he fought the Mexican Army alongside his older brother and General Sam Houston at San Jacinto, when he was just thirteen. He had been a bounty hunter and battled the Comanche's throughout most of his life.

Everett never got involved in the Civil War. He was down in Mexico for much of it. It always seemed like a distant battle to him and really none of his business. When they were kids, his little brother had trouble pronouncing Everett's name. It always sounded like Ebrett. His kid brother shortened it to Eb and the nickname stuck.

Eb was in his forties when he decided to settle down and take up a safer profession. Tired of hunting wanted men below the border, he went to work as a cowhand for Coop Cooper on the Busted Wheel Ranch.

Eb's hair was nearly white. He wore it shoulder length and he had a neatly trimmed beard. He always wore a fringed leather shirt. His britches were tucked into his high-topped boots and held up by suspenders. He carried a large knife on his belt along with a .44 caliber, 1860 Colt Army percussion revolver. His constant companion was a double-barreled, twelve-bore made by W.W. Greener of New Castle, England.

Eb was at the Cantina, in the little border-town of Coyote Flats, enjoying a warm beer when Bolt walked in and went to the bar.
"Can I get a cool glass of water?"
Nearly everyone in the place laughed out loud. Most of the men in the cantina were Mexican cowboys. They didn't think too much of the gringos that stole this land from their grandfathers and they never missed a chance to humiliate one of them.
"We only serve a man's drink in here," one of them said.
"Si, Gringo," another one added, "If you want water, go to the well and ask one of the old women to draw it for you."

Eb was watching all of this with little interest. Most of the Americans that came into this cantina would leave quietly without any trouble. The Mexicans knew of Eb's reputation and they left him alone.

Being hot and thirsty, Bolt was in no mood to laugh, and it wouldn't be long before he would have a bellyful of these Mexican cowboys.
"Alright give me a beer," he told the bartender. Bolt wasn't much of a drinker, but at this point, he needed something wet.
There was a hot little chili-pepper of a waitress moving around the clientele that afternoon and she spotted Bolt right away. She brushed by him, and when he ignored her, she pushed herself up against him and spoke something in Spanish.
"Pardon me, ma'am," Bolt said.
The chili-pepper flung her arms around his neck and tried to pull him down to her. Bolt had seen prettier women, but the chili-pepper was the best in sight. He had been on the trail from San Antonio for well over a week and his encounter there with Sarah stirred up some long-dormant fires. He wasn't about to disappoint this new lady.

"Name's Bolt," he said, putting his hands on her waist. "I'm not from around here."

Most Mexican men weren't very tall. The long-legged Tennessean stood out in a crowd and evidently the Mexican women liked what they saw. She pressed herself against him while offering up her mouth like she wanted to kiss him.

Bolt could feel the heat from her body against his. Having never known women like these Texans, Bolt figured either Texas was a real friendly place or he must be irresistible. He put his arms around her, closed his eyes, and bent down to kiss her.

Just as his lips touched hers, Bolt was spun around by a huge hand on his shoulder. It belonged to a big heavy-set Mexican named Raul Ramirez.

"That is my woman you are kissing," Raul said, just before he hit Bolt right between the eyes.

Bolt was caught completely off guard. A good sized dust cloud was billowing off of him as he stumbled backwards across the room and landed in the middle of Eb's table.

"Howdy," Eb said, rescuing his beer just as Bolt fell on the table and it collapsed to the floor. "Watch out for Raul, he's got a knife and a temper."

Lying in the floor, Bolt's head was spinning. He couldn't remember ever getting hit that hard.

"Yeah, thanks," he said. Shaking the cobwebs out of his head, Bolt struggled to his feet. He wasn't going to quit just yet and he went back at the big Mexican.

Raul was standing at the bar laughing about the Gringo and holding the chili-pepper under his right arm. When he heard Bolt approaching, the big Mexican turned around and pulled a knife.

"You do not want any of this, my Gringo friend," he said waving the blade under Bolt's chin.

Bolt drew back like he was going to hit the big Mexican, but instead, kicked him between the legs. Raul never saw it coming. Bolt knocked the knife away as the big Mexican doubled over in pain.

Once again, Bolt drew back and hit Raul as hard as he could. When Raul dropped to his knees, Bolt pulled him back up and slugged him with another hard right. The big Mexican went to the floor for good.

Bolt stepped over Raul and grabbed the chili-pepper who had been watching all of this. He pulled her up close and kissed her hard on the lips. As he was kissing her, he held her up to him with both hands on her butt.

She didn't try to struggle. The chili-pepper was getting into this dusty drifter and she started to wrap her legs around him. Just before she was able to get a good hold, his hands went up around her waist and he tossed her onto the nearest table. Her legs and petticoats were flailing in the air when she landed. She was cursing him in Spanish as the table crashed to the floor.

Some of the other Mexicans began getting to their feet, intending to teach this gutsy drifter a lesson. Bolt had his blood up, he was more than ready to take on any or all of them. He pulled Davy's knife just as Eb got up.

"That'll be just about enough of that," Eb said, holding the Greener on the Mexicans, "It was a fair fight up until now. You boys just have a seat."

Bolt noticed one of the Mexicans by the door slip out and run down the street.

"Welcome to Texas, we got to go," Eb said, motioning toward the door, "That big Mexican has lots of family and they'll soon be headed this way."

Bolt and Eb were just getting in the saddle when a crowd of Mexicans came from down the street with guns drawn. Their bullets were whining around Rufus while the big horse spun in the street. Bolt had no idea why this cowboy was helping him, but it was obvious he wasn't welcome in this town anymore. He put Rufus up in the wind and followed Eb away from the dusty border-town.

"I appreciate the help back there," Bolt said, after they were clear of town and slowed the horses to a walk.

"Think nothing of it. That bunch of bandits thinks they own that town."

"Looks to me like they do."

"I suppose they do at that. What's your name?"

"Ashton…Bolt Ashton."

"Pleased to meet you, the name's Everett Monday, my friends call me Eb."

"It's good to meet you."

"You must be new to these parts," Eb said.

"I guess you could say that, how'd you know?"

"Never ride a pale horse; too easy to see in the dark."

"I won't be getting rid of this horse anytime soon."

"Suit yourself. What are you doing out here?"

"Looking for work. I heard some of the ranches around here might be hiring."

"You don't look like a cowpuncher."

"I'm not," Bolt said, "not yet anyway."

"What were you doing before you got to Texas?"

"I did a little farming back in Tennessee, been fighting Johnny Reb for the last four years."

"Fighting Johnny Reb…and you're from Tennessee."

"It's a long story."

"I suppose it's really none of my business."

"I suppose not."

They rode along quietly for a while until they came to the gateposts of the Busted Wheel Ranch.

"Who named this place?" Bolt asked.

"Ms. Cooper, the owner's mother, when he was just a nipper. The family was looking for a place to settle when their wagon smashed a wheel on a rock. Ms. Cooper figured the good Lord was trying to tell them something so they stayed right here."

It was several more miles before the ranch house came into view. The Busted Wheel was a rundown bunch of buildings being held together by little more than dust. The only women living there was a Mexican cook named Corazon and her daughter, Angelia.

The daughter was a fine looking young woman. Corazon kept all the cowboys at bay with a large butcher knife and the threat of removing certain parts of their anatomy if she ever caught them with Angelia.

Coop Cooper, the owner of the Busted Wheel, came out of the house as they approached. His given name was Toussaint Charbonneau Cooper. His mother named him after a legendary French-Canadian Explorer she read about when she was a young girl.

Charbonneau was an interpreter for the Corps of Discovery and husband to several Indian women, including Sacagawea. Very few people knew about Coop's real name and he planned to keep it that way. Coop was in his early forties with graying hair and clean shaven. He wasn't a tall man but he was powerfully built.

"It's about time you got back here," he said to Eb, "Who's this you got with you?"

"The name's Ashton," Bolt said, "Bolt Ashton."

"Step on down and get out o' the sun," Coop said.

When he shook Coop's hand, Bolt noticed it was hard and callused, belonging to a man who knew about work. Bolt liked him right off. Coop looked at Eb and saw he was empty handed.

"Did you get those things I sent you into town for?"

"No, we may have to put that off for a day or two," Eb replied.

"You went to that damn cantina again, didn't you?"

"Yeah, but it weren't my fault this time. It was Bolt here that started the. . . ."

"If you'd been where you were supposed to be, there wouldn't have been any reason for you to be involved in this boy's fight."

"I suppose not, but. . . ."

"No buts about it," Coop said, ending the conversation with Eb. "Come on in and have a seat," he said turning to Bolt. "Don't pay any attention to anything that man tells you and you just might live through the day. The ornery cuss would rather fight than eat."

"I'll remember," Bolt said.

Eb walked away in a huff, talking to himself.

"Ornery cuss, that's what I get for not minding my own damn business."

After they were inside, Coop offered Bolt a seat.
"What brings you to Texas?"
"Things aren't good back home. I always wanted to see the frontier, so here I am."
"A drifter?"
"Yes sir, but I'm looking for a job."
"You know anything about cattle?"
"Not much, I'm afraid."
"How about horses?"
"I managed to outrun Johnny Reb for the last few years without falling off, but according to Eb, my horse is the wrong color."
"I wouldn't worry about that, unless you're planning to be a rustler or a horse thief. You got any sand?"
"Sand," Bolt repeated.
"Yeah, you know, grit, guts."
"I've fired a few shots in anger."
"If you were in that damn war, I'm sure you did," Coop said. "Bolt, I think you might just fit in around here, its thirty dollars a month with a bunk and a biscuit.
"Sounds good to me, Mr. Cooper."
"It's just Coop."
"I appreciate that, Coop, but there's one more thing."
"What might that be?"
"I think you should know. I'm wanted for murder back in Tennessee."
Coop studied Bolt's face for what seemed like a long time.
"Are you guilty?"
"I killed 'em alright, but they had it coming. It wasn't murder. There was four of them and they were about to do the same to me."
"Then we got no problem," Coop said, "The work is hard and dusty around here. Don't get too attached to the place, I ain't gonna be here forever."

"I'm not afraid of hard work. I'll do my best for as long as I'm here."

That night at supper, Bolt was introduced to the rest of the crew on the Busted Wheel.

An old cowpuncher sitting across from him extended his hand. "I'm Bo Boudreau,"

"His name's Spud," Eb said, "crazy old Cajun chef from the bayou country, came out here years ago, running from the law."

"It is true, I'm afraid," Bo said.

"What were you wanted for?" Bolt asked.

"Probably for poisoning half the people in. . . ."

"It was an affair of the heart," Bo said, ignoring Eb. "There was a duel. My rival lost. He was an important man. I was not. Alas, here I am."

"I'm glad to know you." Bolt said, "What should I call you?"

"Everybody calls me Spud. I'm afraid Bo Boudreau is dead to the rest of the world."

"How'd you get the name, Spud?" Bolt asked.

"I know many ways to prepare the humble potato."

"Yeah," Eb interrupted again, "but he only uses two of 'em, boiled dry or fried to ashes, both taste about the same."

"So you're the cook around here?" Bolt asked.

"I was, until Corazon and Angelia came along. Coop figured they could do a better job, now I'm just a cowpuncher, like all the rest of this bunch."

Eb dropped his cup on the table, spilling some of the contents. "Cowpuncher, you ain't even. . . ."

Eb was interrupted when a beautiful Mexican girl suddenly appeared with a tray piled high with bowls of stewed meat, tortillas, and beans. She wasn't exactly heavy, but she was definitely full grown. Bolt's pulse quickened when she bent over him, pressing her left breast against the back of his neck. She placed a tortilla on his plate and filled it with meat and beans.

"Thank you," he said.

"You are welcome."

The curvaceous beauty never made eye contact with Bolt, but she pressed her hip against his shoulder while she served Eb. Bolt's face was starting to glow before she finally moved away down the table.

The temptress stirring Bolt's blood was Angelia, the cook's daughter. She was barely twenty-years-old, but her beauty was something Bolt had seldom seen. He was growing fond of these Mexican women and this one was the best yet.

Eb leaned over to Bolt and pointed at Angelia with his fork. "Don't get too interested in that. She's too young for you and her momma will geld you with a rusty spoon if she catches you anywhere near her."

"Thanks," Bolt said with a grin, "I'll try and remember."

Angelia was sixteen years younger than Bolt, but he was smitten with her beauty at first glance. In spite of the warnings about Corazon's knife, Bolt was determined to get to know this girl.

Over the next two weeks Bolt saw Angelia every day. They even passed a few words when her mother wasn't around. She loved to tease by shooting him looks at mealtime and brushing his back as she moved about the table. When she was serving across from him she would lean over and expose part of her ample charms.

It was obvious to him the attraction was mutual. One dark night, against Eb's advice, Bolt went to her room in the cookhouse. Corazon's room was right next door. Trying to be quiet, he tapped on Angelia's window.

She was barely dressed in a little cotton nightshirt when she helped him in. Moist with sweat, the clingy nightshirt revealed every soft curve of her body. She spoke a little English, Bolt didn't know any Spanish, but there was no communication problem that night. They both knew exactly what the other needed. With the nightshirt gone, her body was breathtaking lying there in the moonlight on that sweltering Texas night. Corazon must have been a heavy sleeper to have not heard them.

It was breaking day when Bolt heard Corazon get up to start breakfast. He just made it out the window when she opened the door to Angelia's room to get her up.

Bolt got to the bunkhouse carrying his clothes and hopping on one leg after stepping on a sandspur with his bare foot.

Hearing Bolt come in, Eb rolled over in his bunk. "Boy, you don't know how close you just came to singing soprano for the rest of your life."

It was a month later when Eb and Bolt were moving cows from the main ranch to the river. There was more grass along the shallow stream and Coop needed every blade he could get.

Eb called a halt when they reached the stream bank. Dismounting he sat on a log in the shade. "You're a hard man to figure."

"Why do you say that?"

"You don't drink, you don't use tobacco, and you rarely swear. I ain't sure I can trust a man like that."

"Well, I'll tell you. I don't drink anything but a beer now and then, that's true enough. Smoking and chewing make me sick, and my granddaddy always told me cussing makes a man look weak."

"I'll be damned."

"Probably," Bolt replied with a grin. "Grandpa Boston said if a man is sure of himself and his words are true, he doesn't need to swear to make people listen to him, but I have to admit, there are times."

Eb didn't know Bolt well enough to know about his dark side. He would come to find out when Bolt started to swear, somebody was about to have a real bad day. Regardless of how angry Bolt ever got, he never used the Lord's name in vain.

"You may not do any of that, Mr. Peaceable," Eb said, "but I know you like the ladies, and I know you're slipping around with Angelia. Many a cowboy has tried to get close to her, but she's never out of sight of her mother for very long. Sooner or later, she's gonna catch you. Besides, Angelia is years younger than you are, she shouldn't be having anything to do with the likes of you."

"Not that it's any of your business, but age has nothing to do with love. Angelia is a beautiful woman, if she wants to spend time with me; I'd be a fool to turn her down."

"That may be, but I think a lot of that girl. I know it ain't any of my business what you all do together. I just don't want to see her hurt when you decide to head out for. . . ."

The first bullet ricocheted past Eb's head before he could finish. The cattle were running in all directions, stirring up a cloud of dust, and providing enough cover for Bolt and Eb to make it to a driftwood log on the bank of the river.

"Who do you think is out there?" Bolt asked while lying close to the log. "Why are they shooting at you?"

"Me! They ain't shooting at me! They're here to kill you. You and your damn womanizing. It's likely that bunch from the cantina."

"The cantina! All I did was beat that Mexican in a fair fight and show him up in front of his lady friend." Bullets were kicking up sand, and knocking bark off the log they were bellied down behind. "I got no argument with this bunch. I sure as hell, don't want to kill any of . . . ." A sharp pain shot across Bolt's upper arm just before he saw blood soaking the brand-new hole in his shirt sleeve.

"Are you hit?" Eb asked.

"Those low-down, dirty sons o'...they shot me!"

"How bad is it?"

"I'm alright," Bolt said, pulling his pistol, "it's just a scratch."

There were six Mexicans out in the brush shooting at Eb and Bolt, but they had underestimated their foe. The bandits thought it would be easy to ambush and kill these two cowboys. Their family honor had been soiled, now they intended to make them pay.

The first of the brothers caught Bolt's first shot right under the nose and died instantly. When the second one got hit, they began to think this ambush had been a real bad idea.

"Are you hitting anything?" Bolt asked, "Or are you just poking holes in the air?"

"You just got lucky. And the next time you start a fight in a saloon you can for damn sure leave me out of it. I got better things to do than being a target just for hanging around with you." Eb had just finished when several shots rang out behind them. "They're getting around behind us," Eb warned, looking over his shoulder.

Eb's fears were eased when he spotted several friendly faces riding up behind them. The Mexicans abandoned the fight and lit out as Coop, Spud, and five other cowboys rode up.

"I send you boys to move a few head of cattle and you go and start a gunfight with the locals!" Coop said.

"We never started any fight," Eb said. "It was that bunch of. . . ."

"Mount up and get after them," Coop said, "I don't want that bunch thinking they can come on this ranch anytime they please. Next thing you know, they'll be out here stealing the stock."

"Hell, we stole half of it from them," Eb said under his breath.

"That'll be enough of that," Coop said, "Go on, get after 'em. We'll gather up these cows."

"You boys want any help?" Spud asked.

Eb got to his feet and brushed himself off. "I reckon we can handle it."

After binding up Bolt's arm, Eb spent the better part of the afternoon tracking the Mexicans off the ranch. Bolt followed along behind watching the brush for an ambush.

The tracks faded at the edge of town, but the brother's horses were tied in front of the El Toro Rojo Cantina, the very place where this feud had started.

"I don't know how many others are in there," Eb warned.

Bolt pulled his Remington and checked the caps. "I suppose it doesn't really matter."

"I suppose not."

Bolt dismounted as Eb swung down from his horse. Eb pulled the Greener out of his saddle scabbard, checked to see that it was capped, and cocked both hammers.

Donning a long duster, Eb put the shotgun under it. Nodding to Bolt that he was ready, they walked in the door.

The music was loud as usual and there were sounds of laughter. All eyes were suddenly on Eb as the place fell silent. Raul was at the bar with the three remaining gunmen. The fear was plain on their faces.

"You boys left a little unfinished business out at the Busted Wheel," Eb said.

"We're here to settle up," Bolt added.

Eb was watching Raul's eyes, figuring he would be the one to throw down on them first. The silence was deafening in the room. They stood facing each other at less than a dozen feet. Finally, Raul broke the tension.

"My friends, we must not do this thing. . . ." Raul was trying to be clever, but he was too fat and slow to be a gunfighter. While he was speaking, he went for the gun hidden under his vest.

Bolt pulled his revolver and fired at Raul, putting a bullet in the big Mexican's chest. In a blur, Bolt turned, cocked the hammer and fired, killing the first brother before the startled Mexican could fire his pistol for the first time. Eb raised the shotgun from under his duster and yanked both triggers. A swarm of buckshot slammed the remaining brothers back into the bar as the glassware and the mirror behind them were blown to bits.

The smoke was thick as Eb dropped the shotgun, drew his pistol and cocked it. He was watching Raul, the only one left standing. Despite being wounded, the big Mexican was clinging to the bar. In desperation, he turned back to them and raised his gun. Before Raul could fire, Eb killed him with a bullet from his Colt.

With Raul on the floor, Eb waited to see if anybody else wanted in on this fight. No one moved. If any one of them moved, they would die in short order.

When all remained quiet, Eb picked up the shotgun. Bolt went out first, and Eb slowly backed out the door. When they were safely in the street, they mounted up and rode out of town.

When they got back to the ranch, Angelia was waiting for them. She put her arms around Eb as he stepped off his horse to make sure he was alright and then went to Bolt.

She could see that his sleeve was bloody. She helped him into the kitchen and stripped off his shirt. She cleaned his wound and bandaged it. Angelia was patching up cowboys as a regular routine. The others didn't get the attention that Bolt got that night, however. It was past midnight when Bolt slipped into the bunkhouse and finally turned in.

Time went by quickly as Bolt settled into a life of punching cows. He learned a lot from Coop and the others, and he made some good friends in Texas. A strong bond of trust and respect grew between him and Eb. Bolt's romance with Angelia continued as the two of them met in secret whenever possible.

The Busted Wheel crew got through the winter of 1866 without any big problems. By the spring of 1867, Bolt had become a good cowhand. It was after supper on a warm spring evening when Coop stopped to talk with Bolt in the corral.

"Bolt, you ever seen Montana?"

"No sir, never been any farther west than right here."

"I hear tell it's something special."

"I suppose," Bolt said.

"Come on over to the house when you finish up."

"I'll be right there," Bolt replied as Coop turned and walked away.

When Bolt stepped into the parlor, he found Eb, Spud, and a couple of the other cowboys were already there.

"Boys," Coop said, as Bolt found a seat, "I've asked you all in here to share some news." Pausing, he went to the cabinet and poured himself a slug of mescal. "I'm leaving Texas," he said, turning back to them. He tossed the mescal into the back of his throat and swallowed it as he allowed the news to sink in.

"You all know we've been gathering cattle and horses for a while now," Coop said, with a glance at Eb. "We got more critters than this dry country can feed. I'm moving the whole outfit north to the Montana Territory."

There was another grumble of voices as the hired hands debated the news. They quieted as Coop continued, "I want all of you to go with me. It'll be a long tough trip, make no mistake about that, but the country up there is wide open and waiting for us to take it. The grass plains go on forever and I want to see it. What do you say?"

Things were quiet for a spell until old Spud spoke up. "Well, I'll be going, I guarantee. I sure ain't staying here all by my lonesome."
"Good, you can be the cocinero again. Corazon wants no part of this."
"I'm in," Eb said, "never been nowhere but Texas and Mexico. It's about time I see some new country, when do we leave?"
"Right away," Coop said, "the grass is already drying up in this heat. I've got a feeling this summer is gonna be hotter than hell on a Saturday night. The cattle will start to suffer if we wait much longer. If we leave soon, maybe we can get up there and build a cabin before the snow flies. What about you, Bolt, you haven't said much."

Bolt was growing restless after being in this one place for a couple of years. This was his chance to see the big country he always dreamed about. He didn't want to leave Angelia, but his wanderlust was stronger than the love he was beginning to feel for her. That kind of love only meant pain for him in the past and it was time to go.
"I'm going with you all," he said, looking over at Eb, "The Indians will probably get this old brush-popper if I'm not there to protect him."
"That'll be the day," Eb replied.
The Busted Wheel crew left Texas and started the herd north just over a week later.

Chapter Four:
1876, The Lonesome Wind

Weeks turned into months and months into years until a cold night finds Bolt all alone on a frozen expanse of Montana buffalo grass. Daylight was still just a promise in the predawn darkness. It was bitter cold as Bolt lay shivering in his bedroll. He was older now, but his heart was still haunted by memories of lost or abandoned love, and he was very much alone.

It was February, moon of the popping trees to the Sioux. The winter sky was clear over Bolt's head as the sliver of a sinking new moon hung in the west. He was camped on the frozen snow-covered expanse of the Lonesome Wind Ranch.

The ever-present wind from the day before died at sundown. The clear sky allowed the temperature to drop considerably during the night. Bolt guessed it was near zero.

He raised himself up on one elbow and tried to shake off the last vestiges of sleep. Even with a double bedroll it had been a miserable night. He was awake every couple hours throwing wood on his fire.

When he looked around to reassure himself all was well, he was greeted by a grumble from his big gray horse. The old horse's breath was forming billowing clouds of vapor in the still air.

"Morning, you old outlaw," Bolt said, "You still think it was a good idea coming up here?"

Rufus was pawing through the snow to get at the grass underneath, but the old horse needed some grain to help fill his belly. The thick hair of his winter coat was standing on end to offer greater insulation against the cold. The big horse looked huge in the fading moonlight. That coat worked so well, a layer of frost formed on his back overnight.

Bolt made his camp in a dry wash next to a fallen cottonwood trunk. The giant cottonwood had been a good-sized tree when William Clark came down the Yellowstone, seventy years before. Its spreading branches provided shade for the buffalo, early Spanish and French explorers, mountain men, and Indians. The hungry ponies of the Sioux and Cheyenne fed on its corky bark when times were hard during the bad winters.

The ancient tree finally succumbed to the unrelenting forces of time during a summer thunderstorm just two years before. Even in death the big tree was still giving shelter and comfort to wayward travelers. Its branches provided a plentiful supply of dry wood and the big trunk was a good backdrop to reflect the heat from his fire.

Bolt sat up and placed a few small branches on the still-glowing embers of his feeble campfire. The dry branches began to smoke and pop as tiny flames flickered among them. He tossed a few larger pieces onto the growing flames and soon had a good fire.

Bolt sat close to the growing flames to soak up some much-needed warmth. He stretched his old muscles to work out the kinks left from sleeping on the frozen ground. The flickering light and warmth from the flames were comforting there in the darkness.

In spite of the cold, Bolt was content. He loved the solitude of this country. He figured this high lonesome cathedral was left empty so God would have a quiet place to rest without anybody to bother him.

Bolt never had much use for organized religion, but he always stayed close to the Almighty. He considered himself a Christian. His faith was unshakable, but quiet, personal, and private. He talked to God almost every night but he never made a big show of it. That simple faith gave him great comfort and courage. It made him a strong, quiet, and gentle person. It also made him an extremely dangerous man to those who would do him wrong.

Bolt still had a lean build, but now his hair and mustache showed definite traces of gray. Seeing no need to shave every morning, he usually had several days of stubble on his chin. There were a few deepening wrinkles around his blue eyes, but he was still a force to be reckoned with.

Bolt was in his mid-forties and still unmarried. He wore high-waist brown trousers with galluses and a tall hat with the gold braid and tassels of a Union Cavalry officer. The large bone-handled sheath knife was still there on his right side, but the old Remington was tucked away in his saddlebag.

Bolt purchased a nearly-new 1873 Colt Army revolver just the year before. The big .45 cost him twenty-three dollars, but he was glad to pay it. The Colt used metallic cartridges which made it much easier and faster to reload than his old cap-and-ball Remington, and it was pretty much weatherproof. He carried the Colt in the same cross-draw holster on his left.

It was still over an hour until sunup, but he was too cold to sleep anymore. He pulled the lid off of his little coffee pot and turned it bottom-side-up. The left-over coffee from the night before was rock-solid in the bottom. Turning it back over, he poured in a handful of fresh grounds. The water in his canteen wouldn't be coming out until April, or at least until it sat by the fire for a couple of hours. Bolt packed the little coffee pot with snow and put it on to boil.

While Bolt waited on the coffee, he leaned back against the fallen Cottonwood. As he absorbed the warmth from his fire and the aroma of cowboy coffee beginning to heat, he thought back to the long journey that brought him to this vast empty landscape.

It had been nine years that past October since they drove nearly two thousand head of Busted Wheel cattle across the Yellowstone River. Coop set a pile of rocks and a stake to mark the southern border of his new ranch. "We start from here."

Coop looked up at the old Cajon on the wagon seat. Spud was bundled up, trying to shield himself from the wind-driven sleet, "What was that word you used back there at home about staying alone?"

"All by my lonesome," Spud replied.

"Lonesome, that's what this place is," Coop said. "Boy's we're all by our lonesome up here. We haven't seen anyone since leaving Rapid Creek over three hundred miles back."

"You're right about that," Bolt said, "There's nothing up here but the wind."

"Damn this wind," TJ Burke complained, "Does it blow like this all the time?" Burke was a young cowpoke that joined the crew in Nebraska.

"This wind has teeth, I guarantee," Spud said.

"That old man at the trading post in Rapid Creek said we were headed for the high lonesome," Coop said, "I been thinking on that for weeks, and I think that fits pretty well. Boys, welcome to our new home, the Lonesome Wind Ranch."

They carved the Lonesome Wind out of the rugged high plains of Eastern Montana, a vast and desolate wilderness. The Lonesome Wind covered 300 square miles of wide-open spaces north of the Yellowstone River. There were deep canyons and shallow Coulees. The only trees were the Cottonwoods growing along the creek bottom and a few lonely cedars.

The high plains were covered by buffalo grass, sagebrush, greasewood, and prickly-pear cactus. Looking out across its great expanse, one could get the idea there was nothing but grassy flats and gentle rolling hills as far as the eye could see.

In truth, there were thousands of sharp cutbanks, deep gullies, and sinkholes. A million places for the deer, coyotes, and an occasional Indian to move about unseen.

There were numerous sandstone bluffs that showed no perceptible evidence of the constant erosion process removing them from the landscape. In contrast, were the huge grassy buttes with primordial rock running up through their heart and jutting from the top. Those rocky promontories were streaked with white where great brown eagles sat to survey their world.

Around the base of those rugged mounds could be found numerous frost-shattered remnants of stone ranging in size from fist-sized rocks to boulders as big as a buffalo. Loosened by eons of rain, wind, and ice, those fallen rocks had finally succumbed to the relentless pull of gravity and tumbled from their perch.

The Sioux were latecomers, arriving just a century before. The Cheyenne, Crow, and other Plains Indians had called this place home for hundreds of years. They lived as free-roaming hunter-gatherers from mobile camps.

Those halcyon days were coming to an end for the various tribes of the west. The former masters of the plains were on a collision course with the invading army of white settlers. It wouldn't be long before their nomadic way of life would only exist in the stories of their old men.

Bolt was brought back to the present when the coffee began to boil. He put his memories away and got back to the day at hand. He was riding the north range, something he did every month or so during the winter. Most of the other hands preferred to stay close to the ranch house during the bitter-cold months. Bolt enjoyed being alone from time to time. It allowed him time to think.

It was desolate on this part of the ranch. Most of the cattle were wintering fifty miles south, between Cherry Crick and the Yellowstone, where there was flowing water.

Bolt was watching for any kind of trouble or squatters who might try and carve off a piece of the Lonesome for themselves. Normally he would be staying in a line shack with a bunk and a wood stove to keep him warm.

Bolt had been to Medicine Lodge Coulee, a deep canyon on the far-northern boundary of the Lonesome, just to make sure all was well. When he finished up the day before, he was nowhere near the shack. He bedded down in the dry creek bottom to get out of the wind.

During the winter months, other people were few and far between on the range. He was forty miles from the ranch house and over seventy from a town with a decent saloon. Not being much of a drinker it was hard to explain his love of saloons. The nearest one was the Jersey Rose in the little town of Coulter Creek, Montana.

After it started to get light, Bolt had a bite to eat. Breakfast was a few corn dodgers, a stale apple fritter, and several cups of cowboy coffee. He knew just about then Spud was cooking breakfast back at the ranch. He would be serving up hot biscuits and gravy along with beef sausage, eggs, and fried potatoes.

Bolt saddled his horse and rolled up his bedroll, leaving the fire for last. Just before he put the bridle on Rufus, he heated the bit over the embers for a few moments. He knew better than to put a sticky-cold frozen bit in his horse's mouth. It was painful on his old gums and would probably peel some of the tender skin from inside his jaw.

Bolt kicked snow onto his campfire, stepped up on Rufus, and rode up over the edge of the creek bottom. He headed southeast as the first rays of the sun broke over the distant hills. The squeaky powder under Rufus' hooves and the stiff breeze on Bolt's back promised another cold day.

"Tonight we'll be at the line shack in the dancing grounds and you can get a good feed of grain and hay," he told Rufus. Bolt loved the Great Plains, but winter was a tough time to be a cowpuncher. Work was hard to come by on the frontier. Bolt knew he was lucky to have a steady job on a good outfit.

Spring came slow to Montana. It was well into April before the weather moderated and the temperature got much above freezing. The grass would soon turn green and the country would come to life. Northbound waterfowl had been flying overhead and the ice was going out of the Yellowstone.

Now that Bolt was settled on the Lonesome Wind, the thought of drifting held little appeal to him. He couldn't imagine finding any place that suited him better than Montana. He occasionally thought it might be nice to have a family. He was too old to start having kids, but a good woman would make his life complete. The chances of that happening, however, looked pretty slim.

There were a few women on the frontier. Most of them were hard and worn-out from the difficult life on the plains. There were the soiled doves in town that would share their charms for a price, and most cowboys were more than happy to oblige them.

Those women were never much of a temptation to Bolt. He possessed a big jealous streak and he wasn't interested in sharing a woman with half the territory. He missed the sweet smell of pampered southern belles and the embrace of the passionate women that he had known for only a short time in Texas. He wouldn't admit it to anyone, not even himself most of the time, but Angelia was still on his mind and Carrie Lynn was always in his heart.

When he and Coop came up to Montana, most of their horse stock was descended from Spanish mustangs. They had heart, but most of them were on the small side. Bolt's working string of cowponies was made up mostly of tall horses. He looked out of place on one of those little mustangs.

Even though he was one of the oldest horses still working for a living on the Lonesome, Rufus was still amazingly fast and surefooted over rough ground. Bolt fed him well, rode him often, and kept him in shape.

Bolt always rode the big outlaw on the long circles. Rufus had a good head, and he wasn't prone to going home every time Bolt turned him loose at night. Rufus was a lot like the man who rode him, ageing, but still quite a bit more than a handful.

It was June when Coop asked Bolt to step in the main house. Coop went to the sideboard to pour himself a shot of whiskey. He held an empty glass up for Bolt, but Bolt shook his head and declined the offer.

"Don't mind if I do," Spud said from across the room. He was relaxing in a chair after finishing the dishes.

"Get it yourself, you old biscuit-roller," Coop said, "I ain't here to wait on you. Sit down, Bolt; I want to talk to you."

Spud got up and poured himself a drink while Bolt and Coop found a seat. The old coosie went back to his chair grumbling.

"Been feeding him three times a day for fifteen years, you'd think he'd. . . ."

"What was that?"

"Nothing."

"Bolt," Coop said after taking a sip from his glass, "I've been in touch with a horse breeder back in Kentucky. I'm investing in some thoroughbred mares."

"That right," Bolt replied.

"Yes sir, I got a wild idea, been working on it all winter. I think it just might be the start of something real special. We need a horse that'll have the size to survive these Montana winters on grass alone and not much pampering. They'll still need heart, guts, and a sturdy foundation to do the job demanded of them up here, so I want to keep the Mustang blood."

"I want you to travel to Kentucky to oversee those horses getting back to the Lonesome. I know this won't be easy. I figure it'll take the best part of a month to get them back here."

"To be honest with you, I ain't looking forward to it," Bolt said. "But I'm game to go. Is Eb or any of the boys going with me?"

"I can't spare any of them right now. We got plenty to do before those horses get here. The horse breeder…ah. . . ."

"Canary," Spud said, sensing Coop's confusion, "its hell getting old, ain't it?"

"Carson Canary," Coop continued, ignoring Spud's remark, "He passed-on just recently, but some of his family will be there to meet you. One of Canary's wranglers will be coming back with. . . ."

"Wrangler…aaack!" Spud was suddenly beet-red and choking on his whiskey.

"What in blazes is the matter with you?" Coop asked.

The old coosie coughed a few more times and finally got his wind, "Wheweee…noth…ahhmmm…nothing. Just…had a little trouble swallowing, the wrangler…nothing…I'm fine."

"It'll be a chore," Coop said, turning back to Bolt, "but you're the man for the job."

Bolt was suspicious as he eyed the old cook. "A wrangler, you say?"

"I'm told they're a pretty good hand with horses," Coop said. He shot a stern look over at Spud before he continued. "They'll be here awhile to help with the breeding and such, may just stay on. You'll be fine. The two of you shouldn't have any trouble. We should see you back here before the middle of July. Send us a telegram from down the line when you're a week out of Rapid Creek, I'll send a couple of the boys to meet you and help out the rest of the way."

"Alright," Bolt said, getting to his feet, "I guess I'm headed for Kentucky."

As Bolt was about to leave the room, Coop offered him a suggestion.

"You're gonna be mighty close to home. If you want to go down to Tennessee for a spell before you start back, it'll be alright with me."

"I don't know. I appreciate it, but I don't think so."

"It's been years, things may be different now."

"Maybe, but I don't think I want to risk it. Be seeing you. So long, Spud."

"Good luck, pardner, you're gonna need it," Spud muttered under his breath after Bolt was out the door.

"I feel sorry for him sometimes," Coop said, "Except for us, he's pretty much alone in this old world."

"He'll be alright," Spud said, "You better be feeling sorry for us."

"How's that?"

"I still think you should've told him the truth about this deal."

"Well, you did everything but tell him!"

"I just couldn't swallow that wrangler yarn you were spinning."

"It was mostly true. I just left out a few details. You know that hardheaded hillbilly as well as I do, if I'd told him the whole story, we couldn't a dragged his ornery carcass to Kentucky."

"Well, when he finds out the truth about the wrangler that's going to meet him, and we knew about it, he'll probably come back here and shoot both of us!"

"Yeah, you could be right. But I'd sure like to be watching from a safe distance when he finds out."

Bolt could hear laughter coming from Coop's parlor as he walked back to the bunkhouse.

The trip back east would be a long one for Bolt. It was three hundred miles to the railroad in Rapid Creek, then fifteen hundred more to Kentucky. Bolt saddled his horse early next morning and headed southeast toward the brightening sky.

The ride to the Black Hills was uneventful until Bolt approached the Belle Fourche River and spotted a group of Indians. He reined Rufus up into a thick stand of pines to watch them pass by.

The group was made up of twenty-five or thirty people. There were a few men, mounted on fine looking ponies. The rest were women and children. Most of them were leading heavily-loaded packhorses and a few dogs.

They appeared to be the Sioux, as far as Bolt could tell. They were moving west away from the Black Hills. It appeared they were headed to the southern grass ranges of the Montana Territory. He figured they must be fleeing the army and life on one of the recently established Indian Agencies.

Bolt didn't know it, but these Indians were headed to the Valley of the Greasy Grass to join Sitting Bull. The Black Hills were the center of the Sioux universe. Ruthless forces were at work in the white man's world to steal the hills from the Sioux and a bloody conflict was coming.

Bolt never talked about it, but he felt a strong connection to the Indians. He didn't understand why, but it had been there most of his life. He was never close to any Indian except one old man that used to live on the Lonesome.

Bolt stayed out of sight until the Indians were gone over the horizon. He saw no point in starting any trouble. He knew the sight of a white man might draw them into an unnecessary confrontation.

It took Bolt two more days to reach Rapid Creek and the railroad. He left Rufus in a livery stable, seeing no reason to subject the old horse to a three-thousand-mile round-trip standing in a cattle car.

"Take good care of him," Bolt told the man who ran the livery.

"I'll do just that. He'll be right here waiting for you when you get back."

Bolt relaxed in his seat as the train rumbled east. In his wildest dreams, he couldn't have imagined the radical life changes that were about to occur or that the lovely catalyst for those changes was cautiously awaiting his arrival in Kentucky.

Chapter Five:
Scarlett Canary

Spring in the South was like his boyhood memories. The grass was green and the flowers were blooming all around. Most of the damage from the war was gone and Kentucky was thriving.

Bolt thought about being just over a hundred-and-fifty miles from his home in Smith County. He briefly considered Coop's offer for him to go home for a visit. His parents were gone now. He wondered about the rest of his family, but being tossed into a Tennessee jail was one thing he planned to avoid. As far as Bolt knew, Trace was still around Smith County. Bolt hoped his brother was doing well. Someday he would try to get in touch with him.

As soon as he arrived, Bolt's disposition changed for the worse. Even though it had been years since he'd seen her, he thought of Carrie Lynn, just over a hundred miles south in Nashville. He could almost feel her presence. If he took the train, he could be there the next day.

For a brief moment he allowed himself the fantasy of going down there, telling her he was alive, and taking her back with him. His common sense overcame those thoughts, but the renewed pain in his heart told him he hadn't gotten her out of his memory after all.

Scarlett Canary was an attractive southern belle, raised in the lap of luxury that was the old south before the Civil War. Her father owned several thousand acres and nearly fifty slaves. Roland Canary was a good man and treated his slaves well compared to many. His passion was horses and Kentucky was prime horse country.

Scarlett was an only child. Her father raised her much like he would have raised the son he never had. She was five-feet four inches tall, well built, and attractive. She was an accomplished horsewoman and a good shot with rifle and pistol, but the casual observer would never know it to look at her.

That strength and independence made it difficult for her to ever find a lasting relationship. The men that drifted in and out of her life were often intimidated by her when they got to know her. Scarlett settled for a wealthy soft-handed gentleman once, but it would never happen again.

Rowland Canary had entered into an agreement with Coop to raise horses for the Lonesome Wind Ranch. Without the slave labor, the plantation was falling into ruin. His holdings were being sold off a few hundred acres at a time to cover his mounting debts and he was ready to seek his fortunes in the west.

Canary's plans were cut short by his untimely death. In his seventies when it happened, the doctors figured it was probably his heart. It was now up to Scarlett. She knew the plantation was all but lost, and she had no choice. All she had left in the world was several thousand dollars from the sale of the land and thirty brood mares. The horses were worth a fortune, but she couldn't bear to part with them. That was the main reason she was following through on her father's dream to take them to Montana.

The afternoon found Scarlett weeding her flower garden for what was likely to be the last time. The new owners were due any day and she didn't want the place to look unkempt. She was troubled about leaving behind everything she had ever known and the only home she ever lived in.

Scarlett was expecting a stranger to arrive there and he was overdue. She was uneasy about leaving with this man and traveling to Montana. Mr. Cooper's letter assured her that Bolt Ashton was someone she could trust. Cooper warned her however, Bolt was a man of few words.

She pictured Bolt in her mind many times. She knew from Coop's letters Bolt was in his forties. She was expecting some illiterate, tobacco-chewing old cowpuncher, like the ones in the dime novels.

Regardless of what Bolt turned out to be, she was ready to go with him. Her destiny lay in a big new country in the west. She only planned to be with him for the train ride. Coop and some of the others were going to meet her in Rapid Creek.

Scarlett knew she was taking a big risk, going into business with a man she never met and moving to a country she had never seen, but she refused to allow herself any moments of self-doubt or uncertainty. She read stories about the frontier, now she was determined to see it for herself.

Bolt rented a horse in town and rode out to the farm where he was to pick up the brood mares. It was an old plantation house with big barns and several outbuildings that housed the slaves that worked the land. A touch of pride went through him when he realized he was part of the reason those cabins were standing empty now.

Bolt was coming up the lane to the house when he saw her. She was standing in a little flower garden with a hoe trying to keep back the weeds. The last thing Bolt expected to find there was an attractive woman. Coop left him with the impression that everyone from the family was gone except the horse wrangler he was to meet.

Bolt had been on the frontier for a long time. He couldn't remember having seen a woman like this one for quite a spell. He had seen his share of good-looking women, but this one was different. She didn't possess the sharply evident good looks of a twenty-year-old, or the stark, but sometimes phony beauty of a powdered and painted lady.

This woman was natural and simple. Her beauty perfected by time and life. She wasn't wearing any powder on her face or color on her lips. Her auburn-red hair hung haphazardly around her face, and she was wearing a simple cotton dress. The afternoon sun shining through that dress was giving him a good indication of her body. The sight of her stirred something deep inside him.

The lady looked up from her work as Bolt got off his horse. He removed his hat and introduced himself.

"Ashton, ma'am, Bolt Ashton."

"Mr. Ashton," she replied, "I'm Scarlett Canary."

Her eyes were like nothing Bolt had ever seen before, the color of a mountain waterfall. Not really blue, not exactly green. Bolt felt drawn to those lovely eyes at first, but quickly put up his guard.

Bolt figured her to be about thirty-years-old. She had a firm body from what he could tell. It was obvious that she took care of herself. She was making small talk as the old cowpuncher explored her in his mind, not hearing anything she was saying. She explained about her father's passing and that she was fully prepared to carry on with her father's contract to go into business with Coop in Montana.

Bolt was snatched back to reality when he realized what she just said.

"Whoa, just a minute," he blurted out, "Go into business with Coop!"

"Yes, Mr. Cooper and I are going to raise horses together. Why else do you think you're here? And by the way, where have you been? I was expecting you last week."

"Expecting me!"

"Mr. Cooper said you were leaving on the fifteenth."

"I did leave on the fifteenth. It's a long way from the Lonesome to Rapid Creek. I got a good horse, but three hundred miles of rough country ain't like riding into town on Sunday afternoon."

"Be that as it may, you're late."

Bolt was fuming at this new revelation. Now he understood Coop saying this trip would be a real chore. He was there to do more than just move a bunch of horses back to Montana. The conversation in Coop's parlor was suddenly becoming crystal clear.

This brazen woman was moving lock, stock, and barrel to the Lonesome Wind. Bolt wanted no part in that. He had finally gotten comfortable with the fact he was going to live out his life alone. This woman was above him and obviously would never have any interest in him, but he sure didn't want her around to remind him of what he was missing. Then he remembered the laughter from Coop's house that evening just before he left.

"I'm gonna skin both of those old. . . ." he mumbled under his breath.

"I'm sorry?" Scarlett said, unable to understand what he was saying.

"No, I'm sorry," he said out loud, "there's been a mistake. Coop said there was a hired hand going back with me, not a...a...."

"A what?"

"A...well...that is to say...a woman."

"I can hold up my end. And besides, Mr. Ashton, you're the hired hand. You're working for me now and you best remember it!"

"That'll be the day," Bolt mumbled.

"What was that?"

"There's no way I'm gonna be roped into this plan with you and that no-good, Coop Cooper! It's a long hard trail back to the Lonesome and I can't see that you're up for it."

Scarlett was standing with her hand on her hips. "Let me remind you once again, Mr. Ashton, it's not up to you. My horses and I are going to Montana, whether you go along or not!"

"When I get my hands on Coop Cooper," Bolt mumbled under his breath, "I'm gonna. . . ."

"I'm sorry," she said. "I can't hear you."

"I wish Coop had sent a few more hands."

"I'm sure Mr. Cooper knows what he's doing. We leave first thing in the morning."

"Oh yeah, he knew alright," Bolt mumbled, "the no good. . . ."

After things quieted down a little and Bolt cooled off, Scarlett spent the afternoon showing him the horses and mules that would be going with them. The Union Army confiscated many of their best horses. The payment promised had never come.

"Those blue-belly Yankees took our finest horses as remounts," she said. "That Union script they paid us with wasn't worth the paper it was printed on."

"Yes ma'am," Bolt replied. "You know. . . ."

"Know what?"

"It's not important."

By that evening, Bolt and Scarlett had become nearly civil with each other. She fixed a nice supper for him. They talked about the Lonesome Wind and Bolt's plans for getting there.

"Thank you, Ms. Canary," Bolt said as he finished his second piece of pecan pie. "That was the best supper I've had in some time. I love country ham, but we don't get much of it in Montana."

"You're welcome, Mr. Ashton; it was a pleasure to cook for company again in this house."

"We're going to be together for a spell. You might just as well call me Bolt."

"Alright, Bolt, you can call me Scarlett. Don't you have one of those colorful nicknames, like the cowboys I've read about?"

"What have you read?"

"In all of those stories about frontiersmen and desperados, they all have a nickname."

"I don't know about a nickname, but the Indians call me Buffalo Grass Rider."

"I like that, why Buffalo Grass Rider?"

"It started with an old Arapaho we found living alone when we first got to the Lonesome. He was so old he couldn't travel with the rest anymore. They figured he wouldn't make it through the winter, so they left him to take care of himself."

"That seems harsh."

"It's their way. We decided to build the main house not too far from where he was camped. Coop made sure the old man had plenty of firewood to keep him warm. I'd shoot him a deer now and then, and every time we butchered a beef, we'd take him a big piece of it."

"What did he have to do with your name?"

"It turned out the old man was pretty spry. We didn't have any idea how old he really was, but he was tough. None of us could pronounce his real name so we got to calling him Hard Tack, because he was always down on his luck. He could speak English pretty well. Hard Tack would come up and stay with us when the weather really got bitter. We had a lot of long talks about the old days and Indian ways. One night I told him about meeting Davy Crockett when I was a kid."

"You met Davy Crockett?"

"I was seven-years-old. He was on his way to Texas."

"That's some story. What about your Indian name?"

"I explained to old Hard Tack that Davy originally put the idea in my head about coming to the buffalo grass and Hard Tack started calling me Buffalo Grass Rider. Once in a while, when I was going to town with a wagon, I'd take the old man with me. He liked the ride and

I'd stock him up with tobacco. He told the other loafer Indians around Coulter Creek about my Arapaho name and now they all call me Buffalo Grass Rider."

"It's a very colorful name. Will I get to meet Hard Tack?"

"The old man died about three years ago," Bolt said, "He must have been close to ninety-years-old. We did our best to give him a proper Arapaho send off. We built his scaffold under a big cottonwood next to Cherry Crick, right where his camp had been for all those years."

"That's a shame. I'd like to meet a real Indian."

"You'd be better off not meeting most of them. Things aren't too good for the Indians right now."

"Why do you say that?"

"Gold has been discovered in the Black Hills and despite the treaty the government wants to open it up for settlement. The army won't rest until all the Indians are penned up on an agency, even if they have to kill most of them to do it."

"Seems like a shame," Scarlett said.

"It is, but there's little anybody can do about it."

"Will we run into any of that trouble?"

"Not likely. We'll go by rail to Rapid Creek in the Dakota Territory, meet the other's there and travel overland about three hundred miles to the Lonesome. The weather's good, we shouldn't have much trouble. No offense ma'am, but are you sure you're up for this trip?"

"I can take care of myself, you just worry about showing me the way, and I'll be right behind you with my horses."

Next morning, Bolt awoke with the sunrise. When his head cleared of sleep, he remembered he was in a barn in Kentucky faced with a difficult job that he never asked for. Scarlett offered him a room in the main house, but he didn't think it right to stay under the same roof with her.

Inside the house, Scarlett lay in her bed for what was to be the last time. Her mind was full of possibilities for the adventure ahead of her. She wished her dad was still with her. She loved the old house, but she couldn't afford to keep it up. Her future was in the west. Scarlett was excited, and ready to put her old life behind her. She was grateful for the man that had ridden up her lane the day before. Scarlett was confident in the outcome of their journey and her intuition was telling her this big man from Montana would play a significant part in that future.

Outside, Bolt was wasting no time. There were thirty brood mares, a couple of saddle horses, and a pair of mules to use as pack animals. The big items that Scarlett wanted to keep would be shipped by rail. Her personals would be put on the mules and packed to Montana.

A couple of men in a wagon showed up that morning. They were to pack and load her possessions to be shipped at a later date. Coop made arrangements with the railroad for two stock cars to carry the horses and mules back to Rapid Creek. Scarlet and Bolt would travel on the same train.

Bolt wasn't looking forward to the trip. Not being prone to conversation, he would be out of things to say in about ten minutes. It was five or six days to Rapid Creek and another two weeks to drive those horses to the ranch.

Bolt was saddled and ready to go meet the train. The horses were milling in the corral near the house as he waited for Scarlett. The men from town were just beginning to go to work when she emerged from the house and stopped on the porch.

"Be careful with those things," she warned, "I want it all in one piece when it gets to Montana." She was wearing a split riding-skirt that once again got Bolt to considering things he didn't need to be thinking about.

"Morning," he said with a tip of his hat when she got to the corral.

"Good morning."

In his mind, Bolt wondered how he could protect this woman from the men whose paths they were bound to cross. He also wondered if he possessed the strength of character to remain a gentleman all the way to Montana.

That skirt was stirring up some strong feelings in the old cowboy. Bolt was trying hard to put those thoughts out of his mind and just focus on the job ahead when he noticed Scarlett was carrying something wrapped up in an oily cloth.

"What do you have there?"

She opened the cloth and showed him an 1847 Colt Walker revolver. The old cap-and-ball .44 looked brand new.

"It was my father's. He carried it in the Mexican war."

"Do you know how to use that thing?"

"You'd best hope you never have cause to find out."

Scarlett wrapped the old thumb-buster back up and placed it in her saddle bag. She took one more look around and got up on her horse. She swung her leg over, straddled her mount, and hooked her boot in the stirrup.

Bolt groaned a little at the sight of her butt on that saddle. Doing his best to put it out of his mind, he rode over to the corral and swung the gate open to release the mares.

"C'mon girls, let's go to Montana."

Scarlett was impressed with the man she was about to ride off with, but she still wasn't sure of him. She wanted to be able to trust him, but many men seemed to be one thing and turned out to be another. She wouldn't let her guard down for a long time. Her intuition told her safety lay in staying close to him, but she sensed a little danger there as well. She sunk the spurs in her horse's flanks, turned him down the lane, and never looked back.

The train station was like a beehive. Bolt found the rail cars reserved for the mares and began to load them. The stock handlers helping him were both wearing old confederate uniform jackets.

"Where you from, Son?" one of them asked.

"Tennessee, but now I live out in the Montana Territory."

"Were you in the war?" the younger Johnny Reb asked.

"Yeah, I fought several campaigns up through Virginia as well as Gettysburg," Bolt replied.

"You were at Gettysburg," the older man said. "That must have been one heck of a battle."

"A lot of good men died in those three days, that's for sure," Bolt said.

"Abe Lincoln made a big speech after it was over and tried to cover up the fact it was his fault in the first place," the older one complained. "He should o' just left us be!"

Johnny Reb was all puffed up. "Just like a bunch o' Damn Yankees. Think they know better than we do how to run our own lives."

"You look awfully young to have been in the war," Bolt said.

"Yeah, well maybe so, but I know all about it."

"You don't know anything about it. Abraham Lincoln held this country together through the darkest days of its history. This is going to be the greatest nation in the world someday and men like President Lincoln are the reason why."

The older man was clearly in a state of disbelief as he stared at this tall stranger. It was only then he noticed the *U.S.* on Bolt's hat band.

"Just exactly which side did you fight on?"

"The winning side, I was a captain in the Second Brigade, Third Cavalry, under George Custer."

"A Damn Yankee and we're helping him load these horses!" the old man screeched, "He probably stole them from Ms. Scarlett."

"Did you just call me a horse thief?" Bolt asked, suddenly in the old man's face.

"That, and a lot worse!" young Johnny Reb exclaimed.

Bolt was a hardheaded son of Tennessee and he wasn't going to take that. Before either of them could make a move, Bolt lashed out at the nearest ex-confederate, which happened to be the older of the two, hitting him square in the nose. The old soldier stumbled backward and fell out the door of the boxcar.

The younger one spun around, grabbed a pitch fork, and lunged at Bolt in an attempt to pin him to the wall of the stock car. Bolt dodged the fork and slugged Johnny Reb hard on the chin. While he was still stunned, Bolt grabbed him, spun him around, and booted him out the door. The kid went flying out into the gathering crowd of onlookers, landing on his friend in the mud and manure.

Hearing the commotion, Scarlett walked up just in time to see Johnny Reb come flying out of the boxcar.

"If you're quite finished, Mr. Ashton," she said, glaring at Bolt, "I'd like you to join me up front. The train is about to leave."

"Yes ma'am, be right there." Bolt loaded the last three horses and secured the door of the car. He made his way past the grumbling onlookers to join Scarlett on the train.

"What was all that about?" she asked when they were seated.

"We were just talking about politics and Mr. Lincoln's contribution to the country."

"It didn't look like you were talking from where I was standing. What about Mr. Lincoln?"

"I never discuss politics with a lady. We have a long way to go, so let's just relax and enjoy the ride."

Chapter Six:
The Frontier

As the train sped across the flat prairie of Nebraska, everything was going fine. Scarlett sat reading a book and Bolt was snoring in the seat across from her. They would be in Cheyenne, Wyoming Territory by the next day, change trains, and if all went well, arrive in Rapid Creek in three days. The trip, so far, had been easy. Scarlett was much more relaxed and happy with her decision to go west.

Bolt was just ready to get it over with. He knew the hard part was still ahead. Not driving those horses overland to Montana, but living day to day on the same ranch with this most attractive woman.

If Scarlett had been just some woman he met on a train, Bolt would have already made a move on her, but he held back. She was going to be around him every day after they got to the Lonesome and he would live to regret doing anything less than honorable.

The train rolled into Cheyenne early the next morning. The high plains weather was typical for early July. Every day was hot with abundant sunshine and low humidity. Cheyenne was a wild frontier town, the likes of which, Scarlett had only read about.

Bolt procured a room in the hotel and asked Scarlett to stay there while he made arrangements to go north to Rapid Creek. Scarlett wasn't happy about it, she wanted to see the west and look around town.

"I'm not staying all cooped up in this room," she said.

"Begging your pardon, Scarlett, but you will stay here until I get back. This is a tough town; you won't be safe on the street all alone. You're not in Kentucky anymore. Once we're gone from here, you can do whatever the.... Please, just stay here."

"Alright, if you insist, but don't be gone too long."

"Yes ma'am, right away ma'am, whatever you say ma'am," he mumbled to himself as he went out the door.

"I heard that," she said to the door as it slammed behind him.

Bolt returned with bad news. He planned to haul the horses to Rapid Creek by way of the narrow-gauge railroad that ran north out of Cheyenne, but that plan had fallen apart.

"There's been heavy rain in the Black Hills since I came through there," he explained. "Several bridges have been washed out. It'll be at least a month before any rail traffic can get to Rapid Creek from here."

"What can we do? I don't want to sit around here for a month."

"I don't intend. . . ." Pausing, Bolt took a deep breath, "Our choices are to go back east to Kansas City, then north and west across the Dakota Territory to Rapid Creek. That'll take at least two weeks and we'll still be three hundred miles from home."

"Whatever you think," she replied.

"There is another option," he said. "There's a new stage route that's been opened from here to Deadwood, up in the Black Hills. Its two hundred and sixty miles, but we wouldn't go all the way to Deadwood. I'd have to kill somebody over these horses if we go up there with them. Deadwood's a rough place, I've been told. We don't need that kind of trouble. It's a little out of our way, but I've got to pick up my horse in Rapid Creek. We'll leave the coach road south of Deadwood and take the trail toward Custer. It's on the way to Rapid Creek."

"That's a long way, isn't it?"

"Yes ma'am, but I believe it's the only real choice we've got. We can unload the stock here, drive them north through the Black Hills to the Belle Fourche River, and on to Montana. These are your animals, so it's really your decision."

"If you think we can do that, I'm for it, but you already sent word to Mr. Cooper. He'll be expecting us in Rapid Creek in a few days."

"Yeah well, about that. I never sent it, guess it slipped my mind."

"Slipped your mind, I can't believe you forgot, of all the. . . ."

"They got a telegraph office here."

"Very well," Scarlett said, "Please see to it that we get word to Mr. Cooper. These horses are as much his as they are mine."

The horses were in a corral near the rail yard. Bolt was staying nearby to watch over them. The mares were valuable horses and the west was full of no-accounts that would love to take them off his hands.

As Bolt sat in the cool night air, he could hear the sounds of a nearby saloon. He wondered if Scarlett was alright. He asked her to stay in the room until he returned for her in the morning. He found himself worrying more about her as each day passed.

He was tempted to mosey up the street to the bright lights but he held back. This was important to Scarlett and she was important to him, though he would never admit it to anyone else.

Back at the hotel, Scarlett was awake. She could hear the noise downstairs and out on the street. She was also thinking about Bolt down at the rail yard. She wasn't comfortable being away from him in this strange place. Of course she would never tell that hardheaded cowpoke about that. She tried to make him believe she would only tolerate his company as far as the ranch.

Scarlett finally drifted off to sleep for a couple of hours, only to be awakened by the sound of boots coming down the hallway to her room. She recognized the walk and she was happy it was Bolt. Opening the door to let him in, her first impulse was to put her arms around him, but she recovered her senses before she could follow through on it.

"We need to get those horses out of town early so everybody in the territory won't know where we're headed," he said.

Scarlett got her things together and followed him out into the gray light of early morning. She had no idea where they were going, but she was glad to be with him. Reminding herself this was only business, she stepped up on her horse and followed Bolt out of town.

Bolt purchased enough supplies to last them the month or so he figured it would take to cover the five hundred miles to the ranch. He hoped Scarlett could survive on beans and salt pork, along with whatever game he could kill along the way.

The one thing in his favor was the weather. It was warm and mild, there would be plenty of grass and water for the stock, and sleeping out wouldn't be too tough on his companion. He was anxious to be clear of towns and get through the Black Hills as soon as he could.

Bolt wouldn't have been so anxious to leave the relative safety of Cheyenne if he had known the telegraph wires were singing about a massacre that morning. It was July sixth. The steamboat, Far West, arrived at Fort Abraham Lincoln, in the Dakota Territory, the day before. She was carrying dozens of wounded, and news of a tragic defeat.

Lt Colonel Custer and a large contingent of the Seventh Cavalry had been wiped out on the twenty-fifth of June in the Montana Territory. The dashing boy general of the Civil War was gone. The shock of that news spread across the country like wildfire.

Johnny Carlton was a two-bit outlaw that hung around southern Wyoming. He was wanted down in Denver and had come up to Cheyenne to escape the Colorado law. Johnny felt the world owed him a living, if he wanted something, he just took it. Killing men, or women for that matter, didn't bother him in the least.

Johnny's brother, Bart, and his saddle partner, Riley, had been in the hotel when Scarlett checked in. They overheard the desk clerk talking about her journey and the horses at the rail yard.

"It'll be an easy payday for us," Bart said, when he found Johnny, "It won't be hard to take those horses away from a woman and one cowboy. We can sell the horses in Newcastle, and have our way with the woman."

"You should've seen her," Riley added, "she's a looker for sure."

"Who's with her?" Johnny asked.

"Just one old cowpuncher," Riley said, "he won't be no trouble for the three of us!"

The northern plains were full of men who would be happy to force themselves on an innocent woman, especially one as desirable as Scarlett. The outlaws heard about Custer's defeat, but failed to grasp the consequences. Johnny planned to follow the horse herd at a distance until sundown and jump Bolt late at night while he slept. This was hard country and these three misfits were about to find out just how hard it could be.

The high plains of Wyoming were very similar to Bolt's home in Montana. Scarlett was once again relaxed being back with this cowboy she was coming to trust completely. She had never seen anything as wide open as this country. There were mountains in the distance that would take two days to reach on horseback. The first day went well, the horses figured out they might just as well go where Bolt pointed them and save themselves a lot of trouble. The new coach road made it fairly easy to keep the horses moving along.

Johnny Carlton and his partners left their horses quite a ways back from Bolt's camp that night. They could see his fire through the trees, but very little else. They planned to wait until Bolt was asleep before they approached his camp.

Around midnight, Bart was ready to get on with it, after having Scarlett on his mind all afternoon.

"C'mon, Johnny, he's bound to be asleep by now."

"Alright, easy does it. Be careful of the woman, I don't want her hurt."

"Don't worry," Bart said, "and I want her first."

"You'll take your turn when I say so," Johnny warned.

Riley was still closely watching Bolt's fire. "Will you two shut up. I don't mind going last, but nobody's getting anything if that cowboy hears us."

The three outlaws began to slip through the trees towards Bolt's camp. Everything was going according to their plan until Riley stepped on a dry stick. In the quiet stillness of the night it sounded like someone cracked a whip. All three outlaws froze in their tracks as one of Scarlett's horses grumbled out in the dark.

"Be careful," Bart whispered.

"Sorry," Riley whispered back, "He couldn't have heard that, we're too far away."

Bolt lay quiet after being awakened. He wasn't quite sure what was bothering the horses but his subconscious had registered some faint noise. Scarlett was asleep about ten feet from him completely unaware of the danger nearby. Bolt reached for the familiar grips of his Colt and his thumb settled on the hammer.

The fire had burned down to barely glowing coals. Johnny wasn't sure which sleeping form was Bolt and which was Scarlett. He dared not shoot the woman.

"I can't tell which one is which," Johnny whispered.

"He's a lot bigger than her," Bart said, "step up on that rock, you can get a better look."

His eyes more accustomed to the dark now, and his head clear of sleep, Bolt was straining to hear the slightest sound or see any movement in the inky blackness when he noticed the silhouette of a man step up against the starlit sky. The dark figure was holding a rifle.

Bolt rolled out of his bedroll just before the night was split with the report of the rifle. The rifleman's bullet scattered dirt where Bolt had been only a split-second before. Coming up on his knee, Bolt pointed the Colt and fired. The rifleman went down, only to be replaced by two more dark figures.

"You shot my brother…you. . . ." one of them shouted, just before Bolt's second shot hit him square in the chest. The dark figure sagged with the impact, firing his pistol into the ground, but didn't go down until Bolt's third bullet slammed into him.

The third one turned to flee, but it was a futile effort. It seemed the intruder was running away, but Bolt didn't care. They came at him in the dark and he intended to kill all of them. The Colt roared for the fourth time. The fleeing gunman was slammed face first into the ground when 250 grains of red-hot lead hit him between the shoulder blades.

Yanked out of a sound sleep, Scarlett had no idea what happened or if her companion was alive or dead. Bolt reached her in a flash, holding her in the darkness, shielding her from further danger with his body.

Just as suddenly as it had begun, all the movement ceased out in the dark, and the night was silent again. The only sounds were fading hoof beats as the horses scattered. Bolt replaced the four empty cartridges with fresh loads and stared into the darkness watching and listening for the slightest sound or movement. With now razor-sharp senses, he waited for any more nightriders that might be coming in on them.

Bolt relaxed after everything remained quiet for several minutes. Scarlett could feel him trembling as the adrenalin began to wear off.

"Are you alright?"

"I'm fine," he whispered, "everything's fine."

Scarlett tried her best to calm down. She was a strong woman, but this was the first time she had ever been in a true life-and-death struggle.

"Who were those men? Why...why did you shoot them?"

"They intended to kill us and take the horses."

It was the first time Scarlett had seen the violent side of him, but now she knew this man was more than able to protect her no matter what might come her way.

"I'm sorry I got you into this," Bolt said, "I knew this was dangerous country. I may have been wrong in trying to travel cross-country with you along. I'm used to taking care of myself and not worrying about anyone else."

Scarlett was holding her face tight to his chest. It was the first time she had ever been this close to him. She was breathing in the essence of this big man from the buffalo grass. Bolt was different than the lilac-scented gentleman that called on her back in Kentucky. He was a hard man and capable of extreme violence. Scarlett was little bit afraid of him, but his scent and the sound of his voice together were quite sensual. She wanted to stay close to him.

"It was my decision as well as yours. I'll hold up my part. I know we'll be alright." Bolt held her close to him until dawn, hoping things would seem better in the daylight.

Sunup was rolling over the eastern ridgeline when Bolt left her side to look at the men he killed. He had no idea who they were or how they knew about him and the horses. He assumed they had seen Scarlett in town and followed them all day. He tried not to think of Scarlett's fate if they had been successful. Once again, he began to doubt the wisdom of his decision to try for the Lonesome overland and alone, but it was too late to turn back. He did his best to cowboy up and went back to Scarlett with a confident air about him.

Scarlett was trying to pull herself together. It was hard for her to believe there were men who would kill two people over a herd of horses. The man she was with was quiet, but obviously, no stranger to violence.

Bolt never mentioned what these men may have had in store for her. He never would speak of this night again. He took no pride in killing his fellow man, even those that needed killing.

Bolt was wishing Rufus was with him as he went out to round up the scattered horses. That old gray horse was the best watchdog there ever was. He would never have let those outlaws get close without making a fuss.

The Kentucky thoroughbreds weren't used to ear-splitting noises in the middle of the night. They spent their lives behind white rail fences, the wide-open spaces and freedom was strange to them. When the gunfire started, they left the country in a wild panic.

It took all morning to find the lost horses. Locating all but one, Bolt took them to a little meadow about a mile from their camp. He found the last one about an hour later.

She had shattered a bone in her foreleg. Bolt had no choice but to shoot her. He knew it had to be done, there was no way for her to travel and she was in pain. Bolt knew if she didn't die of infection, her suffering would be brought to a violent end by falling prey to a cougar or the wolves.

It was never easy for him to put down a horse, he knew they were just animals, but they were so much more to him. His oldest and most trusted friend was a horse, he dreaded the day when he might lose him.

By the time Bolt got back, Scarlett had packed as best she could. The dead bodies were very disturbing to her and she wouldn't go near them. Bolt hobbled the mules at night so they were nearby. It was already after noon, the smart thing would have been to camp there again for the night. Bolt wanted to put some ground between them and this place. He was worried the nightriders might have friends who would come looking for them.

The decent thing would have been to bury the outlaws to keep the animals off their bodies, although, Bolt doubted they would have done it for him. Bolt didn't invite those men into his camp. He felt no remorse for their deaths.

Bolt left the nightriders lying where they fell. The time it would have taken to dig three graves was time he didn't have to spend. Scarlett was watching him as he tied the nightrider's horses together with lead ropes. He secured the lead horse to the last pack-mule so they would be forced to go with him. Gathering the outlaw's guns, he put them in a pack on one of the mules.

"Aren't you going to bury those men?" Scarlett asked.

"Bury 'em," he said without even looking up, "Buzzards got to eat too."

Disturbed by his attitude, Scarlett got on her horse and rode to the other side of the herd, away from the bodies. She was upset by the dead men and the loss of her mare. This journey was proving to be much more trying than she ever expected it to be.

Bolt was putting on an act for her benefit. He wasn't actually as callused as he was letting on. He was anxious to put as much distance between this place and Scarlett as he could. They hadn't met another soul on the road so far, but he knew that could change at any moment.

They only made about ten miles that afternoon before darkness overtook them. Bolt set up camp quite a ways off the road. There was a small stream of water where Scarlett was able to clean up a little.

After five more days, sundown found them camped in a little valley of grass on the southern edge of the Black Hills. Scarlett would have been content to stay right there and homestead a place for herself. There was plenty of grass and good water surrounded by a pine forest for logs to build a cabin. Scarlett didn't know it, but the little valley was sacred ground to the once mighty Sioux Nation.

The nightrider's horses were all geldings. They became herd bound to the mares after three or four days, and Bolt turned them loose to travel along with the herd. He was far enough away from the ambush sight, if one of them decided to go home, it wouldn't make any difference. Scarlett was relieved of the burden of dragging them along with the mules and hobbling them at night.

A few days later, Bolt sat on a hill looking out over the endless mountains that make up the Black Hills. The dark green of the Ponderosa Pine trees gave them the name. From a distance they looked black. Set in the midst of the trees were granite spires that shot up through the timber and could be seen for miles. It was nearly a hundred miles from where he was to the northern edge of the hills and the Belle Fourche River. Uneasy in the cover of the trees, Bolt was anxious to get off this road and back out on the buffalo grass.

After several more uneventful days, they left the Deadwood Road and took the trail toward Custer City. Bolt wanted to avoid Custer altogether, but Scarlet insisted on sleeping in a bed and having a bath with hot water.
Against his better judgment, Bolt gave in to her wishes and rode into town. He found a small livery with a corral and left the horses. It was close enough to the town's one hotel that Bolt could keep an eye on them from the room.
Custer was a typical frontier town. There were a dozen small false-fronted buildings lined up on an exceptionally wide, but muddy Main Street. A few log cabins and a tent city had sprung up around the outskirts. The place was crowded with prospectors, buffalo hunters, drifters, and dreamers headed to Deadwood Gulch. The resident population was made up mostly of gold seekers with claims nearby.
Custer had only been a town for just over a year. It was the site of a major encampment for General Custer's expedition of 1874, and the first public gold strike in the Black Hills. The town of Custer was less densely populated, making it a little safer than Deadwood, but not by much.
Closely following the prospectors was the people intent on taking gold from the hills without having to get their hands dirty. Among them were the saloon owners, storekeepers, and professional gamblers. Painted ladies by the score were in town to take care of the citizen's

personal needs. A few Chinese residents catered to the other necessities with their laundry, bath houses, and the opium trade.

Bolt had never been a worrier, he always took what came his way and dealt with it. He was changing since he met Scarlett. Being her protector wasn't a job he asked for, and he wasn't happy about being in this raucous frontier town.

"Well, this is a real fine mess," Bolt mumbled. He was looking out the second story window of the little hotel where he and Scarlett found only one room available.

"What did you say?" she asked.

"Sorry about the room, I hope you don't mind sharing."

"We've been sleeping next to each other every night. I don't see where this will make any difference just because we're under a roof."

Scarlett was hiding the fact she didn't want to be far from him in this rowdy town. The cramped little room consisted of a wash stand and a single bed.

"Where are the facilities?" she asked.

"Out back."

"Out back! You mean we have to share them with everyone else in this hotel."

"Yes ma'am."

"What about a tub?"

"Down the street, at the Chinaman's place."

"Down the. . . . What kind of city is this?"

"I tried to tell you."

"This is your fault," she said.

"My fault!"

"The next time you try to tell me something…try harder."

The talk around town was of the Seventh Cavalry. Bolt heard the news and he was worried about continuing with his plan. He was sorry to hear about the General. They were never close friends, but he admired Custer.

Bolt knew they couldn't stay in Custer. He had no choice but to push on and hope for the best. He figured if the Indians did get after him, he'd let them have the horses and just get away with Scarlett. If they got their hands on a fine bunch of mares, maybe they'd forget about running him down.

Bolt was still looking out the window when he spotted a small café down the street. Scarlett was lying on her bedroll. Bolt wasn't sure how often the sheets got laundered in this rough hotel. He warned her if she didn't want to share anything with the former tenants, it would be a good idea to sleep in her bedroll. The straw-filled mattress under her was lumpy, but still softer than the ground.

"Would you like to have supper?" he asked.

"That would be nice. I'm a little tired of fatback and beans."

"Are you complaining about my cooking?"

"Oh no, you're a wonderful cook."

"Well come on," he said, ignoring the sarcasm.

"I have to get ready."

"Ready for what, we're just going to eat."

"Never you mind, just go downstairs and I'll be down in few minutes. I need to get out of these clothes."

"A few minutes, you look alright to me…I don't see why. . . ."

"Downstairs, Mr. Ashton, if you please!"

Bolt was on the planked sidewalk outside watching the townsfolk passing by when he spotted a couple of over-dressed women approaching. They were wearing heavy makeup and headed toward the saloon down the street. When they got close, he tipped his hat.

"Good evening, ladies."

One of them touched his arm as they passed, "Come down to see me later." Bolt just gave her a smile and turned away.

Bolt was growing more aggravated and impatient as he stood around outside the hotel. It seemed like an hour had passed since he left Scarlett in the room. He walked over to the corral and checked on the horses and took a few lessons about finding gold from an old prospector that passed by.

"Where in blazes can she be?" Bolt asked himself as he paced up and down the sidewalk, rattling the boards under his boots. "She could've made a dress by now."

Finally, at the end of his patience, Bolt went back inside to get her. As he crossed the lobby, Scarlett appeared at the top of the stairs, wearing a nice dress. Her hair was up and she put on a little makeup. Everyone in the lobby was watching as she got to the bottom step and took Bolt's arm.

"I'm ready now."

They walked down the street without talking and found the café. A lady showed them to a table in a far corner, thinking they were lovers. A noticeable hush fell across the dining room when they entered. All eyes were on the cowboy's lovely companion.

Bolt's jealous streak was showing and he was preoccupied with being extra protective of Scarlett. Several men were watching Scarlett and talking among themselves. Bolt figured it was just a matter of time before one of them said something to her and the fight would be on.

After taking a seat, Bolt ordered a beef-steak for both of them as the buzz of conversation returned to the dining room. Bolt was anxious to get Scarlett back to the room and away from these people. He was never comfortable in a crowd, he longed for the solitude of the Lonesome.

"What's the matter with you?" she asked as they ate, "don't you like your steak?"

"I'm fine. I just don't like being here with you."

"I'm sorry my company is so distasteful to you," she replied with her head down. She was surprised and a little hurt by his remark.

"No...no, that's not what I meant. It's just...this is a rough town, and you're...very attractive."

"Well, thank you," she said, quickly recovering, "I didn't think you'd noticed."

"I noticed. Women like you are rare around here. You attract a lot of the wrong kind of attention and I worry about your safety. You're important to me...that is, this job's important to me. It's my responsibility to get you back to the Lonesome."

"I understand, and I accept your apology."

"What apology?"

"You just said you didn't mean it."

"That wasn't an apology."

"Oh, I think it was," she said with a slight smile.

"Let's just finish our dinner and get back to the hotel before there's any trouble. This is a tough town. I want to be away from here by first light in the morning."

"Whatever you say," Scarlett said, looking across the table at him, "So, you think I'm attractive?"

"I meant, compared to this bunch."

Scarlett's smile suddenly faded to a frown and her attention went back to her dinner.

Bolt knew from experience being with a lady as pretty as Scarlett was just asking for trouble. At his age, he figured fighting over a woman was a thing of the past. Now here he was, expected to defend the honor of Scarlett if it became necessary. He hated towns and the trouble that always seemed to be brewing.

After finishing their dinner, Bolt settled up with the waiter. Ten dollars for a steak was a huge waste of Coop's money, but he didn't care. If it wasn't for Cooper, he wouldn't be there in the first place.

Bolt was deep in thought on the way out the door when he ran into a man coming in to eat. The gentleman was carrying a mug of beer from the saloon next door and some of it splashed up on him.

"Sorry about that, friend." Bolt said.

Glaring at Bolt, the man brushed himself off. This stranger had hard eyes. There was something familiar about his long dark hair and rangy mustache. He wasn't as tall as Bolt, but he was not a man to be overlooked. Bolt's eyes were drawn to the ivory-handled Colt Navy Revolvers in a double cross-draw rig.

The café was quiet as everyone waited for the outcome. Scarlett finally broke the silence by offering her hand to the stranger. "I'm Scarlett Canary from Kentucky, Sir. This is Mr. Ashton of Montana. I must apologize for my clumsy escort's complete lack of manners."

The stranger relaxed when he took Scarlett's hand. Placing his drink on a nearby table, he removed his hat, "James Butler Hickok, at your service, ma'am."

"Mr. Hickok, do you live here in Custer?"

"No, Scarlett, I'm on my way to Deadwood to do a little prospecting. I just stopped here for the night."

"I think I've heard of you, but by something. . . ."

"I'm called Wild Bill by some."

"Of course, it has been a pleasure, Mr. Hickok."

"It was indeed my pleasure, Scarlett. I hope to see you again." Releasing her hand, Hickok replaced his hat, picked up his mug and walked away.

Bolt's first instinct was to inform Hickok that Scarlett was with him and he could forget about seeing her again. He decided speaking up would make him look foolish in her eyes and he didn't want to give Scarlett the idea he cared who she was with.

Bolt was familiar with Hickok's reputation. He wasn't afraid of him, but there was no need to instigate an argument. Swallowing his pride, he remained silent as they left the café.

Back in their room, Scarlett retired to the bed and began to scan a copy of the Bismarck Tribune she picked up in the lobby. Bolt was lying on his bedroll in the floor next to her.

"The Indians out here are worse than animals," she said.

"Why do you say that?"

"It says here, the Indians did horrible things to the soldier's bodies at Little Bighorn. Mutilations, I can barely stand to read this."

"Don't be too quick to judge, they may have had good reason. Did you ever hear of the Sand Creek Massacre?"

"No, I don't believe I have."

"It was during the war, around '64, I believe. Seven hundred Colorado Militiamen led by a man named Chivington massacred a village of peaceful Cheyenne Indians. The Indians had signed a treaty. They were even flying an American flag. The militiamen killed practically all of them. They took trophies from the dead, women and children included. Decorated their horses with body parts and rode through Denver to show them off. It was disgusting, brutal, from what I hear."

"What is wrong with people out here?"

"It's hard country. The Indians believe a mutilated body will remain that way in the afterlife. It's a form of eternal revenge and punishment for their enemies. What Chivington did will never be forgotten."

"Well, it's just horrible, simply horrible."

"I'm not a bit sleepy," Bolt said, trying to change the subject, "Think I'll get a beer."

"Go ahead, but don't stay out all night. We need to get an early start in the morning." Scarlett was smiling to herself as she listened to him going down the hall grumbling.

Rattlesnake Jake's Saloon was crowded and loud. Bolt managed to find a table in the back corner and ordered a beer. There was every kind of person in the saloon, miners, gamblers, cowboys and some of the roughest looking women Bolt ever laid eyes on. The air was full of cigar smoke and the talk was loud.

Bolt caught a look from Bill Hickok at a poker table. Bill nodded and went back to his game. Bolt was on his second beer, which is just about his limit, when the door to Jake's swung open and a cowboy stepped in holding a double-barreled shotgun.

"Hickok, you bushwhacker!" the cowboy shouted, "You killed my brother over in Kansas, now I'm here to do the same for you!"

"Who the hell are you, Boy?"

"That don't matter. Get up and face me, I want you to see this coming."

As Bill slowly rose to his feet, Bolt noticed a man at another table. The man pulled his pistol and held it out of sight under the table. Everyone was watching the ranting cowboy in the door and didn't notice the other gunman.

Bolt had never seen a man as fast as Bill Hickok. He drew and fired both guns before the cowboy in the door could pull the trigger. The impact from the twin .36's knocked the gunman partially back out the door. When he hit the floor, the fall caused him to pull the trigger on his shotgun, blowing one of Jake's swinging doors right off its hinges.

The gunman at the table started up with his pistol, but before he could fire, Bolt pulled his Colt.

"Let it drop, Mister," he warned.

Bill heard Bolt and spun around to level his pistols at him. When the second gunman dropped his gun, Bill realized that Bolt had prevented him from being shot in the back.

"Stand up," Hickok said to the back-shooter. "Let's make this a fair fight…pick it up whenever you're ready." The blood drained from the back-shooter's face and he began to tremble. "That's what I thought," Bill said, "get out of town tonight. If I see you after sunup, I'll kill you whether you draw or not." The back-shooter stepped over his dead friend and hurried off into the night.

After things quieted down, Bill walked over and shook Bolt's hand. "Thank you, my friend, you probably saved my life." This time it was a firm handshake of mutual respect.

"Can I buy you a beer, to replace the one earlier?"

Bill put his hand on Bolt's shoulder. "I appreciate it, but you've more than made up for that." Bill and went back to his card game as Bolt sat down to finish his beer.

Bolt was about to leave when the woman he'd seen on the street came over and tried to make conversation.

"I'm glad you came in," she said, taking a seat at the table. The woman wasn't that attractive, her hair was rumbled and her makeup was smeared a little. Bolt knew if he was inclined to go upstairs with her, it wouldn't be her first trip of the night. It was clear from her odor that she was an opium user. Bolt was in no mood for anything she was offering. He was never into sharing a woman and he was ready to get back to Scarlett. "Looks like you could use some company, would you like to go upstairs?"

"No thank you," Bolt replied.

"I have a nice room where we can be alone. I'll make you feel real good."

"No thank you ma'am, I feel just fine right here."

"Now cowboy, I won't take no for an answer." The lady was in need of another pull on an opium pipe. She was growing more than a little aggravated with this cowboy's reluctance to pay up. "Now come on upstairs with me," she said, reaching across the table to grab Bolt's hand.

"Sorry ma'am," Bolt said, jerking his hand away and getting to his feet, "I got to go." They were starting to create a scene, and he wanted no part in it.

Bolt was making his way to the door when a big man came out of the crowd and grabbed him by the shirt. The man shoved Bolt backwards and slammed him down on the floor, as a smaller man tripped Bolt from behind.

"What's the matter with you, Mister?" the big one shouted in Bolt's face. "You should've gone upstairs with that girl and given her a little money, 'cause now you're gonna pay me."

Bolt was caught off guard by this foul-smelling skirt herder and his sneaky little partner, but he'd taken all he was going to from this bunch in the saloon.

"I wouldn't go upstairs with her if she paid me," he said, "and I damn sure ain't paying you."

Bolt hit his attacker as hard as he could, right in the nose. The blood was pouring out of the skirt herder's nose and his eyes were watering so bad he couldn't hold onto Bolt.

While the skirt herder was groaning in pain and trying to straighten his broken nose, Bolt managed to get to his feet. The skirt herder was still on his hands and knees trying to clear his head when Bolt grabbed the nearest empty chair and broke it over his back, knocking him unconscious.

Seeing his partner go down, the little man was trying to get away when Bolt reached out and grabbed him by the collar. Bolt spun him around and slugged the little man, sending him sprawling across the sawdust covered floor. Several stacks of chips toppled over when he piled up under the roulette wheel.

Next morning, Scarlett rolled over in her bed and looked down at Bolt on the floor. She pretended to be asleep when he came in, and didn't know the details of the night before.

Bolt moved and let out a groan. His rib cage was black and blue, and his hand was swollen and throbbing.

"Let's go, cowboy," she said. "It's late and we have a long way to go. If you hadn't stayed out all night drinking, you wouldn't feel so bad now."

Bolt struggled up from the floor grumbling.

"A bossy woman…just what we need on the Lonesome." Rolling up his bedroll, he pulled his boots on and followed her out the door.

It was an easy ride from Custer to the edge of the Black Hills. Bolt made it plain to Scarlett they were going to be in Rapid Creek just long enough to get Rufus. As soon as that was done they would be back on the trail to the Lonesome. He wanted nothing more to do with any towns.

"Will Mr. Cooper be meeting us in Rapid Creek?" Scarlett asked.

"If he isn't there by now, we're not waiting around for him."

"I believe your instructions are very clear about that. We are to wait there for Mr. Cooper."

"Coop told me to get these horses to the Lonesome and that's what I'm going to do. If he got that first telegram, he should already be there. But, if he isn't and you want to stay there, be my guest."

Scarlett was riding behind him and she had a little bit of a mad on herself. She was displeased that her hired hand refused to do as he was told. She knew he was in pain, but she wasn't about to give the hardheaded cowpuncher any sympathy.

"Maybe you should stay out of saloons and take up reading or something less demanding for a man of your age."

"I'd like to show you what a man of my age could do for you," he mumbled.

"I beg your pardon."

Scarlett heard him, but she wasn't quite sure how to respond to that.

"Is there anything else I can do for you?"

"No, I'm fine for now. I'll let you know as soon as we get to town."

"You best forget about town. There are no more damn towns. We're going to Montana, that's the end of it."

Earlier that same morning, two men had been in the livery stable at Rapid Creek trying to buy fresh horses. Jonas Hollingsworth and his brother, Ben, were on their way to Montana from Illinois.

Ben Hollingsworth, along with his wife and children, was traveling in a heavily-loaded wagon. It had been a hard trip and their horses were worn out. The Hollingsworth party was on its way to find their fortune in the gold fields.

"Is that big gray stud for sale?" Ben asked Albert Cantrell, the man at the stable.

"Nope, he belongs to a cowboy from Montana, should be along anytime to pick him up."

"Too bad, he's a fine animal."

"I got some good stock out here in the corral. I'm sure you can find something to suit your needs." After they were outside, Cantrell was curious about what brought them to the Dakota Territory. "Where you folks headed?"

"To the gold fields in Montana," Ben said. Jonas gave him a stern look to let him know he shouldn't be telling everybody their business. "For goodness sakes, Jonas," Ben said, "It ain't no secret there's gold in Montana."

"Have you folks heard the news about Custer and the Seventh Cavalry?" Cantrell asked.

"What news?" Jonas asked.

"Custer and his entire command were wiped out by the Sioux, just over in Montana."

"What's that got to do with us?"

Cantrell pulled off his hat and scratched his head, "What's it got to do with you? Every Indian on the Plains is out for blood. It ain't safe out there."

"We haven't seen any Indians," Ben said.

"That's just the trouble. When you see 'em, it's too damn late!"

The Hollingsworth brothers picked out four horses from the group in the corral and settled up with Cantrell. They hitched the new animals to the wagon and were preparing to leave.

"You got a fine little family there," Cantrell said to Ben when he thought Jonas couldn't hear him, "Why don't you all stay here for a few weeks until the army can get out here in force and deal with those damn redskins?"

"We've got no time to lose," Jonas said, interrupting the conversation, "There won't be any claims left if we don't hurry and get there."

"Them little ones are worth more than all the gold in Montana," Cantrell said.

"We'll be alright," Ben assured him. "I appreciate your concern, but we need to be moving on." Being swayed by his big brother's greed, Ben got up in the wagon seat and picked up the reins. "Get up!" he yelled to the team as he rolled the reins across their backs. Mrs. Hollingsworth had a worried look on her face as they drove out of the corral.

"Good luck, Ma'am," Cantrell said, tipping his hat.

The next day, when Bolt walked into the livery stable, he heard his old horse stomping around in his stall. Rufus already picked up Bolt's scent and he was glad to be getting out of horse jail.

"Well, I see you made it back," Cantrell said when he saw Bolt.

Bolt was scratching Rufus's ears and rubbing his head.

"How you doing old horse, they been treating you alright? Thanks for taking care of him," he said, turning to Cantrell, "what do I owe you?"

Scarlett was waiting outside with the horse herd, while Bolt saddled his horse.

"Would you care to sell any of those mares?" Cantrell asked her when he walked outside with Bolt.

"No, these horses are headed to Montana."

"Why in blazes is everybody going to Montana?"

"That's where I live," Bolt said. "These horses are going to the Lonesome Wind Ranch, up near Coulter Creek."

"Well, it's a mighty fine bunch of horses you got there. You folks be careful out there and watch out for the Indians."

"We'll do that," Bolt said, "you haven't seen any new cowpunchers around town in the last week or so?"

"Can't say that I have, are you looking for someone?"

"Friends of mine…you'd know if they were here. Where's the telegraph office?"

"It's right down the street, across from the saloon, but you're wasting your time going down there."

"Why do you say that?" Scarlett asked.

"The Indians have cut the lines all over the territory. The repair crews are too scared to go out and fix anything since we heard about Custer."

"I guess that takes care of your telegram," Bolt said with a look at Scarlett. "So long, Cantrell."

"So long, pardner, good luck to you."

It was two days ride to the Belle Fourche River. From there Bolt would turn northwest toward Montana. There would be no more towns until Coulter Creek, nearly three hundred miles away.

In the weeks following Little Bighorn, the Indians scattered. Many returned to the agency, some went north toward Canada, but a few were still roaming the plains and they were not to be taken lightly.

Bolt and Scarlett were still a day's ride from the Belle Fourche River. Just a few miles away from their location, a Sioux raiding party sat watching a solitary settler's wagon. The Indians were hidden by the trees growing around their vantage point. This bunch had ridden east with He Dog after the battle at Little Bighorn. They were part of several small groups attempting to drive the miners and settlers out of the Black Hills. Crazy Horse was nearby, but he wasn't part of this raiding party. The wagon they were watching belonged to the Hollingsworth family.

Jonas Hollingsworth was a strong willed, but foolish man. He disregarded Cantrell's warning as idle rumors, figuring they were meant to keep people away from the gold. This little band of gold seekers hadn't seen an Indian since they left Illinois, unfortunately for them, that was about to change.

Being woefully short on food and ammunition, the Indians saw this wagon as a possible source of the things they needed.
"Let us take this white man's wagon," Wolf Walks Alone said.
"There is not much honor in killing two foolish white men," Gray Bull replied.
Fresh from Little Bighorn, Wolf Walks Alone was feeling invincible. He was ready to spill more white blood and he didn't care about the circumstances.
"There is honor in killing all whites," Wolf Walks Alone said, "They will have food and we can take the horses."
"What about the little ones?"
"Did Long Hair spare the little ones at Washita Creek?"
"No, he did not, but we are warriors, not butchers."
Without answering, Wolf Walks Alone raised his hand as a signal. When he dropped it, the whole bunch started off the hill.

Ben Hollingsworth was driving the wagon and Jonas was on horseback when they heard the yelling. Ben slapped the reins across the horses' backs in an attempt to outrun them. It was a futile effort in the heavy wagon. The Indians were on him before he could get a hundred yards. Wolf Walks Alone shot Ben right out of the wagon seat, but the bullet didn't kill him. Gray Bull grabbed the harness of the lead horse and pulled the team into a sharp turn. Mrs. Hollingsworth was screaming as the wagon rolled over, spilling her out on the ground and crushing the life out of the children in the back.
Jonas came back to help them and was immediately killed by several rifle bullets from the Sioux. Jonas and the children were the lucky ones. This war party was out for blood. There was no mercy for Ben or his wife. Their screams could be heard echoing through the hills before all was finally quiet.

The Indians tore the wagon apart looking for whatever they could use. They took the horses, the food, all the guns, and cartridges. Before they left, they set fire to the wrecked wagon.

Not far away, Bolt heard the distant gunfire. His first instinct was to just let it go, but he knew the area was a powder-keg. If trouble was brewing, it would be better to find out before it got to Scarlett and the horses.

He left Scarlett and the mares hidden in the thick timber and rode out to investigate. Sound travels a long way in the dry air of western Dakota, and he wasn't sure from how far away it had come.

Bolt had just come across fresh wagon tracks when he spotted a slender column of smoke rising in the sky. After riding up into the timber, he left Rufus and slipped up the ridgeline to look over the edge. What he saw almost made his stomach turn. The war-party was still there, but the bodies lying all around told him he was too late to help any of their victims.

Bolt's first impulse was to ride down and kill as many as he could, but he knew there was too many of them. He might have chanced it if not for Scarlett. The raiding party was yelling and having a grand time celebrating killing a bunch of helpless people.

Bolt could see the bodies of two men and a woman. He could only imagine what that woman's last few minutes of life must have been like. Each body was festooned with arrows. The final image was almost too much to bear when he saw the bodies of the two young children. There were no arrows in the children, but it was obvious they were dead.

Bolt was a strong, hardened man, but he nearly wept at the sight of those little bodies. He had no way of knowing how they died. Whether Wolf Walks Alone would have actually killed them would never be known.

Two throbbing veins popped out on Bolt's forehead and his face got red. The warrior spirit that had been quiet for many years was beginning to stir. He vowed to himself that before the sun rose again, these Indians would all be dead.

After the Indians finally rode off to the west, Bolt walked down to the scattered remains of the wagon. There were picks, shovels, and other prospecting gear thrown out on the ground where the wagon had turned over.

Bolt knew there was little he could do for these people except give them a Christian burial. He washed the dirt and blood from the little one's faces and arms with water from a canteen, wrapped them in some blankets and buried them together in one grave. He found a cloth doll on the ground and wrapped it up with the little girl.

A smoldering rage was burning brighter with every shovelful of dirt he dropped on those little bodies. The demon spirit was screaming to get out as he went about his work. Bolt's head was aching from the pressure of holding back his fury.

After removing the bloody arrows, and burying the adults, Bolt said a word of prayer over them in the flickering light of the smoldering wagon. He felt a little guilty praying to the Almighty, while planning to kill at least ten men.

The sun was long down before Bolt got back to Rufus. He stepped up in the stirrup and rode for Scarlett. When he got back to her, Bolt explained what happened.

"A war-party murdered a family of settlers nearby. We have to be quiet with no fire tonight. They rode off in the other direction, but there's bound to be more around."

"What if they come back for us?"

"We'll be alright. They'll camp somewhere tonight and tell each other how brave they were to kill so many whites. I'm going after them."

"Going after them; you can't take on a war-party all alone!"

"Hopefully, they've found some whiskey and they'll be drinking when I catch up with them."

Scarlett wanted no part of his plan. She wanted him to just ride for the ranch and get out of the area as soon as possible. She didn't know the whole story and she never would.

"Saloon brawls are one thing, going after a war-party single handed is quite another."

"It has to be done, I've got no choice."

"Please don't do this," she pleaded, "It's not your responsibility."

"Stay here and be quiet, I'll be back before dawn, whether I find them or not, I promise." He started to walk away, but paused and came back. "If this goes really bad, leave the horses and head southeast. It's not that far back to Rapid Creek."

Scarlett was nearly overwhelmed by the thought of being left out there alone, but she remained silent. Unknown to her, Bolt really wanted to stay with her. He could have justified it by telling himself he was keeping her safe, but he was compelled to do otherwise. The warrior spirit was determined vengeance would be wrought that very night. The images of those innocent children were burned into his mind. Now that the warrior spirit was stirring, only blood could put it to rest.

It was past midnight when Bolt found the Indian's camp. He was on a ridgeline above them when he saw their fire through the trees. They were camped down below him next to a small stream. It appeared they had indeed found some whiskey on the wagon as most of them were sleeping soundly. The ones that were still up were in bad shape. It didn't seem quite fair, but it was ten to one and these Indians needed killing.

Bolt left Rufus in a little stand of pine trees. He pulled his rifle from the saddle scabbard and quietly levered a round into the chamber. He replaced that round with one more in the magazine. He needed his rifle fully loaded to do what he was about to do. After making sure it was loaded and capped, he stuck his old Remington pistol in his belt.

His initial rage had cooled into a deep dark need for vengeance. The warrior spirit was going to kill each and every one of the men sleeping in the camp down below. Their lives were going to end violently that very night. There would be no warning or the slightest shred of mercy.

The sleeping Indians had no idea that an ancient and merciless warrior curse was descending upon their camp. They were peacefully spending their last moments on earth when Bolt stepped into the light of the fire.

Awakened by one of his horses, Wolf Walks Alone turned over and looked across the camp. Seeing Bolt, he let out a cry of rage and tried to get to his feet. Bolt killed him while he was still on his knees, and began shooting each of the others as they tried to get up.

The Indians got off a couple of shots, but they were too startled and too terrified to hit anything. When the Henry went dry, Bolt pulled his Colt and finished the job. Gray Bull was still alive when Bolt walked up to him. He holstered his empty Colt and pulled the Remington from his belt. The Indian had a sucking chest wound, but was still full of fight.

"You're not so brave," Bolt said as he pulled the hammer back, "You're a woman killer, but there are no women or children here now. Kill me…if you can, Woman Killer."

Hurt too bad to get up, Gray Bull reached for his rifle lying nearby, but Bolt kicked it away. The dying warrior spit blood at Bolt and cursed him in Sioux. When Bolt touched the trigger, the Remington belched fiery vengeance. A .44 caliber hole appeared on the Indian's forehead as his body was knocked prostrate to the ground, his face burned black by the powder.

There were a couple others who were badly hurt, but still alive. Bolt spoke to each of them as he killed them one by one. He was hoping they would feel the same terror those people felt earlier that day while waiting their turn to die.

Bolt wasn't satisfied after all was quiet. The brutal warrior spirit was loose and determined to make these Indians suffer even more. Bolt knew they were dead, but the spirit wasn't finished with them.

Bolt wanted all to know these men died a bad death with no honor. While looking over the camp, he found a saber, no doubt a souvenir from the battlefield. Remembering the bloody arrows, and driven with determination born of rage, he went first to the body of Wolf Walks Alone. With one savage blow he separated the warrior's right hand from his body.

Bolt moved from one body to the next, repeating the brutal amputations. He was violently sick to his stomach a couple of times during this barbarous act. His subconscious was begging him to stop, but the warrior spirit was in control and determined to render a terrible vengeance.

Just as he finished, Bolt spied a whiskey bottle. Dropping the bloody saber, he turned it up and took a drink, thinking it might make the horror of this night more bearable. The whiskey was like fire in his throat and he choked on it. Spitting it out, he hurled the bottle at the fire, smashing it to bits in a flash of flame. He made no attempt to hide his tracks as he left, if these Indians had any friends who might want to try and kill him, they were welcome to follow.

It was a two-hour ride back to where Scarlett was waiting. Picking his way through the darkness, Bolt was holding so much in, his head was about to explode. Finally giving in to a moment of weakness, he allowed himself to weep over the savage events of that day. His tears were as much for the dead warriors as the slaughtered whites. Like every other time before, the demon spirit abandoned him, leaving Bolt to deal with the horror and guilt alone.

After a while, the pressure in his head eased off and he began to feel a little better. Bolt knew he was as much a savage as those men he just killed. Still sick to his stomach and lightheaded, he stopped by a creek and washed his face. He scrubbed the blood off his hands and out of his clothes as best he could so as not to upset Scarlett.

She was glad to see him when he finally found her in the dark.

"Please don't ever leave me like that again." She had been crying, this time she didn't hesitate to put her arms around him and hold him close.

"It's alright," he whispered, "those Indians won't ever hurt anyone again."

"I don't care about that. I just want you here with me."

"I'm here now," he said, taking her in his arms, "And I'll be here from now on."

Bolt held her close to him until daylight. Scarlett didn't protest. She was never more secure than when she was pressed tightly against him.

Chapter Seven:
Lone Elk

Lone Elk was an Oglala Lakota. At Little Bighorn, he fought alongside Black Moon and Big Road to turn Benteen's men away at the south end of the camp. When that engagement was over, he joined the fight in Medicine Tail Coulee, never making it to the ridgeline where Custer was slain. Lone Elk was more than willing to fight the soldiers, but he didn't participate in the desecration of their bodies afterwards.

Lone Elk lost his family years earlier in the Dakota Territory. The cavalry attacked his village early one morning while Lone Elk was away hunting. His wife and young son were still asleep when the army stormed through their lodges. The white soldiers killed every Indian they could find. It didn't matter how old or young. When Lone Elk returned from the hunt he found the entire village in ruin.

The bullet-riddled bodies of his family were in the ashes of his burnt lodge. He placed them on elevated burial platforms and spent three days mourning them. He had every reason to hate the whites and he killed his share of white men.

This mighty Sioux could never bring himself to kill women and children. He would see the faces of his family and know these young ones were innocent and not his enemy.

Lone Elk was with a small group of Oglala warriors, northwest of the battlefield, when word came for him to meet his cousins at a camp thirty miles to the north of Custer City, near Wolf Creek. They were with He Dog and Crazy Horse, wreaking havoc on the mining camps in the Black Hills.

It was evening when Lone Elk and his friends arrived at the rendezvous point. A feeling of dread came over him as he rode near the camp. Something was very wrong, the horses were there, but there was no smoke from the cooking fires and no sound coming from the camp.

Sliding off his horse, he called out, "Wolf Walks Alone! Gray Bull!" There was no answer. As they drew nearer he could see the remnants of burnt rifles, bows, and arrows lying atop the cold ashes of their campfire. Before the Indian could figure it out, he spotted the first body.

Lone Elk couldn't believe once again the white man had taken away what was left of his family. When he realized the right hand had been removed from each warrior, his stomach turned, and he was overcome with rage and contempt.

"It must have been the long knives," one of his companions said.

Lone Elk was quiet as he sat by his cousins. Most of the bodies had but one bullet hole. Several more had two wounds. Powder burns indicated Gray Bull had been shot at close range, looking into the eyes of his killer.

It was becoming clear this wasn't done by a large group of soldiers. There would be multiple wounds in each body had it been a large battle. There were no tracks from the iron-shod horses the cavalry rode. Tracks around the camp made it very clear this was the work of one lone man on foot.

Each of Lone Elk's companions was thinking the same thing as they attended to the bodies. Whoever was responsible for this was more than just a mortal man. Only a spirit warrior would take on ten armed braves in a close-quarters fight? What possible reason did the spirit have for hating these Sioux so much that he made sure none of them would be able to draw a bow in the next life? They would never say it out loud, but none of them wanted to ever meet this spirit warrior face to face.

Lone Elk and his companions rode out at sunup to track the man down and kill him. They were but a few and none of them really had much heart for what they were setting out to do. The Sioux had great respect for bravery wherever they found it. They knew the man they sought, if he was indeed a man, was among the bravest they would ever face. They found where the man had ridden off the ridgeline and tracked him to the little valley where he met up with a herd of many horses and headed north.

That morning, the weather was warm and dry. The horse herd was just south of the Belle Fourche River and making good time. It was still over two hundred miles to the ranch. It would take at least another ten days to complete the journey.

Scarlett was glad to see the end of the Black Hills. She was learning a lot about her cowboy escort. Believing him to be a man she could trust, she had grown comfortable sharing her thoughts with him.

If he wanted to, Bolt could have taken advantage of her several times when she was afraid and wanting to be near him. Scarlett had a feeling he was pursuing her all the same. She hoped he would continue until she finally decided to let him catch her.

Bolt was dozing in his saddle when Rufus jumped to one side. At the same instant he heard a thump in the dirt beside him. He saw the little puff of dust from the bullet, just before he heard the report of the gun that fired it.

Swinging around in the saddle, Bolt saw six Indians bearing down on him. Scarlett was looking back at Bolt when he yelled at her.

"Leave the stock and get out of here!"

Scarlett released the mules, but stirred the mares up into a run. She had no intention of leaving her horses for the Indians.

"Don't stop and don't come back, no matter what happens!" he shouted after her as the horses lit out across the plains.

As Bolt turned Rufus around to face the oncoming Indians, he pulled his Henry rifle and stood in the stirrups. "Steady, Boy, steady." Settling his sights on one of the Indians, he fired. The warrior took Bolt's first bullet in the chest and was driven off his pony. The warrior on his left took the next bullet.

Bolt dropped back in the saddle, turned Rufus away, and touched him with his spurs. He fired over his shoulder as Rufus got up in the wind. The old horse was always fast, he ran with his big head stretched out in front of him, his nostrils flared wide open as he pumped massive volumes of air to his lungs. Once Rufus got up to speed, he was as smooth as glass, allowing Bolt to let go of the reins to just concentrate on his shooting.

Bolt fired and one more of the Sioux went down. Two of the remaining three Indians seemed to be slowing down. The lead Indian, however, was still coming on. Bolt worked the lever on his rifle, turned in the saddle and drew a bead on the pursuing warrior.

With the report of the rifle, Bolt saw the lead Indian's pony stumble, throwing the Indian to the ground and rolling over him amid a cloud of dust. After seeing their companion go down, the two remaining Indians seemed to abandon the chase and head away toward the west.

When the remaining Indians gave up, Bolt eased Rufus to a trot. The old horse was blowing hard and Bolt didn't want to wear him out completely. Once again Rufus had outrun the devil and saved Bolt's life.

Realizing the shooting had stopped, Scarlett could see Bolt coming along behind. She headed her mares into a circle and slowed them down to wait for him. She was becoming a pretty good hand, although she would never hear that from her companion.

While she watched him approach, Scarlett was thinking about how many people seemed willing to risk their lives to put a bullet in Bolt, and remembering the times that very thought had crossed her mind.

They made camp by the Belle Fourche River that afternoon. "I'll go back and look for the mules at first light in the morning," Bolt said.

After the long run, Rufus was enjoying a chance to rest and a splash in the cool water of the Belle Fourche.

When the sun was down, the coyotes started singing and the temperature began to drop. Lone Elk's pony was dead after taking a bullet from Bolt's rifle. The Indian wasn't too far from it himself. His arm was broken and his hip was dislocated. He was in terrible pain and all alone. His broken ribs made it painful to breathe. As badly hurt as he was, Lone Elk vowed he would see this white man again someday and finish this fight. As his head cleared, the mighty Sioux realized he was going to die if he lay there much longer.

Lone Elk hurt all over, his entire body was stiff, but he had to fix his hip before it swelled anymore and became impossible to put back in place. Dragging his injured leg, he crawled over to some sagebrush. When he was close enough, he sat up and pulled a leather thong from his vest.

Ignoring the pain, he managed to tie his foot to a greasewood bush. When his foot was secured, he fell back to rest for a minute. Regaining some strength, the Indian reached out and got his hands around the trunk of another sturdy bush. When he was stretched out between the bushes, he took a deep breath and gave a mighty yank. The pain was too intense for even the Sioux to bear and he passed out again. Remarkably, he was successful. His hip was back in its socket.

When Lone Elk awoke again, he was chilled and thirsty. He was nowhere near the river or any other source of water as far as he knew. There was a stiff breeze blowing and he was lightly dressed. Unable to stand on his injured hip, he managed to drag himself into a nearby coulee to rest out of the wind.

The mighty Sioux was lucky. Up in the head of the coulee was a low spot, eroded away by the runoff water falling from the cutbank above it. A small puddle still remained from the heavy rains of several weeks before. The ground surrounding the puddle was snow white from the heavy mineral deposits left by the evaporating water.

After he managed to crawl to it, Lone Elk found the cloudy liquid thick with alkali and full of mosquito larva. None of that mattered, he needed moisture.

The Indian tried to strain the concoction through his clenched teeth as he sucked it in. Each time he got a mouthful and swallowed it, he would spit the wrigglers out on the ground.

The adult mosquitoes seemed out for revenge as they swarmed around him. Lone Elk's only choice was to endure their attacks, there was nowhere else to go and little he could do about it.

When his thirst was somewhat abated, he crawled away from the water to a place under a short cutbank. He was out of the wind, but it was blowing just above him, sweeping away some of the mosquitoes. There was nothing to do for his arm except hold it to his chest and avoid moving it. He didn't have the strength to try and set it, he could not endure any more pain that night.

Bolt was sitting by the fire, enjoying the warmth. It was July, but nights were still cool on the plains. The night breeze was brisk. The dry air of the plains holds little heat, when the sun goes down the air cools rapidly.

Scarlett hadn't been too shaken by the Indian raid, she was getting used to being with this man that seemed to attract trouble everywhere he went. She moved to Bolt's side and sat down. She knew he was far away in thought, staring into the flickering flames.

"How old are you?" she asked, trying to start a conversation with the quiet man.

"I'm forty-six."

"How about marriage, have you ever been married?" Bolt didn't answer at first and her heart sank. He didn't wear a ring, but could it be possible he was already taken? "Are you married now?"

Marriage was a hard subject for Bolt to talk about. He hadn't been avoiding her question, just looking for the right thing to say. He wasn't going to get into any details about his past.

"I wanted to marry once," he finally said, "it was years ago. She was the love of my life I think. I was determined to see the frontier, but she wanted no part in pioneering. Her father was determined to keep us apart. Then the war came along. . . ." He hesitated, it was the first time in years he had spoken of Carrie Lynn to anyone.

"And what?"

"When the war broke out and I went north…she married… someone else"

"When you went north?"

"I fought the war in the Union Army."

"You were a Yankee, I'm surprised. . . ."

"It's true, a Captain in the Third U.S. Cavalry, and I'm not apologizing for it."

"I don't expect you to," she said. "I'm sure you did what you thought was best. I won't presume to judge you for that, I'm not surprised you were an officer."

Scarlett had come to admire this big man so much she really didn't care what his reasons were for fighting for the north. Bolt was surprised at her attitude, he expected a lot worse from her when the truth finally came out. In reality, the people of Kentucky were never part of the Confederacy. Some of them were loyal to the south, but many of them weren't.

"So, she was the only one?" Scarlett asked, getting back to his love life, "That was so long ago; I can't believe there hasn't been other women in your life."

"There was a girl down in Texas I might have married if things had been different," he said, "but that was years ago. I guess I'm too old to be much in demand with the ladies anymore. I try not to think about being alone. Besides, what have I got to offer a woman? All I own is that old horse, a fifty-dollar saddle, and a Henry rifle."

That was more than he had said at one time since starting their journey. Scarlett was encouraged to try for more, she moved closer to him. He instinctively placed his arm around her to share some warmth. It felt good to both of them to have some contact with each other.

"How about you?" he asked.

"Are you asking how old I am, or have I ever been married?"

"I know better than to ask a lady about her age."

Scarlett pushed herself up against him and laid her head on his chest. She loved to hear his deep voice. She could feel his words vibrate in his chest when he spoke to her and she loved the scent of him.

"I was married once. I thought I could change all his bad habits, but I was young and he only got worse as time went on. His family was pretty well off, his idea of love was to own me like I was just one more of his a possessions. As I grew older it became more than I could bear.

"That was years ago, since then, each time I've thought I was in love, that's been in the back of my mind. And for your information, Mr. Ashton," she said looking up at him, "I'm thirty-eight-years-old."

Bolt assumed she was much younger. She was so pretty and she was still firm and shapely. He had only held her close to him during moments of stress, but he still noticed her body when it was pressed close to him.

Now it felt good to have her on his chest. Her warmth and the scent of her hair were stirring things that had been out of his mind for a long time. He thought he was passed that, but now he wasn't so sure.

He held her there in the firelight until she fell asleep, and gently covered her with his bedroll. *"Cowboy, you may be in big trouble,"* he thought to himself as he leaned back into his saddle and drifted off to sleep.

Out in the dark, Rufus was stomping around on a picket rope. Bolt very seldom tied the old horse. He depended on him to stay wherever he put him. Bolt knew some of these mares were in season and a terrible distraction to Rufus, he wasn't taking any chances. Rufus was snorting and grumbling all night, he would be in a foul mood come sunup.

Bolt went to search for the pack mules right after daylight. He was leading one of the nightrider's horses in case he found a disabled mule and had to transfer the pack. It didn't take long to find them. They hadn't run far from where the chase started and everything was intact.

Rufus was acting strange most of the morning. He was extra ornery and almost bucked a couple of times. Bolt figured he wasn't happy about the strange horse being so close to him.

As they started back along the trail to Scarlett, Bolt was hoping to sleep in Wyoming that night. If they could get started soon, it would only be two or three more days to the Montana Territory.

Bolt passed the bodies of the Indians killed in the running battle the day before. He felt bad about killing them, but he couldn't let them get to Scarlett. Reining in Rufus, he got off.

He knew Indians don't want to be buried, they prefer to be scattered far and wide by the birds and animals. Bolt didn't hate Indians. In fact he always felt a strange connection to them. He knew they were fighting to keep their land just like he would if placed in the same circumstances. He didn't want these brave men to lie scattered across the plains.

Bolt took some blankets off the mules and wrapped their bodies in them. After dragging the bodies up into the timber, he laid them all side-by-side facing east. He cleaned their faces and arranged their weapons alongside them. When he was finished, he took the mules and rode for Scarlett.

It had been a bad night for Lone Elk, he was in constant pain. Hunger, cold, and the marauding mosquitoes had taken a toll on him. The only reason he was even alive was the puddle in the coulee.

The wounded warrior knew he was facing almost certain death. There was no way he could walk out of there for several days. Without food he would never have the strength. If a white man or the army found him, he would be shot to death. He almost wished it would happen soon, he had very little to live for as it was. His grandfathers must have been watching over him. The mighty Sioux's prayers were about to be answered, but not in the way he expected.

Not long after he left the bodies of the Indians, Bolt came upon the remains of an Indian pony. It hadn't been dead too long. He figured it was the one he hit during the running gunfight. There was no sign of the pony's rider, Bolt assumed he survived and was picked up by the others.

As they passed a little coulee, Rufus spooked away from the edge. Bolt thought the old horse was still just being ornery until he saw the Indian lying in the bottom of the coulee. Bolt drew his Colt, not knowing if the Indian was dead or alive. He could see the Indian was armed only with a knife.

Bolt dismounted and went down to investigate. The Indian was in bad shape. His arm was broken. He was cut and bruised all over. Bolt figured he was the one that fell off the dead pony, and he tried to speak to him.

"What's the matter? Are you shot?"

The Indian didn't seem to understand anything Bolt was saying.

"Io-wacin," the Indian said, but Bolt had no idea what that meant. The Indian pulled his knife and tried to get up.

Bolt pointed his Colt and cocked the hammer.

"Don't push it."

Being too weak to press the attack, the Indian dropped the knife and fell back. Bolt got closer to him and kicked the knife away.

"Easy," Bolt said, "I'm not here to hurt you."

The Indian seemed to relax a little when Bolt holstered his pistol. It was easy to see the Indian's arm was broken. Bolt had seen broken bones set in the war. He thought he could do it for this Indian. After gathering some sticks to fashion a splint, Bolt set the Indian's arm.

His pain was evident, but the Indian never made a sound. Bolt cut one of Scarlett's petticoats into strips and used it to secure the Indian's broken arm and bind up his ribcage.

Bolt brought the Indian some jerky and a canteen of water. He fashioned a rope halter for the nightrider's gelding and helped the Indian up on it. Bolt returned the Indian's knife when he was mounted.

Bolt knew this warrior was practically helpless. If he ran into any kind of trouble, he wouldn't be able to defend himself. Bolt thought for several moments before going back to the pack mule. He took one of the rifles out of the pack and gave it to the Indian. He put a handful of cartridges in the pouch with the jerky.

Lone Elk couldn't believe this white man's kindness. "Thank you, my friend," he said in Sioux, but the man couldn't understand. Lone Elk had no idea he was in the presence of the spirit warrior. This man was very different from most of the whites Lone Elk ever encountered. There was something in his eyes that touched Lone Elk. It was almost as if he already knew this white man.

When they parted, Lone Elk rode off to the west and Bolt went north to return to Scarlett. The mighty Sioux rode passed his dead companions and saw them arranged on the hillside. He knew it must have been the work of the white stranger that helped him. Lone Elk was surprised and grateful this man had taken care of his friends.

"This man knows the Indian ways," he thought. Another dark thought crossed his mind for a moment, but it couldn't be.

"You're a fool to waste a good horse and a rifle on a half-dead Indian," Bolt said to himself. He knew he did the right thing. The Indian seemed like a man not a monster. Bolt knew he was right in trying to save him.

Scarlett was sitting in the sun next to the river waiting for Bolt to return with the mules. *"He's late as usual,"* she thought. *"Probably ran into somebody who wanted to shoot him. There certainly is no shortage of people on that list."*

The Belle Fourche is a small shallow river. The cool water looked so inviting; Scarlett decided to take a bath. Being alone, she felt safe going in the nude. She washed out all of her undergarments and hung them on a limb. Then she just sat down in the cool running water. She thought about last night and how Bolt seemed almost human for a couple of hours.

Bolt rode up over the crest of the little hill where he left Scarlett and the horse herd. He was deep in thought about the night before and how good it had felt when Scarlett was lying on his chest. He was all mixed up inside, but he wasn't going to let his guard down over one little show of affection.

He saw Scarlett just as she stepped out of the river. Feeling like an intruder, he wanted to look away, but he couldn't tear his eyes from her. The cold water was having a noticeable effect on parts of her. The reality of her wet naked body was even more than he had imagined.

Scarlett saw him at last, "You are no gentleman, Bolt Ashton," she said, but made no attempt to hide herself. Bolt turned away, trying not to look over his shoulder as she calmly went about drying off and getting dressed. He had no idea what to say, he didn't plan to ride up on her or to invade her privacy. If he had any idea where she was, he would have announced himself in plenty of time to for her to get out.

"I didn't know. I didn't mean to look. I mean…I know…I looked, but…I…I wouldn't have looked." For once in his life, Bolt was at a loss as to what to do.

Unseen by him, Scarlett was smiling. She hadn't planned for him to see her body, but she wasn't sorry he had. She managed to put a big crack in Bolt's defenses and she didn't compromise her morals to do it.

Bolt fixed supper that night and they ate in silence. He started to apologize again, but finally decided to just turn in. They still had a long way to go, and this would eventually blow over.

Bolt had a difficult time going to sleep that night. Every time he closed his eyes he could see Scarlett's body in his mind. Cursed to a life without lasting love, he wondered if this independent, but very desirable woman, had come into his life to drive him completely loco, or would she be the one to finally break that curse.

Two nights later, a small band of Cheyenne Indians sat around a campfire telling stories of bygone days of glory. They were making every effort to avoid the white man's army. The cavalry was further south in the Dakotas chasing Crazy Horse, and they felt safe in the area east of Devil's Tower. One of them told a story he heard from a Sioux a few days before.

"A young Sioux warrior had been with a war party that killed several settlers. After they made camp, they began to drink the whiskey they stole from the settler's wagon.

"This Sioux storyteller was very young. Having never tasted whiskey, he became ill and slipped away into the brush so the others wouldn't see him be sick. He was afraid they would think he was sick from the killing.

"This Sioux was lying in the brush trying to clear his spinning head when he heard the first shot and the screams coming from the camp. He managed to crawl to the edge of the brush to see what was going on.

"What he saw was a tall, white spirit warrior, as big as a grizzly, standing in the midst of his companions and killing them one by one. Flame shot from his hands as Indians fell like stalks of grass before the buffalo. When all were dead, the spirit cut off their hands.

"This young Sioux was too afraid to fight and too sick to run. He lay paralyzed with fear, hoping this spirit warrior would pass over him. He knew it was a bad thing to kill women and children, he vowed never to take part in another raid.

"The spirit seemed to float through the camp when the killing was over, then faded from sight in a flash of fire. When daylight came, the young Sioux fled west to Devil's Tower. This story must be true; a Sioux would never tell of his own fear without great provocation."

Lone Elk was going to live, but he was exhausted. The food and water given to him by the white man saved his life, but it was about gone. He hoped to find a Sioux camp somewhere to the west. It was well after dark on the third day, when he heard the sounds of voices. The voices were speaking Cheyenne. The Cheyenne were still pondering the story of the Spirit Warrior when Lone Elk rode into the firelight. He slid off his horse and collapsed in a heap from pure exhaustion.

After recovering from their initial fright, the Cheyenne pulled him to the fire and covered him with a blanket. They had no idea where this Sioux had come from, but they knew he must have encountered a white man because of the linen bandages. They were worried the whites may be tracking this lone warrior and they slept very little that night.

Chapter Eight:
Eb Monday to the Rescue

Morning comes early on the Lonesome Wind. Coop's rule is breakfast at five, work by five-thirty. The cowboys who work for Coop had just finished eating and were headed out to the corral and go to work. They would be digging postholes and finishing up the new corral.

The corral was next to the new barn Coop had them build over the last few weeks. All this was for the Kentucky horses that Coop thought should have already been in Rapid Creek.

Coop was a horseman. He grew up raising good ranch horses with his dad. Coop never worked a horse until it was five-years-old. After they were weaned, they would be turned out on their own to grow up and enjoy life until he was ready to begin training them.

Those five-year-olds were big and hardheaded, but they had the bone and muscle to do anything he demanded of them. Coop preferred to avoid gelding them. His dad was of the opinion a gelding didn't have the stamina or the legs a stud or even a mare would have, and whether it was true or not, Coop still held to it.

From the time those horses were five and well up into their twenties, they were ready for anything. Coop believed in working them hard. If a particular horse proved difficult to deal with, Coop just rode him that much farther and harder. He always said, "Wet saddle blankets would cure most rank horses."

All of the cowboys on the Lonesome were good horseman. They had to be, to keep up with their boss. Most of them had a string of six to eight good horses they would alternate riding, depending on the job that needed doing.

As a rule, each of them had two mounts they kept fed with grain through the winter until green-up. The rest were turned out on grass to take care of themselves. Those grain-fed, legged-up mounts were the ones they depended on when things got tough or they were faced with a big difficult circle.

They were well into summer and Coop was anxious to get on with breeding the thoroughbreds. Wanting to see what his investment had gotten him, he was frustrated with week after week of waiting and no word from Bolt.

"That hardheaded Bolt may have just turned around and rode off after meeting Ms. Canary and learning the truth about this deal."

"Bolt is a no account, skirt-chasing saddle bum for sure," Spud said, "But I reckon he'll do this job just like he does everything else, his way, in his own sweet time. I just feel sorry for that poor girl traveling with him."

The old Cajon was looking through the kitchen window when he spotted a rider coming in the main gate. The stranger rode up to the house and delivered a rumpled envelope to Coop's hand.

"The telegraph lines were down from Cheyenne for more than three weeks," the stranger said, "the Indians keep cutting the wires and this just came in."

"I don't know anybody in Cheyenne," Coop said, "What is it?"

"Beats me, I was coming this way and the telegrapher asked me to drop it off." Coop thanked him for his kindness and offered him a cup of coffee before he would be on his way.

"It's a telegram from Bolt," Coop said, after opening the envelope. "It's over three weeks old and. . . ." Coop's face got red as he read on, "I'll be damned. He's trailing those horses overland from Wyoming, all by himself."

"Why?" Spud asked.

"Damned if I know."

"Does he want any of us to meet him in Rapid Creek?"

"Doesn't say he's coming back that way. That damn hillbilly wouldn't ask for help or wait till any of us could go to him. If he gets Ms. Canary hurt, or loses those horses, I'm gonna shoot him myself."

"What's that you say about shooting somebody?" Eb asked. He saw the stranger ride up and had just walked up on the porch in time to catch the last bit of Coop's conversation.

"I'm talking about that hardheaded partner of yours."

"Where is that no-good loafer? Here we are slaving away on this barn and corrals while he's off on a picnic with a woman." Coop handed him the telegram. "I should've gone with him," Eb said after reading it, "somebody's liable to shoot him if I'm not there to look after him. That lady is probably ready for some company other than that hardheaded ridge-runner by now."

"He's got bigger problems than that," Coop said, "The country west of the Black Hills and north to the Powder River is a bad place to be right now, and Bolt's headed right for it."

"I ought to be with him," Eb said as he walked away.

"You better go pack him some grub," Coop said, turning to Spud.

"Where's he going?"

"To find Bolt, unless I miss my guess."

Coop went to check on the progress of the corral as Spud disappeared into the house.

"So long," Eb said as he rode passed the boys working on the new corral.

"Where are you going?" TJ asked.

"To find a fair damsel."

"You might just as well," Coop said, "you ain't worth a damn around here for much of anything."

"You'll be singing a different tune after you spend a week or two with nobody here to do the work, except these wet-behind-the-ears baby cowboys."

"At least it'll be quiet, and I still got Spud."

"That old biscuit-roller, I'd be surprised if he can even get on a horse."

Eb was riding a big eight-year-old roan named Buster, and leading another, younger horse that he called Banjo, the strongest horses in his string. As Eb was talking, Spud walked over to the corral and handed him a cotton sack containing coffee, sugar, and salt. The old cook added a few corn dodgers, dried apples, and jerky as well.

"Much obliged," Eb said as he took the bag from Spud.

"You won't get fat, but it'll keep you alive for a few days. Just what put the notion in your head that you can do anything for Bolt, he can't do his own-self?"

"He's probably out there lost and that lady is in need of rescuing about now. I'm just the cowhand to do it."

"You never rescued anything, except maybe the last drop of red-eye out of a busted bottle," Spud said, "She'll probably take one look at you and head right on back to Kentucky."

"That won't amount to a grunt in a buffalo herd after she sees what she'll have to face every morning serving her breakfast."

"Well, you danged old horse thief, I don't see it keeping your ornery carcass from being the first one at the table every time I pour the gravy."

"Are you gonna stand here and jaw all day?" Coop asked, looking up at Eb. "Go on, if you're going. We all got work to do. If you don't find Bolt inside a week, you turn around and get back here, you ain't on a holiday."

"You watch your hair out there," TJ warned, "the Sioux have their blood up after killing Custer."

"Damn a bunch of Indians," Eb said, "they better watch out for me." With that, he pulled Buster's head around and spurred him out the gate.

"If he finds Bolt, it'll be completely by accident," a young cowboy said from behind Coop, "I guess he's got to try, that's what partners do."

"I suppose," Coop said, "those two are a pair, that's for sure."

Spud had his foot up on a rail as he watched Eb ride away. "I pity any Indians fool enough to run afoul of either one of 'em."

The young cowboy standing in the corral with Coop, Spud, and TJ was Logan Penny. He showed up in Coulter Creek one cold day about four years earlier. Logan was an orphan and just fifteen-years-old at the time. Coop happened to be in town when he spotted the ragged and hungry youngster and brought him to the Lonesome.

Logan was twenty-years-old now, and the Lonesome was his home. The kid had grown into a fine young man, a top hand, and the best horseman on the place. Logan was slight of build, light weight, and tough as a rusty cut-nail.

Logan recently acquired a young Mustang stud from old Bill Weems, a horse trader in Coulter Creek. The Mustang cost him half-a-year's wages, but Logan knew as soon as he saw the little horse he had to have him. Coop covered part of the cost with a promise from the youngster to pay him back.

The Mustang was a light buckskin color with a black dorsal stripe, black mane and tail, and a black stocking on each foot. Logan named him Sandy. He wasn't a big horse. He was stocky and sturdy, and quicker than greased lightning. With Logan in the saddle, it was like they became one animal. There wasn't a brushed-up heifer on the Lonesome that could get away from them.

"We'll be shorthanded with Eb gone," Coop said, "You boy's better get busy. Those mares should be here soon, and we'll need this cavvy corral.

"I think I'll get Sandy and ride up to the Dancing Ground," Logan said, "We need to check. . . ."

"Son, I may be getting' old, but I ain't feebleminded."

"No sir."

"I think you want to take a ride for a couple of days to get out o' digging post holes."

"Yes sir, you might be right, but. . . ."

"No buts about it, this can't wait." Shielding his eyes with his hand, Coop looked skyward, "You boys see the sun up there?"

"Yes sir," Logan and TJ said together.

"When you can't see it anymore, you can quit. Now grab that posthole digger and start sweating." Logan reluctantly picked up the digger and started on a new hole.

Coop was smiling as he and Spud began to walk toward the house.

"Cowboys," he said to Spud, "If they can't do the job from a horse, they don't want any part of it." Satisfied everybody was busy; Coop went back in the house to have another cup of coffee.

Eb knew Bolt would come north from Cheyenne, through the Black Hills to Rapid Creek. Bolt would pick up Rufus even if it was out of the way. He figured Bolt would turn northwest from there to Coulter Creek. If the telegram was three weeks old, Bolt should be somewhere near the northern end of the Black Hills by the time he could get there.

Eb was dragging the spare horse to cover more ground. Riding one animal for half-a-day and then switching, he could make fifty or sixty miles every day, if he wanted to push them. He would be near a rendezvous point with Bolt in three or four days without hurting his mounts.

The old cowboy was anxious to meet Ms. Scarlett. None of the men on the Lonesome had any idea what Scarlett looked like. They just knew she was a fairly young woman from back east.

It was full dark when Eb made camp by the Powder River. He had been riding for two long days. "We're getting too old for this kind of punishment," he said to Buster. "If it weren't for that mule-headed Bolt, I'd be at the Lonesome sitting down to supper right now."

It would be a cold camp. The weather was warm and there were Indians in the Powder River country who were determined to remain free. Only planning to sleep a short while and rest the horses, Eb would make do without a fire.

Bolt had been quiet since seeing Scarlett in the river. He tried to apologize several times, but Scarlett would roll her eyes and give him this look that almost drew blood.

It was getting on toward evening the next day and he was looking for a place to camp. They were far from the river, on the open plains. Every coulee was just about like the last one.

He finally found one with a small cutbank and a few sandstone caprocks on the edge. It was a good spot to hide his campfire and get out of the wind. Bolt reined in and stepped down.

"This is as good a place as any."

Scarlett thought he would never stop. She wouldn't say a word, but she was done-in and wanted to get out of the saddle. It was as if he thought as long as he kept riding, he wouldn't have to look her in the eye.

She was never angry with him. She was, in fact, quite pleased with his reaction to her naked body. She pulled the saddle off her mount, spread her bedroll on the ground, and dropped onto it. It felt good to just lie there for a few minutes.

Bolt was searching around for a little greasewood or buffalo chips for a fire. The Coyotes were starting to sing to one another, getting ready for a big night. It had been a warm day, but the temperature was going down.

They ate a light supper and turned in without saying much to each other. Bolt lay on his back looking up at the vast array of stars over his head. The nights in the open allowed him time to think. The darkness and the quiet always stirred old memories of love lost or abandoned. As he lay there, his memory drifted back to Texas and the first time he ever saw Angelia. Talking about her the other night brought the beautiful Mexican girl back to his mind. He thought about her beauty and the passion they shared on those hot Texas nights.

Bolt was brought back to reality when he heard Scarlett moving around in the dark. To his surprise, she came over and lay down beside him.

"I wanted to say I'm sorry for yesterday. It was my fault, and I've been pretty hard on you." Bolt placed an arm around her and pulled her over closer to him.

"It's alright. I was surprised to find you like that, I should have looked away, I'm sorry…I. . . ."

Scarlett placed her fingers on his lips to stop him from saying anything else. She gave him a soft kiss on the cheek, and started to get up. Bolt wanted more of her mouth, he tried to gently hold her down, but she resisted.

"We have an early day tomorrow," she said, "get some sleep."

Bolt lay in the dark after she was gone, feeling more alone than ever. Just on the other side of the fire, Scarlett was snuggled in her bedroll feeling very much in control. Her plan to snare this big cowboy seemed to be working perfectly.

Out in the dark, Rufus was waiting for everything to settle down for the night. Bolt tied him to some sagebrush, as there were no trees to tie a picket line to. The sagebrush hadn't been grown that could hold Rufus and the big outlaw knew it.

He waited until after Scarlett lay down and he could hear Bolt snoring. The old horse pulled back until the rope was tight, then just sat back. When all of his fourteen hundred pounds hit the rope, the sagebrush popped right out of the ground, and the big gray outlaw quietly made his way over to the mares. It was quite a night for both testosterone pumped studs. Only one of them got lucky, the other one tossed and turned all night.

Bolt was awake just as the sky was turning bright. He sat up and stretched his muscles. Scarlett was still sleeping soundly.

"You're quite a woman, Ms. Scarlett," he said to himself. Bolt could see Rufus, but he wasn't where he had been tied, and the old horse seemed to be watching the horizon.

Before Bolt could figure it out, the ground started to tremble. The horses began to stir around as an ominous rumble filled the camp. Spotting a rolling dust cloud on the horizon, Bolt shouted for Scarlett to get up. Sprinting to her side, he helped her up against the cutbank behind the caprocks. The moment they made it to the cutbank, hundreds of shaggy beasts topped the rise in front of them.

Bolt shielded her body to protect her as best he could as the first buffalo thundered through the coulee. It seemed to take forever for the buffalo to pass, as Bolt and Scarlett huddled against the bank. Dirt and gravel were pelting them as a rolling torrent of animals engulfed the camp. Scarlett was afraid, but unhurt, thanks to Bolt's quick reaction and their being close to the shelter of the caprocks.

After it was over, Bolt got up to look for Indians, but there seemed to be no apparent reason for the stampede. Rufus wasn't far away. He simply moved out of the way and let them pass. The mares were nowhere to be seen. The pack mules were dead. Being hobbled, they were unable to escape. The buffalo pulverized them along with most of the camp gear and food.

Scarlett was shaken, but unhurt. After going through their meager supplies to salvage what he could, Bolt caught Rufus and went to look for the mares. He would spend the best part of the morning getting them all back together. They hadn't gone far and they were all in good shape.

Bolt put what was left of their gear into one pack and strapped it on one of the remaining nightrider horses and started the herd toward Coulter Creek, still two hundred miles away. Bolt wasn't sure, but he thought he was back in Montana.

With most of their food gone, it would be up to him to feed them with what he could kill along the way. There wouldn't be any more sugar, salt, flour, or coffee until they got to Coulter Creek. Little did he know; being without coffee would become a serious problem. Scarlett liked her morning coffee. It wasn't safe to talk to her until she had her first cup.

Lone Elk was mending well with the help of the Cheyenne. He heard the story of the spirit warrior who killed his friends, but Lone Elk wasn't as superstitious as a lot of other Indians. He knew some things could not be explained, but he was sure one white man, not a spirit, was responsible for the death of his cousins.

He often thought of the white man who saved his life. Why hadn't this man just killed him and why did he take time to prepare his dead companions? This stranger was unlike any white man Lone Elk had ever run across.

The mighty Sioux wanted to meet him again. He wondered if their trails would ever cross and if they would know each other. He also wondered what would happen if fate brought them together on the field of battle.

Lone Elk often thought of the man who killed his friends, the so-called spirit warrior. Maybe this man was the family of the settlers his renegade cousins killed. He could almost understand this man's hatred of the Indian, but Lone Elk would do his best to kill this man if he ever found him. He had no idea the two men in his thoughts were the same person.

Lone Elk decided to stay in the company of the Cheyenne until he could join some of the free-roaming Sioux. The Cheyenne were traveling north to the Powder River country to hunt. Buffalo were still found in good numbers along the Powder River. It would be a ride of several days, but the weather was good and the army was to the south. It was a time to heal for Lone Elk.

"You are one sorry excuse for a guide, Bolt Ashton," Scarlett snapped. "Thanks to you, we have no breakfast, no flour for biscuits, no sugar for coffee, of course that doesn't really matter…because we have no coffee! I'm not happy about any of this! If I wasn't a lady…I'd…I'd shoot you myself."

It was the first morning after the stampede destroyed their camp and Bolt was walking as if on egg shells.

"You picked the very coulee used by the buffalo migration."

"Buffalo migration, where in hell did you hear that?"

"I read books and don't swear at me."

"Sorry, I just meant. . . ."

"Some frontiersman you are. You probably don't even know where we are…do you? Are you listening? For all I know we could be riding around in circles, or headed for Canada. I wouldn't be surprised to see an iceberg pop up in front of us."

"I think Icebergs are out in the ocean."

"You know what I mean, and don't change the subject." Scarlett had a throbbing headache from the lack of coffee and she had been impossible to deal with ever since sunup.

Bolt was trying to keep busy as he broke camp and saddled the horses. He was doing his best to keep his mouth shut, knowing anything he said would not help his situation. He was thinking he should have grabbed the coffee and hid it behind the cutbank instead of his outspoken companion. He wondered if Coop would mind if he just gave her to the first bunch of Indians that came by.

"The Indians have suffered enough," he mumbled to Rufus, "I wouldn't want to inflict that much pain on them."

"What was that?"

"Nothing; I'm just talking to my horse."

"That's just fine. He's the only one that will be talking to you from now on. I'm finished."

"Thank you, Lord," Bolt whispered under his breath.

Bolt planned to stop early that afternoon and take time to hunt. They needed food and he needed to get away from Scarlett for a while. That part of the Montana Territory is open plains with little wooded hills scattered around. It is great country for the pronghorn antelope and mule deer. It would not be much of a chore to get some fresh meat for their supper.

It was about five in the afternoon when Bolt pulled up and stepped off. "We'll camp here tonight." After unsaddling the horses, he laid out the bedrolls on the edge of a tree-lined hillside. It was cool there in the shade with plenty of firewood for a change.

"You'll be comfortable here," he said, "I'm going to get our supper." Pulling the Henry out of his scabbard, he walked down the hill. "Just fire off that old Walker, if you need me," he said over his shoulder.

"I'll fire it off alright," she said to his back, "but you might not want to be around when I do."

Bolt crept to the edge of the hill and peeked over into the grassy swale out in front of him. There was a small group of doe antelope. Most had tiny fawns with them. Antelope aren't big animals and the does are almost dainty.

Bolt wouldn't shoot one of the does because he didn't want to leave any little ones alone for the coyotes. He was hungry, but not that hungry. He continued on until he found a bachelor group of antelope bucks.

He was going to have to put the sneak on the bucks. They were out of range, feeding on sagebrush in a big flat. Bolt didn't want to shoot more than once. A single shot is hard to place, but two or more make it easy to locate the direction they came from. He didn't want any company that night, white or red. Getting down on his hands and knees, he slowly advanced toward the antelope.

Knowing the pronghorns use their big bugged-out eyes as their main means of defense, Bolt stayed low in the grass in order to get close enough for a shot. He loved the smell of the grass and the sagebrush when he was crawling through it. He was always on the lookout for the prickly-pear cactus growing down in the grass.

Bolt crept ever closer to the antelope until he was within easy rifle range. Pulling the hammer back on the Henry, he laid the blade of the front sight on the buck's shoulder and slowly squeezed the trigger.

Just over a mile away, Jack Sprigg pulled up hard on his horse's reins.

"Did you hear that?" he asked his two saddle partners.

"I heard a shot," one said.

"Where'd it come from?"

"I don't rightly know."

"Keep your eyes open," Jack warned. "It could be redskins and there ain't enough of us to tangle with them devils."

Sprigg and his friends tried their hand at gold mining in the Black Hills, but they never struck any ore. Prospecting turned out to be more work than they were used to. Now they were on their way to Coulter Creek to seek their fortunes.

After dark, Bolt was roasting antelope back straps and tenderloin on the fire while Scarlett sat quietly, waiting for supper. She was feeling better and apologized for her tirade that morning. Tonight would be just meat. Everything else was lost in the stampede. The Indians survived on a diet of mostly meat for thousands of years. Bolt figured she could make do for a few days.

In addition to the back straps, he had two racks of jerked antelope meat drying by the fire, planning to save it in case game was scarce farther on. Scarlett was hungry and the antelope smelled good. Bolt was tending to the roasting meat when he heard Rufus grumble out in the dark.

"We may have company," he said to Scarlett.

"Hello in the camp," a man called out. The stranger's voice was coming from the darkness beyond the fire, "Can I come in?" Bolt was an easy target in the firelight and he was several steps from Scarlett. He had no choice but to play it out friendly, and see what would happen.

Without waiting for an answer, a man wearing rumbled dirty clothes walked into the light. His hands were empty, but the tie-down on his holster was pulled back.

"Name's Jack," he said, "Jack Sprigg." The stranger was talking to Bolt, but he couldn't take his eyes off Scarlett. "Howdy ma'am," he said, touching the brim of his hat, "you sure are a pretty thing to be out here all alone."

"She isn't alone," Bolt said.

When Sprigg got close, Scarlett noticed his breath and the smell of old sweat. In the firelight she could see tobacco stains in the corner of his mouth and on his shirt.

"We saw your fire. Thought we'd ride over and be neighborly."

"Who's we?"

"My saddle partners and me," Sprigg replied.

As Sprigg was talking, two more men walked in behind Bolt, they were each carrying a rifle. Scarlett started to move closer to Bolt. She was nervous being around these strange men, remembering the night the Carlton's attacked them in the Black Hills.

"You just stay still, Missy," one of the others warned, pointing his rifle at Bolt's back.

Bolt couldn't believe his misfortune. It seemed like every low-life in the territory was following him around. He knew this was going to get serious. This bunch was there for more than just a visit.

"We ain't gonna hurt nobody," Sprigg said, sensing Bolt's uneasiness. "We just want to share your meal and maybe some whiskey, course now that we've seen your woman, we might just share her too."

Sprigg thought he had the power over this one lone man and his beautiful companion. The thought of being with the woman was making his pulse quicken. He couldn't believe his luck. Here was a lovely woman, a herd of fine horses, and only one man to prevent him from taking it all. The two-bit outlaw thought it was his lucky day.

Bolt's mind was racing to find a way out of his predicament. He knew exactly what was on Sprigg's mind, but he couldn't draw on him. The two behind him would shoot him in the back and have their way with Scarlett.

The warrior spirit was stirring, but Bolt had to stay calm if he was to have any chance at saving her life. In spite of his wrinkled brow and reddening face, he played with Sprigg's mind by acting timid.

"We don't want any trouble, friend," Bolt said.

"Ain't gonna be no trouble," Sprigg said, "as long as you behave. Now pass out some of that meat and get your whiskey bottle."

Reading the signs in Bolt's face, Scarlett knew a storm was brewing.

"We don't have any whiskey," she said to Sprigg, trying to defuse the situation. "My husband and I don't abide the demon rum. Please, just eat your fill and be on your way."

Scarlett was trying to convince Sprigg she was a married woman, hoping it would change his mind about anything he was planning to do to her. Unfortunately, that made absolutely no difference to these outlaws.

"We're gonna have our fill, ain't we boys," Sprigg said to his partners, "Then we're gonna have you ma'am."

"I want her first," one of the men behind Bolt said. Scarlett was genuinely afraid after hearing that, and looking to Bolt for reassurance.

Two throbbing veins popped out on Bolt's forehead when Sprigg mentioned having Scarlett. He was struggling to control the demon awakened by these intruders. Bolt already knew, no matter what happened in the next few moments, the now raging warrior spirit was coming out, regardless of the odds or the outcome. This bunch wasn't going to hurt Scarlett as long as he was alive. Bolt looked into her eyes for a moment and turned back to Sprigg.

"You touch a hair on her head, and I'll kill all of you."

It was inevitable now; the spirit was loose. Sprigg was already dead; he just didn't know it. Bolt's hand was easing toward his Colt when he heard Rufus making a fuss out in the dark.

"Big talk," Sprigg said, "we got you three to one. We'll do whatever we want with her. Ain't nothing you can do about it."

"Why don't you quit fooling around?" one of the men behind Bolt said, raising his rifle, "Just get on with . . ." he was interrupted by a flash of steel and a wet thump.

The gunman looked down in horror to see a large knife buried in his chest. The stricken outlaw's knees buckled and he toppled over. Before the outlaw even hit the ground, Sprigg heard a loud voice from the darkness.

"Reckon you sons-o'-bitch's better count again!"

In desperation, Sprigg spun around and fired in the voice's direction. Unfortunately for him, his one remaining partner did the same. That gave Bolt the opening he had been waiting for. Bolt got one knee under him as he drew his Colt and put two quick shots into Sprigg's chest. The first bullet was to eliminate the threat. The second was for Bolt's temper. While he was killing Sprigg, two bullets zipped right by Bolt's head. One came from the darkness, the other from the man still on his feet behind him.

Bolt spun and fired at the one remaining target, the one that wanted Scarlett first. The already-bleeding gunman took Bolt's third bullet in the chest. He was still on his feet, struggling to work the lever on his rifle when Bolt's fourth bullet slammed into him and put him down for good.

Bolt got to his feet and shot the gunman once more as he lay on the ground. The last remaining load in the Colt went between the still opened eyes of the man with the knife in his chest.

"Take her now, you sons-o'. . . ." Bolt didn't finish, he realized Scarlett was lying on the ground nearly frightened to death. Bolt knew she was watching him and he didn't want her to see his rage.

Silence returned to the camp as Bolt reloaded his empty pistol and tried to calm down. Once again the warrior spirit had been victorious and Bolt's enemies paid the price. Now the spirit needed to go away for Scarlett's sake.

Scarlett had seen Bolt change before, but not to the extreme she just witnessed. She was disturbed by his temper and brutality. Now she was afraid of whoever was out there in the dark. Looking to Bolt for an answer, she saw him holster his Colt.

"Are you through, or are you gonna shoot 'em a few more times?" the voice asked.

"I'm done," Bolt said. Scarlett began to relax when she noticed a slight smile cross his lips. "It took you long enough to do something. You damn near shot me trying to kill that one behind me."

"Stop your whining. I was wondering how far you were gonna let this go before you lost your temper. You never knew I was out here anyway, I snuck in here like an Indian."

"You couldn't sneak up on a blind buffalo. I heard you out there stumbling around for the last five minutes."

"You never done no such thing. I have once again saved the life of the great Buffalo Grass Rider, who has a knack for finding people who want to shoot him. It's getting to be my life's work."

"Well you're done now, so get back on your horse and let us eat supper in peace."

"Not likely. I'm coming in."

Scarlett noticed the stranger walking into the firelight was lean with a white beard and long snow-white hair. He was wearing a fringed leather shirt, a tall hat, and a red silk scarf around his neck. The knife sheath on his belt was empty.

"The name's Monday, ma'am, Everett Monday," he said removing his hat, "my friends call me Eb."

"Thank you for helping us," Scarlett said.

"It was indeed my pleasure."

"Do you two know each other?"

"Looks like I got here just in time to save you," Eb said.

Bolt just grunted and smiled at his partner, "How the devil did you find us?"

Ignoring him, Eb helped Scarlett down on a log and sat down beside her.

"You see ma'am, when you're out in this country with outlaws and Indians, you don't build a bonfire so everybody within ten miles can see your camp." Bolt just shook his head as Eb continued, "I've been trying to school this boy about getting along out here, roping, riding, but mostly how to treat ladies. I'm afraid he's a slow learner ma'am, real slow." Eb looked back across the fire at his partner with a puzzled look, "Did you get married while you were back east?"

"No," Scarlett said, "I was just trying to make those men think. . . ."

"I didn't think so," Eb said, the firelight revealing a grin on his face.

"What's that supposed to mean?" Bolt asked.

"Nothing...I only meant. . . ."

"Meant what?"

"Well, I'd be surprised if you had gone and...I mean after all the other...you know...you got 'em everywhere."

"What in blazes are you talking about? Got what everywhere?"

"Are you gonna offer a feller a cup of coffee or not?" Eb asked, unwilling to answer Bolt's question.

Scarlett was watching Bolt's reaction to Eb's question. She was thinking maybe he hadn't been completely honest about his love life.

"I'm sorry," she said turning back to Eb, "we don't have any coffee to offer you. We lost it all in a buffalo stampede."

"A buffalo...well I got plenty in my saddle bag."

That was the best news Scarlett had heard in several days. She put her arms around Eb's neck and hugged him. Eb winked at Bolt over her shoulder. He'd only known this lovely lady for a few minutes and she was already in his arms.

After dragging the bodies away from camp, Bolt and Eb got back just as the coffee started to boil. Eb made himself comfortable beside Scarlett once again and asked about the buffalo.

"The migration came right through our camp," Scarlett said, "all our supplies were trampled into the dirt."

"A migration, you say. Who picked the campsite?" Scarlett pointed at Bolt, "Figures."

"It wasn't a damn...ah...darn migration, it was a stampede," Bolt said, "There was no way I could've known. . . ."

"I was in a stampede one time," Eb said, "we were moving a herd across the Llano Estacado...near two...no...maybe, three thousand head of longhorns as I remember it."

"That's a lot o' corral dust," Bolt said.

"They weren't in no corral."

"Really," Scarlett said, ignoring Bolt's comment, "Three thousand head. What's a Llano Esta. . . ."

"Estacado, it's a huge piece of flat ground south of the Canadian River in the Texas panhandle. As close to the middle of nowhere as any place I've ever been. There's nothing up there, but cactus, coyotes, and blood-thirsty Comanche's."

"Comanche's," Scarlett repeated.

"The worst kind of Indians," Eb said moving closer to her, "They're always up to no-good. They came at us late one night, trying to cut out a few steers for themselves."

"The Indians attacked you at night?" Scarlett said, "I've read they never. . . ."

"Yeah, a whole murdering bunch of 'em, must have been a hundred o' them savages, two hundred maybe."

Bolt wasn't buying it. "There hasn't been two hundred Comanche's in one spot since. . . ."

"They skedaddled when I come up with my Colt," Eb said, "but the cattle quit the country after the first shot."

Bolt hung his head and sat quiet. Eb was too far into this windy now, and there was no stopping him.

"They must o' run ten miles before we managed to get 'em turned and milling," Eb said, "but it was too late for young Billy Bird."

Scarlett's eyes were wide as she listened, "What happened to Billy?"

"We found him at daylight, flatter than a flapjack. The whole herd must have run over him."

"My word!"

"We didn't need a coffin…just slipped him between two boards and buried him."

"How horrible!"

"Where'd you get the boards?" Bolt asked.

"Where'd we…well…we just had 'em."

"I thought you were out in the middle of nowhere. You brush-poppers always carry a few boards around with you, do you?"

"No we don't carry no…never you mind, Mr. Particular, we done it. That's all that matters."

"I've heard enough," Bolt said, "I'm turning in."

Daylight seemed to come early the next day. Eb kept Scarlett amused with his stories late into the night. Bolt was ready to be on his way but she was still sleeping soundly. Eb was making coffee and frying antelope chops in a small black iron skillet.

"Morning," Bolt said to his partner.

"Morning yourself, how'd you sleep?"

"I hardly slept at all with all those yarns you were spinning for Scarlett. When did you leave the Lonesome? How'd you know where I'd be?"

"We only got your telegram five days ago. I've been riding the Owl Hoot Trail ever since to get here and lend you a hand."

"Missed me, did you?"

"Nobody was fretting over your ornery hide. Coop was worried about Ms. Scarlett and those horses. He couldn't figure why you changed the plan."

Bolt explained about the bridges and the long delay if he backtracked to Kansas City. "This was the best I could come up with and I just went ahead."

"Something smells good," Scarlett said, stirring in her bedroll, "What's for breakfast?"

"Antelope steaks, and hot coffee," Eb said. He was in his element, taking care of wandering damsels in distress. Grabbing a piece of sizzling meat from the skillet, Bolt went to saddle the horses.

Scarlett sat down to have her first cup of the day. The steaming brew perked her right up. She was glad Eb showed up when he did, not wanting to face another day without her coffee. Bolt could hear Eb and Scarlett laughing as he walked back to the fire.

"If it's not too much to ask," he said, "we need to mount up and get out of here."

"Pay him no mind," Eb said, "He has no tolerance for the finer things in life, like a good cup of coffee."

"I suppose he's right," she said, "We should be going. Thank you so much for breakfast and the stimulating conversation last night. That man hasn't said ten words to me in a week."

When they were all packed, Eb saddled Banjo and put Buster on a lead rope. Turning Buster loose with the mares would have created a non-stop rodeo all the way back to the Lonesome. Every time Buster got too close to Rufus he would squeal and try to bite him. The competition for the mares had already started.

Bolt turned Sprigg's horses loose to follow along or go away. They were rode-down, lean, and not worth fooling with. When he got up on Rufus, he could tell Scarlett had something on her mind.

"What is it?"

"I assume you aren't going to bury those men."

"Bury 'em," Eb said before Bolt could answer, "Buzzards got to eat too."

Bolt had a grin on his face as Scarlett rolled her eyes.

"Nobody asked them here," Bolt said, "they got exactly what was coming to 'em." Poking Rufus in the slats, he started the horse herd northwest toward the Powder River.

The western sky grew darker as the day went on, promising rain by sundown. They were making good time with an extra hand to keep the horses moving in one direction. It was late in the afternoon when a cold rain began to fall.

"Scarlett, did you ever seen that big scar on Bolt's backside?" Eb asked out of the blue.

"Of course not."

"Oh, I didn't mean to imply that you had."

Scarlett was curious, and she wanted to hear more about Bolt's butt.

"Where did it come from? Or should I say; who gave it to him?"

"We need to find a campsite with some shelter," Bolt said, trying to change the subject, "looks like it's going to blow up some heavy rain tonight."

"We'll find a place," Eb said, "what's the rush? I'm not finished with my story."

"If you'd spend as much time thinking about work as you do talking, we might get back to the Lonesome before the snow flies."

"The man has no tolerance for fun," Eb said with a wink at Scarlett. "He is way too serious, be an old man before his time. I can see him now, sitting on his front porch thinking back on all his missed chances for a good time."

"I'll most likely be watching you trying to remember if you ever did a full day's work in your entire life."

They camped in a grove of cottonwoods near a small stream that night. Eb heard a turkey gobbling back up the creek and went to try and get supper.

"That's alright," Bolt said, "I'll unsaddle the horses. Don't you never mind about setting up camp or building a shelter to keep the rain off. You just go hunting and I'll start the fire."

Bolt could hear Eb mumbling as he went out of sight. Scarlett was busy laying out her bedroll and finding her slicker. The weather had been fine all along, but that was about to change.

"Eb, I believe that was the best roast turkey I ever ate," Scarlett said as they sat around the fire that night, "It was so good of you to provide us with supper."

"It must have been blind and deaf for him to ever get close to it," Bolt mumbled.

"What," Scarlett asked.

"Good," Bolt replied, "real good."

The night cooled quickly as a steady rain began to fall. Eb and Scarlett were huddled together under a slicker. "Please finish your story about Bolt's scar and where he got it."

Bolt was quiet. He knew nothing he said would keep Eb from telling the story. Sitting there in the rain, he wondered if anyone would miss Eb if he never made it back to the Lonesome.

"It happened when we were working on a ranch down in west Texas," Eb said.

"That was years. . . ."

"It was hot weather and the nights were sweltering," Eb continued, ignoring his partner, "Bolt had a thing for this little Mexican girl who worked on the ranch."

"Why Bolt you never mentioned a little Mexican girl to me before," Scarlett said, using her best southern drawl.

"Yes I did, just the other. . . ."

"Our boy, here, was sneaking out of the bunkhouse at night," Eb said, "We all knew where he was going and we knew there'd be hell to pay if he ever got caught. This girl's name was Angelia. Her mama always slept in the next room. Bolt would sneak in to spend most of the night with Angelia and then get out before her mama woke up."

"My word, Mr. Ashton, you're a scoundrel after all."

"You don't know the half of it," Eb said, "One night they got real loud. We could hear 'em from the bunkhouse. Angelia's mama woke up and came through the door waving a butcher knife. Bolt was going out the window when she swiped at him. She missed the part that was vital, but she cut a big gash down his cheek."

"His cheek," Scarlett said, studying Bolt's face.

"Not that cheek, the one he's sitting on." Bolt was bright red and Scarlett was laughing with tears running down her face. "I had to sew him up with a needle and thread. It left quite a scar and he rode his horse a little funny for several days. Corazon didn't get a good look at his face, it was dark and she only saw his skinny hillbilly backside disappearing out that window. That was the last time this boy went tom-cat'n at night. I think they still got together after that, but no one knows where or how."

"That was a long time ago," Bolt said, "I haven't seen her since we left Texas."

The brunt of the storm hit around ten that night as the three of them huddled under the lean-to. Scarlet was lying in the middle, as close to Bolt as she could get. The fire was long since drowned out and cold. Only the flashes of lightning offered any illumination. Bolt had his back to her, but he could feel her there in the dark. He was glad she felt some sense of security being near him. He vowed he would never let her down or give her any reason to doubt him. Love wasn't really part of what he was feeling, but this woman had become about the most important thing in his life.

He lay awake for quite a while thinking back to Angelia and Texas. He wanted to tell Scarlett that Angelia was a part of his past and not important anymore. Bolt wondered if it made any difference to her one way or the other. Turning over, he put his arm around her.

Scarlett moved in closer to him, put her face into his chest, and went right back to sleep. He gently kissed her forehead and dozed off with the rain falling all around him. His dreams were scented by the sweet smell of her hair and the rhythmic rise and fall of her breathing.

Earlier, the week before, a wide-eyed young boy arrived in San Francisco. The crowded waterfront and bustling city were very different from his small village in Mexico. The boy was eight-years-old, tall for his age, and handsome. He was lighter skinned than most of the children of his village. He could speak English and Spanish equally well.

The boy's mother was a strikingly good-looking woman. She had a difficult trip from Mazatlan north to California. The ship's crew was constantly trying to win her attentions. She made the trip alone as she never married. She hated old Mexico. The poverty, heat, and dust were not what she had in mind for her son. When her mother passed away, she sold everything they owned and used the money she had been saving for years to pay for their passage to California.

Her plan was to travel on the Central Pacific to Ogden, Utah, then by stagecoach to Coulter Creek, Montana. She knew Coop had settled on a piece of land somewhere around Coulter Creek. She felt sure she could find him from there. Coop was an old friend, and she hoped he would help her start a new life.

The train ride was uneventful to Utah, but the stage was a different matter. It was days and days of bouncing on rough roads with blowing dust and heat. The coach was often crowded with passengers. Men were constantly propositioning her.

The coach slowing down signaled the end of another long day. It was evening and they were going to spend the night at a way station.

The boy's mother found a small room for them and went in to have supper. She was anxious, being only a few days from Coulter Creek, and a possible reunion with her friends.

That night, she lay awake, wondering about a man that frequently walked through her dreams. It had been years since she had seen him, but he was seldom out of her thoughts.

The youngster was only half Mexican. Being quite different in appearance than most and fatherless, he had been picked on by the boys of his village. That treatment only served to make him tough, hardheaded, and mature beyond his years. Possessing a violent temper, he never backed down from anyone.

The rain stopped about an hour before daylight. Scarlett was lying in the lean-to looking at her cowboy. Her bedroll was wet and she was ready to get out of it, but he was still asleep. She wanted to know him better, but she was afraid to be too forward. She moved closer to his face and kissed his bottom lip.

"Good morning, Cowboy."

"Good morning, Ms. Scarlett," a gruff old voice said from behind her back. She had completely forgotten about Eb. Quickly recovering, she moved away as Bolt started to stir.

Bolt was dreaming that he was kissing Scarlett when Eb woke him up. He rolled out of his bedroll and stretched his aching muscles.

"With any luck we'll make the Powder River today," he said. "We're only about a hundred miles from Coulter Creek when we get to the river. We should be on the Lonesome in few days."

It was late afternoon when Lone Elk and his companions found a small herd of buffalo quietly grazing the tall grass along the Powder River. Their group included two young Sioux warriors who joined them when they left Devil's Tower. One of them was the storyteller that watched Bolt kill the renegades.

Lone Elk questioned him in detail about the events that led up to the killings. He was disappointed in his cousin's savagery toward the white settlers, but it was hard to define the line between defending your land and just killing whites for revenge.

Normally they would ride down and kill all the buffalo they could. Their group was only eight strong and they couldn't eat a whole buffalo in several days. Lone Elk convinced them to just take one small bull. They could eat their fill and stay in the country to rest. Lone Elk and one of the Cheyenne slipped into a coulee to work their way close to the herd. The Cheyenne made a good shot, and the young bull fell in his tracks.

Eb heard the shot, but it came from a long way off toward the west.

"One shot usually means somebody's hunting supper. You all keep going; I'll ride over that way and check it out. We don't want any unexpected company in this country." Eb rode over a little hill and disappeared from sight. Bolt and Scarlett continued northwest with the horses.

When Scarlett was alone with Bolt, she rode up near him to talk.

"I slept pretty well last night. It was nice being so close to you in the rain. If Eb hadn't caught up with us would you have made a pass at me?"

She had never been so bold, but there wasn't much time before Eb would return.

"Yes ma'am, I believe I would have."

"Well, we're alone right now."

Bolt reined in Rufus and waited for her to pull up beside him. When she was close enough he reached out to pull her over to him and kissed her. It was the first real kiss that ever passed between them.

"Indians," Eb said behind them. Flustered by the attention from her cowboy, Scarlett pulled away from him. "It's a small bunch. They're cutting up a buffalo, couple of miles away in a little coulee.

"We got no quarrel with them," Bolt said, "But we need to get far away from here, as fast as we can. If the Indians spot these horses, we'll have to fight to hang on to them."

Unknown to Bolt, Eb had been spotted by the young Sioux. He was on a hill as a lookout for the rest of the party. The Sioux followed him back to the horse herd. His blood ran cold when he recognized Bolt. He wasn't a spirit after all. This was the white man that had slain his friends all alone on that dark night. After slipping out of sight, he rode as hard as he could back to his companions.

Lone Elk was roasting the tongue and hump from the buffalo. The aroma was filling their camp and they all were looking forward to a big meal. The young Sioux came in at a gallop, slid off his pony, and went straight to Lone Elk's side.

"I have seen the white man that killed your cousins."

"You said a spirit killed them, and you were not able to help."

"That was true…the spirit had a face. I have seen it again, with the horses."

Lone Elk had only seen Bolt from behind at a distance. When his pony fell he lost track of him. When Bolt helped him the next day, he never saw Rufus and he didn't notice Bolt's clothes. Lone Elk still had no idea the man who helped him was the same man he had been chasing.

"We will camp here tonight and go after him in the morning," Lone Elk said. "He won't travel far tonight, we don't want him to know we are after him. This man is dangerous. He will not be easy to kill."

Being a small group, the Cheyenne wanted no part of this plan. After eating, they loaded as much meat as their ponies could carry and headed west.

Bolt pushed on toward the Powder River, not planning to stop until well after full dark. "It's a cold camp tonight. No fire for cooking or coffee. We can get by on antelope jerky until we get to town. Hopefully, those Indians will stay put, and we'll be on our way as soon as it's light enough to see."

The Powder River was running high from the rain, but they had no trouble crossing it. Even when it was low, the Powder River was thick with eroded soil. It was as if the river was determined to move most of Montana down to the Missouri.

Eb was tempted to fill his canteen, but decided against it.

"This stuff is too thin to plow, but too damn thick to drink."

"You don't need that canteen," Bolt said, "just grab up a couple of handfuls and put 'em in your pocket."

That night, Bolt was restless as he sat watching and listening in the darkness. He wanted to push hard for the next couple of days and get the horses to the Lonesome without any further conflict. He had no idea the Indians behind him knew all about him and what he did that bloody night in the Black Hills.

Eb was snoring in his bedroll about twenty feet away from Bolt. He volunteered to take the first watch, but Bolt insisted he get some sleep. Bolt agreed to wake him about midnight, and try to sleep until dawn.

As Bolt sat on his bedroll in the dark, he could hear Rufus making a fuss about being tied. He was trying to get to Buster and start a fight.

"You better be quiet and listen for Indians," Bolt said, "You'll be painted up and wearing feathers in your tail if they get you, old horse, unless they decide to eat you." The big outlaw grumbled as if he understood.

Everything was quiet, even the wind was still. Scarlett came over to Bolt's side and sat down beside him. Covering them both with her bedroll, she snuggled up close to him in the dark.

They were both fully clothed right down to their boots in case they had to leave in a hurry or make a fight with the Indians. Scarlett's body was warm against him and he was happy to have her so close. As Scarlett lay in his arms, she pulled herself up to return the kiss he gave her earlier that day.

"I think I've developed some feelings for you. The more I get to know you, the more I want to know about you. When we get to the ranch, will I get to see you, or will you be off on another adventure?"

"I think you'll see plenty of me."

It had been a long time since he used the word love toward anyone and he wasn't about to use it right then. Bolt wasn't sure if he could ever use it again. He held her close until time to wake Eb.

Chapter Nine:
Logan, Creek, and TJ

Coop was sitting at the breakfast table the next morning wondering where Bolt and Ms. Canary might be and if they were alright. "Eb should have caught up to them by now."

"Bolt's alright, he'll get them horses here eventually," Logan said.

"Eventually, I wanted them here two weeks ago, not eventually. And by the way, why are you still in here when everybody else is at work? What are you doing with that old bow?"

"It's the one Hard Tack gave me before he passed. I think it needs a new string, but I don't know exactly where to get one."

"The Indians used buffalo sinew."

"What's sinew?"

"I'll have to show you. Put that thing away for now and go get TJ and Creek out of the creek bottom. You boys ride to Coulter Creek and see if there's any word from Bolt or Eb at the telegraph office. I don't think the Indians are this far north, but if you happen to run into some, a couple more guns will come in handy. Get to town and right back here with any word, and don't get in any trouble." Logan grabbed one more of Spud's apple fritters as he went toward the door. "You're gonna get fat eating all those sweets," Coop warned.

"Fat," Spud said, "if the boy closes one eye now, you'd take him for a needle!" Logan went out the door laughing.

TJ Burke was a young cowboy in his late twenties. TJ was short for Thomas Jefferson. He was a stocky, tough young man with a big smile that was always there. He was everybody's friend until they proved to be otherwise. A few men had taken him for granted and tried to walk over him. They all soon learned he was not to be trifled with. He could use his fists and his gun equally well.

Creekmore Cagle was thirty-five, tall and with dark hair and a big mustache. He came from old money back east. Having grown frustrated with his high-society friends, he felt there had to be more to life than just easy living around a bunch of spoiled blue-bloods. None of them knew anything about hardship or being cold or hungry. Few had ever done a day's work in their life.

Creekmore was on his way to California when he met Eb and Bolt. The coach he was riding in was held up by road agents. They killed the driver and the man riding shotgun. Creekmore made a fight of it, even though he was badly wounded. There were two women on the coach and Creekmore was defending them at all costs.

Creekmore was down to his last few rounds when two riders appeared on a distant ridgeline and began firing at the road agents. After three of the outlaws were hit by the approaching riders, the other two took off.

"Don't shoot," Eb said opening the door to the coach, "We're friends, just take it easy and we'll get you some help."

Being only a few miles from Coulter Creek, they got Creekmore back to the doctor, and he never left Montana. He was part of the family now and a trusted friend. It didn't take long for the cowboys to change Creekmore to Creek for short.

Creek and TJ had taken the buckboard that morning to carry all the wire and posts. They were just beginning work on the fence around the creek bottom meadow, when Logan rode up on Sandy.

"Boys," he said, "Coop's got a job for us to do."

"What's he got?" TJ asked, "Another hundred postholes for us to dig?"

"Yeah or maybe throw up another barn before suppertime," Creek added.

"Coop wants us to ride into town and check on any word from Bolt, but if you're too. . . ."

"We ain't," TJ said, before Logan could finish.

"We're going with you," Creek added.

"Saddle up boys, the saloon's open late. If we hurry, we can get there by sundown." Logan didn't need to say another word. The cowboys jumped in the buckboard and headed for the barn. A couple rolls of wire and a shovel bounced out as they rattled across the pasture. They were in the saddle and gone in a few minutes.

"I wish those boys would move that fast when it's time to work," Coop said as the three disappeared down the road in a cloud of dust.

Creek was the oldest and the level-headed one on the threesome. Coop figured he would do his best to keep the younger cowboys out of trouble.

Lone Elk had been following Bolt's trail since sunup. The white men fooled him by traveling into the night. Bolt was several miles ahead and Lone Elk would be hard pressed to catch him that day. The young Sioux was the only other person with Lone Elk. It would be an even fight when they attacked Bolt and Eb.

"We'll be in Coulter Creek by tomorrow afternoon at this pace," Eb said. "First thing I'm gonna do is head for the Jersey Rose. I know Charity will be glad to see me. If I was the marrying kind, she'd be the one."

Charity Austin was an attractive woman in her mid-thirties and the owner of the Jersey Rose Saloon in Coulter Creek. Despite the difference in their ages, Eb had a pretty big yearning for her.

"If you were the marrying kind, you'd already be married, and we wouldn't have to listen to you go on all day about it," Bolt said. "Besides, if Charity saw you coming with a wedding ring, she'd be on the first stage back to Kansas."

"Is that right?"

"That is right."

"Well I'll tell you one damn thing."

"There ain't nothing you can tell me that I haven't heard a hundred times before," Bolt said.

Late afternoon found them only twenty-five miles from Coulter Creek. Bolt could see a dust cloud up ahead and riders coming their way.

"They aren't Indians," he said.

"Looks like the army to me," Eb said.

A young captain was in the lead as Bolt rode out to meet them. After a few minutes the captain motioned the troop on and they rode off down Bolt's back trail.

"Some Indians are causing trouble over in Wyoming," Bolt said, when he was back with Eb and Scarlett, "the army thinks they may be part of the bunch that killed Custer. That troop is headed for the Powder River to poke around."

"That'll keep them redskins off our trail," Eb said.

"Even so, we'll push on till dark. Tomorrow night, we can sleep in a bed in Coulter Creek.

Lone Elk was getting close to the white men and horses. He wanted to just ride in and fight, but he knew the man they called the spirit warrior and his companion were not to be taken lightly. He was planning his next move when the first shot was fired from the cavalry scouts on the hill above them.

Whirling their ponies around, Lone Elk and his companion fled back toward the Powder River. As bullets swarmed around him, Lone Elk knew he allowed his hatred of this one white man to cloud his judgment. He hadn't counted on the army being anywhere around and it cost him a chance to kill the white man. It would be days before the two Indians managed to elude the troopers.

Logan and his companions rode into Coulter Creek around sundown. The noise from the Jersey Rose meant things were just getting started. It was too late to get any word at the telegraph office so the boys decided to have a beer. They found a table and ordered drinks. Ms. Charity was looking her best. As always, she was the center of attention at the Rose.

"That's the woman for me," TJ said, watching Charity.

"She wouldn't give you a second look," Creek said. "You're just a kid, I'm the man for her and that's for sure."

"Eb thinks she's in love with him," Logan said with a grin.

"Eb thinks every woman he meets is in love with him," Creek said. They closed the place up around two-thirty and went to their room at the hotel to grab some sleep.

Twenty miles south of Coulter Creek, Bolt lay in the dark with Scarlett close by. Eb was on watch out near the horses.

"We've been lucky on this trip," he said. "We only lost one horse, managed to get out of several close calls, and we're still in one piece."

"And I didn't have to shoot you."

"Yeah that too. We'll be in Coulter Creek tomorrow afternoon and at the ranch late the next day."

"I can't wait to see the Lonesome Wind."

"Bolt, take over the watch if you ain't gonna sleep," Eb said as he walked up on them, "I need my beauty rest to look my best for Ms. Charity tomorrow night."

A stagecoach rolled into Coulter Creek shortly after ten the next morning. It was going to be another hot summer day and the road had been dusty. The boy and his mother were worn-out from their long trip. They retrieved the luggage and checked into the Range Hotel. After some rest and a bath, she planned to try and find out about Coop and his ranch.

Having drunk a little more than they were used to the night before, the boys had just gotten up. They never got to sleep late on the Lonesome and they had taken advantage of it that morning. As they made their way down the stairs, Creek was holding his head and trying to shield his eyes against the bright sunlight in the lobby.

"I need coffee," Logan moaned, holding his gut. "I never felt…this…never this bad."

"I'm ready for breakfast," TJ said. Unlike his companions, he seemed to be suffering no ill effects from the night before. "I'm thinking half a dozen eggs, still runny, and bacon, not too crisp."

"Will you shut-up," Creek begged.

"He ain't human," Logan said. "Nobody can drink that much and still. . . ."

"What's the matter," TJ teased, "Ain't you boys hungry?"

"No dammit," Creek said, "I ain't hungry. I don't want to think about it and I'm tired of. . . . Sorry ma'am," he quickly apologized for his outburst to the lady and young boy suddenly appearing on the stairs in front of him.

"Let me help you with that ma'am," TJ said, tipping his hat to the lady. She was struggling with the heavy luggage.

"Always the knight in shining armor when there's a pretty lady needing help," Creek said as his partner followed the lady to her room.

"I'm going to the telegraph office to check on word from Bolt," Logan said, "I'll meet you at the cafe." Logan stepped out into the sunshine and made his way down the street. Creek waited for TJ in the lobby and the two of them went off to find some coffee.

Just south of town, Bolt could see Coulter Creek from the hill he had ridden up on. "We'll be there in about thirty minutes. We can get some rooms and take a bath."

"A bath sounds wonderful," Scarlett said, "I haven't had a real bath since Custer, unless you count that afternoon at the river."

"What happened at the river?" Eb asked.

"We'll get an early start in the morning," Bolt said, ignoring Eb, "if we push 'em hard we'll be at the ranch tomorrow night."

"Early start, look here, Bolt, we ain't getting no early start. I'm going to enjoy myself tonight and we might just stay two nights before we go back to work on the Lonesome."

"I think he's right," Scarlett said, "We deserve a little rest after what we've been through."

"Alright, I can't fight both of you. I guess I could use a little time off before going back to work myself."

"Let's ride," Eb said, "Charity's waiting for me."

"I'll have to meet this Charity that you all talk about so much," Scarlett said.

"That saloon is no place for a lady like you," Bolt said.

"Neither is a trail drive with two old, worn-out cowboys, but I got through that alright and I'm going to that saloon with you two."

"Old," Bolt said.

"Worn-out," Eb added.

Logan was standing in the telegraph office inquiring about his friends, when Bolt rode into the south end of town.

"Sorry Son," the telegrapher said, "there's nothing here for Coop Cooper from anybody." Logan thanked the man and went to find Creek and TJ.

After putting the horses up at the livery, Bolt spotted an Indian friend of his. Bolt gave him some tobacco money and asked him to keep an eye on the horses. Lame Deer was a Mandan Indian that occasionally came into Coulter Creek for supplies. Bill Weems, who owned the livery, allowed Lame Deer to sleep in the stable when the Indian was in town.

Bolt checked them in at the Range hotel. He got three rooms, Scarlett could have some privacy, and he wouldn't have to listen to Eb snore all night. It felt good to lie down on clean sheets, but he would miss being near Scarlett.

"It's too late to ride back this afternoon," TJ said, "Coop won't care if we stay one more night and head out bright and early in the morning."

"I think he's right," Logan agreed, "We don't get to town that much and a message might come in tonight from Bolt. We can check first thing in the morning."

"Alright," Creek said, "but Coop is going to skin us alive if we don't get back tomorrow night." Creek was giving in against his better judgment as the trio headed off to the Jersey Rose.

The boy could hear the sounds of the street outside as it began to get dark. His mother found out Coop had settled about a day's ride northwest of Coulter Creek. Being practically out of money, she was glad to find her quest nearly over. There were three nice young men staying down the hall from her. She planned to ask them about guiding her to Coop's ranch.

The boy and his mother made their way down the stairs and up the street to the café. She wanted to have supper and get back to their room before the streets were full of cowboys looking for a good time. The boy was curious about all the noise from the saloon and he stuck his head in the door. He was mumbling something as his mother got him by the collar and shuffled him into the café. The waiter sat them at a corner table. The boy sat facing the door.

Hearing a gentle knock at her door, Scarlett opened it to find two very clean and handsome gentlemen waiting to escort her to dinner.

"You boys clean up pretty good," she said.

"Don't get used to it," Bolt said, "We don't dress for dinner at the Lonesome."

"Ignore him," Eb said. He was polished and his white hair was shining. They made their way to the café up the street from the hotel.

Eb spotted the small boy in the corner as the waiter showed them to a table. The boy smiled back at him as Eb took a seat.

"We want three of your best steaks and don't take all night getting 'em out here," Eb said to the waiter, ordering for the three of them.

Bolt nodded passed Eb's shoulder. "Look who just walked in."

Charity Austin, from the Jersey Rose had stopped for dinner before going to work. Eb stood up and reached out to her. "Charity it's always a pleasure to see. . . ."

Before Eb could finish, Charity rushed right past him and threw her arms around Bolt's neck.

"Where have you been, cowboy? I've been asking everyone from the Lonesome about you for weeks now. I've missed you and I thought you might not love me anymore." Bolt was bright red. Scarlett had suspected all along that he was probably too good to be true, and now she didn't know what to say as Bolt introduced her.

"Charity," he said, "This is Scarlett Canary from Kentucky."

"Scarlett, it's a pleasure to meet you. How did a lady like you get hooked up with the likes of these two?"

"It's a long story," Scarlett replied, being in no mood for polite conversation with the saloon girl in the arms of her cowboy. Bolt was in shock, he didn't think Charity even knew his name. Much less that she might have been missing him.

"Don't you leave town without coming to see me, Bolt Ashton," Charity said as she released her hold, "And don't wait so long before your next visit. You too, ornery," she said turning to Eb. Charity left them standing there and went to her table.

"How do you figure that," Bolt said, "she never…I never…that's the first time she ever. . . ." Struggling for the right thing to say, Bolt wasn't having much luck. They all sat down again, but the mood had changed around that table. Eb was mad that Charity was hanging onto Bolt and not him.

"That's the damnedest thing I ever saw, who would've thought?"

Scarlett thought Bolt might actually be in love with her. Now she knew he was like all the rest, with a girl in every saloon. Bolt was in big trouble, and it was about to get even worse. Having finished his dinner, the boy that had been sitting across the room walked by their table and Eb spoke to him.

"What's your name, Son?"

"My name is Joaquin Rafael Everett Maximliano, Sir."

"Everett," Eb repeated, "well I'll be. My name's Everett too. My friends just call me. . . ."

"Eb!" the boy's mother exclaimed, as she threw her arms around his neck.

Bolt was dumbfounded, it couldn't be, but it was. She was older, but still the same beautiful woman that he remembered. He got to his feet and stood behind Eb.

When Angelia released Eb, her eyes met Bolt's. Her heart nearly stopped when she realized she was finally face to face with the man that haunted her dreams for so many years. Releasing all of her pent-up emotion, she rushed into his arms. Bolt couldn't speak, he just held her as she cried.

After regaining her composure, Angelia sat down to tell them about her journey. She told them about her mother's passing, Mexico, and her desire to raise her son in Montana. She wanted to go with them when they left Texas, but she had to stay behind. Angelia went on and on, she couldn't believe she found them so easily. She was wondering about Scarlett, but wasn't going to ask.

Bolt was trying to make eye contact with Scarlett, but she was studying Angelia. It was obvious she was still in love with Bolt. Scarlett already knew about Bolt's past with this beautiful Mexican woman. She had been laughing about it just a few nights before, now she could scarcely believe Angelia was actually sitting at the same table with them.

Next door at the saloon, the three friends were once again drinking beer and trying to impress the girls who worked there.

"I thought you weren't going to drink anymore," TJ teased.

"That was this morning," Logan replied.

The boys weren't exactly ladies men and they weren't having any luck. They bought drinks for the two girls who were sitting at their table. Logan was using every line he ever heard Bolt use on a lady, but they weren't working as well for him.

"I wish Eb was here," Creek said. "I miss that old fart when he's not around. Do you think he found Bolt and that lady yet?"

Two ragged wolf trappers came in about then and walked to the bar. One of them was a small man. The other one was over six feet with a big barrel chest. They ordered shots of whiskey and tossed them down. The little one pulled out a can of snuff and took a big pinch. Thinking he was tough, with the big man to always back him up. The little wolver packed his bottom lip with snoose and spit into a cuspidor on the floor near him.

He wiped his mouth on his sleeve and looked right at TJ. "That's my girl, you're holding there, Sonny."

"Why do they always pick me out of a bunch?" TJ asked.

"It's that sweet little face of yours," Creek said.

"Very funny, I suppose you're just gonna sit there and let me take 'em on all by myself."

"You started it," Creek said with a grin.

"I never said a word to them coyote skinners."

"Coyote skinners," the big one repeated, "Are you talking to me, Boy?"

"No sir," TJ said, "I'm talking to that little snooze-dipping runt next to you."

"Who you calling a runt?" the suddenly bristling little man demanded.

"I believe he was talking to you," Creek said with a grin.

"Don't help me," TJ said.

"You cow nurses had best just keep your mouths shut," the runt warned, "Unless you want a taste of my skinning knife."

"Cow nurses," TJ repeated, suddenly on his feet. "Who in hell are you calling cow nurses?"

"We don't want any trouble, Mister," Logan said as the hunters approached. He was trying to avoid what he knew was coming, but it was too late, TJ had lost his temper. The big Nebraska cowboy threw his beer in the little one's face. Creek threw a left hook at the big man's jaw while he wasn't looking and the fight was on.

Creek's punch had very little effect on the big wolver. Creek grabbed a chair and broke it over the big man's back as the wolver was busy smashing Logan's face. Logan went down hard, but came right back up with a hard right to the wolver's gut.

The big wolver wasn't even phased by the chair. He turned around and grabbed Creek planning to tear off his head as several drunken spectators joined in. They knew these boys from the Lonesome Wind were a proud, arrogant bunch of cowboys, and it was high time somebody put them in their place.

The two painted ladies were right in the middle of the brawl with no way out. One had a small derringer in her garter and made the mistake of pulling it out. TJ, not knowing who she intended to shoot with it, shoved her backwards over a chair and sent her sprawling.

The big wolver landed a smashing blow that knocked Creek senseless. Creek was struggling to stay on his feet when the big man grabbed him and threw him out the door. Three other cowboys threw TJ out next, and Logan right behind him.

Moments before, Eb had gotten up from the table thinking it would be a good idea to go back to their rooms. Bolt was ready to get some air and try to get Scarlet alone to explain that Angelia was only a part of his past.

As Eb walked by the saloon, a battered cowboy with a big mustache came crashing out the door, knocking him into the dusty street. Lying in the dirt, Eb had a hold of the cowboy's shirt as he tried to get back on his feet. Drawing back to hit him, Eb recognized Creek, just as two more bodies came out the door and landed on him in the dirt.

"Eb, where the heck have you been?" Creek asked as they got untangled.

"Are we glad to see you," Logan said, brushing himself off. "Coop was worried about you. He sent us in to check for another telegram. He's been real anxious to hear from you two."

"We thought the Indians might have got you," Creek said, "they've been murdering settlers and stealing horses in that country between the Black Hills and the Powder River."

TJ he shook Bolt's hand. "We're glad to see you back." All three of them were looking at Scarlett.

"Boys, this is Ms. Scarlett Canary and Angelia Maximliano," Eb said. "Ladies meet Logan, TJ, and Creek from the Lonesome Wind Ranch."

"We're mighty glad to meet you ladies," Logan said.

TJ took his hat off to Angelia. "It's nice to see you again, ma'am."

"And this is Joaquin Rafael Everett Maximliano," Eb said with his hand on the boy's shoulder.

"Everett," Logan repeated.

"That's right," Eb said, "Everett."

"If you'll excuse us, ma'am," Creek said to Scarlett, "we have a little unfinished business inside the Rose."

"Nobody throws the Bunch from the Lonesome Wind out of no saloon," TJ boasted.

"Begging your pardon," Logan said with a tip of his hat. "We need to go back inside and finish a little something we started a few minutes ago." TJ tipped his hat and the three started back in the Rose.

"I better go with them," Eb said, "just to make sure it stays a fair fight."

Being the first one in the door, Logan leaped up on a table and jumped on the big wolver's back before he could turn around. The big man tried to reach around and pull him off, but Logan was stuck like a wart on a witch's nose. The youngster had the big man in a chokehold and spurring him at every jump.

"You got him?" Creek asked as the big man stumbled around and around.

"I got him!" Logan yelled, "Do something!" Staying on the big man's back was like trying to ride a grizzly.

Creek's mustache was turned up in a big grin. "Are you sure you got him?" The wolver was bug-eyed and turning a bluish-red as he tried to shake Logan off. He was reaching out trying to grab Creek.

"I got him, dammit!" Logan shouted, "Hit him with something!" Creek picked up a bung-starter that was lying on the bar and smacked the big man right between the eyes. Blood was pouring out of the gash on his face when the wolver finally passed out. Logan rode him all the way to the floor.

TJ and Creek were beating on the rest of the cowboys that had thrown them out. With the big wolver out of the fight, things were a little different. One by one, the boys from the Lonesome Wind tossed their attackers into the street.

Realizing he was going to take a beating, the runt started to pull his belly gun. Eb shoved the barrel of his Colt up against the back of the little man's head and cocked the hammer.

"Let's make this a fair fight mister, you pull that pistol, it'll be your worst day." The little man handed his gun to Eb, and started slinking toward the door. TJ saw him trying to escape.

"Come here you little snoose-dipper," he said, grabbing the runt by the shirt collar and dragging him back inside. The little man took a swing at TJ, but missed. TJ slugged him, turned him around, and tossed him out the door.

Bolt walked Angelia to her room to say goodnight. She held her arms around him and kissed him.

"I'm so glad I found you," she whispered. Bolt kissed her back, but it wasn't the same kiss he used to give her on those hot Texas nights.

"I'll come back for you in the morning," he said, "We'll all go out to the ranch together."

She slipped her hand inside his shirt and rubbed his chest. "Won't you come in for a little while? Rafael will be asleep in a few minutes."

"Not tonight...I...I need to find Eb and the boys. We...we need to move the horses...first thing in the morning."

"What horses?"

"Scarlett's...that is...Coop's and Scarlett's. They're all going to the Lonesome."

"Goodnight," she said as she reached up and gave him another soft kiss. Tickling his lip with the tip of her tongue, she was doing her best to turn it into something else when Bolt pulled back from her.

"Goodnight," he said, "I'll be back in the morning." He went to Scarlett's room and knocked on her door, "I'd like to explain if you'll let me."

"You have nothing to explain. I'll see you in the morning." She shut the door and Bolt walked down the hall.

"This has been one heck of a night," Bolt thought, as he walked back to the saloon. When he got back to the Rose, he could see five men lying sprawled in the street. He stepped over the largest of the bodies, went in the door, and found the boys sitting around a table. Charity was cleaning the wound on Creek's cheek with a damp bar towel.

"You three take the mares and head out at first light," Bolt told the young cowpunchers, "If you push them, you should make it before dark. Leave Banjo and Buster, it'll be a lot easier without them along. We'll need one of the extra saddle horses for Angelia and her son. I'll follow you a little later with Scarlett. Tell Coop we'll be in late. Thanks for coming to check on us."

Bolt was ready to get home and try to sort things out as best he could. He smiled a little when he thought about the group that was riding to Coop and the Lonesome Wind Ranch. It was going to be a real interesting summer.

Chapter Ten:
Whiskey Hill, Montana

Sheriff John Baker left his office and started across the muddy street, he had business in the Silver Dollar Saloon. Baker was the only law in the little town of Whiskey Hill. It sat just west of the Crazy Mountains, in the Montana Territory.

The saloon was owned by a man named Rex Star. He had been in Whiskey Hill for about six months. Star arrived about the same time Baker learned the army was coming to establish a new Indian Agency.

Most of the folks in this little town weren't thrilled about living so close to hundreds of Indians, but the businessmen thought it would be profitable. There would be troopers in town on a regular basis and that would be good for the saloon. The gamblers and the painted ladies that worked in the Silver Dollar would profit as well. The merchants planned to cash in as there would be civilian support people and they would need goods and services from town.

Rex Star was a good looking man about forty-years-old. He was well groomed and usually dressed in fancy clothes from back east. His prematurely gray hair was always perfect. Star seemed out of place in a town like Whiskey Hill.

There had been several unsolved murders since Star came to town, the original owner of the Silver Dollar, Dan Walton, for one. He balked at selling out to Star at first. When Walton's wife went missing, he accused Star and his gang of being responsible. Dan tried to confront Star, but before he could get to him, one of Star's hired guns, Garrett Frye, called him out.

The witnesses all testified Walton went for his gun first. Sheriff Baker was forced to turn Frye loose. He knew most of the witnesses worked for Star, and he was sure Dan and his wife had been murdered, but he never found her body and couldn't prove anything. With no family left to pay the mortgage, Star managed to pay off the bankers and take over the Silver Dollar. Sheriff Baker had been working to get something on him, but so far he hadn't been able to.

"Morning Sheriff," Star said as Baker walked in the Silver Dollar, "What can I do for you?"

"I want to see Garrett Frye."

"He's not here right now."

"Where is he?"

"I'm not real sure," Star said, "I think he's out towards the ranch or maybe at the agency. What do you want with him?"

"I've got a warrant for his arrest."

"Arrest, that can't be right. What's he done?"

"There was an Indian found murdered out at the agency last week. Some of his kin say Frye did it."

"That's hard for me to believe."

"I don't give a damn what you believe. He was having his way with a young girl and her father tried to stop it. Frye shot him down like a dog in front of his family."

"What day was that?" Star asked.

"Last Thursday evening."

"Well, there you go, Frye was here all night last Thursday. Isn't that right?" Star asked turning to the bartender.

"That's right, Sheriff," the bartender said, "Garrett was in here all afternoon, stayed until closing time."

"You're a flannel-mouthed liar, but a liar none the less." Shaking a finger in Star's face, Baker warned, "If you think you can come in here and take over my town, you got another think coming!"

Baker was hoping Star would pull the fancy pistol he wore under his coat. Then he could just gun him down and be done with it. Star was too coolheaded to try and take on the sheriff.

"Your town," Star said, as he looked over at the bartender and smiled, "I think you better leave now, Sheriff. I don't take threats very well."

"That was no threat. I'll be back for Frye."

Around ten that evening, the Silver Dollar was going strong. Star was moving around through the crowd and talking to his customers. He was really good at making people like him. The buzz of conversation quieted as a shot was fired outside. It was followed by three more in rapid succession. The sound of pounding hooves could be heard as several horses thundered out of town. A few seconds later, a man stuck his head in the front door of the saloon.

"Sheriff's been shot!" Most of the crowd ran out into the street to see what had happened.

Sheriff Baker was lying dead in the street. He was on his back with his gun still in his hand and two bullet holes in his chest. It appeared that Baker managed to get off only one shot before he was killed.

Star went over and stood over his body. "Well, that's a shame," he said to the crowd around him, "I suppose we should get him off the street."

Several of the townspeople picked up Baker's body and took it to the barbershop. The barber also served as the town undertaker. The rest of the crowd followed Star back to the saloon like nothing ever happened.

The next day, Star got word the town council was in a meeting trying to decide what to do about a lawman. Star went down and barged in.

"Good afternoon, Gentlemen. I have a suggestion that I would like to put before you."

Most of the men on the town council were business people. They really didn't have a lot of power in this small frontier town. They all knew Star and they knew about the men that worked for him. None of them planned to stand up to him, fearing they'd end up just like Sheriff Baker.

"What's your suggestion?" Charles Hesson asked. Hesson was the town barber and unofficial chairmen of the council.

"The town is growing. We need a good lawman that can stand up to the people who threaten our wellbeing."

"I think we all agree on that," Hesson said.

"Then since we're all agreed, I'd like to nominate Garrett Frye, as our next sheriff."

"Frye," Hesson repeated.

"That's right, he's good with his gun and people around here respect him."

"Respect him, you mean fear him."

"Well that's pretty much the same thing isn't it? And to show my civic pride, I'll continue to pay him out of my own pocket."

The council knew they had little choice but to go along with Star's plan. They were businessmen and shopkeepers, not gunfighters. None of them wanted any more trouble.

"Would you please wait outside, Mr. Star," Hesson asked, "Give us a moment to discuss this issue."

"My pleasure, Gentlemen, I'll be right out front."

After several minutes of debate, the council reluctantly agreed to go along with Star. Hesson went out to tell him.

"Mr. Star, we've decided to appoint Frye as sheriff."

"Splendid, I'll go tell him."

"He can move in the sheriff's office whenever he wants."

It was one afternoon about a week later when Star and Sheriff Frye were sitting in the Silver Dollar having a drink. They were interrupted by loud voices coming from the street. Frye got to his feet and went to look out the door. A small crowd was forming down at the stage line office. A man came hustling by and Frye stopped him.

"What's going on?" Frye asked.

"Stage was held up! A bunch of masked highwaymen stopped them just outside of town."

Frye walked back to the table where Star was still sitting, finished the remainder of his beer, and picked up his hat.

"I guess I better go on down there, somebody just robbed the stage."

"That wouldn't be the stage with the monthly payroll for all the civilians out the agency, would it?"

"I believe it was."

"Tough luck for them, I guess we'll be extending some more credit to those poor people. We can't let them stop drinking over one little holdup."

"I suppose not," Frye said, "see you later."

When Frye got down to the stage, he found two very attractive young women who were both in tears.

"What's going on here?" he asked.

"We were robbed," one of them said, "they took everything we had. We were on our way to San Francisco, now we're stuck here with no money."

"I'm Sheriff Garrett Frye, maybe I can be of some assistance." Frye was thirty-years-old and he wasn't bad looking. If not for being a cold-blooded killer, he could have passed for a decent man.

"Thank you, Sheriff," one of the girls said, "We don't know what to do."

"Well come with me. I have a good friend who owns the saloon down the street. We can put you up there for now, I'm sure he'll think of something. Everything will be all right."

The next day Star rode out to call on the colonel at the agency. After waiting for a few minutes, a sergeant appeared. "Come in Mr. Star, the Colonel will see you now."

Star was there to see Colonel John Harding. He had been given the assignment to build the new Crow Indian Agency. His headquarters were just outside of town.

"Come on in Rex," Harding said, "It's good to see you again."

"Colonel, how is everything?"

"Things are going fine. I've been given the go ahead to award you the contract. Some of the men at Indian Affairs are acquainted with your family."

"That's good news."

"Are you sure you can supply that much beef? We'll need nearly a hundred head a month when we get up to capacity."

"You let me worry about that."

"Where's your ranch? I haven't seen any big cattle outfits around this valley."

"It's to the south about ten miles, but there isn't any cattle out there as of yet."

"Well, you best be getting your hands on some, and soon. They'll cancel the contract if you can't deliver."

"Nobody's canceling anything," Star warned, "They're all getting paid too well, including you."

"That may be true, but we have to feed these Indians. If we don't, the word will get out eventually."

"I have some men out hunting buffalo right now. That should hold you until the cattle arrive."

"There are damn few buffalo left around here."

"Maybe so, but I'll have some cattle in here soon."

Star got to his feet and left the Colonel's office. Several men were waiting outside on horseback. Star mounted up and started back to town with them.

"LeConte," Star said, "I need those cows in here right away. There's a lot of money at stake here. Are you ready to go?"

Bloody Bill LeConte was a French-Canadian, Ojibwa Indian, mixed-blood. He was partners with Star. It was his responsibility to secure the cattle needed to fulfill Star's contract with the army.

"We'll leave at first light in the morning. It shouldn't take much more than a week to get back here with the herd."

"A week. Where do you have to go to get them?"

"You're not back east anymore," LeConte said. "This is a big territory. It takes time to cover this country."

"I don't care about that. I need those cows here right now."

LeConte was accompanied by his friend, Sean Marceu, another French-Canadian, and a drifting cowpuncher named Pete Watson. Watson worked for Cooper during the roundup the fall before. He was familiar with the Lonesome Wind's widely scattered herds of cattle.

"Are you sure about those cows being up on the northern end of Cooper's ranch?" LeConte asked turning to Watson.

"They're up there alright. Cooper keeps them on the Dancing Grounds all summer. He saves most of the grass along the Yellowstone to winter on."

"The Dancing Grounds," Star repeated.

"They call it the Devil's Dancing Grounds. It's over twenty miles from the house on the western border of the Lonesome."

"How many men will we have to face?" Sean asked.

"None, if we're lucky," Watson said, "Cooper only checks on the herd every couple of weeks. Even when he does, he only sends a couple of riders."

"Sounds like a good plan," Star said, "How many head are up there?"

"Four or five hundred, most of the time. We should be there and gone with them before anybody even knows they're missing."

"What about the future? Can we get any more cattle from Cooper?"

"If you have enough men, Mr. Star, we can get all you want. Cooper's the largest cattle producer anywhere around. He only has six or seven regular hands and the Lonesome is huge. It shouldn't be any problem to take 'em all, but we have to gather them quick and get out of there."

"Why is that?" Star asked.

"Some of those boys on the Lonesome are…well, nobody we want to face in a fight."

"We can handle a handful of cowpunchers," LeConte assured them.

"Do whatever you have to do," Star said, "if this works out, there will be a big bonus in it for you."

"It'll work out," Watson promised.

When Star and his hired guns arrived back in town, Star got off his horse in front of the saloon.

"Good luck, Bill. Get back here as soon as you can."

Chapter Eleven:
Home

It was nearly dark when Coop heard horses coming down the road. He stepped outside just in time to see three riders pushing a herd of thoroughbreds into the cavvy corral.

"Where did you boys find these horses? Where's Bolt? Did you see Eb?" Coop was asking questions faster than Logan could answer them.

"We ran into 'em in Coulter Creek last night." Logan said, "They're on their way here, Bolt, Eb, and the ladies. Oh and a kid's with one of the ladies."

"What other lady is with them besides Ms. Canary?"

"A Mexican lady named Angelia and her son," TJ said, "The boy's named after Eb."

"Named after Eb. Angelia…not the Angelia that used to cook for us in Texas?"

"Yes sir, that's her, she was real glad to see Bolt," Creek said.

"Yeah, I bet she was. Was Bolt glad to see her?"

"Come to think of it," TJ said, "Bolt seemed to be unusually quiet when they were all together."

"Yeah," Creek said, "He didn't have much to say."

"Well I'll be…Angelia," Coop said, "What a small world."

TJ pulled the saddle off his sweaty mount and tossed it over the top rail. "No sir. Her being here ain't no accident."

"That's right," Creek said, "She came by way of sailing ship from Mexico to California and then by stagecoach to Coulter Creek. She's looking for you."

"Looking for me," Coop repeated.

"She wants a job and a chance to raise her son here on the Lonesome," Logan said.

"You bet she can have a job right now. She's one of the best cooks I ever knew. I've been missing that Mexican cooking. The boy's named after Eb you say?"

"Scarlett," Bolt said as they rode along, "Welcome to the Lonesome Wind Ranch. We're still ten miles from the house, but we're on the Lonesome."

It was wide open country the likes of which she had never seen. It went on for miles, you could see the clouds come up from the horizon, go over head, and go down the other side of the Earth. Scarlett was happy to be here at last, but she wasn't quite sure what to think about Angelia and her history with Bolt.

Scarlett had begun to think of him as her cowboy and she wasn't about to give him up this easily. *"Does he still love her?"* she thought, *"Can we begin a relationship with her always around?"* Scarlett's mind was full of questions. She had a nagging feeling little Rafael was part of the history between his mother and the man she was beginning to have strong feelings for.

It was full dark when Bolt and the rest climbed down from their horses in the corral at the ranch house. Coop came out to welcome them home.

"Ms. Scarlett, it's good to finally meet you," he said.

Angelia ran up to Coop and hugged him. Then she grabbed old Spud and kissed him on the cheek.

"I can't believe I've found you all alive and well," she said, "I hope you have something for me to do to earn my keep."

"Lord a mercy, Angelia," Spud said, holding her around the waist, "it's good to see you again."

"It's good to finally be here. I've missed you so much."

"I've been feeding this ungrateful bunch for too long, I can sure use some help. What a fine little fellow you have there, he looks familiar somehow. Ms. Scarlett," the old Cajon said, taking her hand, "I hope you won't judge all of us by them two you been keeping company with."

"I certainly won't," she said with a smile, "and I'm very happy to make your acquaintance."

After the introductions, Spud led Scarlett and Angelia toward the main house.

"We've been holding supper for you all," he said, "I'll have it on in a few minutes. You ladies come on in and freshen up." After he had the ladies fixed up with a wash basin and towels, Spud walked back into the kitchen where the rest of the cowboys were sitting around the big table. "It's about time you loafers got back to work," he said to Bolt and Eb.

"We been working, you old biscuit-roller," Eb replied, "A lot harder than you, I suspect."

Spud paid no attention to the insult.

"What happened to your eye, Creek? Logan, you and TJ get kicked by the same mule, or what?" The old coosie was having a good time making fun of the boy's bruised and battered faces, "Logan, who gave you that purple eye?"

"Not that it's any of your business," Logan said, "but nobody gave it to me, I had to fight for it."

"Ya'll are a fine bunch of cowhands," Spud finally said, "Go get cleaned up; supper will be on directly." The old man looked back at Bolt and grinned, "How about that wrangler?"

"You got one coming, old man," Bolt said, getting to his feet, "you definitely got one coming!"

When they were all gathered for a late supper, the boys were taking turns trying to out-story the other. They wanted to make the newly arrived women think they were the best bunch of cowpunchers between the divide and salt water.

"I saw a big rattlesnake out behind the barn this evening," Creek said during a lull in the conversation.

"A rattlesnake," Scarlett said with a startled look, "Do you see them often?"

"No," Creek said, "almost never. This one got into the weeds behind the outhouse before I could find a shovel."

"Probably never see him again," TJ said, "he's down in the creek bottom chasing mice by now."

"Son," Coop said, dismissing the snake story and turning to Rafael, "Run your name by me one more time."

"Joaquin Rafael Everett Maximliano," Rafael said.

"That's a mouthful. We need to come up with something. . . ."

"Not Eb," Spud said, "One of them is too many."

"At least I ain't named after some vegetable," Eb said.
"What's wrong with Rafael," Bolt asked.
"Too long."
"How about Rafe," Logan said.
"Rafe," Coop repeated, "Now I like that."
"How about it, Son," Spud asked.
"I like it," Rafael said.
"How about you," Coop asked looking over at Angelia.
"It's a new country and a new life for my son. I think his a new cowboy name will be fine."
"Then Rafe it is," TJ said, "The newest addition to the Bunch from the Lonesome Wind."

"Scarlett," Coop said, "We built you a nice little house that's fit for a lady with all the comforts of home. It's just a short walk from the main house and I know you'll be comfortable."

"Angelia, there's a real nice room on the back of the house here," Spud said, "There are two beds; you and the boy will be just fine in there." Spud was acting like a rooster with two new hens to watch over. "You cowboys stay away from these ladies," he told the men around the table, "finish your supper and get back out to the bunkhouse where ya'll belong."

When they were finished, Bolt got up from the table and motioned for Scarlett to join him. "I'll show you to your house. We fixed it up nice as we could, but it still needs your things to make it home."

Scarlett said goodnight to her hosts and followed Bolt out the door. It was a cool night, typical for the high plains.

"There's a wood stove in your place if it gets too cold for you at night," Bolt said.

He opened the door and struck a match to light her lamp. She looked so good in the golden glow of the lamp. He pulled her to him and kissed her the way he always wanted to. She kissed him right back and held him for a long time. Bolt wanted to take her to bed right then, but he would wait and not try to be too forward.

"This may take a little time," he said, "but everything will work out just fine."

"I have plenty of time, and thank you for getting me here safe and sound. You're one special man, Buffalo Grass Rider."

"Shucks it weren't nothing ma'am," Bolt said with his best cowboy drawl. It was the first time she ever used his nickname. He gave her another quick kiss and disappeared into the darkness.

Angelia was watching them from the window in her room.

"You will never have him, Ms. Southern Belle," she thought. *"He needs a strong, young woman. I'm the one he will want when he finds out the truth."*

Bolt could hear laughter and conversation coming from the bunkhouse as he approached. Eb was telling the boys how he saved Bolt from the Sprigg gang and how Scarlett had taken such a shine to him.

"Don't you all believe anything this old man tells you," Bolt said as he came through the door, "There were only three of them and I already had them on the run."

"On the run," Eb repeated, "That bunch had you dead-to-rights, if I hadn't come along. . . ."

"Bolt, how did you and Scarlett get along before Eb showed up?" TJ asked before Eb could finish.

"Ms. Scarlett is a true southern lady and that's all you boys need to know. We had several kinds of trouble and she handled all of it just fine. Scarlett's a special kind of woman, I'm proud to know her."

"Yeah, that's just about what we figured," Creek said with a grin. All the rest were laughing.

"What about Angelia?" Logan asked when things settled down. "We hear you were pretty close to her down there in Texas."

"Good night boys," Bolt said as he stretched out on his bunk.

"The only two women on this whole place and they both want that old codger," TJ said, "beats all I ever saw."

"They're just using him to get to me," Eb said, "either way; you boys don't stand a chance." Bolt smiled from his bed as they all laughed.

Rufus was glad to be in his favorite pasture. The old horse was due a rest, and happy to be home at last. The mares were all down in the creek bottom and he could keep watch over them. He felt safe here. He didn't need to keep his guard up all night like he did out on the trail.

Bolt was glad to be in a familiar bunk. Sleeping out on the ground wasn't as much fun as it used to be. He lay there thinking about Scarlett being only a short distance away. She was everything any man could want. He wanted to be with her every night out there on the trail. Her body was constantly on his mind since that day at the river. He had done his best to be a gentleman, but he longed to know her much better.

Then there was Angelia. She was vibrant and beautiful. Her body was as he remembered it from those hot Texas nights. He could go to either one of them that night, but he was staying right where he was until he sorted this out. The love he currently felt for Scarlett was stronger than his memories of Angelia.

That night along the Tongue River, Lone Elk was huddled under a sandstone outcropping trying to stay out of the cold rain. He finally eluded the army and was back on the trail toward a fight with the white man.

He knew the man he sought was likely headed to Coulter Creek with the horses and the woman. Lone Elk could never show his face in Coulter Creek without being shot on sight. He had to find a way to discover this man's whereabouts.

The young Sioux that had been with him continued on to the Red Cloud Agency. He wanted no more to do with Lone Elk or the white man. Lone Elk's hatred had turned into an obsession. They were both nearly killed by the army because of it. Lone Elk swore he would never rest until the spirit warrior was dead.

The mighty Sioux would ride for miles in a wide circle around the town just to see what was there. Maybe he would pick up a trail left by the horses. He had plenty of time, it was still summer. He didn't know about the arid country north of the Yellowstone River, where water and shade were equally scarce.

It was five a.m. when Coop came through the door of the bunkhouse.

"Good morning, Girls. Get your lazy butts out of those bunks. Bolt, I want you to spend the day showing Scarlett around the ranch. You both need a little rest so take it easy today."

"We could use a rest, thanks," Logan said from his bunk.

"You boys have about five minutes to be at the table for breakfast. You already had your days off. Now get out of that bed. Old man, that means you too." Eb just ignored him and rolled over in his bunk.

Bolt was sitting at the table having his breakfast, listening to the conversation, and realizing how much he missed this morning ritual while he was gone. Creek, TJ, Logan, and Eb were all at the table along with Coop and Spud.

"I saw that big rattler again this morning," Logan said, "back there by the outhouse. Funny, he'd be out so early in the morning."

"Well, with this hot weather, I guess they're out all night," TJ said.

Eb peered at TJ over his coffee cup. "Damn a rattlesnake. I better not see him, I won't be looking for no shovel."

Bolt thought it strange a snake had come up in the conversation during the last two meals. Noticing a twinkle in Logan's eye, he watched the youngster for several minutes. Logan wouldn't make eye contact with him. If he was hiding something, he was doing a good job of it.

"Boys, I want you three to ride up to the Dancing Grounds today and check on the cattle up there," Coop said. Laying out the day's work assignments at breakfast was a normal part of his daily routine. "Make sure that seep has water in it. It's been mighty dry the last few weeks. I don't want to stress any of those cows."

"It's twenty miles up there," Creek said.

"I ain't running a damn debate," Coop said, turning to Creek, "And I think I know how far it is to the Dancing Grounds."

"I didn't mean anything by it, I just thought. . . ."

"Take enough grub and water to last you a few days," Coop continued, "Cover that rough ground and make sure all the cows are doing well.

Take a packhorse with a load of salt for them. You should be back in three or four days."

Bolt left the table and went to wake Scarlett with her breakfast. Knocking on her door, he let himself in. She was still in bed, but she was awake.

"Morning," he said as he sat down on the edge of the bed.

Scarlett was dressed in a cotton nightshirt. Bolt wanted to just crawl in with her, but he would fight that urge and be a gentleman. Scarlett pulled him down to her and kissed him.

"Morning, cowboy," she said.

"Mr. Bolt," a small voice said from the open doorway, "My mama told me I would have to earn my keep around here from now on. She said anytime I see you around Ms. Scarlett's house I should come over to help you."

"Well, Rafe, how are you this morning?" Scarlett asked. She wasn't surprised to see the boy. His presence meant the struggle for her cowboy had already begun, but she wasn't going to do or say anything that might hurt Rafe's feelings.

"When I need your help there, mister, I'll ask for it," Bolt said. He had no experience with kids and he wanted to be alone with Scarlett.

"You don't have to be such an old grump," she said. "Little boys need men to look up to, be glad you got one who wants to be with you."

"Sorry kid. Meet me outside in a few minutes; we'll saddle a couple of horses or do some other fun stuff."

Rafe went out the door grumbling, "That doesn't sound like. . . ."

"Now where were we?" Bolt asked.

"You were going outside to saddle my horse and I'm going to eat breakfast, now get out of here."

Bolt went out the door grumbling, "I could think of something a lot more. . . ."

When Bolt was outside, he noticed Creek, TJ, and Logan hiding behind the new barn with their horses. All three of them were peeking around the corner. Slipping up behind them, he grabbed TJ.

"What in blazes are you all doing?"

"Dang it, Bolt," TJ gasped, "you scared me out of a month's growth."

"Shhh," Logan whispered, "here he comes."

They all watched as Eb headed to the outhouse for his morning constitutional. He was humming as he walked along like he didn't have a care in the world. They could see him paying close attention to the weeds along the path when he got close to the privy. He never noticed the fresh dirt by the back corner.

Bolt shook his head. "I hope you all know what you're doing."

Unknown to anybody, except the three scheming cowboys, Logan killed a huge rattler down in the creek bottom when he ran the mares down in there the evening before. The three of them, knowing how Eb hated snakes and knowing his morning routine, had rigged the now headless rattler up in the rafters of the outhouse. It was suspended over the twin holes on a narrow pine board. TJ rigged a trigger to drop it. The snake carcass could be pulled down with just a tug of the string running to the barn where they were hiding. They watched the latch slide over after Eb went in and shut the door.

Coop had saddled one of his rank young horses right after breakfast that morning. The horse was standing hip shot, tied to the rail in front of the house. Coop planned to spend the morning wringing him out.

After things got quiet in the outhouse, TJ yanked the string. The snake fell out of the rafters, and all hell broke loose on the Lonesome.

The privy began to rock and rattle as all manner of knocking and stomping began. "Yeee-aaahhh!!" Eb screamed, "Son-of-a. . . ." Four quick shots echoed inside the privy. Wood chips and dirt were flying around the outside as .45 slugs came through the walls and hit the ground.

Coop's horse came unglued with Eb's first couple of shots. He jerked back, tearing the top rail right off the hitching post. After Eb's third shot, the horse pulled away from the house and quit the country. The wild-eyed young stud was doing his best to get away from the gunshots and the bouncing rail chasing him down the road.

Coop and Spud exploded out the front door of the house with guns in hand. With all the yelling and shooting, they figured they were under an Indian attack at the very least. Coop got outside just in time to see his horse disappear down the road with the hitching rail.

"What in blazes is going on!"

Logan fell to the ground laughing as the latch on the privy hit the dirt in three pieces and the door flew open. Eb tumbled out butt-first with his britches down around his high-top boots. The old cowboy was scooting across the ground on his bare butt as he finished emptying his Colt into the outhouse.

Bolt, TJ, and Creek were holding their sides and roaring with laughter. They were trying to get out of Eb's sight, but they couldn't move. They finally got Logan up from the ground and climbed on their horses. The three boys galloped around the barn as if they were startled by all the shooting.

"What's…going on?" Creek asked. He was about to explode, chocking back the laughter. Tears were still flowing from Logan and TJ. They couldn't even pretend to be surprised.

Coop shook his finger at them and started back in the house.

"You best go catch that damn horse!" He followed Spud back inside and slammed the door behind them.

"I'll get him," Logan said. He touched Sandy with his spurs and lit out after the runaway. They could hear him laughing until he was nearly out of sight.

A half-hour later, Logan and TJ were horseback, sitting in front of the house. They were ready to head up to the Dancing Grounds.

"C'mon, Creek, we need to go!" TJ hollered at the house, urging his partner to mount up. Both cowboys were looking around, watching for Eb, but they hadn't seen him.

Where's your partner," Logan asked, looking over at TJ, "I want to get out of here."

"He's in the kitchen saying goodbye to Angelia."

Logan was ready to put some country between them and Eb. "We got a long ride ahead of us, let's go."

Creek came out the door with another biscuit in his mouth. He hit the saddle and the three cowboys rode off to the north.

"Where's Eb?" Creek asked after they were away from the ranch.

"We ain't seen him," Logan said.

"That ain't good."

The Devil's Dancing Ground is an arid, rough piece of ground covering about fifty square miles. It's made up of gumbo hills, gravel slopes, steep-walled cutbanks, and eroding rock. The ground on the flats is rock hard, only scattered clumps of salt sage grows there. There is one low-growing juniper tree clinging to the top of one of the hills, right out in the middle. A man on horseback can see that tree from ten miles away.

In the old days, buffalo would pause on their northern migration trek, the salt sage made good grazing for a short spell. They would wallow on the hard ground to shed their winter's coat.

It had been a battleground where the Crow, Cheyenne, and Sioux fought for hunting rights. There is a mineral in the ground that attracts lightning, making it no place to be during a summer thunderstorm. Lightning bolts slam into the ground and roll across the flats on a regular basis.

It's said, if you're there on a quiet night, with a horse-thief moon overhead, you can hear the rattling hoof beats of mystic warriors riding their painted ponies across the salt sage flats, challenging each other for the right to be there.

The Dancing Ground is thin-grass desert country. The buffalo grass, wheat grass, wild onions and parsnips, white and black sage, and blue joint are better suited to mule deer, antelope, and maybe wild horses. There are sage grouse, sharp tails, badgers, coyotes, and the dark-brown eagles that ride the thermals overhead.

Farther up in the hills, there's a little more grass in the coulees, but it's a tough place for a cow to make a living. It is frozen, windblown, and desolate during the winter.

The Dancing Ground makes up a big chunk of the Lonesome, so Coop tried to take advantage of the limited forage during the summer months when living was easier for his cows. They would winter farther south where there was flowing water and more grass.

In addition to the cattle, Coop's young horses lived there in the summer. The cowboys referred to them as the wild bunch. The Dancing Ground belonged to the north-wind and the wild critters from November until May.

The name comes from the dust devils that whirl around on the flats when the sun is high. It's rough up in the hills with lots of rugged low ridges, gumbo mounds, and coulees leading up to a great escarpment.

Those ridges and mounds are covered with jagged pebbles and crumbling rocks. The tiny rolling stones are slick as ice when underfoot and hard on the hands and knees of anybody trying to sneak around. When you reach the western side of the high escarpment, it drops off into a huge flat basin that goes on for miles and miles. The steep drop-off is only negotiable in a few places. That escarpment is the western boundary of the Lonesome Wind.

There is only one water source in the whole area, and it occasionally goes dry in the hot years. The water seeps out from under a gravel cutbank at the head of Badlands Coulee. The cattle can drink it, but any cowboy that ever tried it, would spend a couple of days in the bushes with his britches down. A few swallows of that mineral-laced water would sure enough flush his pipes.

"If the seep is dry, we'll find most of those cows down along Porcupine Creek," Logan said as they rode along, "There should still be water lying in there."

"That Angelia is one good looking woman," Creek said out of the blue.

"Where did that come from?" TJ asked.

Logan was chuckling. "His mind ain't on the cattle."

"I'm just saying she's a good looking woman."

"Angelia wants Bolt," TJ said, "Anybody can see that. You might as well forget it."

"Bolt don't act like he wants her. He's much more interested in Scarlett if you ask me."

"Well, time will tell," TJ said.

Angelia was cleaning up the breakfast table when Spud joined her in the kitchen. "Please fix some of that left-over roast and some biscuits for Bolt and Scarlett to take with them today. Bolt will keep her out all day if I know him. They'll need a canteen of fresh water too if you don't mind."

"Mind, yes I do mind. I mind a lot." Angelia was keeping her thoughts to herself since it was her first day on her new job. "I'll be happy to," she replied out loud.

Bolt was standing in the barn with Rafe. "Have you ever saddled a horse, kid?"

"No sir, we never had a horse in Mexico, so I don't know much about them."

"The first thing you need to know about horses is never turn your back on one or start to think they're you're friend. Horses are noble beasts, but they got very little sense when they get spooked. A horse can kill himself and anybody that's around him when he blows up."

Scarlett walked into the barn and stood to listen as Bolt continued with Rafe.

"Now you take old Rufus here. We've been together for many years and we know what each other is going to do at any given time."

"So you don't have to be careful around Rufus?"

"It takes years to earn the trust of a good horse. Maybe someday you'll have a horse like old Rufus. Until then, you do what I tell you and watch 'em close."

"Are you cowboys ready for our ride?" Scarlett asked as she made her presence known.

"Yes ma'am," Rafe replied.

"Hold on there, kid, you ain't going anywhere. You got chores to do and you need to help your mama get settled in."

"Yes sir," Rafe replied. As he went out the door, Rafe kicked a dried-up piece of horse manure. Bolt could hear him grumbling. "I'll get my own horse…then I'll show him."

"What was that?" Bolt asked.

"I said have a nice ride."

Scarlett was smiling. "Kind of reminds you of someone, doesn't he?"

"The little peckerwood reminds me of a smart-mouthed kid."

Scarlett sat horseback, amazed at the distance she could see when they rode out on top of the rimrock. "This is the most spectacular view I've ever seen,"

"This is my favorite place on the ranch," Bolt said, "I come up here to be alone and think about things when I get lonesome."

"Are you lonesome right now?"

"No, I'm feeling pretty good to tell you the truth."

"I hope that has something to do with me being here."

"It has everything to do with you being here."

Bolt got off Rufus and walked over to Scarlett's horse. Helping her off, he cradled her in his arms as he slowly lowered her feet to the ground. He gave her a hug and kissed her.

"You know how to get a girl's attention don't you?"

"No ma'am, I'm usually quiet and a little shy, but it's different with you. I can't remember when I didn't know you. I feel completely comfortable with you and I want to tell you what I'm thinking."

Scarlett put her arms around him again and stood on her tiptoes to reach his mouth. She pulled him down to the ground as she was kissing him. Just about the time her butt hit the ground she let out a yell. Unknowingly, she had sat in a little patch of prickly-pear cactus.

"It's a rattle snake," she exclaimed, jumping to her feet, "I've been bitten by a rattler!"

"It's not a rattle snake," Bolt said, "You've just had your first butt-full of cactus. It's everywhere out here and you'll learn to watch for it. Turn around; I'll see what I can do."

Scarlett was squirming in her riding skirt as the spines worked deeper into her skin. "Do something," she begged.

"I have to pull this skirt down to get to the spines that have broken off in the fabric. If I don't, we'll never get them all out. You'll have to walk back to the house and it's a long way."

"You just want to see my butt!"

"I won't deny that, but I seem to recall it won't be the first time, and besides, this is an emergency. Just think of me as your doctor."

"Some doctor you'd make. Oh alright get it over with." Bolt took hold of her skirt and gently pulled it down to expose the spines. Scarlett let out a yell, "yow … that hurt!"

"Yes ma'am. Do you want a bullet to bite on?"

"Yeah, and gun to put it in. Just get on with it before someone comes by and sees us." Scarlett wasn't having much fun, but Bolt was really enjoying the moment.

"I think you're ready to ride," he said when he was finished. Bolt helped her back on her horse, but she was still in pain. "Some of those spines broke off under your skin; they'll work back out in a week or so. Next time; watch where you put your backside."

"Thank you for your advice, even if it is a little late." Scarlett threw her leg over and gingerly eased down on the saddle.

They spent the rest of the day looking around the Lonesome. Scarlett was happy she made the trip west. This ranch was everything she dreamed it would be and much more. It was the most breathtaking place she had ever been.

The vistas were like nothing she ever experienced back in Kentucky. There seemed to be something new to marvel at over every hill. Mule deer were plentiful and she was especially taken with the beauty and speed of the pronghorns.

It was late afternoon when the three cowboys arrived at the dancing grounds.

"We'll camp along the creek bottom and head up to check the cattle at first light," Creek said.

Logan was a fair camp cook, and he went to fixing supper. They were having sage hens roasted on a spit. Logan killed them with his bow that afternoon right after they made camp. Along with the fresh birds there were beans and some left-over biscuits Angelia packed for them.

"Man there is no life I'd rather lead than being a cowboy," TJ said, as they stretched out under the big star-filled sky.

"Amen," echoed the others. The night was clear, the fire felt good, and the boys were soon asleep.

The sun was up over the horizon by the time the cowboys had their last cup of coffee. They saddled up and rode west into the Dancing Grounds.

"You could hide an army in here," Logan said.

TJ was standing in his stirrups with his hand up to his brow, but there wasn't a cow in sight. "It'll take all day to find this bunch of cows. If there's any water in these coulees they'll be scattered all over."

"Let's split up and each cover a section," Creek said, "we'll meet up on the ridgeline this afternoon. If you find any cows just keep track of the number and we can get out of here tomorrow. Spread the salt up in the head of Badlands Coulee, where the cattle can find it. Sooner or later they'll all move in there to water."

"Sounds like a good plan, let's go," TJ said. "See you boys up on top this afternoon." TJ sunk spur and rode off to the west leading the packhorse. He was going straight up the edge of Badlands Coulee. Logan went south and Creek went north. After a couple of miles they each turned west and headed up into the Devil's Dancing Grounds.

Logan was watching the coulee ahead of him when a mule deer buck jumped up and stood staring at horse and rider. Still in velvet, the big buck stood for only a moment before bounding over the hill behind him. "I wish I had time to hunt that big boy." He made a mental note to come back up there in the fall when the bucks are in rut and not quite as spooky.

TJ was further west than his companions and starting to see signs that made him worry. The country gets very little rainfall. Tracks can appear fresh for weeks. It takes a trained eye to pick out the fresh from the old.

Next to Eb, TJ was the best tracker on the Lonesome. He was seeing signs headed toward the northwest. The thing that worried him most was the horse tracks among the cattle. They were wearing iron shoes. He guessed there were at least ten riders in this bunch. TJ reached the ridgeline first and waited for his friends. The tracks he had been following went out across the big basin toward the Musselshell River.

"I haven't seen a single cow all day," Logan said as he rode up to TJ.

"I think we got us some rustlers to deal with, and there's a bunch of 'em."

Creek got there about an hour later and he had the same thing to report.

"I saw some buffalo and twenty-five or thirty of the wild bunch, but there ain't a cow within ten miles of here."

"Rustlers got em, I'm pretty sure," TJ said.

"Rustlers," Creek repeated.

"There hasn't been anyone from the Lonesome up here in two weeks," Logan said. "Those tracks were made by some riders that don't belong here."

"The tracks look to be about three, maybe four days old," TJ said, "There's a lot of country out there and only three of us to find em."

"Are you scared?" Logan asked.

"Hell no, but we knew we need to get word back to the ranch. We'll be missed in a day or so and no one will have any idea where we are."

"Logan, you ride to the ranch tonight," Creek said, "Take the pack horse with you. TJ and I will stay here. We can't track 'em at night, but we'll start after them at first light. You get Coop, Eb, Bolt, and get back on our trail as soon as you can."

"I'll get 'em," Logan said, "you boys go careful."

Dragging the pack horse, Logan headed southeast toward the ranch as the sun was setting in the west. Logan knew the country and he would be at the ranch long before daylight. He planned to change horses and be on his way back with the rest by sunup.

Creek and TJ built a fire in a little coulee and had a bite to eat. They would be long gone by the time Bolt got there the next day. Creek knew Eb would be able to follow their trail and would catch up to them in a day or so. It was a long way to the Musselshell, and he couldn't understand why these rustlers had chosen that direction to travel.

Bolt was still asleep when Logan rode into the yard at the ranch house. He jumped up on the porch and started banging on the bell Spud used for calling them to supper.

"Who's making that racket?" Eb asked from his bunk.

"Sounds like trouble," Bolt said, "get a move on."

Coop came out of the house with only his nightshirt and boots.

"Boss, somebody has stolen the whole herd out of the Dancing Grounds," Logan said.

"Stolen."

"Yep, gone. Every last one of them. Creek and TJ are after the rustlers. There are tracks from maybe a dozen riders. TJ thinks they're headed for the Musselshell. We got to go help 'em."

"Saddle up boy's," Coop said, "We got to get that herd back."

"Logan, are you going?" Bolt asked.

"I'm not going to miss this." Logan left them on the porch and made his way to the corral to get another horse.

Spud was packing some grub as the men were getting saddled. Angelia came out of her room and asked what was happening just about the time Scarlett walked in the door.

"Rustlers up on the Dancing Grounds," Spud said. "They got almost five hundred head and went west. Creek and TJ are after them. The rest of the boys are going to help 'em."

Everyone was saddled and ready when Coop came out, tied his bedroll and slicker behind the saddle, and stepped up on his horse. Scarlett was holding on to Rufus' bridle and asking Bolt to be careful.

"We'll be fine," Eb assured her as he climbed on his horse. "I'll take care of this bunch."

The four riders headed out the gate and turned to the north to catch up with Creek and TJ. It would take most of the morning to reach the ridgeline above the Dancing Grounds and they had to spare their horses. There was no way of knowing how many miles they would have to travel.

Early that afternoon, Eb and Bolt made it to the rim of the escarpment. The trail was plain.

"They went off here," Eb said, examining the tracks. "We need to move fast. Creek and TJ won't wait for us. They'll take this bunch on as soon as they get the chance."

"Where are these rustlers going?" Coop asked.

"Let's go ask em," Bolt said. Dirt and rocks were rolling as they descended the narrow trail to the basin.

Later that afternoon, Creek and TJ found the spot where the rustlers had camped. TJ was down examining the ashes from their campfire.

"It's been at least one night, probably two. They could be twenty miles ahead of us."

Sunset found Creek and TJ nearly to the river. The tracks were getting fresh.

"They're turning south," TJ said. "It looks to me like they're headed to Salt Springs."

"There ain't anything in Salt Springs."

"I was through there about a year ago, there's a little trading post run by a French Canadian."

"We're about done for tonight," Creek said, "We'll make camp here and go on at daylight."

"Eb, can you follow these tracks in the dark?" Bolt asked.

"There's a little bit of moonlight and I can see pretty well. If we keep after them all night, we may catch the boy's before sunup."

"We'll have to walk and spell these horses some. They need to be fresh when we catch this bunch."

"If you'd get rid of that old horse, we wouldn't have to worry so much about that."

"If we got rid of everything that's old around here, you'd be the first thing down the road."

"Is that a fact? Well I'll tell you one. . . ."

"Just find those boys," Coop said, interrupting the argument, "We got no time for anything else."

The eastern sky was turning gray when Eb and Bolt bellied up a little hill and peeked over. There was a red glow in the shadows of the dark coulee down below. It appeared to be the coals of a campfire.

"I think it's Creek and TJ," Eb said, "There's just two men down there. I don't see any cows, but it's hard to tell from here." The wind was picking up and rain was a threat. The western sky was still dark. A layer of clouds hid the stars. "It rains once in a blue moon up here," Eb said. "Now that we're tracking these outlaws the rain won't make it any easier."

"Let's get down there and see if it's the boys."

Bolt and Eb slid back down the hill to where Coop and Logan were waiting. The four of them rode into the camp with guns drawn. They were ready if this was part of the outlaw gang that had stolen the cattle. The boys were still asleep when Bolt rode up on them.

"Are we glad to see you boys," TJ said.

"Any sign of the herd?" Coop asked.

"No sir," TJ said, "But it looks like they're headed to Salt Springs."

"Why would they go to Salt Springs?" Eb asked.

"Beats me," Creek said, "It don't make sense."

"Roll up those bedrolls and let's get on their trail," Coop said.

The Bunch from the Lonesome Wind was finally together again and making good time toward the little settlement of Salt Springs. Now, the odds were stacked against the rustlers. There would be hell to pay when they caught up with the herd.

The Bunch made it into Salt Springs late that afternoon. A cold rain was falling, but the signs were fresh. A large number of cows had passed that way and not too long before.

Coop dismounted in front of the trading post and pointed at the younger cowboys. "You three stay here with the horses. Bolt, you and Eb come with me. Let's go in and see what these people might tell us about the herd."

A big man behind the bar greeted them with a smile. "Welcome my friends. Welcome to Frenchy's. What would you like to drink?"

"John Barleycorn all around," Eb said.

"Coffee will do for me," Bolt said.

Coop had no time for the social graces. "We're following a herd of stolen cattle. Did you see or talk to the men who drove them through here?"

"They were here yesterday. They work for a man in Whiskey Hill. The army has established an Indian Agency, and they need beef to feed the Indians"

"Those are my cows, taken off my ranch."

"Oh no, you must be mistaken. It was Bloody Bill LeConte and some very bad men. If they are indeed your cows, perhaps it would be wise to just forget the cows and go home."

"Not very damn likely," Eb said.

"At least now we know where they're going," Coop said.

"Who are we after?" Logan asked when they were back outside.

Eb stepped up on his horse. "Some half-breed named Bill LeConte."

"I've heard of him," TJ said, "he's a bad one."

"He's got about a dozen riders with him," Bolt said. "They're headed to Whiskey Hill with the herd. We need to catch them before they get into the mountains. If we stay on 'em hard, we should find them by sundown tomorrow."

Chapter Twelve:
Scar.

Lone Elk had been searching around Coulter Creek for a week or more. Finding no tracks that would lead him to believe the horse herd passed that way, he still had no idea where the man he was looking for might be.

Lone Elk knew of an Indian camp in the breaks along the Missouri River. The people there were Mandan Indians and the army left them alone. The Mandans sheltered Lewis and Clark during the winter of 1804. They were peace-loving trader Indians and were no threat to the whites. Lone Elk decided to head to their camp and rest.

He arrived worn-out and hungry after two days of hard riding. The Mandan camp was full of children talking and playing. The fires were lit for the night and Lone Elk could smell roasting meat. He had not experienced this scene with the Sioux in many months.

The Mandan village was very different from the Sioux camps. The Mandan were farmers and traders rather than roving hunters. Their big lodges were made of dirt and sod, and very much permanent.

There was a famous old woman that lived among the Mandans. Her legendary wisdom and visions were strong medicine among the Plains Indians. Lone Elk planned to seek her counsel about the white man he was sworn to kill.

The Indians in the village were surprised to see a Sioux warrior riding into their camp, but they made him welcome and invited him to eat and rest.

The woman Lone Elk sought was Wind in the Grass. She was older than anyone else in this village. She claimed to remember Lewis and Clark very well. Wind in the Grass told stories of the winter they spent in her village. She was a young woman at the time and she was attracted to the strange white men with blue eyes. It had been over seventy years, but it was clear in her memory.

She nursed the sick and dying during the smallpox outbreak in 1837. The runny face sickness decimated the Mandans, but despite repeated exposure, she never became infected. The old woman never married. Many people thought she waited for one of the white men to return to her.

Lone Elk spent a quiet night and sought an audience with her the next day. As he entered her lodge, Lone Elk slipped off his moccasins and left them outside as a sign of respect. He called her grandmother, and brought her a gift of tobacco.

Wind in the Grass was ancient, her hair was snow white, and her face deeply wrinkled. She was the oldest person Lone Elk had ever seen, but her eyes were bright and her mind was sharp.

"What is it that you want from me?"

Lone Elk told her the story of his friends and family being killed by a white man.

"This was no ordinary man. He fought alone against ten men." He continued to tell about falling from his pony and being saved by a white man. "I found my enemy near the Powder River, but I was chased away by the long knives. He went to Coulter Creek with another man and a woman. How can I find this man and kill him?"

Wind in the Grass took the tobacco Lone Elk had given her and packed some of it in a long ceremonial pipe. A woodpecker scalp was tied to the bowl. She pulled a smoldering stick from the small fire in front of her and lit the pipe.

She puffed on the pipe until it began to billow smoke. After it was lit, she offered the stem to father sky, mother earth, and the four winds, beginning in the east. She studied Lone Elk's face as she smoked. The mighty Lakota sat silent.

After several minutes, she laid the pipe down with the stem pointing to the east. There was a basket with small braids of sweet grass next to her. Placing one of the braids on the coals in front of her, she used a hawk's wing to brush the smoke across her face and over her head.

After much ceremony, she appeared ready to speak. "The spirit warrior is a strong heart. The spirit warrior was driven to kill by a need for vengeance. I feel his courage and his strength, but he has a dark and terrible spirit. Death rides with him, for he has killed many men. You cannot kill this man, even though you will face him one day. I feel you live because of this man. Your spirit and his are bound by an ancient and powerful force, like the force that binds brothers."

"That cannot be, Grandmother, this man is a white man."

"I can only tell you what I see and feel." Sensing she was finished, Lone Elk got to his feet and started to leave her lodge. "Before you go," she said, "take this." Wind in the Grass handed him a small pouch. "When you have fasted for two days, make an infusion with this and drink it. If your mind is open, and your spirit true, you will have your answer."

"Thank you, Grandmother."

The old woman touched his arm and looked him in the eye. "Lone Elk, if you find the vision you seek, be warned; you may not like what is revealed to you. The truth is not always what we want it to be."

Instead of answers, Lone Elk only had more questions. The old woman, however, had said all there was to say and she was finished with him.

There was an Indian in the village that had been to Coulter Creek many times. The town's people considered him to be just another loafer Indian and he was left alone. Lone Elk sought him out to ask if he was there around the time the white man and his horses were in town. Lame Deer listened to Lone Elk's story and thought back. He was in Coulter Creek and he had seen Bolt with a woman and a herd of fine horses.

"The man you seek is Buffalo Grass Rider. He lives on the Lonesome Wind Ranch, a long day's ride northwest from Coulter Creek. He is a good man. The whites and the Indians respect him for his honest ways."

"Buffalo Grass Rider, why is he called that?"

"He befriended an old Arapaho many years ago. The old one gave him that name."

"Can he really be the man I seek?"

"He was with the horses you describe." Lame Deer watched Lone Elk for a moment and then offered some advice, "I know you are a brave man with a warrior's heart. I hope you will also be my friend, but hear my words, Lone Elk, for I speak only the truth. If Buffalo Grass Rider killed your friends, he had a good reason."

In spite of the steady rain, Eb was down off his horse studying tracks. The sun was long gone and it was going to be a miserable night. The pungent smell of crushed sagebrush and fresh manure filled the heavy damp air around them. Eb knew they were getting close.

"They're not far ahead now. We should catch 'em soon."

"Let's keep after 'em," Coop said.

Bolt was uneasy. "We need to go slow. These horses are worn out and we're all tired. We don't want to let these rustlers know we're on their trail until we're ready to fight. We can't risk riding into an ambush. They could be watching their back trail."

"Alright, we'll rest a couple of hours, before we start. . . ."

Coop paused when Bolt held up his hand for silence. The rain pattering on his hat brim made it difficult to hear as he concentrated on the distant sound. "I think I hear 'em."

When calves get separated from their mothers during a drive, the cows will turn around to come back to look for them. If the calves get completely lost, they'll head back to where they suckled last. By stopping now and then to let the calves, mother-up, the drive will make better time.

It was bad luck for this bunch of rustlers they picked that moment in time to stop. Bill LeConte was sitting by the smoking fire in his slicker, drinking coffee and trying to warm up. The outlaw lowered his head to take a sip of coffee, allowing a trickle of rain water to run off the brim of his hat into the steaming cup.

"I hate this damn rain. I don't like being in these mountains, there's too much cover for anyone on our trail."

"That bunch from the Lonesome may not even know these cows are gone yet," Watson said, "by the time they find out, this rain will have washed out all our tracks and we'll be home free."

"You don't know that," another of the men said, "Cooper and his men won't let this go. When he finds out, they'll be after us, you can count on that. He may be coming up our trail right now for all we know."

"We'll camp here until daylight, and then move on toward Whiskey Hill," LeConte said, "The Mountains will slow us up a little so we need to get an early start."

Sean was a little more timid than LeConte. "We don't want to tangle with Cooper and his men if we don't have to."

LeConte pulled his slicker up around his ears and leaned back against a pine tree. "Relax, Sean. We'll all sleep a lot better when we get this herd delivered."

The rustlers were intruders in the pristine valley. Little did they know, but the undisputed king of that valley was nearby and on the prowl. The Indians called him, Scar. He was a huge boar grizzly that lived in the Crazy Mountains for more than twenty years. The Indians named him for the blonde streak of fur down the side of his head covering an old burn injury. This old bear was over nine feet from head to tail. He was half-a-ton of bad attitude with a hair-trigger temper. The Indians gave Scar's home territory a wide berth. The short-tempered old bear was bad medicine and to be avoided at all costs.

The driving rain was making Scar restless. He was out looking for a meal when he caught the scent of an animal similar to a buffalo. This bear had never seen a cow or had much contact with white men. He knew little of firearms or their dangers. He was moving in the direction of the scent when he began to hear the sounds of the herd. The big bear went on full alert. Despite his size, he was silent as a mouse slipping along the wet forest floor.

Bob Stanley was a young cowboy that fell in with the wrong crowd. He was looking for work when he hired on with LeConte. He knew what he was doing was wrong, but he stayed for the money.

Bob made the mistake of drinking from the seep at Badlands Coulee. He'd been suffering with a stomach problem ever since and his gut was in bad shape. Feeling sick, he left the fire to go to the woods.

Bob was alone in the dripping forest when he sensed something near him. He spun around just as a hulking apparition slammed into him. Before he could make a sound, Bob's neck was shattered by a blow from a huge paw.

Scar sniffed the body of the man he just killed. He had killed Indians before, but this man smelled different. Scar had no intention of eating him. His heart was set on a big meal of buffalo. He continued on until he saw the fire. Scenting more of the stinking white men, he began to get angry. This was his range, these strangers had no place here.

Scar crept forward, silent as death, as he advanced on the intruders. His raised hackles revealed ivory canines the size of a man's index finger. Testing the air, the despised odor of smoke made his hair stand on end as old memories of being burned in a forest fire were rekindled. Quickening his pace, the enraged grizzly closed on the unsuspecting men.

Ignorant of the grizzly's presence, the men from the Lonesome Wind were picking their way along a game trail just above him. They were on foot leading their horses through the thick timber. Down below, they could see the flickering light of a campfire through the trees. The rustlers were resting in the head of the little mountain valley. Bolt wanted to get as close as possible to the rustlers and do it without being discovered. The sounds from the cattle and the falling rain were covering any noise they may have been making.

As they picked their way along, another storm approached with rolling thunder and crashing lightning. The surrounding timber was pitch-black until a jagged streak of lightning would transform the lodge pole pines into a ghostly stockade. The intensity of the storm was making the cattle restless and they began to mill around. It was the perfect setting for the terror about to befall the outlaws.

Bill LeConte and his men were dozing around their smoky fire, unawares that a thousand pounds of primal vengeance was coming toward them in the dark. A burning pain in his shoulder awakened the first outlaw. Scar snuffed out his screams with one bite to his neck. The rest awoke in the middle of a nightmare.

Lightning flashes revealed a huge grizzly, scattering rustlers left and right. Scar was roaring as he tossed men like matchsticks. A couple of them managed to get off a desperate shot or two, but the giant grizzly was moving so fast, they were doing more damage to each other than their attacker. The loud reports and blinding flashes from the gunfire startled the big bear. Breaking off the attack, he retreated to the safety of the dark timber.

Eb was standing close to Bolt in the dark. "What the devil is that?"
"I don't know. It sounded like a grizzly roaring in the middle of all that yelling."
"What's going on?" Logan asked TJ, "Can you make it out?"
He and the others were listening in the dark. The shouting and shooting died down until men could be heard talking aloud. Cattle were bawling as some of them began to smell the bear. The whole herd began to scatter in the trees.
"Sounds like the devil himself is after that bunch," Eb said.
"It wasn't the devil, but if it was a big bear it was just as bad," Bolt said.
"I never heard men screaming like that," TJ said,
"Tighten your cinches boy's, be ready to ride," Coop said, "If whatever was after them comes up this way, I want to be able to get out of here."
Logan was spooked, "I'm ready to go right now!"
"I'm with you," Creek said.
"Hold those horses," Bolt warned, "if they get a snoot-full of grizzly they'll be half-way back to the ranch by morning."

Bill LeConte was scared nearly witless. He had faced many men in gunfights and never been afraid, but this was different. The big bear came out of the black of night as if intent on killing all of them. It was no chance meeting. The grizzly planned to attack them. Coming upon them silent as a wraith, the rustlers had no idea he was around until he was in their midst.
Three of LeConte's men were dead from the bear and one from a stray bullet. There were only five healthy men besides him to round up the herd and continue on. Those men just about decided the life of an

outlaw had not worked out the way they planned it. The first outlaw to speak was Pete Watson.

"LeConte; that bear could come back here any minute. The best thing for us to do is forget these cows and ride out of here, tonight."

"Nobody rides anywhere without this herd. Any of you try running out on me, I'll shoot you myself."

"Maybe Pete's right," Sean said, "This is a bad spot we're in. A killer grizzly out here in the dark with us and that bunch from the Lonesome Wind behind us somewhere."

Badly frightened, Watson was tossing more and more wood on the fire and talking fast. "If Ashton and Monday are on our trail, we may be in trouble. It'll take a day or more to round up this herd; they'll catch us for sure. With only six of us left to fight 'em off…it ain't good."

"We can't give up now," LeConte said, "It's a good payday when we get these cows to Whiskey Hill."

"We can't get this many cows through the mountains alone with no rest," Sean said, "None of us can sleep with that bear out there in the dark and those cowboys on our trail."

"Nobody's on our trail," LeConte stormed, "and nobody run's out on this job, I mean it, Sean."

Up in the timber, Bolt was figuring a way to take advantage of the outlaw's misfortune. "That bear may have provided us a way to get this herd back without much of a fight."

"How's that," Eb asked.

"Those outlaws are beat up. Some of them may be dead. They won't be expecting us tonight. If we hit 'em in the dark, we'll have the advantage. That big fire they got going will hinder them from seeing us coming."

"Suppose that bear is still around?" Logan asked.

"He's long gone after all that shooting. Logan, do you have your bow with you?"

"Yes sir, I do."

"Get it and come with me." Turning to the others, Bolt laid out the plan. "When you boys hear me start shooting, come on in, we'll surprise this bunch and take our cattle back tonight."

"What are you gonna do with a bow?" Eb asked.

"Sneak down there and shoot a couple of them in the dark."

"I never killed anybody," Logan said as he strung the bow.

"They'll damn sure kill you if they catch us," Bolt warned, "Just follow me and go quiet." The others watched as Bolt and Logan faded into the gloom.

Scar was lying about three hundred yards below Coop and the others and less than a hundred yards from the clearing where the outlaw's fire was blazing. He was confused, after being stung by one of the wild shots during the confrontation. This big grizzly had grown old by being careful and not taking any chances with the unknown. He would stay hidden and watch before he made another attack. The smell of more men hit his nostrils as Bolt and Logan approached.

"What if that grizzly is out here in the dark?" Logan whispered, "He could be watching us right now."

"You're going to get old before your time if you don't stop that worrying." Bolt was putting on a good show, but he was just as scared as Logan. He knew if the bear came after them they were done for. Bolt had his rifle, but it would be of little use if the bear got close before he could shoot him. "How far can you shoot that bow?"

"About thirty yards is my limit."

Scar was less than fifty yards from Bolt and Logan when they went by. He was lying near a blow-down and invisible in the dark. The big bear stayed put as Bolt and Logan slipped right by him on their way to the fire in the clearing. Bolt never knew how close he was to the killer grizzly.

Bolt could feel the hair on the back of his neck standing up. He knew something was watching, but he tried to ignore it. His sixth sense was telling him he was in a bad spot. Logan's guardian angel must have been sneaking along with them there in the dark, Scar never moved from his vantage point.

"This should be close enough," Bolt whispered when they had crawled as close as they dared, "Shoot the big one by the fire."

With the firelight reaching out almost to their hiding place, Logan rose up on one knee, drew his bow, and let the arrow fly. The shot was a little high, but still effective. The arrow hit LeConte in the shoulder and knocked him over backwards into the fire. He let out a yell as he rolled away from the flames. The other rustlers began firing blindly into the dark forest. Bolt started shooting back and managed to drop two of them.

That was all Watson and the other remaining outlaw needed to see. They weren't getting paid enough to face all this trouble. First the weather, then a monster grizzly, and now Indian's attacking in the middle of the night. Abandoning the wounded LeConte, they hit their saddles and never looked back.

Coop and Eb started off the hill with Bolt's first shot. Eb's horse nearly bucked him off when a huge dark shadow passed right behind them on its way up the slope. Eb had his hands full just staying in the saddle and couldn't tell what it was. A couple of rustlers went by just as Coop and Eb burst out into the clearing. A flash of lightning illuminated the scene for a moment and Eb recognized one of them.

"Pete Watson, you cattle stealing son-of. . . ." Eb was drowned out by the roar of his Colt.

Having picked a different path getting off the ridge, TJ and Creek were off to Coop's right by fifty yards. They heard Eb yelling and shooting and saw two strangers riding right at them as they cleared the trees. The boys didn't know the outlaws were running away. Two rifle shots rang out and both outlaws tumbled into the wet grass.

Scar had heard enough, the woods seemed to be teaming with these strange white men. The running horses in the timber and the gunfire were making him uneasy. He continued up the mountain, went across the ridgeline and down into a little valley to a more peaceful setting.

Bolt and Logan walked into the firelight just as Coop and the rest arrived on horseback.

"Don't even think about going for that gun," Bolt warned LeConte. The outlaw's wet clothes were still steaming from rolling through the fire. Sean was holding his hands in the air. Logan got their guns and tied the outlaw's hands behind their back.

Coop was ready to shoot both of them on the spot. "Do you skunks think the world owes you a living? What makes you think you can just take anything you want with no regard for the rights of others?"

Bolt took out his knife and heated it over the fire. Logan was using steel arrowheads he made himself. Hard Tack showed him how to turn old wagon-wheel rims and strap steel into arrowheads. LeConte grimaced from the pain as Bolt cut the arrow out of his shoulder and cauterized it with the hot blade.

"He'll be alright," Bolt said after tying a bandage over the wound.

"Alright, hell," Eb said, "we ought to hang both of them."

"There's been enough killing in this valley tonight. We'll turn these two over to the law."

"What law?" Eb asked, "There ain't a marshal within a hundred miles of here."

"Well, we aren't going to hang 'em," Bolt said, "That would make us no better than them. We'll figure it out in the morning. I'll take the first watch, the rest of you get some rest. We got a long day when it gets light."

"There's no way I can sleep knowing that bear is still around," Creek said.

Eb was squatted down looking at Scar's footprints in the mud.

"This bear is a monster. I've never seen tracks this big. I bet he's close to ten feet."

"Ten feet!" Logan and TJ said together.

"Throw some more wood on that fire and pray for daylight," Creek said.

The storm eventually blew itself out and the sky began to clear. There were dead men scattered all around the camp.

"Let's get these bodies moved away from here," Bolt said, "We'll bury them in the morning." It was late before they were done with the rustler's bodies and settled down to get some rest.

"Are you asleep?" Creek asked TJ after things had gotten quiet.

"Heck no, are you?" he answered from somewhere in the darkness.

"You boys be quiet," Logan whispered, "I'm listening for that bear,"

"Have you ever seen a ten-foot grizzly?" Creek asked.

"I never seen any kind of grizzly," TJ said. "They were killed out of Nebraska long before my time."

"He's lying out there right now deciding which one of you he wants for breakfast," Eb warned, having a little fun at the boy's expense.

"I'll be glad to get back to the plains and out of these trees," Logan said. "There ain't no bears out there."

Scarlett was awakened by a bad dream and a feeling that all wasn't right with her cowboy. It was the middle of the night and she had no idea where he was or if he was safe. She lay awake in the dark for a long time, feeling all alone in her empty house and remembering those nights when he was always nearby.

She wanted to come to him many times on their journey. The nights were difficult for her. She felt safe in his arms and she longed for his touch. If she could have had her way, she would have slept pressed against him every night. Scarlett decided when he returned, she would find a way to let him know how she felt. She was ready to tell Bolt that she loved him and the woman in her wanted him in her bed.

Dawn came without another confrontation with Scar. The valley was flooded with brilliant sunlight and the high-country air had a bite to it. The warmth from the rekindled campfire felt good to the boys as they emerged from their wet bedrolls. Logan was already up and fixing breakfast with the outlaw's supplies.

"As soon as we eat; you three start digging graves," Coop said, warming his hands at the fire. "Bolt, you and Eb start looking for the cattle. When we're done here we'll help you."

"What about us?" LeConte asked.

"You'll just sit there and keep your mouth shut, if you know what's good for you," Eb said.

After eating and indulging in a cup or two of coffee, Bolt and Eb saddled their horses and rode off toward the western end of the valley. The boy's fed the outlaws and tied them back up.

"Logan, you stay in camp while the rest of us go round up the herd," Coop said after they had finished with the dead men. "You did a good job last night with that bow, Son."

"Thanks Boss."

"Keep your eyes open, fire a shot if you need us back here. We won't be far away." Coop stepped up on his horse and turned to Creek and Rye, "Let's ride boys. I want out of here by tomorrow."

"I'm all for that," TJ said.

Scar was lying in the morning sun, drying out from the rain. He hadn't eaten the night before and he was hungry. A grizzly feeds heavily in late summer and early fall. They do it to prepare their bodies for the winter. Bears don't really hibernate. It's more like a long slumber. They can wake up, stir around, and then go back to sleep.

Scar had a really fine place to spend the winter. It was a small, but deep cave up in the rimrock. The winter winds would howl outside, the temperature could drop to forty below zero, but the fire in the bowels of the earth would keep his cave comfortable. The old bear would simply snooze away the bitter cold high-country winter.

With his belly rumbling, Scar got up and began to backtrack to the herd. The scent of cattle was strong on the morning thermals coming up the mountain, and a cow would keep him happy for days.

"It's not as bad as we first thought," Eb said, "The cows aren't scattered after all. The timber and the steep slopes must have kept them together last night."

"That's a break for us," Bolt said, "I'm ready to get out of here and get back to the ranch."

"You just want to get back to Scarlett."

"You might be right about that."

"Well never let it be said Eb Monday ever stood in the way of true love. Let's head this bunch of cows back down to the valley then go find the rest. I hope Coop and the boys are having the same kind of luck we are."

"One more night in here is one too many as far as I'm concerned."

"That bear got you spooked has he?"

"That bear is the boss in these mountains and I'm ready to let him have 'em back," Bolt said. "I got no quarrel with him. I just don't want to face him. He softened up those rustlers for us; we really owe that bear some thanks."

By late afternoon, they had most of the cows gathered back in the valley.

Coop was on horseback, making a quick count. "Near as I can figure, we only lost about thirty head. Eb, you and Bolt, take one more turn around the hills to the north there, see if there's any more strays around."

"I'll have supper ready in an hour," Logan said, "be back before then."

"If we run into that bear we'll invite him back for a sit-down," Eb said, still teasing the boys. Just then a cow could be heard bellowing about a mile up the valley. "Let's ride partner, I think our bear's back," Eb said as he spurred his horse. Bolt and Rufus were right behind him. After about five hundred yards, Bolt could see a dozen or more cows running toward them from the hills.

He slowed Rufus to a walk and continued on slow and easy. The old horse was nervous. Being downwind, he could smell Scar and fresh blood, and he wanted no part of either one.

They dismounted when they reached the trees and continued on foot. Bolt knew even Rufus couldn't be expected to stand still if a grizzly got after him. Bolt tied the reins to the saddle horn so Rufus could run if he had too. Bolt pulled his Henry rifle from the saddle scabbard and levered in a shell.

Hearing a struggle up ahead, it was apparent the bear had taken at least one cow. Coming in from downwind, the two of them crawled up to a moss-covered log and peeked over. Just down in a little hollow, they could see the bear tearing big chunks of meat out of a freshly killed cow. Brush was torn up for twenty yards in every direction. It was obvious that a savage struggle was played out there. The big bear's muzzle was covered in blood as he fed on the cow's carcass.

"Shoot him," Eb said in a loud whisper.

Sensing their presence, Scar went on full alert. He stood up on his hind legs to get a better look. Being nearsighted, it was standard grizzly behavior. The shifting breeze was blowing away from him so he didn't pick up Bolt's scent. The huge blood-covered grizzly was the most formidable beast Bolt had ever seen.

"Shoot him before he gets after us," Eb whispered.

"He doesn't know we're here."

"It don't matter, I don't want to spend another night watching for him."

"I'm not sure I can kill him. He'll be on us in a flash if I just wound him." The already tense situation changed for the worse when Bolt felt a falling thermal of cool air on the back of his neck.

Scar got a whiff of Bolt and started to emit a low growl. He knew the man scent from the night before. The old bear dropped down to all fours as Eb kept insisting that Bolt shoot.

"Here he comes, shoot him…shoot him!'

"I don't think so," Bolt whispered.

Scar remained where he was. After a moment, he lowered his head, ripped off another hunk of meat, and swallowed it. He turned back to stare in the direction of the man scent until his eyes found Buffalo Grass Rider's.

Bolt felt a chill as he made contact with the great bear's eyes. It was as if their spirits were locked in some primordial exchange, bridging the gap between their species. After what seemed like a long time, Scar seemed to relax. The bristling hair on his hump settled. He let out a loud woof, just before turning away to waddle up the mountain.

"Let's get back to camp," Bolt said, letting the hammer down on his rifle. He wasn't sure what passed between him and the great bear. It had been powerful and primitive, but it wasn't fear. Whatever it was, he would never speak of it to anyone.

Bolt and Eb got back to camp just in time for supper. Logan had done a good job and soon everyone was full and ready for sleep. As the others snored, Bolt lay awake watching the glowing embers of the fire. He was deep in thought as his mind went back to the ranch with Scarlett. He thought about that day at the Belle Fourche River when he saw Scarlett coming up out of the water. She was the most perfect woman he had ever seen. For the first time in many years, there was no room in his heart for the memory of lost loves.

Bolt could see the stars, as the high country air was clear. He often lay under a blanket of stars and wondered who else in the world might be looking up at the same big sky.

Tonight, he would be happy to know Scarlett was standing on her porch at the ranch looking up at the sky over her head. She wondered about her cowboy. Was he all right? Was he on his way back to her or still pursuing the rustlers? She wanted him home with her. She was in love with him and she was ready to tell him.

Logan got a fire going just as the stars were fading and the eastern sky was growing light. Coop was trying to get all the boys up and ready to ride.

"I want this herd out of these mountains today. If we push hard we can be home in four or five days."

"That was a short night," TJ said.

"We may just as well get up and get moving," Creek said, "Maybe tonight we can sleep without that bear to worry about."

When the cowboys finished their breakfast, it was time to make a decision.

"Coop, what are we going to do with these outlaws?" Bolt asked.

"I'm not sure what to do. Eb's right, there's no law around here and we don't need to watch them all the way back to Coulter Creek." After a moment of thought, he turned to LeConte. "Take your friend and ride out of here. I'm giving you a chance to save your own life, but listen close. If I ever see any of you near the Lonesome again, I'll shoot you on sight. You go back to Whiskey Hill and tell your boss to stay the hell off my land or he'll suffer the consequences."

"You mean we're just turning them loose," Eb said.

"That's right," Coop replied, "That's the only thing that makes sense right now."

The boys gathered the outlaw's horses and helped them to mount up.

"Are you gonna give us our guns?" Sean asked.

"No, we ain't giving you no guns," Eb said.

"We can't travel in this country without some protection," LeConte pleaded.

"That's the life of an outlaw," Eb said. "Now get out of here before we change our mind and hang you."

When the outlaws were out of sight, Coop climbed up on his horse.

"Logan, you and the boys saddle the rest of those horses and gather up the guns. We'll take them as payment for our trouble."

"Yes sir," Logan said.

"Alright boys, let's go the house," Creek said over his shoulder as he headed out to the herd.

"The Lord must be watching over the boys from the Lonesome," Logan said as they rode along, "We faced a bunch of outlaws, a killer grizzly, got most of the cows back, and none of us got a scratch."

"Amen," Coop added with a grin.

The next two days were quiet. After crossing the river, Coop made a wide detour to the south of Salt Springs. He didn't want the Frenchman to know what happened. Coop felt he was a little too friendly with LeConte and Marceu.

When the herd hit the big basin they were only three days from home. The high escarpment, northern gateway to the Lonesome, was plainly visible, even though it was more than forty miles away.

Coop pulled up and sat until Creek rode up to him. "Creek, take TJ and Logan, keep this herd moving. Leave them in Cottonwood Creek when you get there. The rest of us are going on ahead, we'll see you in a few days."

Chapter Thirteen:
Love on the Lonesome Wind

Angelia was cleaning up the dishes from supper when Coop, Eb, and Bolt rode into the ranch yard.

"Spud, they're back!" she shouted to the kitchen. Bolt was getting down from the saddle when she came off the porch and threw her arms around his neck. Scarlett was in the barn when she heard the commotion. She stepped out just in time to see Angelia hanging onto Bolt.

"I'm so glad you're safe," Angelia said.

"It's good to be home," Bolt said. Scarlett started walking to him as he peeled Angelia off and straightened himself up. He met Scarlett halfway and pulled her into his arms.

"Thank goodness you're alright," she said.

"We had a lot of luck, everyone's fine. The boys are with the herd, they'll be in the day after tomorrow."

Scarlett reached up to his mouth and kissed him.

"I missed you."

"I missed you too," he replied.

As Coop and Eb walked toward the main house, Coop was telling Angelia about getting the herd back and the men they faced. "I've got some good men working here. I'd stake my life on any one of them."

"You're a good man yourself," she said, "I'm sure they all feel the same way about you."

"Got any supper left?" Eb asked, "I'm hungry enough to eat a parboiled buzzard."

"Come on in when you're through with those horses!" Coop shouted to Bolt, "We'll get something to eat."

"I'm not unsaddling all these horses!"

"Come on," Scarlett said, "I'll help you."

That evening at supper, Scarlett sat next to Bolt at the table while they ate.

"That was mighty good eating," Coop said, "Better than that old biscuit-roller dishes out," he added with a glance at Spud.

"It'll be quiet in the bunkhouse tonight," Bolt said, wiping his mouth with a napkin, "If you ladies will excuse me, I think I'll get some sleep. I won't be worrying about that grizzly tonight."

"What grizzly?" Scarlett asked.

"Rafe will be glad to see you in the morning," Angelia said before Bolt could answer. Scarlett rolled her eyes, but kept quiet.

"Be glad to see him too," Bolt replied over his shoulder as he went out the door. Scarlett got to her feet and excused herself.

"Goodnight everyone," she said. Hurrying outside, she caught up with Bolt. "I'll be awake for a while if you want to come by and talk later. I still want to hear about the grizzly." Bolt touched her hand for a moment before heading to the bunkhouse to clean up.

It was after ten and the ranch compound was quiet. Scarlett changed into a silky lace-trimmed nightgown in anticipation of what she hoped might happen. She was sitting up reading a book when she heard boots on her porch and a knock at the door. She could see Bolt as she opened it to let him in.

"I saw your lamp, and I wanted to say goodnight." Taking her in his arms, he gently kissed her lower lip. "I want to assure you I know you're a lady. I'm not here to make you…that is, I don't expect you to do anything you're not ready to do."

"I know that." Taking his hand, she led him over to her bedside. "I don't have much furniture, my things haven't arrived yet. I hope you'll be comfortable sitting here."

Turning down the lamp, she came back to stand directly in front of him. She was only five-foot-four and he could reach her mouth while sitting on the edge of the bed.

Scarlett bent down, helped him out of his boots, and tossed them into the corner. Bolt pulled her to him until his cheek was pressed against her chest. He could feel the firm round curves of her body in the nightgown. The soft silky material left little for him to imagine. He let her go long enough for her to unbutton his shirt and toss it away.

Bolt began to undo her nightgown down the front. She didn't protest as he pulled it off her shoulders and let it fall to the floor. Bolt held her close to him then lay back on the bed.

He pulled her down on his chest and began to rub her back as she kissed him. Neither of them exactly planned this, but it was what they both wanted. He caressed the small of her back, and moved his hands farther down her body.

"Why...Mr. Ashton," she said, teasing him.

"Just checking for cactus, you can't be too careful." Scarlett tried not to, but she had to laugh. "I can't believe we're together for the first time and you're laughing about it," Bolt said.

Scarlett was more than ready to release all the emotion she had been holding back. She wanted him for some time, and now he was finally lying beside her. She was still in his arms when the clock on her mantle struck one in the morning.

"It's been a long time since I was with someone like this," she whispered. Scarlett was comfortable with him. It felt like the most natural thing in the world to be there with Bolt. It was like she had been making love to him forever. One minute they were making passionate love, the next, they were laughing out loud at something Bolt said. She had never seen the playful side of him and she loved it.

"I've often thought about being with you," he said.

"Oh really, I thought all of you cowboys were gentlemen."

"If I wasn't a gentleman, I would have been chasing you around the fire every night out there on the trail."

"There were a few nights I wished you had."

"Well now's a poor time to tell me that."

"I'm glad you made it back in one piece," she said as she propped herself up on one elbow, "now tell me about that grizzly."

Bolt told her about the bear attacking the outlaw camp and how he and Logan were crawling around in the rain.

"You were out there in the dark with a grizzly," she said, "I'm glad I didn't know anything about that little adventure, weren't you afraid?"

"Shucks, it weren't nothing ma'am," Bolt said in his best cowboy drawl.

They lay in each other's arms, talked, and laughed until the eastern sky began to turn gray.

"I've got to get going," Bolt said, "I don't want anyone to find me here. It's not the right time for them to know about us."

"What about us?"

"Well I kind o' like having you around."

"I like being around." Bolt kissed her one last time and went out the door. Completely drained, Scarlett was sound asleep in two minutes.

Bolt got to his bunk and fell into it.

Roused from sleep, Eb rolled over. "Where have you been?"

"None of your damn business," Bolt mumbled into his pillow, "go back to sleep."

Coop was up at daylight just like always. He put on a pot of coffee and read a week-old newspaper until Spud and Angelia got up to start breakfast. Eb and Rafe were the only ones at the table when the sun popped over the eastern ridgeline.

Folding his paper, Coop looked across the table at Eb. "Where's Bolt and Ms. Scarlett?"

"I don't know about Scarlett, but Bolt's still in his bunk."

"I'll go get 'em for breakfast," Coop said, getting to his feet.

"Sit down and eat before it gets cold," Spud said, "Bolt's bound to be worn out and he deserves to get some rest. He's no kid you know. Ms. Scarlett is a grown woman; she'll get up when she's ready."

"I guess you're right," Coop said, returning to his seat. "Do you think I could get another cup of coffee?"

"Get it yourself, I'm busy."

Bolt woke up about nine, he couldn't remember the last time he had been asleep that late in the day. When he stepped out on the porch of the bunkhouse, he saw Scarlett and Coop at the corrals.

"We need several of your best mustang studs," he could hear Scarlett saying, "We can start breeding these mares right away. The foals will be born in warm weather. That will eliminate at least one problem for us."

Bolt walked up and wished them both good morning.

"It's about time you got out of that bunk," Coop said.

"I don't remember ever being that tired."

"You're getting too old to keep up with the youngsters, I reckon. You best try and slow down some and start acting your age."

"I guess you're right," Bolt said, as he caught a slight smile from Scarlett. "Speaking of old, where's my partner?"

"He took the buckboard and went up the creek this morning," Coop said, "said something about a bobcat and a badger hole, or some dang thing."

"A bobcat…their pelts aren't worth anything this time of year. What did he need with the buckboard?"

"He had some kind o' crate in the wagon box. How am I supposed to know what that crazy old man is up to, he's your partner?"

"I'm going to find something to eat and let you all get back to work," Bolt said. Turning away, he went toward the main house.

Angelia looked up from her work when Bolt walked into the kitchen.

"Any leftovers from breakfast?"

"Sit down," she said, "I'll see what I can do." She brought him some cold biscuits and beef sausage, and poured him a cup of coffee. "I'll fix some eggs if you like."

"No, this is fine."

"There's something I want to tell you," Angelia said as she sat down opposite him. "It's been on my mind for years and it's the reason I came all the way to Montana."

Little Rafe came in the kitchen about that time.

"Good morning partner," Bolt said.

"Morning, Bolt," Rafe replied.

"That's Mr. Bolt," Angelia corrected.

"That's alright, my friend's call me Bolt; he can to."

"Rafael, go play outside," Angelia said, "I want to talk to Bolt."

"He's a fine boy," Bolt said when Rafe was gone. "I'm sure you're proud of him. What happened to his father?"

Angelia's eyes began to fill with tears. "That's what I want to talk to you about."

"What's the matter? I didn't mean to bring up any painful memories." Reaching across the table, Bolt took her hand as the first tear started down her cheek.

"It's not that. I came to Montana because I never forgot you. I was in love with you when you left Texas and…I still love you."

"That was so long ago. I loved you too, but I figured it was over when we left to come up here."

Angelia gripped his hand as she looked across the table.

"I've never stopped loving you. I found out I was expecting right after you left Texas. Rafael…Rafe, is our son…yours and mine. He's just like you in so many ways. He acts like you; he talks like you, he even walks like you. He's you made over again."

Bolt was stunned, like he had just been punched in the gut. Angelia broke down and cried.

"I've been carrying that around for so long, it's such a relief now that you finally know."

"Rafe's my son…how do you know? I'm sorry," he quickly apologized, "Of course you would know."

"It must have happened just before you left. I wanted to follow and tell you, but my mother wouldn't hear of it. She said you were a drifter and would never take responsibility for your child. We had a really difficult time after Coop moved out of Texas. There was no work except to sell myself in the saloon. I wouldn't do that. We went back to Mexico and tried to survive."

Spud walked in the kitchen about then. "What's all this about? Is Bolt making you cry? Believe me, he ain't worth it."

Bolt let go of Angelia's hand so she could wipe her eyes. "It's nothing," she said.

"I've got to get to work," Bolt said, as he got up and went out the door. His mind was reeling with the news that he was a father. He felt a little guilty when he was outside. His first thoughts hadn't been about his son. He was concerned about losing his new love. *"What am I going to tell Scarlett?"* he thought.

Rafe was standing near the barn, feeding Rufus grass through the fence. Bolt walked up to him and knelt down on one knee. Bolt put his arms around the youngster and hugged him.

"I'm really proud to finally know you, Son," he said.

Rafe was confused, but pleased the big man had changed his mind and was suddenly glad to have him around.

Supper that night was a real strain for Bolt. He was sitting next to Scarlett as Angelia was putting the meal on the table. Rafe was sitting on Bolt's other side, happy that Bolt was taking such an interest in him.

Rafe never had a man around to teach him the things women don't know about. He wanted to grow up to be just like the big man sitting next to him. He didn't know Bolt was his dad. Bolt would tell him soon, but he had to tell Scarlett first.

Scarlett could feel something was different about her cowboy. He was being a little distant, but she had no idea what was wrong. After dinner, he walked her to her door and kissed her goodnight.

"Do you want to come in for a while?" she asked.

"There's something I have to tell you. I…I don't know how to start."

"Well just come in, let's talk about it," she said, expecting bad news. Bolt went in and sat down on the bed. Scarlett sat beside him and held his hand. "What's bothering you?" she asked.

"You already know Angelia and I were lovers years ago in Texas. When I left there, I forgot about her for the most part and since I've found you, I haven't looked at another woman."

"And you better not, if you know what's good for you."

"I don't know any way to make this any easier. Rafe is my son. He was born after we all left Texas. I had no idea he was even in the world until he showed up in Coulter Creek. Angelia says he's mine and I have to accept that. I have no intention of ever being her husband. I…well…there's you. I'm Rafe's dad and I intend to help raise him right here as long as Angelia will let me. She has no plans to leave. I hope this won't...we can't let it...put an end to what we have."

Scarlett was silent for a time. "I'm not surprised," she finally said, "I suspected it from that first day. I've been doing the math in my head ever since, trying to figure it out. I may need a little time to sort this out. I'm not going anywhere either. It will be uncomfortable with Angelia always around to remind me that once, you loved someone else, but I'm glad you're not the kind of man who would turn his back on a son. Just give it some time."

There was no love making that night. The two of them just held each other. After she was asleep, Bolt left her alone and made his way back to the bunkhouse.

Bolt lay awake for a long time. He had a son and he was happy about that, but at what cost would it turn out to be. Would he lose the woman he loved? *"Maybe I should go over there right now and tell her that I love her,"* he thought. *"No, she'd think I was just saying that to make her feel better about Rafe."* His life was so uncomplicated until he went to Kentucky. Now it was turned upside down and he had no idea what to do next.

Angelia was awake and thinking about Bolt. *"I'm glad I told him,"* she thought. *"Maybe now we can finally be a family."*

Not far away, another woman was lying awake. *"I finally find a man that I can love and now this. I can't just leave here; this is my home now. I love him and I won't give him up because of something that happened long before I met him. Last night wasn't just a fling. There's something very special between us and I'm not going to let it go without a fight."*

The next week was uncomfortable for everyone. Bolt and Rafe were spending time together. Bolt was afraid to go back to Scarlett's bed, worrying she might think he was just using her. Scarlett was afraid to ask him to come to her, afraid he might think she was trying to trap him.

Angelia had wanted Bolt for so many years, but now that she was near him again, she knew he wasn't the pillar of perfection she created in her mind all the years they were apart. She knew her decision to come to Montana was the right one for her son's sake, but it seemed that Bolt had forgotten the passion they once shared. Angelia decided it was time to remind him of what he was missing.

Late the next night, Bolt was outside trying to make sense of his life. The ranch was quiet. He assumed everyone else was asleep. He was lying on a bench in front of the cavvy corral, looking up at the stars and thinking about Scarlett, when Angelia slipped out of the house.

The Mexican beauty was barefooted and wearing only a short cotton nightshirt. The top two buttons were undone allowing it to be partially open down the front. Bolt couldn't help but notice that she was still a supple sensuous woman.

"I saw you from the window," she said, standing in front of him, "What are you doing out here in the dark?"

"Couldn't sleep, Bolt said, sitting up, "Thought I'd come out and get some air."

Moving closer to him, Angelia leaned over to kiss him, but Bolt stopped her. "You're a woman any man would be happy to have in his bed," he said, holding her arms, "but I love Scarlett, I haven't told her, I don't know when I will, but I do. I've messed up so many relationships. I don't want to hurt you, but whatever was between us is different now. You're the mother of my son and I'll always love you, but not in the way you want me to."

"I understand," she whispered, "but that will change in time. You had no way to know we would find each other again. I have all this love I've kept just for you for so many years. Unbuttoning her shirt, she allowed it to fall open, exposing her breasts in the moonlight. "I only want to give it all to you now, think about that."

Still facing him, Angelia threw her leg across and straddled his lap with her arms around his neck. "I know you remember how it was; it can be that way again…every night."

"I remember," he said. Bolt's resistance was crumbling as his hands found the small of her back. He could feel the heat from her body as she pressed her bare breasts against him. Bolt had never been so tempted by anyone in his life and he was struggling with it.

"You will come to love me again after we are together for a while. I know you will. We will be a family one day."

Bolt was outwardly quiet as he held her. Satisfied that she had made her point, Angelia kissed him once more before getting up and starting for the house.

His pulse pounding, Bolt almost called her back, but managed to keep silent until she was back inside. He was glad Angelia let it go as easily as she had. He knew he had just come dangerously close to betraying Scarlett. There was a time in the not too-distant past he could not have refused Angelia's advances.

Bolt was in turmoil as he tried to convince himself he had done the right thing. Maybe he was older and possibly wiser now, or maybe he was truly in love with the auburn-haired fireball from Kentucky.

He pondered the fact that once again, he found himself in a nearly impossible situation involving the love of a woman. He had been alone for so long and now there was not just one, but two sensual women who wanted him in their bed. The old cowboy finally got up and went to his bunk around midnight. His head was beginning to hurt as he tried to get Angelia out of his thoughts.

By the time LeConte made it into Whiskey Hill, his shoulder was infected and causing him real pain. After seeing the local doctor, he went to see Star.

Star was at the bar when the two rustlers walk in. "It's about time. Where in hell have you been? I needed that herd in here days ago. What happened to your arm?"

"I got some bad news," LeConte said, "the men from the Lonesome Wind jumped us in the dark and took the herd back."

"I thought there were only five or six cowboys working on that ranch. You mean to tell me that a handful of cowboys bested all ten of your hired guns?"

"It wasn't like that," LeConte said, "We were attacked by a grizzly that killed several of my men just before that bunch from the Lonesome hit us in the dark. By the time we knew what happened, they'd killed most of the gang and captured me and Sean."

Beside himself with frustration, Star began to rant. "We would have made a fortune with that herd if you would've had the guts to take on those cowboys, a bear…really? You're both fired, get out of my sight."

LeConte's face was blood red, his finger in Star's face. "You can't fire me, you over-dressed son-of-a-bitch!"

As they were arguing, a big man dressed in black walked up and stood beside Star. "You boys get out of here. The man said you were fired."

"Who the hell are you?" LeConte asked, turning to the dark stranger.

"My name's none of your concern. I won't tell you again, now get out."

LeConte went for his gun, but he was weak from the infection in his shoulder and he was no match for this gunfighter. LeConte was shot before he ever cleared leather. Poor Sean wasn't looking for a fight, but he was killed right along with his partner.

"Get these bodies out of here and meet me in my office later," Star instructed the gun fighter.

The gunman in black was known as Latigo Lane. Emotionally flawed and lacking any conscience, Lane had no qualms about killing his fellow man. He was fast with a gun, and he used a knife on his unarmed victims. He hated women. Lane never had a relationship with one due to some inadequacies in his physical makeup. His only source of pleasure came from torturing and killing his female victims.

Lane was in Star's office later that evening.

"I want you to take some of the boys and go down to the Lonesome Wind Ranch," Star said. "Hit them hard. Eliminate all the cowboys involved with killing our men. Make an example of them.

Show them we can take whatever we want and there's nothing they can do about it."

"What about any women or kids?"

"I don't care. If they get in your way...do whatever you have to do. Just make sure we get a supply of beef. Gather up the men hanging around town and get going. We can't wait for the others out at the ranch. I'll send more boys to follow you. They'll pick up the herd. I've got to have those cows in here soon."

Lone Elk was with the Mandan tribe for almost a month. He was rested and well fed. His stay was peaceful, and his talks with Wind in the Grass helped to cool some of his hatred for the white man that he sought.

The mighty Sioux admitted if placed in the same circumstances, he would have done the same as Buffalo Grass Rider. There was a struggle going on inside Lone Elk, his family cried out for revenge, but the reasonable side of him thought the time for hatred was over. His life might be better spent seeking peace instead of revenge. He had proof that all white men weren't to be despised.

There was a woman in this village that was apparently alone, as she had no man. Lone Elk had seen her on several occasions. She was Cheyenne and very beautiful. Her presence in the Mandan village was a mystery to the mighty Sioux. Her name was unknown to him, and he dared not approach her until he knew more about her. Fleeting glances passed between them convinced the mighty Sioux that she had noticed his presence. He lay awake at night remembering his wife and how it felt to be with a woman. He longed for that feeling again.

Lone Elk decided to travel to the Lonesome Wind and face Buffalo Grass Rider. Only by confronting him would he ever know if revenge was what he really wanted. Then, if he was still alive, he would return to this village and possibly begin a relationship with the Cheyenne woman. It would be a journey of many days, but he had no choice.

Bolt was spending time with Rafe, teaching him about manly things. Rafe still didn't know Bolt was his father. Bolt was going to tell the boy soon, but he wasn't sure how to explain why he hadn't been around for the first eight years of Rafe's life.

Creek, Logan, and TJ were teaching Rafe about the outdoors, the cowboy way of looking at things, and being in tune with the plains. Coop was teaching him to sit a horse. No one was quite sure what Eb was teaching him and it was probably best if they never found out.

Angelia was happy to see her son with so many good men. She knew it was the right decision to bring him to Montana. She also knew the closer Bolt grew to Rafe, the better the chance she would eventually become his wife.

Creek and the boys came in late one hot afternoon. They had been working cattle along Cottonwood Creek and were anxious to get cleaned up. When Logan walked in the bunkhouse he saw another familiar face. Virgil Crowfoot had been spending a lot of time down in the south part of the Lonesome.

"Crowfoot," Logan said, "What have you been up to?"

"Riding the Yellowstone Range," Crowfoot said. "You boys got it made up here with all this help. I've been looking out for five or six hundred head down along the river all by my lonesome."

Creek and TJ were the next ones in the bunkhouse door.

"Crowfoot, you old half-breed," TJ said, "It's good to have you back."

"It's good to be back, been looking forward to Spud's cooking."

"Spud ain't doing much cooking anymore," Creek said.

"We got us a new cook now, and she's a looker," TJ said.

"I met Scarlett this afternoon," Crowfoot said. "Now there's a handsome woman. She was with Bolt. I think there's something pretty strong going on between them."

Crowfoot had been working on the Lonesome for about six years. He was from the Arizona Territory and wanted to see it snow. He came north and asked for a job when he arrived at the ranch. Coop gave him a chance and he had been there ever since. He had a special way with horses, he understood them, and they seemed to trust him.

Crowfoot was half Navaho Indian, he knew about the spirit world and Indian legends. He could speak the Navaho and Sioux languages fluently. He was always talking about deep philosophical subjects.

Crowfoot was soft spoken and quiet. He had long black hair streaked with a little gray. He had the thin face and narrow nose of his white father and the complexion and dark eyes of his mother. Crowfoot was in his late thirties, but still slender of build.

Eb was sitting on the porch of the main house when Coop came out and saw him.

"What are you doing over here this time of day?"

"Just getting away from all that noise in the bunkhouse. Thought I'd sit here and enjoy the sunset."

Coop pulled off his hat and took a seat. "Think I'll join you. How 'bout a snort?" He turned to the house and shouted, "Spud, bring us a bottle and a couple of glasses!"

"Get it your own dang self, dammit, I'm busy!"

Scarlett was in the barn when Bolt walked in.

"It's time to knock off for today," he said, "Supper's about ready." She and Coop we're working from sunup to sundown, trying to get all the mares bred in order for the foals to be born in good weather. Ready for her long day to be over, Scarlett left her work behind and started toward the main house with Bolt.

Over in the bunkhouse, TJ was getting cleaned up.

"Man, I need some soap and water and a clean shirt before supper." He went to the foot of his bunk to get a fresh shirt. TJ kept his clean clothes in a trunk that sat there on the floor. Creek was stretched out on his bunk and Logan was taking off his chaps with his back to TJ. Crowfoot was sitting at the table by the opened window rolling a quirley.

Creek rose up on one elbow like he was listening for something far away.

"Do you hear that?" he asked.

"Hear what?" TJ asked as he reached for the lid of his trunk.

"It sort o' sounds like. . . ."

Bolt and Scarlett had just stepped up on the porch when pandemonium erupted in the bunkhouse. The sound of furniture being thrown about, pots and pans banging in the floor, bottle's being smashed, and men yelling could be heard all the way over to the main house. The sounds of a snarling animal were mixed in with the yelling and a muffled war-cry.

Coop jumped to his feet and looked toward the bunkhouse. "What the devil is that?"

Eb was sitting quietly with a grin on his face. Just then, a large ball of fur shot out of the open window of the bunkhouse and disappeared into the creek bottom.

"Payback," Bolt said with a glance at his partner.

The boys in the bunkhouse were late for supper. All four had scratches on their arms and faces. TJ had a bandage on his right hand, and the back of Logan's shirt was shredded. They had very little to say when they finally sat down at the table. None of them would even look at Eb. Crowfoot was still on the warpath, his tobacco supply was scattered all over the bunkhouse.

Scarlett hadn't been with Bolt since he told her about Rafe and she missed him. She lay awake at night knowing he was only a few yards away in the bunkhouse, but it had to be his decision to come to her. That evening after supper, Bolt knocked at her door.

"I've got a horse for you. I'd like to ride up to the rimrock, maybe watch the stars for a while, if you'd like to go."

She got her coat and went out the door with him. The sun was gone, the sky was turning from blue to a deep purple. The fleeting, mare's tail clouds, were tinged with bright gold where the sun was still shining on them from California. It was a cool, clear evening so typical of the high plains.

Bolt got off Rufus and helped Scarlett down from her horse. He had a bedroll with him and he spread it on the ground.

"Be careful of the cactus," she warned.

The coyotes were singing to one another as the two lovers sat on the ground together.

"The last couple of weeks have been lonely for me," he said, taking her hand in his, "I felt like I should wait for you to decide what you wanted to do before I attempted to see you again. I've missed you. I lay awake at night wanting to be with you. I spend all day looking for you, hoping to see you."

"I feel the same way about you. I know you've grown close to your son. I didn't want to get in the way of that."

"I do love that little boy. But the truth is…I'm in love with you, Scarlett. I have nothing to offer you, but I'll love you for the rest of my life if you'll have me."

"I love you too," she said, "I have for a long time, but I wasn't sure that's what you wanted."

He pulled her up against his chest.

"I want you to be at my side, day and night for the rest of my life, that's what I want."

"That's right where I want to be," she whispered, "Are we talking about marriage?"

"I guess we are." Bolt put his arms around her and kissed her. They watched the stars come out one by one until it was dark. He made love to her under the big Montana sky. The two of them laughed, and talked about their future together until after midnight.

It was the best night of Bolt's life. He still couldn't believe this woman wanted to be with him. She was everything he ever wanted, but couldn't find until now. His heart was so full of love for her there was no longer any room for the pain and memories of his past.

Chapter Fourteen:
Death on the Lonesome Wind

Next morning at breakfast, Bolt and Scarlett were sitting close to each other again. Angelia could see Scarlett was in love with Bolt and she had to find a way to keep Scarlett from him. She wasn't aware they were already talking about marriage.

Angelia wasn't sure if Scarlett knew Rafe was Bolt's son. No one else knew the truth about Rafe, but she knew that kind of secret would come out eventually and probably sooner than later.

Everyone was at the table that morning. The cowboys were healing up pretty well from their bobcat experience. Logan was laughing with Rafe and all the boys were talking at once.

"Coop," TJ said, "We need to take advantage of that grass up in the Dancing Grounds. The herd is eating all the forage around Cottonwood Creek and we may need it if this winter gets rough."

"I reckon you're right," Coop said, "You all start them back up there today. Someone will have to stay up there to watch 'em until we ship the calves in October, those rustlers may try again."

"We should have killed that bunch when we had the chance," Eb mumbled.

"I know some boy's in Coulter Creek who would come cowboy for you," Logan said.

"We could use a few extra hands during roundup," Coop said, "They could stay up on the Dancing Grounds until then. Eb, you and Logan, ride into town and fetch 'em back here. Its forty dollars a month, a bunk and a biscuit, but the job will only last through roundup."

"That's a good idea," Eb said, "I need a trip to town."

"Creek, you and TJ, stay with the herd until the new boys get up there," Coop said.

Creek and TJ were in the barn saddling the horses. Creek wasn't happy about leaving Angelia. "You and your big mouth, I was just starting to make some progress with Angelia. Now we got to go nursemaid a bunch of cows."

"That's the life of a cowboy," TJ said with a grin, "And speaking of Angelia, I hate to be the one to break it to you, partner, but you ain't the one she came up here for."

Logan and Eb made it into Coulter Creek that evening. They went by the stockyards and found Logan's friends mucking out stalls at the livery. Tim and Matt Culhane were brothers. The other boy was Bob Miller. They were all in their late teens.

"You boys want a job herding cows on the Lonesome for a couple of months?" Logan asked.

"Yes sir, we do," Matt said.

"Meet us at the hotel at daylight in the morning," Eb said.

"We'll be there."

After checking in at the hotel and having supper, Eb and Logan headed for the Jersey Rose Saloon. Ms. Charity came over and sat with them for a while. She apologized for treating Eb so badly the last time they met.

"I was just trying to make you jealous," she said, "I thought Scarlett was with you."

"That's alright, but you got my partner in a lot of trouble."

"Why do you say that?"

"Bolt and Scarlett have quite a little romance going on. I think my partner is serious about this one."

"Well, I'm glad to hear it, Bolt deserves a little happiness."

"What about me?" Eb asked.

"Your turn will come," she said, "I'm sure of it."

"It better come pretty soon," Logan said with big grin, "he ain't getting any younger."

"Mind your elders, Boy," Eb said, as Charity laughed.

Next afternoon, Eb and Logan got back to the ranch with the new hands. They introduced the boys to everyone and helped them get settled in the bunkhouse. That night at supper, Coop was explaining what he had planned.

"Bolt, you take these three boys up to the Dancing Grounds in the morning and show them around a little. Bring Creek and TJ back with you. We'll get started rounding up the cows on this end of the ranch."

"I'd like to go with you," Rafe said.

"I'd like to see the Devil's Dancing Grounds," Angelia said.

"You go right ahead," Spud said, "I'll take care of the cooking tomorrow night."

Sundown found Lone Elk a day's ride from the Lonesome Wind. He made camp in a little coulee to avoid detection. It was a quiet evening on the high plains. The wind was unusually still. A warm golden glow and an uneasy quiet engulfed the land.

The mighty Sioux had forgone eating for two days as Wind in the Grass instructed. He gathered a supply of greasewood to start a fire and placed a small pot of water in the flames to heat.

Lone Elk opened the pouch Wind in the Grass had given him and emptied the contents into the boiling water. The pouch contained leaves and stems from several different plants. There were dried purple berries, black seed-heads, and bits of dried meat that Lone Elk didn't recognize. He let the mixture steep while the water cooled.

When it was cool enough to drink, he lifted the dark liquid to his lips. It smelled sickly sweet and pungent, like a carcass just beginning to rot. When he took the first sip, it tasted sharp, with just a hint of sweetness. The mighty Sioux turned it up and forced it all down.

The warrior sat alone in the fading light, listening to the silence. When a west wind began to ruffle the buffalo grass, Lone Elk felt anxious and unsettled. It was then the mighty Sioux became aware of a massive buffalo bull approaching from the east. Lone Elk sat and watched as the great bull came right into his camp. Normally, Lone Elk would have taken up his rifle and killed the bull. This time he sat quiet. He knew this great Tatanka was a messenger. The buffalo was pawing the ground and shaking his head as if he wanted Lone Elk to challenge him.

Lone Elk got to his feet to face the great bull. The sky overhead grew dark as the mighty Sioux tried to understand the reason for the bull's presence. His thoughts were cut short when the bull lowered his head and came for him. Stepping aside as the bull passed, Lone Elk instinctively grabbed a handful of hair and swung up on the beast's back. It took all the Indian's strength to cling to the wooly hump as the bull started north across the plains.

When the buffalo came to the end of their journey, he dumped Lone Elk onto an empty salt-sage flat. The ground underneath Lone Elk was bare hardpan. There were brilliant stars showing between fleeting clouds and a full moon. His surroundings were tangible, but not sharply focused. The pale light revealed no colors, only shadows of muted gray and black.

As Lone Elk considered his circumstances, he became aware of a huge grizzly stalking toward him across the flats. The mighty Sioux tried to get up and flee, but he was unable to stand. When the great bear got close, he rose up to tower over the Indian. Lone Elk had never seen an animal to match the one that stood before him now. When the fierce one dropped down, he began to roar. Lone Elk could see his fangs and feel his hot breath as the raging beast came to stand over him. The grizzly was hatred, rage, and vengeance incarnate.

Lone Elk shielded his eyes with a forearm, unwilling to witness the fate about to befall him. He was awaiting the first terrible bite when the grizzly grew quiet and Lone Elk heard the rumble of distant thunder. Finding the courage to lower his am and open his eyes, Lone Elk saw the bear was still with him, but watching something in the distance.

Gathering his wits, Lone Elk sat up. When the great bear turned back, their eyes were mere inches apart. Lone Elk's fear began to fade as he stared into those eyes. The grizzly was the most feared animal on the plains but there was a quiet strength about him. Honor and nobility were there as well. Lone Elk realized this grizzly was his totem, a kindred spirit, and a teacher.

The grizzly had shown Lone Elk what he had once been. Now the bear was telling him it was time to be something else. The grizzly looked back to the north just before turning away.

When the great bear was gone, Lone Elk spotted two figures riding up on him. One seemed to be white men mounted on a gray horse. The other figure wore a flowing black cape. The hood covering his head revealed no discernible features. This dreadful apparition rode a terrible coal-black animal, surrounded by a dark mist. The demon was wearing twin pistols and holding a bloody saber. Lone Elk knew he was about to come face-to-face with the spirit warrior.

Remembering the warning from the old woman, Lone Elk knew he was going to die, and there was nothing he could do about it. He attempted to yell to mask his fear, to die like a warrior should, but he couldn't make a sound.

As the riders drew near, they began to gallop close to each other. Lone Elk watched as the mist dissolved and the two figures became one. When the one man came close, Lone Elk could see that his hands were empty. Lone Elk had seen him before, he knew the one man to be, Buffalo Grass Rider.

"Do not fear the spirit warrior," the one man said, "He is not your enemy. The words of Buffalo Grass Rider are true? Your blood and my blood are one. There should be peace between us."

As Buffalo Grass Rider turned to ride away, Lone Elk tried to call him back. He didn't understand what Buffalo Grass Rider meant about the blood, but Buffalo Grass Rider never looked back.

When Lone Elk was alone again, there was a jagged bolt of lightning and deafening thunder. A driving rain began to pummel the mighty Sioux as he regained the use of his body and struggled to his feet. His long hair swirled about his face as a howling west wind engulfed him.

The great bull emerged out of the tempest and once again, Lone Elk swung up on his back. The buffalo messenger carried him south until the cleansing storm subsided. When silence returned to the plains, the buffalo messenger dumped the Indian in the grass and vanished.

When Lone Elk's senses began to return, he found himself back in his camp. He was lying on the ground, soaking wet, and gasping for breath, his heart was nearly beating its way out of his chest.

When Lone Elk sat up, he was surprised to find a rather heavy-set, but kindly looking old Indian woman warming herself by his fire. The mighty Sioux didn't know her, but she knew him.

"I miss the comfort of a good fire," she said, rubbing her hands together.

"Who are you, Grandmother?" he asked, not knowing if she was part of his vision or if she was real.

The old woman didn't answer his question. Instead, she began to tell him a story.

"Many generations ago, the grandfathers lived in the big forest far to the east. One of your grandmothers was a young maiden when a raiding party of strange Indians came from the south. There was a long fight before the strangers were finally driven away. One of their numbers was a strong and proud warrior known as Bear Heart. He was wounded in the battle, but he fought so bravely, our people took him in to heal.

"After many months with our people, he fell in love with the maiden. They lived happy lives together and had sons and daughters. Bear Heart could speak to the spirits and foretell the future. You, my son, are descended from his bloodline."

The old woman poked the fire with a stick and continued. "Bear Heart was the son of a mighty warrior known as Ten Thunders. He lived in the mountains of the southern forests. Ten Thunders was a holy man and a prophet, but he was first, a feared warrior. His courage and strength were only matched by his savage and sometimes brutal ways."

"Why are you telling me this?" Lone Elk asked.

Getting to her feet, the old woman approached and stood over Lone Elk. She reached down and touched the pit of his stomach.

"Buffalo Grass Rider also carries the blood of Ten Thunders. But, be warned my son, Buffalo Grass Rider has a demon spirit that you do not have. Ten Thunders was possessed by a dark and dangerous demon, a warrior spirit. It was easily called out when he was angered. The demon, once released, would bring death and destruction to anyone who challenged it. That demon spirit made Ten Thunders a legendary warrior, but his fame came at great cost."

"Ten Thunders fought to control the spirit all of his life. After many years of prayer and ceremony, he defeated the demon, but it did not die. Ten Thunders told the people that the spirit would rise again in a future generation, and now it has. The warrior spirit lives within Buffalo Grass Rider."

"He is the most dangerous man you will ever face, but do not fear him. Like Ten Thunders and Lone Elk, Buffalo Grass Rider has a good heart with courage and honor. The same blood flows within you both. There should be peace between you. When you find Buffalo Grass Rider, meet him with empty hands."

When she was finished speaking, the old woman faded away.

The buffalo grass settled as the wind died once again and color returned to the world. Lone Elk still lacked the strength to get to his feet. The spot where the old woman had touched him began to burn and he became violently sick to his stomach. The liquid he spit up was black as pitch. The vile flux was the hatred he had been harboring in his spirit.

After several minutes, Lone Elk finally managed to get up. Brushing his hair back, he found himself completely alone in the perfect stillness and solitude of the vast Montana landscape.

It was a glorious September morning. Bolt saddled Rufus and another horse for Angelia. Rafe would ride double with his mother for a while and then with Bolt.

"I'll miss you until you get back," Scarlett whispered in his ear as he hugged her goodbye. "Rafe, you take care of him for me," she said. "Say hello to Creek and TJ."

Little did Scarlett know, but it was Angelia's plan to finally get Bolt alone with just her and their son. It would be a good chance to show him what life could be like if they were a family. The three new cowboys were ready to ride. They were glad to be part of the Bunch from The Lonesome Wind.

Latigo Lane and his small gang of cutthroats decided to bypass the herd and go directly to the ranch house. They intended to kill as many

Lonesome Wind riders as possible and leave the herd for the other men that Star was sending.

Lane had just six men with him. Not only was he evil, he was foolishly overconfident. The group of outlaws were only a few miles from the house when they spotted Bolt and the others approaching. They put their horses behind a hill and quickly set up an ambush.

Bolt was riding double with Rafe when he heard the first gunshots. At first he couldn't believe his ears, he was in shock that someone would ambush them right there on the Lonesome.

Bullets were slashing through the tall grass as he spurred Rufus toward Cottonwood Creek and down into a little coulee for some cover. He pulled Rafe off the back of his saddle and dropped him into a deep washout.

"Stay there until I come and get you! No matter what happens, you hear me, no matter what!"

Rafe crawled down into the gully and curled up into a ball. He was scared, but he would obey Bolt.

Bolt bailed off Rufus, pulled his rifle, and looked around for the Culhane boys. They had taken cover with him. Bob Miller never made it to cover. He was lying dead in the grass. Angelia was off her horse, lying behind some sagebrush.

Bolt began firing at the outlaws on the hill. Most of the horses had run off except Rufus, he was in the brush nearby. Angelia was screaming for her son.

"He's alright!" Bolt shouted at her, "Stay down and be still!"

When the Culhane brothers stopped firing, Bolt could see they were both hit, leaving him alone to defend his son. Bolt managed to kill two of the outlaws before he got hit for the first time. The bullet went in his thigh just above the knee. Blood was pouring from the hole and the pain was terrible, but there was no time to do anything about it.

Bolt had no way to know how many men were out there. He was glad Scarlett hadn't come with them. He promised to live the rest of his life with her, now it looked like his life might be over. When he saw one man lift up for a better look, he laid the front sight on him and fired. The outlaw died instantly when the .45-60 slug hit him.

Suddenly, Bolt was hit again. This time it was in the left arm. He couldn't fire the Henry anymore so he used his one good hand to pull his Colt. Thinking he was done for, Bolt figured his only chance to save Angelia and his son was to kill the rest of the men on the hill before he passed out or died. The pain turned into rage as the demon spirit came forth. Bolt struggled to his feet and started up the hill.

The unnerved gunmen on the hill launched a blistering string of fire as Bolt came right at them. Two more of them were killed as Bolt charged up the hill yelling at the top of his lungs and firing his Colt. He made it most of the way up the hill before he was hit for the third time.

A wave of weakness and pain washed over Bolt as the bullet slammed into his chest. The strength drained from his body and he fell on his side. Lying in the short grass, he could see Angelia screaming as she ran to him, but he could no longer hear her. It was a new experience. The demon had never been knocked off his feet before. Defeat was an unknown thing to him. Bolt's sight began to fade, but not before he saw the man that shot him.

The outlaw moving toward Angelia was dressed all in black. As bad as he wanted to, Bolt couldn't move or speak. The edges of his vision began to turn dark. He thought of his lover and that he let her down by dying. He thought about Eb, he knew he would take care of her, and then he was gone. Angelia and Rafe were alone and helpless.

Bolt managed to kill four of the outlaws, but not Lane. The gunman didn't give Bolt another thought as he stepped over his body and grabbed Angelia. She was hysterical and clinging to Bolt's body as Lane tried to get her on her feet. Her mind could not accept the fact Bolt was gone, not now, not after all she had been through to find him. She was terrified the gunmen surrounding her might not spare the life of her little boy.

"We don't have enough men to move this herd now," Lane said, as the two remaining members of the gang brought their horses down in the coulee. "We'll take the woman and head back toward Frenchy's. The others can get the cows. If there are any riders left on this ranch, they won't be much trouble. I always wanted one of these Henry's" he said, picking up Bolt's rifle.

In spite of Angelia begging him not to take her, they put her up on a horse and tied her hands to the saddle horn. When Rafe saw them taking his mother, he came out of his hiding place and attacked the outlaws. Lane was already in the saddle when he turned to see the boy coming at him.

When Rafe got close enough, Lane kicked him in the face, sending the boy tumbling down the steep side of the coulee. Lane drew his pistol and fired as Rafe rolled into the bottom and lay still. Angelia was screaming for her son as they led her away

Rafe could taste blood in his mouth when he finally woke up and tried to get to his feet. By some minor miracle, Lane's bullet passed under the youngster's arm, leaving only a bloody streak on his chest as he tumbled down the hill.

When the boy managed to crawl to the top of the coulee, he could see dead men all around him. Lane and the other gunmen were far off in the distance, headed north with his mother.

Rafe knelt in the grass trying to make sense of the unspeakable violence that had just gone on around him. He was alone, but there was no time for feeling sorry for himself. The dirt on his face was streaked with tears, but he wasn't crying. The hot Ashton blood in him was raging. His anger growing by the minute, he knew he had to get help for his mother before it was too late.

The youngster knew he was north of the house, Logan told him how to tell north from south by the sun's position in the sky. The boy knew which way to go, but he needed a horse.

Rafe crawled over to Bolt's body and picked up his pistol. He was on his hands and knees, trying to clear his head and looking around for Rufus. When he pushed against Bolt's body to get up, Bolt groaned. The old cowboy wasn't dead after all and Rafe was filled with hope. He didn't know exactly what to do, but he was a Montana cowboy. He wasn't going to just sit there and let his friend die.

The first two bullets had been flesh wounds. They hadn't hit any bones on their way through Bolt's body, but they were bleeding badly. The bullet that struck him in the chest was from a small caliber pistol, a backup belly gun Lane carried. He emptied his other gun and didn't have time to reload when Bolt started up the hill.

The small caliber bullet had hit a rib, deflected around Bolt's vital organs, and traveled down along his ribcage before coming to rest against his spine. The shock had been too much for his nervous system and it shut down.

Bolt was too weak to speak or move and he lapsed back into unconsciousness. Rafe knew he had to stop the bleeding. He used the neckerchiefs from the others to bind up Bolt's wounds as best he could.

The boy covered Bolt with Matt's duster to keep him warm until he could get to the ranch for some help. Rafe was looking for Rufus when he heard another horse behind him. The youngster spun around and his fear returned in an instant.

Rafe had never seen an Indian like the one watching him now. There were a few Yaqui Indians around his village in Mexico, but they didn't look anything like the warrior looking down at him.

The Indian was dressed in buckskin leggings. He was powerfully built with a bare chest and big shoulders. He had an Eagle feather tied in his long black hair. The mighty Sioux swung his leg over and slid off his pony. He was carrying a rifle as he approached.

Rafe picked up Bolt's pistol, pointed it at the Indian, and pulled the trigger. Rafe didn't know about cocking the hammer before the Colt would go off, even if he had, it wouldn't have done any good, the pistol was empty. When he was close enough, the Indian took the gun from the boy's hands.

"Do not fear me little one," he said in Sioux, "I am not your enemy." Rafe didn't understand the words this warrior was saying, but he understood his meaning.

Lone Elk had been traveling to the Lonesome when he heard gunshots. Being careful to approach unseen, he saw the white man charge up the hill only to go down in a hail storm of bullets. The mighty Sioux watched as the man risked his life to protect the woman and child. The outlaws were gone before Lone Elk could help the woman.

The Sioux inspected Bolt's wounds then rolled him over. He wasn't surprised when he recognized the man from his vision. The wounded man was the same one that saved his life near the Belle Fourche River.

"Buffalo Grass Rider," the Indian said in Sioux, "we meet again."

Lone Elk saw Rufus standing in the brush and realized he was the pale horse he was chasing when his pony fell. It all made sense to him now. Buffalo Grass Rider was the same fearless warrior that killed his cousins, and he had shown that bravery again today.

Bolt's kindness to Lone Elk and his willingness to give his life for his family convinced Lone Elk this man was indeed Ten Thunders descendant and worth saving. After he used the shirts off the dead cowboys to make dressings for Bolt's wounds, he got Bolt's canteen.

Lone Elk found some wild onions growing in the damp ground in the bottom of the coulee. He crushed the bulbs and stems to make a poultice. It would fight infection in Bolt's wounds and stop the bleeding.

Lone Elk built a fire and heated water in a small pot. He placed the leaves and stems of a plant the Sioux called red medicine in it to make an infusion. It would help control any bleeding that was going on internally. Bolt was regaining his senses, but he was too weak to move.

Lone Elk raised Bolt's head up and offered him a horn cup with the red medicine brew to drink. "Yah-tkon," he said. Bolt was barely aware of what was going on around him as he took a sip of the liquid. He drifted away as Lone Elk went to the nearby creek bottom to cut some drag poles.

When the Indian led Rufus up in front of the rig, the big horse balked. Lone Elk pulled the horse's head around, put his face close to the big outlaw's ear and whispered to him, "Ah-bah-yeh-nah chin-yeh." Rufus calmed down and stood firm while the Sioux tied the rig to the saddle and got Bolt up on it. Lone Elk put Rafe up on his pony and swung up behind the boy. Rafe was still a little afraid, but he would never show it. His instincts told him this warrior had respect for brave men.

It was nearly sundown when Spud looked out the window and saw Lone Elk approaching.

"Coop, there's an Indian coming up to the house."

"Probably some beggar looking for a handout," Eb said.

"I don't think so," Spud replied, "he's leading Rufus and he's got little Rafe with him."

Logan yanked a rifle out of the rack in the front room as he ran for the door. They all came out of the house to meet this warrior with guns drawn.

"Don't shoot him!" Rafe yelled, "He helped us, Bolt's hurt bad."

Lone Elk slid off his pony and helped the boy down. He was trying to explain in Sioux. Spud knew just a little Sioux. He was doing his best to communicate with the Indian until Crowfoot came out of the house and spoke to Lone Elk.

"He says some men ambushed Bolt seven or eight miles north," Crowfoot said. "It sounds like it was up around Cottonwood. Bolt killed some of them before he went down. All the other boys are dead, the outlaws have taken Angelia."

They watched as Scarlett came running from her house. She was in a panic when she saw Bolt lying bloody and lifeless on the travois. "Get him into my bed and let's get these bloody clothes off of him."

Lone Elk and Eb carried Bolt into the house. Scarlett began to remove the blood-soaked bandages when Lone Elk placed his hand on hers and spoke to her in Sioux.

"Leave the poultice in place," Crowfoot said, "it's controlling the bleeding. Removing it will start the blood flow again. Cut his clothes off around them and add a clean bandage on top."

After cleaning him up and adding fresh bandages to Bolt's wounds, they made him as comfortable as possible. Scarlett listened with the rest as Lone Elk told them what happened. Lone Elk pointed to the blood stains on Rafe's shirt, they assumed it was from his bloody nose.

"The boy's been shot," Crowfoot said. Scarlett pulled up the youngster's shirt, exposing the ugly open wound as Lone Elk told them about Lane trying to kill the boy.

"Logan," Eb said, his face reddening, "Go to Coulter Creek for the doctor and don't spare your horse. Take two mounts, ride one till he's done and turn him loose. The second one should get you there."

"Yes Sir, I'm on my way!"

"Coop," Eb continued, "You and Spud stay here to protect the place in case they come back here."

"What are you gonna do?" Coop asked.

"Crowfoot and I will get Creek and TJ from the Dancing Grounds and go after them. This time I'm gonna kill 'em all."

"Kill who?"

"You know it was LeConte or some more of Star's men. They're the only ones that would want all of us dead. That Frenchman at Salt Springs must have told them who we were." Eb's face was bright red as he spoke, "Coop, they shot the boy … the dirty sons-o'-bitch's tried to kill that little boy. We should've killed all of them when we had the chance."

"You may be right," Coop said, "I guess this is on me."

"Don't worry, Boss," Crowfoot said, "They ain't gonna get away with this…not this!"

Coop was in the corral helping Crowfoot saddle the horses while Eb went for their gear. Logan came out of the barn leading two horses from his string.

"Aren't you taking Sandy?" Coop asked.

"I'll need him when I get back," Logan said. He swung up on the first horse and put the gut-hooks to him.

"Be careful!" Coop yelled after him.

Logan was gone in a moment, and dragging a second horse just like Eb told him. He wanted to get to Coulter Creek and back as soon as he could. Logan wanted to go with Eb and Crowfoot, but he knew Bolt needed him. He could get to the doctor faster than anyone else there. Logan intended to do whatever was necessary in order to get the help Bolt needed and still be on hand when the killers met the Bunch from the Lonesome Wind.

Eb and Crowfoot left right after Logan. They were galloping north to get Creek and TJ. They would go by Cottonwood and pick up the outlaw's tracks to get a general direction on where they were headed.

Eb already had a notion they were going to Salt Springs. He wanted to get there in time to save Angelia.

Lone Elk was going out the door when Scarlett touched his arm. He was the first Indian she had ever been close to. Spud was translating for her.

"Thank you for bringing him and the boy back here to me."

"Buffalo Grass Rider did the same for me several moons ago on the Belle Fourche River. He is a brave man and deserves to live a long life. Are you his woman?"

"Yes, I am his woman. How do you know his name?"

"He is known to many. He is my brother."

"I owe you a great debt for helping him," Scarlett said. She wasn't sure what Lone Elk meant about Bolt being his brother. She thought it must be some Indian superstition having to do with saving his life.

"You owe me nothing," he said. "A great load is off my shoulders now. The hate in my heart is gone and I will try to live an honorable peace forever."

The warrior wore a single grizzly claw on a rawhide thong. Pulling it up over his head, he turned to Rafe.

"You are a fierce warrior, little one, just like your father and Ten Thunders. I will call you the Fierce One, and my little brother."

Rafe thanked him for the necklace as he walked out the door beside him. The youngster was in awe of this mighty Sioux. Lone Elk was a force of nature and larger than life to Rafe.

"Bolt's not my father," Rafe said as they got outside, "He's my friend. I don't know my real father."

The mighty Sioux placed his hand on the boy's shoulder. "You are mistaken, little one. Anyone can see you are Buffalo Grass Rider's son. You share all his qualities as well as his courage. Our grandfathers are proud of you both."

Lone Elk gave Spud the pouch of red medicine leaves and told him how to make the infusion. He said it would help build back the blood Bolt lost and keep down any infection.

Spud asked Lone Elk to wait for one moment. The old cook rushed to the kitchen and returned with a package. Handing it to Rafe, he motioned toward Lone Elk. It was a small sack of coffee. Spud knew it was a custom of the Sioux to offer a gift in return for a gift. Rafe handed the package to the mighty Sioux.

"Black medicine," Lone Elk said, sniffing the package, "thank you, little brother." The Sioux were familiar with coffee, but had little access to it.

Without any further words, Lone Elk swung up on his pony and rode away. Rafe watched him go until he was out of site. He would remember this warrior for the rest of his life. Scarlett had tears in her eyes as Lone Elk rode out of their lives. Everything she thought she knew about Indians was completely wrong. Lone Elk was a noble and honorable man. Rafe didn't know it at the time, but the blood he shared with the mighty Sioux would draw them back together one day.

Confident they had nothing more to fear, the outlaws made camp that evening by a little grove of trees. The rest of their friends would be along soon and anyone left at the Lonesome would be too afraid to follow them.

"Bring that woman over here to me," Lane said. Angelia was exhausted, nearly in a stupor. She thought Bolt and Rafe were both dead and she had little to live for. Standing over her, Lane tore at her blouse, exposing her breasts. "I'm going to show you how a real man treats a woman." When Lane took out his knife he had strange, almost insane look on his face. Angelia screamed as he started down on her.

As Lane began to draw the blade across her chest, he was suddenly knocked backwards onto his back, his head bloodied from the blow one of the others had just given him.

"Leave her alone you sick bastard," the outlaw demanded. He was still holding the piece of firewood he struck Lane with. "Shooting men and stealing cattle is one thing, but you ain't gonna skin no woman as long as I'm alive."

"That's right," the other man said, "Killing that kid was just plain murder; we never signed on for anything like that."

The first outlaw turned to Angelia, "Get on your horse and get out of here. We'll take care of this one."

Angelia got up and ran to her horse as the first man held his gun on Lane. The outlaw made the mistake of looking away for a moment, prompting Lane to grab for his pistol.

The first gunman fired first, hitting Lane in the upper chest. Even though he was hit and lying on the ground, Lane fired at the man who shot him. The bullet went through the outlaw's chest as Lane fired at the second man. Both outlaws were down and dying when Lane struggled to his feet.

He could see Angelia off in the distance, trying to get away from the gunfire behind her. Lane was too stunned to ride, and he was bleeding badly from his bullet wound. Realizing he would never catch her, but unwilling to allow her escape, Lane stumbled to his horse and pulled Bolt's rifle from the scabbard. The blood-crazed killer laid the rifle across his saddle and drew a bead on Angelia's back.

Logan switched horses after two hours. He turned his first mount loose, cinched his saddle on the second and thundered off into the night. He reached Coulter Creek just before midnight.

Going straight to the Doctor's house, he began pounding on the door. After several minutes the bleary-eyed doctor opened his door.

"What's so all fired important to get me out of bed at this hour?"

"Doc, we need you out at the Lonesome," Logan said, "Bolt's been shot. I think he's real bad."

"I'll get my bag; it'll just be a minute."

"I ain't waiting for you. I got some killing to do."

Logan went down the street to the small house sitting next to the livery stable. He was beating on the door when old Bill Weems yanked it open and pointed a double-barreled shotgun in his face.

"Logan," Weems said, lowering the scatter gun, "What are you doing out at this hour, I damn near shot you."

"I need two fresh horses. A bunch of gunmen ambushed Bolt. They killed the Culhane boys and Bob Miller. I came in for the Doc. I need the best you got to go after them."

"Alright, Son, go pick 'em out, I'll be right there."

Logan pulled his saddle off his lathered horse, grabbed a dry saddle blanket from the rail, and cinched his rig on one of Bill's fresh horses. He threw a lead rope on the other one.

"Take care of this horse," he said, swinging up in the saddle, "put it all on Coop's bill, we'll settle up later."

"Forget that, you be careful," Bill yelled at his back as Logan pulled his horse around and spurred him out into the dark.

The Doc was coming down the street when he saw a lantern at the livery stable.

"I need my horse," he said.

"I already got him saddled," Bill said.

Logan was headed northwest with two fresh horses. A big prairie moon was hanging high over his shoulder, lighting his way. The dark road echoed with rattling hoof beats as the youngster did his best to outrun the galloping shadow just off to his right.

Chapter Fifteen:
Retribution at Salt Springs

Yanked out of a sound sleep, Creek and TJ could hear riders coming hard in the darkness.

"I wonder who that is," TJ said, reaching for his rifle.

"I don't know, but it can't be good news."

"That looks like Crowfoot's appaloosa," TJ said when they got close. "Get saddled, looks like we got work to do."

Eb bailed off his heaving, sweat-soaked horse and pulled his saddle. He cinched it on one of the spare horses the boys had with them.

"What's going on?" Creek asked.

"Ambush in Cottonwood," Crowfoot said, "A bunch of gunmen jumped Bolt. Angelia and the boy were with him!"

"What happened?" Creek asked, "Are any of them hurt?"

"Bolt's hurt bad," Eb said, "Rafe's going to be alright, but the other boys are dead." Eb fastened the chin strap on his bridle and shoved his shotgun down the scabbard. "They got Angelia. I think they're headed back to Salt Springs. We got some killing to do."

"They've got Angelia!" Creek repeated.

"That's what I said. Now get on that damn horse while she still has a chance."

Creek swung up on his horse and followed Eb off the hill. They headed northwest toward the Musselshell and Salt Springs. They had to spare their mounts now, as there were no fresh horses to be had anywhere. It would take the rest of the night and most of the next day to reach the trading post.

Logan made it back to the Lonesome by dawn. His worn-out lathered horse was standing in the corral as he was saddling Sandy. The sun was just coming up when Coop came out of the house. "What are you doing?"

"I'm heading to Salt Springs. That's where I think they'll go, how's Bolt?"

"Bolt's alive, where's the doctor?"

"He should be right behind me."

"Why don't you rest a spell?"

"There's no time," Logan said, "I'm going after Eb. I want to be there when he catches the bunch that did this."

"You're not going anywhere, boy. You need some hot food and a little sleep. You won't be any good to Eb if you can't keep your eyes open."

"Sorry Boss, you're the big augur around here and I owe you a lot. I mean no disrespect, but this is one time I can't do as you say. Bolt's my best…I…I got to go!"

"Logan, hold on!" Spud shouted emerging from the house. When he reached the corral, he handed Logan a freshly-filled canteen and a small pouch of jerky.

"Thanks," Logan said. The young cowboy swung up on his dancing horse, slung the canteen over his saddle horn, and stuffed the jerky in the front of his shirt.

Sandy had already sensed urgency in the man on his back. The little Mustang was wound up tight and ready to run. He was spinning in tight little circles, as Logan pulled his hat down across his eyebrows and leaned into the little horse's neck.

"Get!" he said as he touched the Mustang with his spurs. Sandy came up on his hind legs and lunged forward. They were gone before Coop could say anything else. The hoof beats faded away as horse and rider were swallowed up by a rolling dust cloud.

The doctor arrived two hours later. He went in to Bolt and dressed his wounds with antiseptic. He worked all morning at the delicate job of removing the bullet from Bolt's back. After he was through, he gave Bolt something for the pain and to keep him asleep.

"I don't know what's in those herbs the Indian left for you," Doc said, "but keep using it. I believe in many of their remedies and this one seems to have saved his life. He's lost a lot of blood, but I don't think there's any permanent damage from his wounds.

"If we can keep them from becoming infected he's got a chance. He needs fluids. Give him lots of water and feed him all the hot broth he will take. Give him as much of that Indian tea as he can stand as well. Other than that, keep him in bed and make him rest. He'll sleep all afternoon and most of the night with this drug I've given him, but someone needs to stay with him."

"I'm not going to leave his side," Scarlett said.

"I'll keep the tea and broth coming when he wakes up," Spud said.

"Somebody better get a rope and tie him down," Coop said. "When he wakes up and finds out they tried to kill the boy, he'll be out for blood."

"That bunch of killers made one hell of a mistake when they shot this hardheaded hillbilly, I guarantee," Spud said.

"Thank you for making that long ride, Doctor," Scarlett said, "won't you have some supper and spend the night?"

"Thank you kindly ma'am," he said, "I think I'll do just that. In fact, I may stay for a couple of days. I left word in town where I'd be. I want to check on Bolt and change his dressings until he makes a turn for the better. I think the world of this old boy; we can't afford to lose any more like him."

It was late and all was quiet at the Lonesome. Spud was on guard out by the cavvy corral. Coop was dozing in the darkened living room with the front door opened. The only light was from a single oil lamp in Scarlett's house. Scarlett sat by the bed reading out loud to her cowboy. When she finished, she placed the book on the bed and bent over to whisper in his ear.

"I love you cowboy, don't you go and leave me all alone. Do you hear me?" Kissing him on the forehead, she went back to her reading.

It was nearly dawn the next morning when Eb and the boys met Angelia's horse coming south. They knew things were bad when they found blood on the saddle. It was several hours later when they found the outlaw's campsite. They were in shock when they discovered Angelia's body. She had been cut several times and shot in the back. They had no idea what had gone on, but it seemed as if she was trying to get away when someone killed her.

They didn't know what to think about the dead men. It appeared as if there was some kind of violent argument among the gunmen. Tracks indicated the outlaw's horses had headed off toward the northwest.

"There's nothing more we can do for her now," Crowfoot said, kneeling in the grass. "Let's bury her and get after the men who killed her. We can cry about this later."

Eb wrapped her in his duster. He was wiping his eyes as he covered her body. There wasn't time to bury the outlaws, but they all felt somehow at least one of them must have tried to help Angelia.

Eb almost couldn't bear the thought of throwing dirt in on Angelia. He didn't want to leave her there alone, but there was nothing else to do. The old cowboy couldn't fight it any longer and he finally broke down.

The men with him didn't know what to do. Eb had never been anything but a crusty old wrangler. They were hurting as they turned away from him, trying to give him some privacy.

When they all finally pulled themselves together, Crowfoot said a word of prayer over her grave. Eb stood, hat in hand, but he was praying in his own way.

"Lord, you know I'm not a praying man and you've never heard from me much. My partner puts a lot of stock in you, and I...well, I'm beginning to. I'll try not to bother you too much, but Lord, please guide me to the sons-o'...the men responsible for this and keep these other boys safe while I do what has to be done. Thank you for sparing the little one, and if you will, Lord, please help my partner to pull through. I ain't much good without him."

Eb never said a word to his companions, just wiped his eyes, got on his horse, and thundered off toward Frenchy's trading post.

"I've never seen Eb like this," Creek said.

"There'll be hell to pay when we catch up to these killers," TJ vowed.

"Eb loved Angelia like a daughter," Crowfoot said, "Bolt's his best friend. If he dies, I don't know how he'll ever get over this."

TJ wasn't able to hold back the tears running down his cheek. "What's that kid going to do without his momma? Those dirty sons-o'-

bitches are going to pay dearly for all of this. They're gonna die wishing they'd never heard of the Bunch from the Lonesome Wind."

Creek swung up in his saddle and wiped his nose on his sleeve. "Damn right. It'll be a bad day for their mothers when we catch this bunch."

Spurring their horses, the boys galloped off after Eb.

The sun was down as Eb and the boys slipped up to the trading post in Salt Springs. They left the horses in the trees just down the road and eased up to the porch on foot.

"This is deadly business, boys," Eb warned, "They're all killers and we're outnumbered. I don't know how many are in there, and I don't give a damn. We have to kill 'em all. If you hesitate, you may get yourself killed."

"Don't worry about us," Creek said. "We're with you all the way on this one. This bunch needs killing, and we're the ones to do it."

The men inside were Star's riders who were supposed to get the cattle from the Lonesome. They seemed to be sharing a laugh about something. Frenchy was behind the bar laughing right along with the rest of them. Eb could see him after chancing a glance through the window.

"Near as I can tell, they're laughing about what they did to Angelia."

"Those dirty. . . ." Creek was in a rage, his face bright red.

"How do they know about that?" Crowfoot asked.

"I don't know," Eb said, "But they're talking about a Mexican woman and someone named Lane."

"Kick that damn door and let's get on with it," TJ said.

"Hold on," Crowfoot said, "We need a plan. Eb, you and the boys take the front door. I'll throw this bench through the window on the side to distract them. It'll give you a second to get in the door. I'll come through the window, don't shoot me."

Eb nodded his agreement as he checked his shotgun. He had recently traded his old front-stuffer Greener for a new 1874 Remington 12 gauge double with twenty-inch barrels. The Remington was a breech-loader. Using black powder shot shells, it could be reloaded in a jiffy, and the short barrel length made it deadly in close quarters.

Eb cocked both hammers and walked up on the porch.

"Ready?" he asked. Creek and TJ nodded. Both of them were holding their Colts.

When Crowfoot threw the bench through the window, Eb kicked in the door and fired the right barrel at the nearest table. Creek and TJ began shooting everything that moved.

The outlaws were caught completely off guard. One of them tried to draw on Eb, but he didn't have a chance. Eb shot him in the chest with the left barrel, driving him across the room. Some of the outlaws died without firing a shot. Facing the men from the Lonesome Wind in a fair fight was not what they planned to do that night.

Dropping the empty scattergun, Eb pulled his Colt. After a dozen more shots, the room fell silent. Frenchy was behind the counter holding his hands in the air. He was so frightened he wet on himself.

Eb's face was flushed. Believing Frenchy responsible for most of this, he wanted to kill the Frenchman worse than he ever wanted to kill anybody. "Alright you son-of-a-bitch, who were these men working for?" Frenchy just shrugged his shoulders.

As Eb was speaking, he holstered his Colt, reloaded his shotgun, and fired the first barrel into the wall behind Frenchy's head. The whiskey bottles exploded all over the big Frenchman.

"I'm not going to ask you twice," Eb warned.

"Alright, alright," Frenchy said. "These men work for Rex Star. He runs the Silver Dollar Saloon in Whiskey Hill. Star told these men to make an example of you and everybody at your place. He said other ranchers would be afraid to fight back."

"He don't know a whole lot about cowboys, does he?" TJ asked.

"Which one of these mongrels killed the Mexican woman last night?" Eb asked.

"No one killed a woman."

"She was dead when we found her, along with two other men."

"I suppose the dead men are the ones who killed her," Frenchy said.

"Then who killed them? And who used a knife on her?"

When a knife was mentioned, Frenchy knew who Eb was probably talking about.

"The man with the knife is not here," he said. "His name is Latigo Lane. He's badly wounded and needed a doctor. Lane claimed to have had his way with the Mexican woman and left her behind. He said his men were killed and he was wounded fighting off the riders from the Lonesome Wind."

"He's a lying son of a bitch," Eb said.

"Lane is a seriously deranged man," Frenchy said, "If anyone killed that woman, it was him."

"That's Bolt's rifle leaning in the corner behind the bar," Crowfoot said, "I'd recognize it anywhere."

"Where'd you get that rifle?" Eb demanded, "And don't lie."

"They gave it to me."

"As payment for information, I'll bet," Eb said, "You told them we were here the first time and where to find us. Then you take my best friend's rifle as payment. You sent them to kill a child, a woman, and my best friend."

Realizing Eb was going to kill him, Frenchy made a desperate attempt to reach a gun hidden under the bar. Eb let him have the other barrel of the shotgun, decorating the back wall with the Frenchman's blood.

There was whiskey all over the floor as Eb opened the breech, dumped the empties, and reloaded his shotgun. He noticed a barrel labeled COAL OIL in the corner. He pulled the front trigger, shattering the barrel and spilling its contents. Creek threw a lamp into the spreading oil and flames erupted in the room.

"That'll give them a little taste of hell before they can get there," Creek said.

There was a whiskey bottle still on the bar with several glasses. Eb poured them all a drink to steady their nerves. The flames were getting hot and the smoke was thick as he laid a silver dollar on the bar. Eb poured himself one more and tossed the bottle, smashing it against the wall. Fire flashed across the whiskey soaked logs. Crowfoot picked up Bolt's rifle when he walked past it.

The Bunch from the Lonesome Wind went out the door of the flaming building and got on their horses. The trading post was blazing, lighting up the night sky for miles. The black powder canisters in the storage room were exploding in the heat of the fire as the Bunch spurred their horses away from Salt Springs and into the night.

Logan could see the flashes in the western sky. He knew he was close to finding Eb and the boys. He guessed right about them heading to Salt Springs.

"We'll rest just down the trail and go on toward Whiskey Hill in the morning," Eb said. "Leave Logan a sign to follow, he'll be along soon if I know him."

The four friends eliminated a big part of Star's outfit, now they were on the way to meet him face to face. Rex Star didn't know it yet, but he made a huge error in judgment when he declared war on the Bunch from the Lonesome Wind.

Eb stopped to rest the horses around eight that evening. They put nearly ten miles behind them since leaving the trading post in Salt Springs. The night was cold and Crowfoot built a big fire as the rest laid out their bedrolls.

They planned to camp for a day, hunt for fresh meat, and finally give the horses a good rest.

"I know Logan is back there somewhere," Eb said, "We'll let him catch up. We need some news."

"Bolt's too tough to die," Crowfoot assured him, "you just keep clinging to that."

"He's probably arguing with Coop right now about saddling Rufus to come help us," Creek said.

"I hope you're right," TJ said, "It wouldn't be the same without Bolt."

Eb calmed down a little now that retribution had been delivered to some of the murderers. The men he sought now were unknown to him. He didn't have any idea how many men they would face in Whiskey Hill.

Eb wanted Rex Star and Latigo Lane. Now that he knew their names, he planned to kill both of them. There would be no discussion or regrets, every man with him knew that would be the outcome as soon as they got to Whiskey Hill. They would go slow, planning their moves from here on in. There was no one left to get word to Star, so there was no hurry.

Logan rode past the blazing building and found the small line of rocks indicating the direction Eb had gone from Salt Springs. He was nearly done in. It had been more than thirty hours since he had slept. He had worn-out five horses, and the only food he had eaten was the jerky he grabbed back at the Lonesome.

He was taking it easy on Sandy. The little horse was lathered and tired. He was still willing, but he was nearly worn-out. Logan let him drink a little from the trough at the burning trading post. The heat from the flames felt good after their long cold ride.

After another hour, Logan could see a fire and a camp ahead. He hoped it was his friends. He approached quietly, listening to the conversation. Hearing Eb's distinctive voice, he breathed a sigh of relief.

"Hello in the camp!" he shouted. "It's Logan, don't shoot, I'm coming in!"

"I can't believe you caught us that fast," Eb said, as Logan walked into the light of the fire. "How's Bolt?" he asked, anxious to know about his partner.

Logan pulled the saddle off of his little horse and scratched his ears. After turning Sandy loose, he grabbed a fork and a tin plate lying next to the fire and began scooping beans from the steaming skillet.

"Bolt...was alive...when I left," he said, through a mouthful of beans, "The doctor was...right behind me." After wolfing down a second plateful of beans and a cup of hot coffee, Logan stretched out on his bedroll. The saddle-sore youngster was sound asleep in less than a minute.

"I never saw that many men gunned down before," TJ said, still shaken from the killing in Salt Springs.

"We had no choice," Crowfoot said, "Those men would have killed us all without blinking an eye, just like they did Angelia. Scarlett and little Rafe would have been in terrible danger if they had gotten us. We did the only thing we could to protect the people we all care about."

"He's right," Eb said, "Those murderers had no qualms about killing innocent people for money. They got exactly what they deserved. If we hadn't stopped them back there, Coop and Spud would be dealing with them at the ranch right now. The men we'll face in Whiskey Hill will be just as bad or worse, but they're going to get the same as we gave that bunch back there, I'll promise you that."

TJ was looking around the perimeter of firelight.

"I can't believe we're back in that bear's territory, in the dark again."

"I wish we could have gotten some more coffee and a few supplies back at that trading post before we left," Crowfoot said.

"Now's a good time to think about that," Eb said.

"There wasn't time to think about anything with you and Creek burning the damn place down around us."

"You'll live for a day or two," Eb said.

Later that evening, the clouds covered the moon and the temperature started dropping as a wet snow began to fall. It was September, and snow wasn't unusual that time of year in the mountains. A muffled silence fell across the mountains as the snow began to cover the ground. The only sound was the cracking and popping of the wood in the fire and the sizzle of doomed snowflakes as they perished in the flames.

Having volunteered to take the watch, Creek was feeding wood to the fire while his friends slept. The ground was covered with snow in an hour, making the night seem bright, and he could see clearly for a good distance.

TJ relieved him at one a.m. "Are you alright, pardner?" he asked.

"I'm alright. I just can't imagine what kind of man would hurt a woman like that."

"I don't have an answer for that," Creek replied. "It was just pure damn evil."

"I wonder about the dead outlaws," TJ said, "Do you think they tried to help her and got killed for their trouble."

"That's the only thing that makes any sense to me," TJ said. "This man, Lane…we'll pay him what he's got coming before we're through, that's a promise." Creek said goodnight and tried to get some sleep.

The next morning was cool and clear like so many September mornings are on the plains. Rafe was sleeping near Bolt on Scarlett's bed. Scarlett was worn-out from staying up for two nights hoping for some sign that he would live. Bolt regained consciousness a few times and taken a little liquid, but he would fall right back into a deep sleep.

"Good Morning," Rafe said through a yawn as he sat up in the bed.

"Good morning," Scarlett replied, "how are you feeling this morning?"

"I'm fine, how's Bolt?"

"I'm not sure yet, he's still real sick, but we're hoping for the best."

"Lone Elk called him Buffalo Grass Rider," Rafe said, "he said Bolt's my father. Is that right, Ms. Scarlett?"

"That's something you should ask Bolt."

"What if he never wakes up?"

Scarlett studied the battered and bruised little face in front of her before she answered.

"He's going to wake up, but I don't think he'll mind me telling you," she said, "Bolt is you're father. He didn't know about you until your mother brought you here. He loves you. He would never have left you in Texas if he had known."

"I'm glad to hear that," Rafe said, "if I could pick out a dad it would be Bolt."

"Good morning," the doctor said as he walked into the room, "how is he?"

"He spent another quiet night," Scarlett said, "hardly moved a muscle."

"I want him to rest as much as possible, but he needs some nourishment. We need to wake him up."

"When will we know he'll be alright?"

"He'll let us know when he's ready," Doc said, "Scarlett, you should prepare yourself, Bolt may never be the same. His system took a real beating. He may not be the man he was."

"That'll be the day, you old pill pusher," a weak, but familiar voice said.

Scarlett was fighting back tears as she looked into Bolt's eyes.

"Good morning," she whispered.

"How are you?" Rafe asked.

"I'm fine, Son, how did we get back here?" Bolt's mind was still a blur, he didn't remember Lone Elk. "I'm glad to see you," he said to Scarlett, "I thought I was a goner there for a spell. I was afraid you would end up with Eb."

"You're not getting away from me that easy," she said, "it'll take more than a couple of bullets to keep us apart."

"What happened to your mouth?" Bolt asked the youngster when he noticed it was swollen and bruised.

"The man that shot you kicked me when I tried to help my mom."

"That's not all," Scarlett said, pulling up Rafe's shirt. "He tried to kill Rafe, but the bullet just creased him."

Bolt's face flushed. His anger was rekindled as he remembered the face of the man that shot him.

"I'll kill him for that," Bolt said, "where's Angelia?"

"The outlaws took my mom," Rafe said.

"I got to get up from here," Bolt said, rising up on his elbow, "I got to. . . ." Wincing in pain, he fell back as Scarlett put her hand on his chest.

"You aren't going anywhere. Please, tell him, Doctor."

"She's right," the doc said. "You were only minutes away from bleeding to death when the Indian found you. You've had a serious injury to your back that needs time and bed rest to heal properly. It'll be awhile before you can get around much."

"Alright Doc, I'll give it a day or two. What did you say about an Indian?"

"Lone Elk," Scarlett said.

"Who's Lone Elk?"

"Later, it's a long story."

"What about Angelia?" Bolt asked.

"Eb and the boys are after her. They left right after you got back here."

"Lone Elk told me you're my father," Rafe said.

"This may not be the right time," Scarlett said.

Bolt smiled at the youngster and put his arm around him.

"I should have been the one to tell you, Son, but I'm glad you know. Lone Elk, whoever he is, was right. I knew your mother many years ago, but I didn't know anything about you until you got here. I'm mighty glad you're here now."

"Me too," Rafe said.

Many miles to the north, Eb was jolted awake by the crack of a rifle.

"What the devil!" he exclaimed as he reached for his gun.

"Relax," Creek said. "Crowfoot went after a cow elk that wandered by here just at daylight. He figured we could all use some fresh meat."

"Good idea," Eb said, "I'm starved. That jerky is wearing out my teeth."

Crowfoot deliberately allowed the elk to get away from the camp before he shot her. He didn't want a grizzly to smell the blood and get too close to them. Crowfoot took Bolt's rifle. The .45-60 made short work of the elk. After removing the back straps, he headed back to camp. Logan was still fast asleep. The rifle shot didn't bother him in the least.

The roasting meat got everyone in a better mood and daylight eliminated the worry about the bear. The big wet flakes got smaller as the temperature fell throughout the night. The mountains were covered in a soft blanket of new snow and there was a definite chill in the high-country air that morning.

The warmth of the fire felt good to them in the cold light of dawn. The smell of food finally woke Logan and he was ready to eat.

Crowfoot jerked and roasted meat most of the day. The boy's all ate their fill and caught up on their sleep.

The horses were rested and grazing the lush green grass of the high mountain meadows. They were hard working cowponies and used to getting by on the buffalo grass of the Lonesome. This was a real treat for them, they were doing just fine without any grain.

Bolt was feeling stronger the next morning. He was still in pain from his wounds, but it seemed he would recover. Scarlett watched as he sipped at the red medicine. "What's in this stuff?"

"Lone Elk said it was an old Indian recipe to build back your blood."

"It smells like there's an old Indian still in it."

"I'm glad you think that's funny," she said, "If it wasn't for Lone Elk, you wouldn't be here right now."

Bolt was much more alert now and curious about the man that saved him.

"Who is this Lone Elk you keep talking about?"

"You saved his life along the Belle Fourche River several months ago. He was the Indian you helped and gave the horse to, the same day you found me in the river. You do remember that day, don't you?"

"I'll never forget," Bolt said with a grin. "I suppose it's a small world. Seems kind o' strange him being way up here on the Lonesome."

"He was looking for you. He knew you as Buffalo Grass Rider. Some of his family was part of that raiding party you went after in the Black Hills."

"I don't understand. Why didn't he just kill me when he had the chance?"

"Lone Elk said he followed you here to kill you, but along the way he had grown to understand your reasons for hating those Indians you killed. He found out you were a good man."

"How did he know Rafe's my son?"

"He saw Rafe attack the outlaws that took his mother. Lone Elk said he got his courage from you."

"What did Rafe say to that?"

"He wasn't sure if Lone Elk was right until he asked me if it was true. I told him Lone Elk was correct."

"Well, I'm glad he finally knows. Did you say Eb's after the men that took Angelia?"

"Yes, he's been gone for three days now, all the boys are with him. Logan rode all the way to Coulter Creek for the doctor and back here. He wore out four horses, stopped here just long enough to get Sandy, and headed right out to find Eb."

"That boy has grown into a real curly wolf," Bolt said, "I've got to go help them. I should be there with 'em right now, not lying here in this bed."

"Eb will take care of them; you just lay here and rest."

Chapter Sixteen:
The Bunch in Whiskey Hill

It was just before sundown when the boys made camp for the last time. Being one day out of Whiskey Hill, they were sitting around the campfire figuring how to deal with Rex Star and his gang. Eb was laying out a plan.

"We'll split up before we go in. Too many strangers riding in together will attract more attention than we need. Logan, I want you, Creek, and TJ to stay here one more day before you come in. Get some rooms at the hotel and just hang around town. Listen to the talk at the Silver Dollar. Find out all you can about who works for Star and how many are in with this bunch. Don't ask questions; just keep your eyes and ears open."

"Boys, these are bad men and there's a lot of money at stake," Eb said, "They won't allow anyone to live that might be a threat to their operation. Don't draw attention to yourselves. Make them think you're just three drifting cowboys looking for a job to get through the winter. If you see Star or Lane, be patient, wait for me to get this all together.

"Crowfoot and I will ride to Whiskey Hill in the morning. I used to know the U.S. Marshal in these parts. If it's still Lucas Brody, he's a good man and he may be up against a bad bunch without any help.

"Crowfoot and I will try to find him. He'll be a big help in settling with this bunch. We'll make contact with you at the hotel. If we need you, I'll get word to you. If you see us, remember, you don't know us."

"We'll only get one chance to finish these outlaws," Crowfoot said, "If we don't succeed, they'll kill us all and go back to the Lonesome to finish what they started. Star may have the law in his pocket. We have to be careful to not tip our hand before we're ready."

"You can count on us," TJ said, "we'll be careful."

"If this guy owns the law, how are we going to get away with this?" Logan asked.

"We're going to kill the whole damn bunch," Eb said, "any of them wearing badges will be just as dead as the rest when it's over."

Late evening found Bolt sitting up in Scarlett's bed. He had eaten the first solid food since being shot.

"That was a great dinner; please thank Spud for me."

"You look much better," Scarlett said. "I think you're going to make it after all, cowboy."

Bolt was being pleasant and quiet on the outside, but inside he was seething. Every time he looked at Rafe's bruised face, his anger grew. Scarlett was by his side practically every hour of the day. She slept in the chair next to him each night. Bolt could tell she was almost done in.

"I feel better and I'm getting my strength back," he said. "I need to get out of this bed and move around."

"You're not going anywhere. You'll stay in that bed and rest until I say you're ready to get up." Scarlett knew as soon as he was able, Bolt would go after the man that shot Rafe. She wasn't being fooled by his calm demeanor. She knew her iron will was the only thing keeping him in bed.

"I'll do as you say if you'll sleep here next to me," he said, "I can't rest thinking of you in that chair all night. I'll promise to behave and let you sleep."

"How can a girl turn down an offer like that?" Scarlett put on her nightgown and turned down the lamp. "If you need anything please wake me up," she said. Bolt raised the covers for her. She slipped in to snuggle up next to him, "That's much better," she said.

Her body was warm. It felt good to be close to her. Bolt placed his arm around her to hold her close against him as she put her head on his chest. Scarlett pulled up her night gown, laid her leg across him and fell asleep almost immediately. Rafe was asleep in her spare bedroom.

Lying awake in the dim light of the lamp, Bolt gently rubbed Scarlett's thigh as she slept. He loved the smooth warmth of her body.

"I need to be with Eb and the boys. Here I am warm, rested and snuggled up to Scarlett, while they're out there somewhere in the dark, sleeping on the ground. I have got to get out of here and go help them."

Bolt's wounds were still sore, but he was out of any danger. The doctor had gone back to town satisfied he had done all he could. The red medicine was making Bolt stronger every day.

"I can ride if I can get Rufus saddled," he thought. *"That outlaw LeConte was headed to Whiskey Hill and I bet that's where I'll find the man that tried to kill my son."*

Next morning, the streets of Whiskey Hill were muddy from the melting snow. It wasn't much of a town. There was a hotel and several stores, the sheriff's office, and the Silver Dollar Saloon. As Eb and Crowfoot rode into town, they noticed a small hand-lettered sign at the end of the street that read, U.S. MARSHAL.

Eb and Crowfoot tied their horses outside the café and walked to the end of the street. They went around the back of the building that housed the Marshal's office and opened the back door.

The man inside got to his feet, "Eb Monday, where'd you come from?"

"Lucas, it's been a spell." Eb introduced Crowfoot, and sat down to catch up with his friend. Eb and the Marshal went on and on about old times and the women they had known.

"Crowfoot, does this old fart still think all the ladies are after him?" Lucas asked.

"Yes sir, he sure does," Crowfoot said.

"What about Rex Star and his bunch?" Eb asked. "Are you doing anything about them and their murderous ways?"

"That arrogant son-of-a-bitch is as rotten as they come. The county sheriff has jurisdiction here, and he works for Star. The former sheriff was gunned down in the street. No one was even arrested, much less tried for killing him.

"Star managed to get Garrett Frye appointed sheriff. Frye's nothing but a rustler and a hired killer. His deputies are just as bad or worse. My boss sent me up here to try and figure things out, but it's been a tough road. Star manages to keep his hands clean. He's always got an alibi for himself and his men."

"How can one man take over a town like that?" Eb asked.

"Star has friends in high political places. He comes from some powerful criminal family, back east, New York, I think. My superiors warned me to leave him alone unless I can absolutely prove he's involved with the criminal activity going on around here."

"Everyone in town is afraid of him and his gang. No one will testify against him. The worst of the bunch is Latigo Lane. He's a cold-blooded killer. If half the stories about him are true, he could be the Devil himself."

"Star sent a bunch of rustlers to steal a herd from the Lonesome," Eb said, "We got it back after killing most of his gang in the Mountains with a little help from a grizzly."

"I heard talk about that after LeConte was killed in the saloon," Brody said.

"LeConte's dead?" Eb asked, "What about his partner?"

"Lane killed both of them the very night they got back to town. Sheriff Frye said it was self-defense, no charges were ever filed."

"Lucas, we're here to clean out this whole bunch and we'll do it with you or without you," Eb said, "You know as well as I do, they won't ever give up and go away. It will be a fight to the finish when it starts."

"I won't get in your way. I'll try to find a way to help. If I ask for assistance on an official level, Star will know about it. Take your time; this doesn't have to happen today."

Eb and Crowfoot left Brody's office, took their horses to the livery stable and got a room at the hotel. Eb's first impulse was to just shoot his way into the Silver Dollar and get it over with, but he was taking his own advice to be patient. It would feel good to sleep in a bed and have a few hot meals after several days on the trail.

"Let's go down to the café and get breakfast," Eb said, "Maybe we'll mosey up to the saloon this evening to see what's going on."

The Silver Dollar was jumping when they walked in. Being Saturday night, the saloon was crowded with cowboys, travelers, and a few gamblers. Eb and Crowfoot had just sat down when a tall good-looking man approached their table.

"Are you boys new in town?" Star asked.

"Just passing through on our way to Helena," Crowfoot said.

"Have a good time, boys," Star said as he walked away.

Moments later, Lane walked through the door. He was dressed all in black and carried a big knife on his belt. Lane was more than just butt ugly, he was frightening. He had coal-black lifeless eyes.

Eb noticed the man in black when he walked by their table. The saloon girls normally approached every man coming in the door, but they avoided any contact with Lane. He had pale, almost transparent, skin with a scraggly black goatee. He had a big bruise on the side of his face from the fight with his men and his left arm was in a sling. Lane was always alone at the bar. People could sense evil in his very presence and avoided him like the disease-ridden vermin he was.

With his boot on the rail, Lane placed his hat on the bar. "Give me a bottle, bartender. And none of that poison you make up out back. I want some real St. Louis drinking whiskey." Lane was loud and he loved to draw attention to himself. "This town is too damn quiet for me," he said, turning to the crowded saloon. "What we need around here is a good gunfight. Any of you gutless cowhands want to draw against me?" Everyone continued to ignore him.

Star walked up and placed a hand on Lane's shoulder. "Nobody wants to face you,"

"That man looks like death warmed over," Crowfoot said softly, "He could prove to be a handful."

"I've seen his type before," Eb replied. "I'm for damn sure not afraid of him. If he wants a gunfight, I'll be glad to teach that ugly bastard a lesson he won't live long enough to remember."

"Not yet," Crowfoot said, "your chance will come soon enough."

They sat in the saloon and watched the people of Whiskey Hill come and go until midnight.

"Have you ever seen those two in here before?" Star asked after Eb and Crowfoot were gone.

"No," Lane replied, "I'll check them out in the morning if they're still around town."

"We don't need any strangers around. They may be lawmen here to help Marshal Brody."

"Why don't we just kill Brody and get it over with?"

"We can't just kill a U.S. Marshal. My contacts in Washington can't cover that up. We need to find a way to get him out of office or replace him with someone of our choosing."

Star knew money would solve all his problems eventually. He had no idea that the vanguard for retribution had been sitting at his table just a few minutes before. His time in the west was coming to an abrupt and violent end, if the Bunch from the Lonesome Wind had anything to do with it.

"I want you to start for Salt Springs in the morning and check with the Frenchman," Star said, "Those boys should be there with that Lonesome Wind herd by now. I need those cows, that herd will put big money in our pockets, there's a bonus in it for you when it's delivered."

Logan, Creek and TJ rode into town late the next day. They did as Eb instructed and checked into the hotel. The desk clerk was asking a lot of questions about where they were from and where they were headed.

The boys passed Crowfoot in the lobby but made no attempt to say anything to him. They knew to sit tight and wait for Eb. It was a good opportunity to get a bath and a nap before going to the saloon that night.

Crowfoot and Eb had no further contact with Marshal Brody. He seemed to be missing altogether. The two of them were sitting together in the Silver Dollar that evening, when Latigo Lane hurried through the door and went straight to Star's office. A few minutes later, Frye burst in and went to the office.

"What's going on?" Frye asked when they were behind closed doors.

Star was pacing back and forth, wringing his hands. "Lane got word from a buffalo hunter that Frenchy's has burned to the ground."

"How would a buffalo hunter know that?" Frye asked.

"He passed through Salt Springs on his way here," Star said.

"He said it looked like all the men must have died before the fire started," Lane said, "Their bodies were still in the rubble, burned to a crisp."

"Where's the herd?" Frye asked.

Star slammed a fist on his desk. "There is no herd, dammit!"

"Apparently, our men never made it to the ranch," Lane said.

"That means some of the men from Cooper's ranch probably did it," Frye said, "and they could be headed here."

"I thought you killed all the riders from Cooper's ranch?" Star said turning to Lane.

"I thought we did," Lane said. "Watson said there weren't that many men working for Cooper. Maybe he was wrong."

"I'd say he was," Star said, "I'm beginning to think none of you fools have the slightest idea about any of this." Lane began to swell up, but kept his mouth shut. There was too much money involved to just kill the overdressed dandy. "Any strangers in town could mean real trouble. I want to know about all of them."

"It appears to me there are six or more hired guns in here every night," Eb said as they sat at a table in the Silver Dollar. "They've been going in and out of Star's office all night. They never pay for any drinks or have anything to do with the girls."

Eb nodded to Crowfoot when Creek, TJ, and Logan walked in the swinging doors of the saloon. Two very pretty girls met them at the door to welcome them to the Silver Dollar. The girls led them to a table and brought them all a beer. They were teasing Logan about being too young to drink. He didn't think it was too funny, but Creek and TJ were getting a kick out of it.

These two girls were sisters, Amanda and Alicia. They were not only sisters, but identical twins. The twins had been on their way to San Francisco to pursue their acting careers when they were robbed and left stranded in Whiskey Hill.

They planned to only work here long enough to make the money they needed to get to California. They weren't into anything but being friendly with the cowboys and making big tips.

"I think I'm going to like it here," TJ said as Amanda set a beer down in front of him.

"Are you boys passing through or do you work around here?" Alicia asked. "I don't remember ever seeing you in here before."

Alicia sat down next to Logan and put her arm around him. Logan was blood red and stammering to say something that made sense.

"No ma'am. I mean yes ma'am," he stammered, "We ain't from here. We're just passing through the valley looking for work."

"Well there's plenty of work if you're a hired gun," Amanda said, "The pay is good, if you live long enough to collect it."

"We're not gunfighters," Creek said, "Just cowpunchers." Creek was trying to not draw any attention to them, but it was hard with these two beauties at their table.

Sheriff Garrett Frye came out of Star's office and started looking for a spot at one of the poker tables. His nightly routine was a few drinks, a game of cards, and a cigar. He wasn't a big man, but he tried to be. Logan breathed a sigh of relief as Frye passed by, but tensed up when the sheriff turned on his heel and came back.

"You keep your distance there, Boy," Frye said, seemingly angered about Alicia sitting so close to Logan.

"Who I sit with is none of your affair," Alicia said.

"Where did boys come from," Frye asked, ignoring Alicia. "Seems kind of strange, why would you three saddle bums need rooms for more than one night?"

"Saddle bums," Creek repeated.

"How do you know how many nights. . . ."

"You seem to make pretty good money doing whatever it is you do," Frye said before TJ could finish.

"We're just cowpunchers," Creek said.

"Shut up," Frye said, snapping his head around to glare at Creek. "When I want you to talk, I'll ask you a question."

"Yes sir," Creek replied.

Eb was caressing the grips of his Colt as he listened to Frye's rant. "He's the third one on my list of who gets shot," he whispered to Crowfoot.

"We're just cowboys looking for a winter job," Logan said when Frye turned back to him, "We won't be in town much longer."

"You got no business here," Frye said, "I know you're likely lying to me and I don't want you around here stirring up trouble. I want you to stay away from these girls."

"You worried about a new bull in your stamping grounds," Creek asked.

"I ain't worried about some damn kid, least of all this one. At first light, I want all of you out of my town."

"You can't throw us out of town for talking to these girls," TJ said.

With his face turning red, Sheriff Frye pulled his pistol and shoved it in TJ's face. "I just did. Now you're going to jail for your smart mouth. I'll teach you to respect the law." Hearing the disturbance, six other men, all wearing badges, drew their guns, pointing them at the boy's table.

Creek sprang to his feet, turning his chair over behind him. "Respect the law! You wouldn't make a pimple on a lawman's ass, you little son-of-a-bitch!"

Eb started up as Crowfoot grabbed his shoulder.

"Not now, not now," he warned. "We're outnumbered, and some of those boys will die if we start something in here."

The blood vessel on Eb's forehead was twice its normal size and pulsing. He eased back down in his chair and tried to breathe. All he could do was to sit there as the deputies led the boys away to jail.

"Now what?" Eb asked.

"Let's just get out of here real easy."

Bolt got out of bed and walked around a little that day, he was feeling stronger all the time. He had eaten another good supper with a big helping of solid red meat. Scarlett thought it was too much, too soon.

Eb had been gone for five days and Bolt had a bad feeling things weren't going well for his friends. He asked to see Coop earlier in the day. The two of them talked for a while when Scarlett went to the main house get Bolt a bite to eat.

Scarlett slept in Bolt's arms again that night. She was catching up on the rest she missed while sitting up with him. When Scarlett awoke refreshed from another good night's sleep, sunshine was streaming in her window. She had her back to her cowboy until she rolled over to kiss him.

"Good morn. . . ." Her heart sank as she spied the note on his pillow. "No, no, no," she cried as she read the note. She feared as soon as she let her guard down, he'd be gone, and she had been right.

"SCARLETT," the note began, "EB'S IN TROUBLE. BE BACK SOON. I LOVE YOU, BOLT."

She crumbled the note in her fist, put her face in his pillow, and sobbed. Rafe woke up when he heard her crying and came in her room. He sat beside her on the bed and patted her shoulder.

Bolt and Coop were halfway to the Dancing Grounds by the time the sun was up. They had taken enough food to get them all the way to Whiskey Hill without stopping to hunt or making contact with anyone. The trail was cold, but they would push on and hope they were right.

Bolt was in constant pain from being on horseback. He was trying to keep most of his weight on the stirrups and off his wounded spine, but the hole in his thigh made that difficult at best. It would be a long unpleasant ride to Whiskey Hill. The face of the man who shot him was plain in Bolt's memory and he looked forward to finding him. His burning desire to avenge what the outlaw tried to do to his son was numbing the pain and keeping him strong.

Scarlett pulled herself together as she got dressed. When she and Rafe walked into the kitchen, Spud was sitting at the table drinking coffee.

"He's gone," Scarlett said.

"I know. Coop's with him. Bolt's worried about the boys and he's ready to deal out some justice to the men who shot him. Anybody involved in killing those boys from town and hurting Rafe is going to die. That may sound harsh, but it's a fact. There'll be hell on earth walking the streets when Bolt gets there, I guarantee."

"But he's in no condition to ride."

"I've known him a long time and I promise you, that boy is tougher than a jerked jackrabbit. He'll be alright."

"I wish I could believe that, but. . . ."

"There's something you have to understand," Spud said, "Those men are much closer than any family. They live every day by an unwritten code. Any one of them would gladly risk own his life to defend the others. Course, they'd all laugh at me for saying it, but it's true."

"They should just let the authorities handle this."

"It doesn't work that way out here. You'll come to understand that eventually, if you stay here."

"I'm staying here," Scarlett said, "make no mistake about that."

"That code is the reason a handful of them have been able to hold onto three hundred square-miles of land all these years. Anybody fool enough to try and take it will soon find you can't fight one of them without fighting all of them. Coop is convinced the outlaws are long gone from here. He intends to get the boys and Angelia back home without any of them getting killed."

"I hope you're right," Scarlett said.

"Bolt means a lot to you, doesn't he?"

"They all mean a lot to me, but yes, I love him."

"It's pretty plain to see," Spud said, taking her hand from across the table, "don't worry, he'll be back, that boy is too damn tough to go and get himself killed."

"Well my mom was right," TJ said. "She said if I left Nebraska and rode off with those cowboys I'd end up in jail or hung."

"I'd never seen the inside of a jail until last night," Logan said.

"They can't keep us in jail for nothing," Creek said.

"Seems to me, they can do just about what they want," TJ said.

Over at the hotel, Crowfoot and Eb were packing to get out of town.

"We can't fight this whole bunch here in town," Eb said, "the only chance those boys have is for us to wait until some of those hired guns leave town, we'll jump them out in the hills somewhere. We need a thin out some of this bunch and then come up with a plan when we come back to get the boys."

"It's only a matter of time before they come to get us," Crowfoot said, "If we end up in that jail; it's the end for all of us."

Logan was watching the street through a small barred window in their cell.

"There goes Crowfoot and Eb," he said, "They're leaving us behind."

"You know better than that," Creek said, "They have to get away before they end up in here with us."

"Those two are our only chance," TJ said. "Damn, I wish Bolt was here."

"We might not have Bolt to fight our battles in the future," Creek said, "We got to do what he'd do if he was in our place. Our chance will come. We have to be ready when it does."

Later that afternoon, Crowfoot and Eb were well clear of Whiskey Hill. They overheard some of Star's men talking about a small ranch where he held the cattle before they were sold to the army. Eb planned to find it and get rid of the men working there. He had seen some of Frye's deputies' ride off to the south earlier.

The boys sat in their cell for several days. One of the twins would bring them food twice a day.

One afternoon, Amanda was there and she was worried about Logan. She placed a hand on his shoulder. "Are you alright?"

"No ma'am, I'm not."

"Amanda, do you know what they have in store for us or how long they plan to keep us in here?" Creek asked.

"Frye is convinced you all had something to do with killing Star's men in Salt Springs. He wants to figure out how to prove it and hang you as a warning to anyone else who would defy Star."

"Hang us!" Logan exclaimed, "It was a fair fight, that bunch killed our friends."

"Shut up, Logan," Creek said, "She works for Star. She may be here to get us to talk."

"Trust me," Amanda said, "We want out of here as bad as you do. We work at the saloon, but we don't have any love for Star or his killers. We tried to buy tickets for the stage last week when some of the sheriff's men threatened us. They said we couldn't leave. We were afraid to press it any further. I think we're trapped here if someone doesn't help us."

Sheriff Frye walked into the cell and turned to Amada. "Go back to work. Tell Alicia I'll see her tonight."

"I'm sure that will make her day," Amanda said as she left the jail.

"Boys get up and follow me," Frye said.

"Where are we going?" TJ asked.

"To stand trial."

"For what?" Logan asked.

"Twelve counts of murder."

"Murder," Creek repeated, "We never murdered anybody."

"That's not what I hear. I know you boys were part of the bunch that killed my friends in Salt Springs. Now you're going to pay for it."

The Silver Dollar Saloon was packed with Star's hired guns and deputies. Star had gotten himself appointed a territorial judge and he would be trying the boys. All six of the juror's worked for Star. Latigo Lane was the jury foreman.

The boys were led into the saloon in handcuffs. They were ordered to sit down in front of a makeshift bench. Rex Star was sitting in a high-backed chair, looking down on them.

"You men are charged with the murder of twelve good men," Judge Star said, "How do you plead?"

"There ain't twelve good men in this whole damn town," TJ said.

"One more word from you and I'll have you gagged," Star threatened.

The Jury deliberated for five minutes before coming back with a guilty verdict. Judge Star was only too happy to condemn them.

"I sentence you three killers to be hung by the neck until you are dead. Hanging will be at daybreak, day after tomorrow. The bars open and the jury's drinks are on the house."

That evening, Eb and Crowfoot were lying on a hill overlooking Star's ranch.

"There's at least six of them down in that shack," Eb said, "As soon as it's dark; we hit 'em."

"Are we going to give them a chance to surrender?"

"Surrender," Eb whispered, "You just remember what they did to Bolt, Angelia, and those young cowboys back on the Lonesome. We ain't leaving anybody alive this time."

There was a definite chill in the air after the sun went down. As soon as it was dark, Eb and Crowfoot slipped down off the hill toward the cabin. The gunmen were huddled around a stove inside. Just one man was on watch.

"You get that one," Eb whispered to his partner, "and do it quiet."

"I'll get him," Crowfoot said. The half-breed was silent as a cat as he slipped up behind the guard and killed him with one thrust of his knife.

They met at the door to the cabin. Eb cocked both hammers on his scattergun, and kicked-in the door.

"Reach, or throw down!" he shouted.

Every man went for his gun and Eb let go with both barrels. He dropped the empty shotgun and pulled his Colt as Crowfoot came through the door right behind him. The two of them killed every man there.

Crowfoot took a bullet that plowed a bloody streak across his thigh. It wouldn't kill him, but it was painful. He pulled off his bandana and tied it around the wound to stop the bleeding. After things settled down, Crowfoot noticed another man tied up and gagged in one of the bunks.

"Marshal Brody, is that you?"

"Boys, am I glad to see you," Brody said, after the gag was off. "I was on my way back from Helena when this bunch bushwhacked me. I guess none of them had the nerve to kill a U.S. Marshal so they've been holding me here. I have a warrant for Star, Frye, and Lane. They're charged with defrauding the U.S. Army and conspiracy to kill the sheriff. Now I can add kidnapping a Marshal."

Gathering some supplies from the cabin, Eb did a more permanent job bandaging Crowfoot's leg. "It's not that bad," he said, you'll be sore for a while; just pull up your britches and get over it."

"That's easy enough for you to say, old man. You ain't the one who's shot."

"I heard these men talking," Brody said, "They're hanging your friends in the morning for murder. Did you kill those men in Salt Springs?"

"You're damn right we killed 'em," Eb said, "But it wasn't murder. They were part of the bunch that came to the Lonesome, killed three ranch hands, shot my partner all to hell, and did their best to kill an eight-year-old kid. Lane kidnapped his mother and killed her on the way to Salt Springs."

"Well, I guess you had reason," Brody said.

"Mount up," Eb said, "nobody's hanging those boys."

Chapter Seventeen:
Judgment Day

Logan had been praying for some kind of miracle. He couldn't believe he was going to die at dawn for a crime he didn't commit, he wasn't even there. He wouldn't mind dying so much in a fair fight, but hanging was brutal.

The young cowboy was in deep thought around midnight, watching the darkened street from the window of his cell. His faith was fading as the night wore on. The crushing weight of utter hopelessness had descended on him and he began to give up. He was resigned to meet his death at the end of a hangman's noose as soon as the sun came up.

Logan's faith was rekindled when he spotted a big pale horse coming up the street. He thought he was dreaming at first, until two dark but familiar figures rode by and went to the Marshal's office. Logan could see a lamp burning in the office, the shadows of several men danced on the wall.

"Thank you, Lord," he whispered.

"Well, I'll be damned," Eb said when he saw his partner come through the door. Bolt was weak and pale, but he was standing there, "You ain't dead after all." Eb reached out his hand and Bolt took it in a firm grip.

"I figured I'd find you here," he said to Eb. "Lucas, how are you?"

"I'm good, Bolt. You got here just in time. Rex Star and his gang are going to hang those friends of yours at daylight."

"No, they're not." Still looking at Eb, Bolt said, "It's time we put an end to this bunch, once and for all."

"You're damn right it is," Eb replied.

"Where's Angelia?" Bolt asked.

"I've got some bad news for you," Eb said, "but you need to sit down." Bolt listened quietly as Eb explained about finding Angelia and what they thought happened to her.

Visibly shaken by the news, Bolt was struggling to steady himself. He was already weak from his wounds and the hard ride from the Lonesome, now he had to deal with Angelia's death. His eyes were filling up as the others turned away from him to give him a moment.

After several minutes he turned to Eb, "Who did it?"

"The same black-hearted son-of-a-bitch that shot you and tried to kill Rafe," Eb replied.

"I'm here to kill him."

"I'm going to help you do just that, but it's got to wait for a few hours."

"How are we ever going to explain this to Rafe?" Bolt asked.

"There's only one way and you know it," Eb said, "tell him the truth about his mother and let him deal with it. We'll all help him through it."

"But he's my son, how can I break this. . . ."

"Your son," Coop said, "How do you. . . . When did you find out about that?"

"I would've been surprised if he wasn't," Eb said, "He's just like you, anybody can see that, and he's just the right age. I knew it the moment I laid eyes on him in Coulter Creek."

It was quiet for a few minutes until Crowfoot spoke up. "We need to get some word to the boys in the jail. They must be going through hell."

Coop pulled his hat down low and wrapped a blanket around his shoulders. He was going to try and get a message to the boys. The guard was asleep when Coop slipped passed the jail and dropped a note through the window of the boy's cell.

>   AT EXACTLY ONE...CALL GUARD...COMING IN DOOR
>   MINUTE LATER. KEEP IT QUIET...NO COMPANY TILL
>   READY.

He added a PS at the bottom.

IF YOU LOAFERS AIN"T BACK TO WORK BY SATURDAY…YOU"RE ALL FIRED.

"Wake up boys," Logan whispered after reading the note, "Hell's coming to breakfast."

"What are you talking about?" TJ asked, "Whose coming?"

"Buffalo Grass Rider himself, that's who. He's got Coop and the rest with him."

"Bolt's here," TJ said. "I knew he was too damn tough to die."

"Its pay-back time for these bastards," Creek said.

When the clock on the jailhouse wall struck one, Logan called the deputy.

"What do you want?" the half-asleep guard asked.

"TJ is bad sick, go get a doctor."

"I don't give a damn if he's sick, he's gonna hang in a few hours."

When the guard got close enough to look in the cell, Creek grabbed him by the collar and slammed his head into the bars of the cell door. Just then, Coop, Crowfoot, and Bolt came through the door of the jail. The other deputy in the office never made a sound. He woke up choking on Crowfoot's knife stuck in his throat, pinning him to the back of his chair. Coop let the boys out and got their guns.

"Bolt, it's good to see you," Creek said, "we thought you were near dead."

Logan was shaking Bolt's hand. He was trying hard not to show it, but his eyes were full and he couldn't say anything. Bolt put his arms around the youngster in a big bear hug.

"I didn't know if I'd ever see you again," Logan said.

"That was just wishful thinking," Bolt said, "who'd keep your little butt on the straight and narrow if I wasn't around?"

Eb and Marshal Brody were the last to join the party in the jail.

"What are you all prepared to do now?" Lucas asked.

"We're going to kill as many as it takes to get to Star and Lane," Eb said. "Neither one of those sons-o'-bitches are getting out of this alive."

"Lucas, we can't ask you to take part in any of this," Bolt said.

"That's where you're wrong. The governor of this territory is a good man. He wants Montana to be a state someday and he doesn't want the likes of Rex Star in power. He asked the president to clean this mess up."

"What did Washington say to that?" Coop asked.

"Word came by army courier while I was in Helena. The Justice department wants Star arrested and tried. When he conspired with the commander out at the Agency, it became a federal matter," Lucas said, "all of you raise your right hand and say I will."

"I will," they all said at once.

"Whatever you do now will be legal. You're all deputy U.S. Marshals."

"Do we get a badge?" Logan asked.

"What about Frye?" Eb asked, not waiting for Brody to answer the youngster.

"The governor has suspended all local law enforcement's power and declared martial law. We're the legal power in Whiskey Hill until the army gets here."

"The army's right outside of town," Crowfoot said.

"Like I just said, half that troop is in with Star. The courier came from Fort Benton. They're gonna court martial the whole bunch at the agency," Brody said, "We're waiting for General Miles and the real cavalry."

Rex Star was getting out of bed as the eastern sky was turning light, anxious to officiate over his first hanging. Lane was still sitting downstairs in the saloon. He didn't sleep much and he was looking forward to the hanging.

Across the street in one of the hotel rooms, the twins were packing to get away from Star and Whiskey Hill.

"I won't stand by and let Star hang those cowboys," Alicia said. She was loading three pistols and putting them in a picnic basket. "We'll sneak down the back stairs and go to the livery stable. They're watching the horses so we have to get rid of the guard."

Amanda was strapping on a .45 and she had a plan.

"I'll distract the guard, you hit him with something."

"Hit him with something," Alicia said. "Why don't we shoot him?"

"Why not blow a bugle to let 'em all know we're coming?" Amanda reminded her.

"We haven't much time," Alicia said, "It'll be daylight soon, and it'll take time to saddle five horses, let's go." Amanda opened the door and checked the hallway. All seemed quiet as the girls made their way down the back stairs into the alley.

The deputy at the stable was asleep when Amanda walked in the front door.

"What are you doing here this early in the morning?" he asked, digging the sleep out of his eyes with his fist.

"I'm going for a little ride with my sister."

"No you're not."

"Yes we are," Alicia said from behind his back. When he turned to look, she hit him right between the eyes with an axe handle.

The Bunch from the Lonesome Wind was still laying low in the jail when two pretty ladies appeared at the door. They appeared to be carrying a basket of food for the condemned men. Bolt pulled them in the door and shut it behind them.

"Don't make a sound," he warned. The twins were dressed in riding skirts and boots. It was obvious they were ready to travel.

"I think this breakfast would be hard to swallow," Eb said, looking in the basket.

"We couldn't let them hang those boys," Amanda said, "We planned to spring them and ride out of here with them."

"Their horses are out back," Alicia said, "we're saddled and ready to go."

"You girls sit tight," Crowfoot said, "We'll all ride out of here together in a little while." He turned back to the cowboys and laid out a battle plan, "Logan, I want you and Creek on the roof across the street from the Silver Dollar. When the shooting starts, no one gets out of there alive, you understand?"

"Yes sir," Logan replied.

"TJ, you and I will be watching the street outside the jail, if any of the gang tries to get out of town, we'll have them trapped like rats. This ends here and now. Eb, you and Bolt stay with me until we get the gang bottled up, then you can take your time dealing with Star and Lane in the Silver Dollar."

Bolt was leaning against a chair in the office. It was obvious to everyone in the room he was in pain,

"Sounds like a plan," he said.

"Are you up to this," Eb asked.

"I'm fine," Bolt said, "they made a big mistake by ever setting foot on the Lonesome, but when they killed Angelia, and tried to kill my son. I'm going to kill 'em all."

"Coop," Eb said, "you and Marshal Brody stay here in the jail. When Frye and his deputies come for the boys, shoot all of 'em."

"Give them a chance to give up their guns," Crowfoot said.

"Yeah and then shoot 'em," Eb said, "That'll be our signal to get this party started. Meet us in the saloon after you're done here."

"We'll be there," Coop assured him.

"You might need this," Crowfoot said, handing Bolt his Henry rifle.

"I never thought I'd see this again, thanks."

"We took it off that mouthy Frenchman at Salt Springs," Eb said.

"Yeah," TJ added, "just before we roasted his ass."

Bolt smiled as he levered a round in the chamber and stuffed one more in the magazine. He would never know he was holding the rifle that killed Angelia.

"Alright," Eb said, "let's go spoil a perfectly good hanging."

"Well look at this," Crowfoot said, as he browsed through the weapons in the sheriff's gun rack. He took down a sawed-off, double-barreled, ten-bore scattergun from the rack. "Now this is a gun," he said, stuffing double 00 buckshot in the breech. He dropped some extra shells in his pocket, and followed TJ into the street. "I want my first shot to make an impression," he said.

"Just make sure it ain't pointed in my direction," TJ said.

"Here you go, Kid," Brody said just as Creek opened the door. When Logan turned back toward the marshal, Brody tossed him a badge.

"Thanks," Logan said. He was fumbling with the pin as he followed Creek out into the dark street.

Coop and marshal Brody were back in the cell when four hired gunmen came for the prisoners. The twins were out back with the horses. Marshall Brody told them to ride off if this went bad.

"Drop em boys," Brody said, "you're all under arrest."

Lucas gave them a chance, but they drew their pistols and opened up on him. Coop wasn't a gunfighter, but he was cool under fire and he hit what he shot at. Two gunmen died immediately. When the third one was wounded, the last man threw down his gun and surrendered. Coop took the two outlaws that were alive and locked them in a cell.

Brody was hit in the gut and losing blood. "Go on," Brody said to Coop, "I'll be alright." Amanda went for the doctor while Alicia tried to stop the bleeding. Coop headed up the street to the saloon.

Rex Star was just coming downstairs when he heard gunfire from the jail.

"What was that?" he asked.

"Gunfire," Lane replied as he headed for the door. "Sounds like it came from. . . ."

Lane was turned back as a swarm of rifle bullets smashed the glass and splintered the front doors of the Silver Dollar. As soon as Lane was driven back inside the saloon, several hired guns began shooting from the second floor of the Silver Dollar. Logan and Creek were well hidden across the street and determined to prevent anyone from escaping the saloon.

Eight riders were coming up the street and headed for the saloon, when Crowfoot walked into their path and shouted for them to stop.

"U.S. Marshal, you're all under arrest!"

They opened up on Crowfoot and he let go with both barrels of buckshot just before ducking behind a building.

Two riders and a horse were killed instantly by the blast from the scattergun. TJ was on the other side of the street with his Winchester. Two more outlaws hit the ground when Crowfoot fired the next volley. TJ killed two more with his first few shots. The remaining riders tried to fight it out as their horses were jumping and spinning from the gunfire.

The last two riders went down as Bolt and Eb joined in the battle. The demon spirit was loose and it intended to kill all of them. There was no opportunity for any of them to give up. It was kill or be killed for Star's men, as the Bunch from the Lonesome Wind dealt out some long overdue frontier justice.

Toward the end of the gunfight, TJ was hit in the shoulder and went down.

"How bad are you hit?" Crowfoot asked as he made it to TJ's side.

"I'm alright. It missed the bone, let's get to the saloon and help Logan and Creek."

Crowfoot tied TJ's neckerchief around his wounded arm to stop the bleeding. "That'll hold you for now. We'll go up the back stairs and clean out the bunch on the second floor. The front door's all yours," he said turning to Bolt and Eb. They slipped down the alley watching the spaces between the buildings as they passed each one.

Coop was making his way up the street when shots rang out from the hotel across the street. Diving for cover, Coop found himself pinned down behind a water trough, with bullets throwing water over him.

Logan could see the barrel of the rifle that was shooting at Coop protruding from the window of the hotel, but he was on the same side of the street and couldn't get a shot at the hidden gunman. Coop was trapped. He couldn't rise up to shoot back without getting hit.

A shot rang out from Coop's side of the street just before the stricken gunman in the hotel crashed out of the window. A shower of broken glass and ripped curtains followed him down to the dusty street below.

"Who fired that shot?" Logan asked.

His question was answered when Alicia stuck her head out from between two buildings and waved at him. She was covering Coop with a rifle, freeing him to continue toward the saloon.

"Damn," Logan said, "she's pretty and dangerous."

"Yeah, you better watch your little butt."

Crowfoot and TJ went up the back stairs to the second floor of the Silver Dollar as Eb and Bolt went to the front. Once in the hallway, Crowfoot and TJ dodged several half-naked saloon girls who were fleeing for their lives.

Crowfoot kicked the door on the first room and ordered the gunmen to drop their guns. The outlaws spun around and fired on him. When Crowfoot yanked the triggers on the big shotgun, the room went to pieces.

Logan was still shooting at the gunmen on the second floor when one of the front windows exploded. Two gunmen, shattered glass, and assorted bits of furniture were blown into the street below.

"What was that?" Logan asked.

"It's Crowfoot with that scattergun he took from the jail," Creek said.

Preparing to move on the front door, Bolt and Eb ducked as debris from upstairs fell in the street near them.

"There's one hell of a fight going on upstairs," Eb said.

"It's Crowfoot and TJ, most likely," Bolt said. "Are you ready?"

Eb pulled the hammers back on his shotgun. "More than ready, let's go introduce these sons-o'-bitches to the Bunch from the Lonesome Wind." They stepped up on the porch and pushed their way through the bullet-riddled doors of the Silver Dollar.

Logan watched the street as Bolt and Eb went inside the saloon. "Let's get over there,"

Two gunmen were firing from the second floor balcony when Bolt came through the door. He killed the one on his left, worked the lever on his rifle and killed the one on his right as Lane tried to get to his feet. Eb fired the first barrel of his scattergun, killing a third gunman trying to escape up the steps. Lane froze as Bolt swung his rifle toward him. Bolt instantly recognized Lane as the man that shot him and probably killed Angelia.

Realizing where he had seen Bolt before, Lane stood quiet as Bolt held the Henry on him. Two pulsing veins had popped out on Bolt's reddening forehead as he stared into Lane's eyes.

"You're one butt-ugly son-of-a-bitch," Eb said, still holding the shotgun on Lane, "you wanted a gunfight, now you damn sure got one."

"Do the world a favor," Bolt said, "go for your gun."

"Big talk while you're holding a rifle and a shotgun on me," Lane said.

"That's not a problem," Bolt said, letting the hammer down on his rifle. He leaned it against an overturned chair, never breaking eye contact with Lane.

"You're just about out of business, Mr. Fancy Pants," Eb said looking over at the suddenly trembling Star.

Star was trembling, "Do something, Lane."

"Like what?" Lane asked, still holding his hands in the air.

"Kill these two. That's what I pay you to do."

"Kill 'em yourself. I quit."

Gunfire could still be heard coming from upstairs as Crowfoot and TJ were cleaning up the rest of Star's gang. A few more shots were heard outside and then all was quiet as Logan and Creek made their way across the street. Star wore a fancy pearl-handled pistol in a shoulder holster, but he never got up the nerve to pull it.

"Let's make this a fair fight," Lane taunted. "There's two of you, at least give me a chance to draw."

Eb placed his scattergun on a nearby table. "Whatever you say."

"Alright," Bolt said, his hand lingering over the grips of his Colt, "if you're going to do something, now's the time."

"That wasn't too smart," Lane said, "Now I'm gonna kill both of you old bastards." With a big grin on his face, Lane grabbed for his gun.

Bolt pulled his Colt at the same instant Eb pulled his. Lane was lightning fast, but he was a little unnerved by seeing a man he thought was dead and the wound in his chest slowed him down a little. Lane still fired first, but his bullet missed Bolt by a hairs-breadth and he never got another.

Bolt wasn't as fast, but he was deadly accurate. Lane's head snapped back as Bolt's first bullet went through his brain, right between his black lifeless eyes. An instant later, Eb's bullet plowed through Lane's heart. Bolt's second bullet hit Lane in the chest as the killer was going down. The third and fourth bullets ripped through his chest when Lane hit the floor.

"That's for my son," Bolt said to the bleeding gunman.

Lane's body was in convulsions with bubbling blood spouting from his chest wounds. The killer's eyes were wide open as the last two red-hot slugs from Bolt's Colt ripped through him.

"He died way too easy," Bolt said turning to Eb.

"Well, prop the ugly son-o'-a-bitch up and we'll shoot him some more," Eb said with a grin. Turning back to Star, Eb found him attempting to retreat behind the bar. "That's far enough," Eb warned, leveling his Colt at Star's head and cocking the hammer.

Just then, Crowfoot and TJ came down the stairs. Crowfoot had been hit again, this time in the other leg. He had a neckerchief tied around it to stop the blood and his right arm in a make-shift sling.

Star was horrified after witnessing what Bolt had just done to Lane. Visibly shaken, he threw up his hands and started pleading for his life.

"My family has money and power. I can make you rich men; just…just name your price."

Eb holstered his Colt and picked up his scattergun. "What's your price, Bolt?"

"This nubbin grabber can't afford me."

"That's what I was thinking."

"Do you want to shoot him or do you want me to." Bolt asked, picking up the Henry.

"He's too scared to kill his own wolves," Eb said, "always hired it done. He's the worst kind of coward." Eb cocked both hammers as he continued, "He's the reason our sweet Angelia and about two dozen other people are dead right now."

"I want to kill him," Bolt said, "but I can't just shoot him, and he's too damn scared to go for his gun."

"Well, I damn sure. . . ."

"That's right," Star blurted out, before Eb could finish, "You can't shoot me, I'm a territorial judge, and I'll. . . ."

Star was blown backward into the fancy glassware behind him as Bolt and Eb fired together. Shattered glasses, liquor bottles and shards of the mirror fell on his lifeless body. The portrait of a reclining nude that hung over the bar was swinging from one corner until it fell, covering the fallen outlaw.

Eb opened the breech on the scattergun and two smoking hulls rattled to the floor. "I believe the judge just got...ah...got...."

"Overruled," Bolt said.

"Yeah...overruled," Eb said with a big grin.

Smoke was still thick as Coop came in the front door. "Are you boys alright?" he asked. Logan, Alicia, and Creek were right behind him. Logan's head was bleeding.

"A bullet took off the tip of my ear," he said lowering the stained neckerchief in his hand.

"Gives you character," Eb said examining the bloody ear.

Bolt put his arm around Logan's shoulder.

"You did real good, pardner, I'm proud of you."

"Damn, did you get shot again?" Eb asked, turning to Crowfoot.

"Yeah," the half-breed replied, "and I think I broke my wrist when I cut loose with that ten-gauge."

Amanda was still in the jail with Marshal Brody and the doctor. They laid the lawman in a bunk, and the doctor was working to save him when Sheriff Frye came in the back door. Frye knew paydays were over in Whiskey Hill. He was after the cash he kept in his wall safe.

Amanda heard him fumbling with the combination and walked out to face him.

"Alicia," Frye said, spinning around, "Honey, let's get out of here. We can go to California just like you wanted. I've got plenty of cash. We can live like royalty."

"You're not going anywhere."

"Oh it's you," Frye replied, realizing his mistake, "alright then, saloon girl, have it your way."

With that, Frye went for his gun. It was already too late. Amanda wasn't waiting for him to draw. Her bullet ripped through Frye's chest before he ever cleared leather. Driven to the floor with the impact, Frye lay gasping his last as the petite pistolaro walked up and stood over him.

"I'm no saloon girl," Amanda said, holstering her pistol.

The whole town was silent when Amanda joined the rest in the saloon.

"You all are one sorry looking bunch of gunfighters," Coop said.

"I think we better stick to punching cows," Logan said.

"I think the boy's right," Crowfoot agreed.

"Let's have a drink," Eb said, "It's on the house."

"Have a drink," Bolt said, "I don't know how you're gonna do that seeing how you blew up every bottle in the place with that damn shotgun."

"I was saving your hide with that damn shotgun, Mr. High and Mighty. Maybe next time, I'll just let you handle it, and I'll stay back and watch."

"Saving my hide," Bolt said, "that'll be the day...and staying out o' my way is probably a good idea for somebody as old as you are. Maybe you should do just that."

"Well, maybe I will."

"Well, maybe you'd learn something."

"Learn something. From a hillbilly like you? Let me tell you one damn thing, Buffalo Hump. Just because you went and got yourself shot...don't start thinking I'm gonna. . . ."

"I don't think we're gonna get a drink anytime soon," Crowfoot said to Coop.

"I think you may be right," Coop replied.

A troop of cavalry rode in later that morning to take over the town until a proper lawman could be found. The doctor stopped by and said that Marshal Brody would recover, but his days of being a marshal were probably over.

"What are you girls going to do now?" Bolt asked the twins.

"I guess we'll go on to California like we planned," Amanda replied.

"Why don't you come back with us?" TJ asked, "Coulter Creek is growing. It could use a theater with good looking actresses."

"That's a great idea," Coop said, "I bet Ms. Charity would be glad to be part of that business.

"Sometimes TJ surprises us with a good idea ma'am," Creek said. "We'd be happy to accompany you both to Coulter Creek and introduce you to Ms. Charity."

"We'll be your first customers," Logan said.

"You boys will be without a job if you go running off to Coulter Creek every Saturday night," Coop said. "We got cattle to gather and we're way behind."

The doctor patched up all the boys. None of their wounds were that bad. Crowfoot's wrist wasn't broken, but it was badly sprained. Once again, the Bunch from the Lonesome Wind had come through a deadly conflict without anyone dying.

"Bolt, let's get out o' here," Eb finally said.

"I think you're right," Bolt said, "I'm ready to get back to the Lonesome."

"Saddle up boys," Coop said, "let's go home."

The twins decided to ride to Coulter Creek with the cowboys from the Lonesome. The second night on the trail, they were camped near the spot where Scar attacked the rustlers. Logan was telling the story.

"Yep there I was, crawling down to the rustler's camp to shoot a couple of them with my bow. It was pitch-dark. I knew that grizzly was still around. I took Bolt along in case the bear tried to interfere with my plan. I knew if we could surprise them in the dark, we stood a good chance of running them off and getting our cows back."

"Logan, you are so brave," Alicia said, "I would have been scared to death."

"Shucks, it weren't nothing, ma'am."

"I'm gonna be sick," Creek mumbled under his breath.

Amanda looked across the fire at Eb. "Where were you, when all that was happening?"

"Holding Logan's horse," Eb replied.

"Do you think that grizzly is around here now?" Amanda asked.

"He could be out there watching us right now," Crowfoot said.

TJ moved closer to Amanda and put his arm around her. He winced in pain from his shoulder wound. "Are you alright," she asked.

"It's nothing," TJ said, "and don't you worry, that bear knows better than to mess with the Bunch from the Lonesome Wind."

Crowfoot was sitting on a log next to Eb. "He gets a little scratch and Amanda is holding his hand, asking if he's alright. I get shot twice, my wrist broke, and I'm over here next to this ornery old cuss."

"It ain't broke," Eb reminded him, "Besides, you need to learn how to run faster."

"Old Man," Crowfoot said, "You think you can outrun me?"

"Appears so, I ain't the one who's shot?"

"Throw some more wood on the fire," Alicia said, "I'm cold." Logan put his arm around her to keep her warm. "How's your ear?" she asked as she patted his hand.

"His ear," Crowfoot said, shaking his head.

"You think this is cold," Eb said, "let me tell you about the time I fought the Comanche's. It was forty below zero. . . ."

"It ain't never been forty below zero in Texas," Bolt said, shaking his head.

"Never said I was in Texas," Eb said, "That's just how much you know."

"I know one thing," Bolt said, "I know you're plumb full of. . . ."

"You girls ignore those two," Coop said. "They argue like a couple o' old women all the time." Crowfoot was laughing along with the rest at Bolt and Eb.

It took two more days for the group to get back to the ranch. They had a great time around the fire at night telling stories and laughing. The threat was gone now and they could relax.

Logan and TJ were taking quite a shine to the twins. Bolt just wanted to get home to Scarlett and Rafe. There was no telegraph in Whiskey Hill and he knew they were worried about him.

Late in the evening, Scarlett was sitting on her porch with Rafe. They were watching the sun go down and listening to the wind.

"I know why they call this place the Lonesome Wind," she said, 'I'm about as lonesome as. . . ." She paused when she noticed a group of riders coming from the north. When she recognized the big pale horse that her cowboy always rode, she jumped off the porch and ran to meet him.

Bolt saw her and spurred Rufus to a trot. When she was beside him, he reached down to put his arm around her. Bolt lifted her up across his saddle, held her close to him and kissed her.

"I'm not going to let you go," he whispered to her.

"I'm not going anywhere," she said with her arms around his neck.

Rafe was right behind her. Bolt reached down, took his hands and swung the youngster up behind him.

"Howdy son, you been taking care of things around here while we were gone?"

"Yes sir, I'm glad you're back, where's my mom?"

Bolt's eyes were clouding over as he looked at Scarlett.

"Oh no," she whispered.

"Rafe, I don't know any way to tell you this," Bolt said, "Except to just…tell you that. . . ."

Seeing that Bolt was struggling, Coop rode up beside them. "Son, the outlaws that took your mom…well…they killed her. She was very brave; fought them right up to the end."

"They were bad men," Crowfoot said. "They're all dead now and you're safe here with us. You have all your friends around you and we'll take care of you."

Rafe held his arms around Bolt's waist, trying not to cry in front of the other cowboys.

Eb was mounted on the other side of Bolt. "We're your family now. Nobody will ever come between us. If anybody jumps one of us, they have to fight all of us. That's the code, and you're part of that family now."

Spud came out of the house when they got closer and spoke to them. "Ya'll are a sight for sore eyes. I'm mighty glad you made it back. Where's. . . ."

Coop explained about Angelia, while Spud listened quietly. Coop introduced the girls and told Spud how Alicia saved his life. "Her daddy taught her how to shoot," he said. "Amanda is faster on the draw than most men I know."

"You girls are mighty welcome here on the Lonesome Wind," Spud said, wiping his eyes.

"Thank you, Spud, It's a beautiful place," Alicia said, "We're so sorry about your friend."

"Thank you," Spud said, "You girls come on in the house. We'll get you settled.

Scarlett took Bolt and Rafe home with her. "Rafe, you can stay here with me if you wish."

Rafe still held his arms around Bolt. "I think I'd like to be in the bunkhouse with Bolt if you don't mind."

"Son, you can stay anywhere you like," Bolt said. "If you get tired of listening to Eb snore, then you can stay over here sometimes too. You might need a female to give you a hug once in a while. I know I do."

Late that night, Scarlett lay in Bolt's arms. Rafe was asleep in the bunkhouse. "I hope he doesn't get too much of the wrong kind of education over there with those cowboys."

"He'll be alright. They're good men; they know how to behave when it's called for."

"I suppose it will be up to us to raise Rafe now."

"I suppose, is that alright with you?"

"Of course, I know I can't replace his mother, but I already love him like he was mine."

"I love you," he whispered just before he kissed her and started to unbutton her nightgown.

"I love you too, cowboy. I'm so glad you're home."

Scarlett responded to his touch and slipped her gown off over her head. Her body was warm next to him under the covers. She was never more beautiful than in the soft light of an oil lamp. Bolt wasn't up to any love making so they just cuddled until they fell asleep. She slept in his arms. Bolt could feel her breathing while rubbing her back as he drifted off to sleep.

Fall turned into winter as peace and quiet returned to the Lonesome Wind. Logan got to kill a big mule deer buck with his bow. Eb was teaching Rafe about being a cowboy, cussing, ladies, and such. The boy was settling into his life in Montana just like he was born there.

The Twins went to Coulter Creek and went into business with Charity. Bolt, Crowfoot, and the rest were healed up by the time roundup was all over. Coop had the money to keep the ranch for another year. Soon the cycle would start all over again.

Christmas Eve came at last. Scarlett put Rafe to sleep in his bed in her spare bedroom. She decorated a tree and there were presents for Rafe from all the cowboys on the Lonesome.

Bolt was holding Scarlett in his lap as they sat in her mother's rocker.

"I love you," he said, "This will be my best Christmas ever."

Bolt held her in his arms as he stood up. He put her back down in the rocker and covered her with a blanket. Bending down on one knee, he tucked the blanket around her feet.

"I'm going to step outside for a minute," he said.

"It's freezing out there."

"Exactly."

"If I live to be a hundred, I will never understand you."

"I expect that's a fact," he grumbled as he went out the door.

Outside, the sky was clear and the stars where shining bright. Bolt loved to be alone in the dark and cold of a winter night. Being outside reminded him of the miserable nights he spent sleeping on the ground. It made the warm cabin seem even nicer when he went back in.

Bolt could hardly remember the loneliness he lived with for so long. Now he was happy to have such a wonderful person to share his life with.

"You are one lucky cowboy," he said out loud.

"You sure are, pardner," Eb said from the porch of the bunkhouse. He stepped out to get some air just like Bolt.

"Merry Christmas," Bolt said, walking over to Eb.

"Merry Christmas to you, Eb replied.

"We've made a lot of tracks together over the years. I want you to know you're more than just a friend to me."

"Hell, I know that," Eb said as they shook hands, "I feel the same way about you."

"We got plenty of tracks to make before we're done," Bolt said.

"You're mighty right about that."

The clock struck midnight as Bolt and Scarlett snuggled under the covers.

"Merry Christmas," he whispered.

"Merry Christmas to you too, Buffalo Grass Rider."

The bunkhouse was quiet. Logan, TJ, and Creek were in Coulter Creek attending the grand opening of the Coulter Creek Repertory Company. Coop and Spud were sound asleep over in the main house. Even old Rufus was snoozing in the barn. The Kentucky mares were all snug in their stalls. It was their first taste of a real Montana winter. They were all settled with mustang foals waiting to be born in the spring. All, but one of them that is. She was carrying a big gray colt that would be born a month earlier than the rest. That little pale horse would grow up to be Rafe Ashton's best friend.

Miles away, in the Missouri River Breaks. Lone Elk lay under a buffalo robe with a new wife. He returned to the Mandan village and courted the Cheyenne woman. Her name was Red Calf Woman. After an appropriate courtship, Lone Elk offered her adopted family a gift of six good horses for her hand. In a strange way, the mighty Sioux owed all his happiness to the man he knew as Buffalo Grass Rider.

Scar was snoozing away the winter, snug in his cave high in the mountains. That old bear didn't know it, but he owed his life to that same man.

The buffalo grass was covered in a thick blanket of new snow on that silent starlit night. At least for that brief moment, all was right with the men who called themselves, The Bunch from the Lonesome Wind.

The Legend of the Buffalo Grass Rider seemed to be complete. Bolt found lasting love from a good woman and a son he never knew. In truth, the warrior spirit of Ten Thunders' blood was an ancient and compelling force. It was far from finished with the man known to many as Buffalo Grass Rider.

The End. . . .

For more adventures with the Bunch from the Lonesome Wind, watch for:

Allen Russell's

"Buffalo Grass Rider"

Episode Two

"Blood on the Rosebud"

Coming soon from Rough River Press

www.RoughRiverPress.com

About the Author

Allen Russell is a native Tennessean, a former professional hunting guide in Montana, host of an outdoor TV show, and a cowboy at heart. His experiences living and filming on the snow-covered plains of Eastern Montana, Wyoming, and the rugged Black Hills of South Dakota have supplied the background for the Buffalo Grass Rider Series. As an author, his favorite subjects lie in the rural hills and hollers of the south and the wide-open spaces of the old west.

Other titles available from Allen Russell:

Cowboy Christmas Tales

Mule

The Reno Kid

www.allenrussellbooks.com

CPSIA information can be obtained at www.ICGtesting.com
Printed in the USA
LVOW061057161012

303021LV00001B/5/P